Praise for:

Walking On Uneven Ground

"Ann Jeffries describes her settings so well I felt like I was living the story not just reading it. I loved the concept of strong community ties she developed in this story. The characters seemed so real I wanted to meet them and congratulate them on their successes." —Rebecca Bridges, President, Coastal Authors Network, Secretary, Lowcountry RWA, and member, Carolina Forest Critique Group.

"Once again Ms. Jeffries weaves simultaneous stories into a satisfying conclusion. Walking on Uneven Ground will keep the reader engaged from the first page until the last with action, intrigue, and, of course, Ms. Jeffries' own brand of romance." —Nancy Engle, Author, *Image of Perfection*

"Ann Jeffries knows how to write a story that pulls you in and keeps you turning the pages! Her latest book, Walking On Uneven Ground, shows her finesse in developing characters from all walks of life. Her dialogue and descriptions of life in the inner city are spot on. You'll shudder as you walk along with the boyz through the dark, dangerous streets they patrol to make their community safe. It's a bonus that love finds its way into the storyline!" — J. A. Meinecke, Author, *A Woman to Reckon With*

"Ann Jeffries delivers another engaging read! Walking on Uneven Ground captures heart and soul, to the very last page! A dynamic presentation by a highly gifted writer!" —Bella Fayre, Author, *Maelstroms of the Silent*

"Ann Jeffries' Walking on Uneven Ground captures you from the initial paragraph and keeps you enthralled throughout. You find yourself in a

conundrum wanting to read faster but not wanting the story to end. Her characters seem as if you might meet them on your street and should you, you'd become fast friends! Fast paced and witty, a definite must read!" —Barb Ryan, Carolina Forest Critique Group

"In Walking on Uneven Ground, Ann Jeffries writes a compelling tale that supports the benefits made possible from those working for the greater good." —Carole O'Neill, Coastal Authors Network, Founding Member

The Better Part of Valor

"Ann Jeffries has done it again! Intrigue, greed, power, and romance all combine to make this a real page turner!" —J.A. Meinecke, Author, *A Woman To Reckon With*

"Ann Jeffries never disappoints! Once again she has the reader hooked and wanting more!" —Catherine Lowery, Author, *Bella and the Muddy Puddle*

"Dakota's life is anything, but ordinary. In fact, she lives a life some of us wish to live. The reader can relate to Dakota's wish to rise above her physical injury in order to obtain a goal and to continue pushing to be the person she once was. Along her journey, we learn about a lifestyle most of us only see on television. Author Ann Jeffries takes the reader on a ride filled with twists that will leave you wanting more. In this case she leaves you with unanswered questions that keep your head spinning as you wait for the next novel to be published." —L. S. Casey, Author, *Alma Mater*

"Once again Ms. Jeffries captivates the reader with characters and plot that demand complete attention. She weaves a story full of intrigue, but leaves plenty of time for romance. This book is a must read." —

Nancy Engle, Author, *Reunions Can Be Murder*

Moments to Remember

"Ann Jeffries, once again, puts us on the edge of our seats delivering a compelling storyline, complete with drama, intrigue, and romance! Jeffries takes no prisoners! A must read!" —Bella Fayre, Author, *Maelstroms of the Silent*

An Unguarded Moment

"I love a story that immediately grabs your attention and keeps you involved till the last page. Good read. Highly recommended." — Gayle A. Hopper, MD

"Ann Jeffries does an excellent job of weaving her characters' stories together and keeping the reader captivated." —Nancy Engle, Author, *Murder at Mount Joy*

"Ann has a terrific voice for romance—it [is] light, readable and the characters were a lot of fun." —Kara Cesare, the Richard Curtis Literary Agency

"I loved the story line! A little suspenseful which I like. The story flowed and it felt like I was reading a movie. I enjoyed the book." —Gina, an avid reader

"An engrossing and sensuous love story that immediately grabs your attention and keeps you involved till the last page." —Abraham Leib, Esq.

"My overall view is that this is a good, intelligent read! It's the kind of story you never want to end." —Janice Sims, Author, *This Winter Night*

"I really admire Ann's smooth writing style and the appealing premise of this project." —Mavis Allen, Associate Senior Editor, Silhouette Books

Uncommon Choices

"Ann Jeffries has given us a great adventure and a terrific love story together with characters that immediately come alive and involve us in their searing passion and heartbreaking dilemmas." —Abe Leib, Esq.

Northern Exposures

"Ms. Jeffries never writes a slow read. Her novels are impossible to put down. I can't wait for the next installment of her Wisdom of the Ancestors Series." —Trisha Moriarty, Author, *The Secrets She Kept*

Another Point of View

"Ann Jeffries has done it again! Once you start reading you won't be able to put the book down!" —J. A. Meinecke, Author, *A Woman to Reckon With*

"Another home run for Ann Jeffries! Deftly woven plot twists and the pace of the novel is strong and the story intriguing." —Jessica Tilles, Author, *Loving Simone*

Southern Exposures

"Ann Jeffries definitely has a skill for storytelling. There is vitality and high drama in Southern Exposures. *The author did an excellent job*

with honing in and focusing on the three main, important characters of which the drama surrounds. I fell in love with the Alexanders. Job well done!" —Jessica Tilles, Author/Editor

"Loved the way [Ann Jeffries] described the activities . . . I felt as though I was there witnessing everything [that she was] describing. [She] immediately got my attention with the colorful . . . attention to details. The book is very warm. The characters have to face challenges and each does it in a different way. Loved the focus on loving family— members of the family loving each other and believing in each other." —Brenda Irons LeCesne, Esq.

"There are a lot of promising plots within the story. I thoroughly enjoyed . . . this [novel]. I think [Ann Jeffries'] ability [to] create emotion is a true talent. [She] did a great job creating suspense. The [characters'] stories seemed most authentic and entertaining. Language and dialogue [o]ver all . . . is a strong area for [Ann]." —Karen R. Thomas, President, Creative Minds Book Group

"I always like a happy ending and being the romantic that I am the ending makes me want the continuation to be available for me to see the two characters Vivian and Benny to have the happy ending like KJ with the respective characters Chuck and Stacy." —Sharon Jarrett-Brown Aurora Reading Group

Walking On Uneven Ground

*Another Family Reunion Novel
In The Wisdom of the Ancestors Series*

ANN JEFFRIES

Published and Distributed By
New View Literature
820 67th Avenue N, #7603
Myrtle Beach, South Carolina 29572
www.newviewliterature.com

Cover and Interior design: TWA Solutions
ISBN: 978-0-9915003-6-9 Print
ISBN: 978-1-941603-58-1 eBook
Library of Congress Control Number: 20144909733

First printing March 2016
Second printing January 2017

For inquires, contact the publisher.

To learn more about the author, visit her website:

www.annjeffries.net

ACKNOWLEDGMENTS

I bow in humble gratitude to:

The Creator

<<<<>>>

The Ancestors

<<<<>>>

Jessica Tilles, Editor

<<<<>>>

Abe Leib, I have known for most of my former professional career. He is a friend and mentor to me and to others. I have thoroughly enjoyed the stories he shared about his world travels that sparked the imagination and looked forward to the trinkets he brought back that were reminiscent of each foreign experience.

Again, he has come through with critical comments that improved the content and quality of this story. For that, and many other reasons, I will always be grateful for his friendship, guidance, and eagle eyes.

<<<<>>>

The Carolina Forest Authors' Club is a mainstay for perfecting my craft. Individually and collectively, their guidance, encouragement, and comments are invaluable. I thank each of you who spent your precious time reading this manuscript and providing moral support.

<<<<>>>

Charles Engle is an expert engineer who manages to keep my computer behaving and answering my commands without a hiccup. I appreciate his friendship, his exceptional technical knowledge, and painstaking attention to detail.

<<<<>>>

My Uncle Bubbles, Edward Lawrence Griffis, music writer and tenor saxophone player extraordinaire. Your sweet sounds never fade from my mind.

<<<<>>>

Family, friends, and fans. You are the wind beneath my wings.

<<<<>>>

The journey continues and the struggle for literary perfection shall never end.

To all, I remain faithfully yours.

Ann Jeffries

"Family isn't always blood. It's the people in your life who want you in theirs, the ones who accept you for who you are. The ones who would do anything to see you smile and who love you no matter what."

—www.spiritualthinking.blogspot.com

Titles in Ann Jeffries'
Family Reunion—Wisdom of the Ancestors series

Southern Exposures

Another Point of View

Northern Exposures

Uncommon Choices

An Unguarded Moment

Moments to Remember

The Better Part of Valor

Walking on Uneven Ground

Touch Me in the Morning

Chapter 1

When LaKesha Reynolds reached between his thighs and pulled on his penis, massaging him aggressively, Wesley Greenfield—aka The Iceman or Ice—automatically rolled over onto his back and let her ready his early morning erection for her pleasure. It really didn't matter to him when she slipped the condom on, straddled him, and inserted him into her body. This was her usual morning routine, regardless of whether he was in the mood or not. He wasn't even half-awake and dog-tired in mind, body, and spirit to boot. None of which would matter to LaKesha. She wanted what she wanted when she wanted it. She was not a woman who took *no* for an answer.

It was five in the morning when he came home. He worked a full, eight hours at his community center the day before. It took all five of them—him and most of his boyhood friends—to run his center when it was open. They ensured the safety of nearly one hundred active kids, teens, and sometimes as many as thirty adults, who frequented the center. Keeping them occupied and interested took a lot of patience and ingenuity.

Then, after a quick meal, he closed the center and he and his crew, in two teams of two, or sometimes three, were out on the dark, chilly streets of far northeast, Washington, DC, conducting a night patrol neighborhood watch program in one of the toughest parts of the city.

Ice's life wasn't easy. Never had been. His foreseeable future promised to be another triumph in much of the same.

LaKesha rocked her hips hard against him, riding him until she began to moan and vibrate. She dug her long, sharp, acrylic nails into his flesh, nearly drawing blood. He gathered enough energy, if no real enthusiasm, to help her reach climax. The moment after she did, she hopped off him before he could get his own nut. Sated, she headed for the bathroom in his one-bedroom apartment. Wesley rolled over onto his face and went further into a deeper sleep.

"Hey! Ice! Wake the hell up!" LaKesha screeched, shaking him awake.

"What?" he grumbled, into his pillow.

"I ain't runnin' no flop house and no nursery!"

"What are you talking about, woman?" He lifted his head frowning.

"You got company!" she said, pointing an arrow-straight arm and index finger toward the bedroom door.

Slowly, he rolled out of bed, pulled on the jeans he left on the floor, and walked barefooted and bare-chested out of the bedroom. In the sparsely furnished living room, he found a member of his posse, Peckhead—aka Roscoe Hubbard—on the pullout futon, sleeping soundly and snoring. Two small mounds were on the floor under a sheet and a nine-year-old boy was at the small, round, dinette table in a chair with his arms pillowing his head.

Ice recognized Cole—Coltrane Cooper—and surmised the two lumps on the hardwood floor were Cole's seven-year-old brother, Marcus Harris, and five-year-old sister, Simone Harris. They and their mother, Jakima Harris, lived on the third floor in the same twelve-unit apartment building. Jakima was a part-time singer, part-time server, and a full-time pothead. She would sometimes go missing for days. Her children knew to come downstairs to his second floor apartment if they found themselves alone for more than a day. He had given Cole a key to his apartment for that purpose. Wesley knew when he stumbled into his apartment that morning he had not seen them, so he reasoned they must have come in after he went to bed, just as Peckhead clearly did.

In Peckhead's case, they finished walking their nightly patrols together over an hour ago. His old lady, Francine Briscoe, must have kicked him out of their apartment, again.

Ice sighed and turned to go back to bed. A very agitated LaKesha followed him into the bedroom and closed the door.

"Well?" she asked, rolling her head, fists planted on her impressive hips, clearly annoyed.

"Well what, Kesha?"

"Aren't you gonna kick them people out of my house?"

"This ain't just your place. I pay rent here. You don't. Go to work, Kesha. They won't be here when you get back tonight." He pulled off his jeans and crawled naked back into bed, turning his back to her. He was asleep within seconds and didn't even hear her mumbling curses or when she slammed out of the apartment.

When Ice surfaced again, it was to see small, dirty, bare feet in his face. He raised his head and noticed Marcus and Simone laying crossways in the bed with him, sound asleep. He eased out from between the bedsheets and quickly went into the bathroom to relieve himself and shower. Once done, he searched unsuccessfully for clean underwear, jeans, and a T-shirt only to put on the same dirty jeans, commando style, and the hoodie he wore the day before.

LaKesha wasn't into the domestic life, so when it came to keeping himself in clean clothes and the apartment neat, he was on his own—not that he had that much to work with in the first place. The apartment was only furnished with a futon, dinette table with four chairs, a double bed, chest of drawers, and a nightstand. He had one good suit and dress shoes in a closet jam-packed from top to bottom with LaKesha's TJ Maxx bargains. She allotted one drawer to him in his five-drawer chest where he kept his jeans, T-shirts, underwear, and socks.

Without waking the kids, he gathered soiled bed linens off the bed, his dirty clothes from piles on the floor, and towels from the bathroom hamper. He shoved them all in a couple of pillowcases in preparation for an impromptu laundry day in the basement of the building. Still tired, he resolved to stay with his laundry or it wouldn't be there when he returned. He hoped maybe he could catch a few winks stretched out on the clothes-folding table while the things washed and dried.

As he went into the living room, he found Peckhead still asleep on the futon, but Cole was wide-awake, reading a book, and eating what looked like the last of his Cheerios.

"Where's Jakima?" he asked Cole while filling a pot with water for coffee.

"I 'on't know. She ain't been home since Sunday."

"It's Wednesday.

Why didn't you come before?"

"Had enough food for a few days, so we went to school like normal. We get welfare breakfast and lunch, snacks, too, at school."

"Why didn't you go to school today?"

"Couldn't get in the crib to wash up and change our clothes. Ol' man Jenkins changed the locks yesterday before we got home. Went lookin' for Jakima all night. Didn't find her nowhere by this morning, so we come here."

"I was on patrol last night. I didn't see you."

"We went over by the clubs looking where she hangs out. Then under the bridge on Minnesota Avenue where she gets high."

He just shook his head. "Did you feed Marcus and Simone?"

"Yeah. Gave them cereal, but you ain't got no milk. Just some OJ. They was tired from walkin' all night looking for Jakima, so when I heard big ass Queen LaKesha hat up," he said, factiously, "I told them to go get in your bed."

"I don't mind you sending them to get into my bed, Cole, but I wasn't wearing anything to sleep in."

"So? Ain't a thing. We seen plenty of nekkid dudes with Jakima before."

Nonplussed, Ice just shook his head again. "I'll get Jenkins to unlock the door, so you can get your stuff and then I'll see what I can do to find your mother."

"A'ight, but she probably gone off with the man she be screwin'."

"What man?"

"I 'ont know. She call him Honeybear. Claims he a big-time music producer, but, he a lie. He don't even got a car. Laid up on Jakima for a few weeks 'til the welfare check come. They probably done gone off in her mama car."

Ice looked up as if communing with The Almighty and released a frustrated breath. This wouldn't be the first time Jakima Harris disappeared, leaving her children to fend on their own, but she generally was only gone for a day or two, at the most.

"Want to call your grandmother?"

"Can't. She dead."

"What? When?"

"Couple weeks ago."

"You didn't say nothin'."

"What for? Didn't have no funeral or nothin'."

"You got any other kin?"

Cole shrugged his thin shoulders and continued eating the Cheerios soaked in orange juice.

"What about your father?"

"I 'ont know him. Ain't never seen him. Jakima, she say he just some dude she was screwin' one night when she was high. All she say she remember was she call him Copper like the penny 'cause he had red hair and 'cause his name be like Cooper or somethin'. He ain't Marcus' and Simone's daddy dough. None o' us got the same daddy. She didn't know thems' daddy neever."

That all three children had different fathers was clearly apparent to Ice, but they still had some facial features in common. At least enough to know they were related. Cole apparently carried his father's last name, but Simone and Marcus carried Jakima's maiden name likely because she didn't know who their fathers were.

Ice reached into the refrigerator, and pulled out what was left of a quart of juice, downing it straight from the carton. There wasn't anything else in the refrigerator, except packets of ketchup and grated cheese. LaKesha couldn't boil water, so she never bought groceries unless it was chips, salsa, and a six-pack of beer, so she and her rowdy friends could hang. There was a small can of coffee on the door rack he opened, scooped out enough for a couple of cups of strong coffer, and then dug through the grounds, and retrieved a roll of quarters. He hid his loose change in the coffee can because he knew if he didn't, LaKesha would take his last dime. He needed that change to do the laundry.

First things first, Ice thought, as he pounded on Fred Jenkins' apartment door. When it opened, Rochelle Taylor, a woman who was a year or two older than Ice, stood before him, her flowery kimono falling open, partially displaying her double-Ds and hairy pubis. She made no attempt to cover herself, but a salacious grin grew around her blood-red mouth.

"Well, hello, playa. What can I do you for?"

"Rochelle," he acknowledged. He looked, but had no interest in what she was offering. He never had, though he believed his brother, Isaac, had tapped that many times years ago. "Jenkins here?"

"Yeah, I just finished givin' the old man the best blow job of his life. You ought to let me show you."

Not on a bet, he thought. Just then, Fred Jenkins, the building's super, a man at least fifteen years Rochelle's senior, came hustling to the door. He stepped in front of her, shielding her from view.

"What you want?" Jenkins belligerently asked.

"Why you change the locks on Jakima's door?"

"What the fuck is it to you, ass wipe?" he demanded with bravado.

In a move too swift for the short, rotund Jenkins to anticipate, he was slammed against his front door with Wesley's big hand around his throat. His eyes bulged, as he gasped for air. Rochelle did nothing, as an easy smile played at the corners of her mouth.

"I asked you a question, Jenkins. Don't make me ask twice."

"Rent," he choked out, clawing at Ice's strong grip, but with no success. "She ain't paid her rent the last three months."

Ice pushed the shorter man away from him. "Go get those keys and unlock the door."

Jenkins fled into his apartment and retrieved his heavy, round ring of keys. He sprinted up the steps to the third floor, as fast as his penguin-like body would take him, with Ice on his heels.

Cole sat on the floor in front of the door, his arms resting on his bent knees, his head hung low. *He looks like a poster child for dejection, hopelessness, and despair*, Ice thought. When Jenkins charged up the steps, Cole stood and shifted aside until the door opened.

"Go on in and get your stuff," Ice instructed Cole while he, too, entered and searched Jakima's apartment for some clue as to where she might be or any evidence of other family relations. She was younger than him and his crew and, consequently, he didn't know her family other than her mother.

Finding nothing to help in his search for her or other family members, they dropped one bag of the children's belongings in Ice's apartment. Then, Cole helped carry three trash bags of clothes and tennis shoes down to the basement laundry. He sent Cole back up to his apartment to stay with his brother and sister in case they woke up and worried because they found him gone.

As the clothes tumbled in the industrial-sized washers, instead of catching a nap as he had planned, Ice contemplated what to do with the three youngsters until he could locate their mother. Clearly, leaving a nine, seven, and five-year-old alone in their two-bedroom apartment wasn't going to work. He and LaKesha lived in a one-bedroom. Living there would be difficult for five people, but he didn't want the children to come up on the city's child protective services' radar. They would definitely separate the siblings and stick them in different foster care housing, which, he believed, would further traumatize them. If tough Cole was any indication, the children's sense of helplessness and hopelessness was beginning to set in. He had to come up with another solution, and fast.

When the clothes were clean, dry, and sorted, he carried everything up to his apartment. Since it was nearly noon, everyone was awake, including Peckhead. They sat on the futon, watching cartoons on his small flat screen.

"You ain't got no food up in this joint?" Peckhead accused.

"How much scratch you got on you?"

"I 'ont know. Maybe twenty, thirty bucks."

"Go on down to the chicken place and get a bucket."

"Man, this all I got 'til the eagle fly," he complained, but looked at Ice's set jaw and eyes rolling toward the kids. He got the silent message, got up off the futon accepted cash from Ice, and headed out the door.

Once Peckhead was gone, Ice took his place on the futon and, with the remote, turned off the flat screen. He ran his left hand over his head and down his face, getting his thoughts in order.

The children patiently watched him without expression.

"First, I want you to know you're going to stay here with me until I find your mother and see what's what. You're going to go to school every day, but do not tell anyone Jakima's not home. Do you understand?" he asked, particularly looking at Simone, the youngest. The children silently nodded their understanding.

"You don't want the welfare peoples to come and get us," Marcus said, his small face sad, but earnest.

"That's right. Now, look. You see I don't have a lot of room, so you're going to have to share this futon to sleep on at night. You know LaKesha lives here, too, so you're going to have to be real quiet around her."

"Cuz she don't like no kids," little Simone said just above a whisper, as if sharing a secret.

Ice smiled at the pretty little girl and ran his hand over her bushy hair that needed a good wash. In fact, both boys looked like they could stand to have their heads scrubbed and haircuts. Another detail he knew he would have to cover before they returned to school the next day.

"All right, go wash your faces and brush your teeth. After we eat lunch, we've got some things to do."

"Don't got no toothbrushes. Just use our fingers. No washcloth neever," Cole informed.

Oh, hell, Ice thought, sighing. He saw the threadbare condition of their clothes and shoes and now he needed to add toiletries to the growing list of things they required. He didn't have cash money for everything these children would need over time, but he would find a way to keep them fed, clothed, and together no matter what it took.

Actually, he was not without resources. He still had the utensils, furniture, and equipment in storage he could sell that came from his father's closed ice cream shop and bakery. Also, the twelve-unit apartment building he lived in, he and his older brother, Isaac, Jr., actually inherited from their father. He didn't make much profit from owning the apartment building, particularly when people, like Jakima, didn't pay their rent and repairs were often needed. After all the expenses, including Jenkins' salary, were paid by the management company, and they took their cut, what little monies were left, were put into anonymous donations for the community center, a savings account for his brother, and some was set aside for repairs and maintenance on the apartment building.

No one, other than the superstar basketball icon, his boyhood best friend, J. Roderick Baylor, aka, JRock, knew he owned the apartment building, not even Mr. Jenkins or LaKesha. He handled everything through a management company that thought he was an absentee landlord, Jeremiah Isaac, who lived in Florida.

He couldn't start flashing around a lot of money or LaKesha and his posse would get suspicious. Everyone knew running a not-for-profit community center was a minimum-wage job. He and his crew barely made enough to survive on, but this was their neighborhood, the place where they all grew up.

When others finished high school, got jobs, and moved away, the seven friends stayed behind and together sacrificed to protect and defend their neighborhood against the criminal element. Some, like him, went to trade schools, others to junior colleges or into the military. They never wanted to live anywhere else.

The old neighborhood was admittedly dilapidated and decaying around them. The once vibrant community of well-kept buildings and homes seemed tired, worn out, and sad; some were even abandoned from decades of use and abuse.

He and his posse still held out hope someday they could make it a place where people wanted to move to rather than a place to escape from. His friend, JRock, was working on a plan that might make it happen. Ice knew he and his posse had to hold out and do what they could until times got better.

When Peckhead returned with the bucket of chicken, side orders, and drinks, they ate their fill, and left the apartment on foot. They went to the neighborhood, squat U-shaped, strip, shopping center blocks away.

First, Ice took the children to Bubbles and Billie's Hair Emporium where he had to ring a doorbell before they walked through two sets of electronically controlled, shatterproof glass security doors and metal detectors to gain entrance. Bubbles and Billie Bouchard, a husband and wife, barber and beautician, with a staff of eight, kept fully loaded Glocks and Macs within easy reach, and they were prepared to use deadly force, if called upon to do so. One could never tell from looking at the couple, but Bubbles got his street name because he could blow a tenor saxophone so sweet it was like seeing champagne bubbles rising from the instrument. Billie could sing like her namesake, the famous chanteuse, Billie Holiday.

Bubbles and Billie used to perform regularly in area nightclubs and in the neighborhood theatre with their band for years. That's how they made money to go to cosmetology school and open their own shop. From time to time, they might pull their old band together again to do a fundraising concert at the community center. As popular as Peaches & Herb and Ashford & Simpson, they even recorded albums and toured the country until the babies started coming. They couldn't be on the road constantly sothey came home to settle down and help sustain the neighborhood.

They and others in the shop were humming to their music coming from the wall speakers while they worked. Ice left the kids there enjoying the old school music and went about his other errands.

The neighborhood had not always been fraught with violence. That tense, edgy, and too often, vicious environment seemed to grow when hard drugs were introduced as a means to a fast moneymaking career. When he and his brother were kids, their father brought them to the same barber shop and beauty salon where the door sat wide open and people stopped in just to pass the time and gossip. Back in the day, customers didn't ring doorbells and wait to be scoped before entrance was granted. Now, he and his crew patrolled the shopping center and the surrounding neighborhoods to protect the merchants and citizens alike.

The graffiti-stained, rundown, poorly lit shopping center in the heart of his neighborhood sported pushers, pimps, and prostitutes every few feet, openly selling their wares. Like 7-Eleven stores, they were always open for business.

Old and new gang tats stained the buildings. Homeless men and women moved aimlessly about, weaving in and out of parked cars, pushing stolen grocery carts filled with their worldly possessions, looking to boost a radio or anything of value and dodging the occasional irate motorist.

More recently, the neighborhood experienced an influx of Latinos, Jamaicans, and Africans who squatted in abandoned single-family homes and apartment buildings or abandoned businesses like the closed gas station and the auto repair garage down the block. He knew at least eleven people were living there.

A souped-up Camaro passed, with radio blasting the latest rap group spewing profanity at every other word of their driving beat. On the street, Wesley Greenfield became The Iceman and most people knew not to mess with him. He rarely traveled the streets alone. As he and Peckhead cast their eyes on the cars crisscrossing each other in the parking lot, they noted the men carried guns clearly visible. The Royal Reds drug gang, Ice and Peckhead knew. The gang members talked openly about who was going to 'get got' for blowing another drug deal. When Ice and Peckhead came into view, conversation halted, and the cars quickly pulled away. Relative quiet was restored, but danger still lingered in the cold, brisk air.

Iron bars graced every large, plate-glass window he and Peckhead passed, as they walked the shopping center. The corner drug and general dollar store had two armed guards and metal detectors standing sentry at the doors when he and Peckhead entered. He nodded an acknowledgment to the guards, who he knew were retired police officers, but otherwise wasted no time grabbing a basket and picking up the toiletry items he needed: toothbrushes, toothpaste, combs, brushes, deodorant, body lotion, hair oil, and One A Day children's vitamins. Packets of new underwear, T-shirts, and socks for the kids and some for himself added to the growing basket of goods.

At the next stop, Addie's Attire, a second-hand clothing and convenience store where he and Peckhead made out like bandits on clothes and shoes for the kids. They even bought coats, hats, gloves, and jackets for little or nothing. They lucked-up on terrycloth towels, washcloths, and linens for sale. Less than two hundred dollars secured enough clothes and shoes to cover each child for a few weeks.

When they walked into the grocery store, security required them to check their bags before grabbing a shopping cart. Food cost more, was less well stocked, and came in smaller containers in Burke's Big V mom-and-pop store than other larger grocery store chains outside the neighborhood, but several generations of Burkes, who still lived in the neighborhood, were the owners. For that reason, the posse continued to shop there.

They got the in-store discount flyer and made the best buys they could on sale items and coupons. Two-for-one boxes of pasta and large packages of ground beef were a bargain, including two big bags of collard greens. He grabbed the family-sized pack of chicken wings and legs, stew beef, and splurged on pork chops. He had a taste for corned beef, cabbage, and white potatoes; the leftovers he could turn into corn beef hash for breakfast so he bought that, too.

Eggs were at a premium along with bacon, sausage, and fresh bread. The bread he returned to the shelf. He just needed the ingredients and he could bake his own bread for a lot less money. Considering the cost of dry cereal, he wished he had the time and patience to learn to make that, too. He picked up the off brands instead of the name brands just to save a few pennies more.

A box of oatmeal, a bag of hominy grits, and Cream of Wheat would fill their bellies on cold, early mornings. They picked up a couple gallons of milk and orange juice, hot dogs and cans of beans, fresh garlic, and a bag of onions. The tin of chocolate was too pricey and would have to wait for another grocery day. The prices of apples, oranges, bananas, and lemons were dear, too, but the cost of other fresh fruit, like strawberries and blueberries, were out of the question. So, Ice settled for what he could reasonably afford now. A ten-pound bag of white potatoes and another of yams went into the shopping cart. He would wait for the farmers' market to open over the weekend to buy more fresh fruits and vegetables rather than waste money on the amoebic-looking fare in the reduced price bin. They shopped for other staple items and found free, empty boxes Ice figured the children could use as drawers to store their clothes for the time being. They could use a single trash bag as a dirty clothes hamper for now.

When they left the grocery store loaded down with bags and boxes, Ice didn't even break stride as he passed the boarded up storefront in the shopping center where Icey's Ice Cream Parlor and Bakery used to be. His father, Isaac, Sr., took over the store from his father, Jeremiah Greenfield, but had been dead now for nearly twelve years. His brother, Isaac, Jr., was still doing time in a Montana penitentiary for killing the man who shot and killed their father. He wouldn't see freedom for too many years to come.

Bracing himself against the bone-chilling cold, Ice tapped a coin on the glass-front window of Nana's Nails to get LaKesha's attention. She sat on one of the high-rise pedicure chairs, engrossed in a movie magazine, wearing ear buds, bobbing her head to the music on her iPhone, and popping gum like a cow chewing its cud. It took a few tries, but someone in the shop got her attention and, when she spotted him at the door, she made her way outside.

"What's all this shit?"

"Food and other stuff. I need your car keys."

"What for?"

"What do you think, Kesha?" He sighed.

"Ain't none of that shit for me, huh?"

"You eat, too, don't you? I also got laundry stuff."

"You said them crumb snatchers wasn't gonna stay."

"So, sue me."

"I ain't comin' back if them brats gonna be there."

"Suit yourself, but until I find Jakima, the kids are gonna be staying there. Put the word out I'm lookin' for her and don't get slick callin' social services, Kesha. Now give me your damn car keys."

She reached into the back pocket of her too tight jeans and handed over the keys to her hoopty. She sucked her teeth, rolled her eyes, and flipped her long, fake hair over her shoulder as she flounced away, swaying her big bootie purposely, letting him see what he was going to be missing. He heard Peckhead's whispered *"Daayam!"* under his breath. For a moment, Ice wondered why his dick didn't get hard anymore looking at Kesha's perfect ass. She wore a tight V-neck sweater with her bouncing boobs on display, a pair of skintight, body-hugging jeans, and man-killer, stiletto-heeled, black boots with chains. Something had to be seriously wrong with him not to even get a woody around her anymore.

He and LaKesha hadn't really established boundaries to their relationship. As one of the round-the-way girls, he had been banging her off and on since junior high school. Then one day, about five years ago, she showed up at his apartment, baggage in hand, saying her stepfather wouldn't keep his hands off her. Not even asking whether she could stay with him, LaKesha simply assumed, because of their relationship, she could stay rent-free. She just moved in and had been living with him ever since, never looking for other accommodations. It seemed to be against her religion tolift her hand to clean one room, do her own laundry, or offer to pay one utility bill.. LaKesha pretty much did whatever she wanted with her friends and never pressed him about love or marriage. Having sex a couple times a day was usually enough to keep her happy. She would sex him up when he came home in the morning before she left for work. At lunchtime she usually came home to get him naked again before he went to open up his community center at half two in the afternoon.

LaKesha wasn't the sentimental type by a long shot, so he didn't have any expectations of moral support where she was concerned. She was a manicurist by day and five or six nights a week she stripped and danced with a pole at Sporty's, a titty bar and strip joint off New York Avenue in Northeast, Washington, DC. She had the body for the job and enough sex appeal with her fake hair, eyelashes, and nails to entice men to give up their hard-earned money, placing it in her G-string. He and LaKesha had known each other for a long time, but they were essentially two adults existing in the same one-bedroom apartment with exclusive access to each other's bodies.

After picking up the kids and paying a grip for their hair care services, he, Peckhead, and the kids hauled the purchases up to his second floor apartment. Peckhead left shortly thereafter to return LaKesha's car and then go home before his woman, Francine, got home from her job as a registered nurse in a doctor's office.

While the kids put their clean clothes and newly purchased items into boxes, Ice chopped celery, garlic, green pepper, mushrooms, and onions for the spaghetti sauce he would make for dinner and added it to the mixture of ground beef, ground turkey, and hot sausage meat he browned in a skillet with seasonings, stewed tomatoes, tomato paste, and sauce. He sliced a long loaf of day-old French bread, and let Simone butter it and sprinkle garlic salt and chives on it, preparing it to go into the oven to brown slightly for garlic toast. While the sauce simmered, he started a ham hock to boil in chicken broth for his stock and washed the collard greens in sea salt.

Simone pulled a chair to the counter, climbed up, and watched him work. She carried on a steady Q-and-A about everything he did. He realized, apparently, Jakima didn't often cook for her children, opting for fast food or cereal when times were tough. When she worked at the North East Diner in the shopping center, she brought home restaurant leftovers.

He let Simone stir the fresh squeezed lemons, limes, and honey in a pot on the stove. Then, he poured the mixture, along with ice-cold water, over ice in the plastic jug. As he continued making dinner, he also learned their deceased grandmother cooked for the children when she was forced to take them in. Apparently, they hadn't had regular meals since their grandmother died. He suspected as much, given their nearly emaciated appearance. That's why he splurged and purchased the expensive children's vitamins. He suspected the children were living on the edge of malnutrition, dehydration, and starvation.

They were obedient and didn't make noise as they watched television, but clearly, Cole seemed as if he carried the world on his small shoulders. After dinner, Cole helped clear the table then helped his siblings to bathe and dress for bed. Of the things Cole had taken from his apartment was a bunch of books. Once they settled comfortably on the futon, he read several stories to Marcus and Simone. Since there was no television in Jakima's apartment, reading stories was apparently something Cole often did. It was meaningful to Ice that the books Cole read came from his community center.

By nine o'clock, the children were tucked in and asleep. Ice stood up a folding screen he took from Jakima's apartment and placed it in front of the futon to block some of the light from the kitchen and dining area. He sat at the dinette table, thinking about how he would manage his night patrols with his posse and care for the children in his apartment. He couldn't afford to hire a sitter every night and he knew he couldn't depend on LaKesha. She didn't have a maternal bone in her body.

As the hour grew later, he assumed she was making good on her threat not to come home if the children were there. By one in the morning, when LaKesha had not shown up, he called Sporty's to confirm she had worked that night, what time she left the bar, and then went to bed.

The next morning, Ice made breakfast for them: French toast, using the rest of the now three-day-old French bread, warm syrup, and fresh cut peaches, bacon, and orange juice, and then made sure they were dressed warmly for school and out the door on time. He had washed dishes and was scrubbing the kitchen floor when all three children came trooping back into the apartment.

"What happened?" he asked.

"Mz. Hunter, she say we gotta have a note 'bout why we wasn't in school yesterday or somebody gotta come and explain."

Fuck a duck, Ice thought, morosely. He'd rather take a beating than face his former high school classmate, Rosalyn Hunter, the principal of the elementary school. Steel magnolias would wilt in her presence. She kicked ass and took no prisoners.

He sucked up his courage, threw on his hoodie, and walked the children the block and a half back to the elementary school; the same one he attended as a child. Unlike when he was a kid, they were buzzed into the lobby where they went through a second set of security doors and metal detectors. Rosalyn was waiting just beyond the doors, with arms folded.

"Roz," Ice acknowledged. He dug his hands into his jean pockets.

"Wes," she returned and then to the children, she said, "Here are your hall passes. Go directly to your classrooms."

Ice felt relieved he wasn't going to have to explain after all and took the opportunity to turn to leave. Before he could escape, he heard Rosalyn's voice.

"With me, Wes." Rosalyn turned to go into her office.

He should have known it wouldn't be easy with Rosalyn Hunter.

"You had a call, Dr. Hunter, confirming your date for tonight," Glenda Gray, another old neighborhood girl said, smiling coyly at Ice.

Yeah, he remembered he had tapped that ass a few times back in high school, too.

"Thanks," Rosalyn said, retrieving the message as she continued toward an inner office. She stopped and held the door for Wesley to enter and then closed it behind him.

"What's going on with Jakima?" She parked her butt against the front of her mahogany desk; arms folded below her voluptuous breasts, and crossed her fine, dancer's legs at the ankles.

Ice stayed in a semi-aroused state anytime he was around Rosalyn Hunter. The woman was built like the proverbial brick shit house and had a face and a head full of real hair that made many men humble. She was an exceptional looking woman and smelled of something exotic and sexy.

In high school, he wanted to step to her, but although she lived in the neighborhood, she wasn't a round-the-way kind of girl like LaKesha or Glenda. Rather, she was a high-energy, straight-A, honor-roll student, something he was not. She participated in many extra curriculum activities like the book club, chess team, and student council, took ballet classes and was Vice President of the senior class while he had only lettered in track.

Her parents were both dentists and used to have an office in the same shopping center where his father's store was located. Their daughter was an only child and it was clear they weren't grooming her for some roughneck, corner boy like him. They had big plans for her that included a top university and a stellar career of her choosing.

When his friend, JRock, a super basketball jock with stardom written all over him, asked Rosalyn to be his date for the senior prom, he was surprised she said yes. Ice and JRock doubled-dated; him with LaKesha. They ended up in the early morning hours at the beach near Annapolis, Maryland, sexing it up. After that night, though, his desire for Rosalyn didn't wane as it should have seeing her with JRock, but he stayed away from her for JRock's sake. After graduation, Rosalyn and JRock went away to different colleges or universities and their relationship fizzled. He stayed at home and went to culinary school at the junior college with the belief he and his brother would one day run their father's business. However, two years later, his father was murdered and his brother sent to prison at age twenty-one.

His mother died only a few months after he was born. Though he had plenty of opportunities, their father never remarried. Their father, and his now deceased paternal grandmother, raised Ice and his brother. With Isaac, Jr., incarcerated, if it were not for his best friend, JRock, and JRock's family, Ice would have been left pretty much on his own from the age of nineteen to the present.

"Wes?" Rosalyn said again, snapping him back from his thoughts of yesteryear.

"Uh, oh, uh, yeah, you asked about Jakima."

"Yes, is she gone again?"

"Why do you ask that?"

"Because her children have never looked that clean, neat, and tidy since they started coming to this school for daycare. It had to be someone else's handiwork. Then they wouldn't explain where they were yesterday and you show up with them today instead of Jakima. I just connected the dots."

"Well," he hedged.

"Give it up, Wes," she said, sighing. "I'm not going to go blabbing to child welfare if you tell me you and LaKesha are going to look after them until Jakima comes back."

He hesitated another pregnant moment. "I'm going to look for Jakima and keep the kids until I find her."

"If you don't find her? Then what?"

"I'll figure it out when I have to."

Rosalyn stared at him for a moment. He was so damn handsome and ruggedly built it was hard to keep her thoughts in a row around him. He wasn't a particularly tall man, only standing about six-foot-one or two. His complexion was buttermilk biscuit brown with slightly darker brown naturally wavy hair that he kept cut short, but he had the most beautiful golden brown eyes she had ever seen.

She dearly wished she could peel his clothes off his phine physique and ravage what she had long envied LaKesha for having. Truth be told, she had been in lust with Wesley Greenfield, aka The Iceman, since their early years in high school.

So had every other young girl in their class. He was the cutest and the most popular boy in their school, primarily because of his unusually pretty golden eyes. He ran track and was too sexy by half in running shorts. She had only consented to go to the prom with his best friend, Roderick, aka JRock, because she knew he and Wesley would double date. She would have done nearly anything to be in his company, even foolishly consenting to have sex with JRock, while Wesley was sexing up LaKesha in the back seat of the rental car.

Sex with JRock was her first experience. Before that night on the beach blanket, she was a virgin. It never would have happened with JRock if Wesley had asked her to be his date to the prom instead of LaKesha, or acted on any number of the other openings she gave him to ask her out. As a young girl, she dreamed her first time having sex would be with Wesley Barrett Greenfield. Back then, she was into good-looking bad boys . . . and she still was.

More than a decade had passed since high school, but she often still craved Wesley in her empty bed at night.

"Roz?"

It was her turn to snap out of her daydream. "Yes, well, let me know if you need any help with the children. Generally, they are good kids and good students. I'll see what I can find out discretely about where Jakima might be."

"That'll help. Thanks."

"Uh, you and your crew still doing neighborhood watch at night?"

"Yeah?" A bit of suspicion was evident in his voice.

"If LaKesha needs a sitter sometime while you're out on patrol or she's working at Sporty's, let me know."

"That's not necessary. I'll handle it, so if there's nothing else, I got to roll out."

"Uh, sure. That's all for now, but keep me posted if you hear anything about Jakima."

"Yeah, sure. See you around, Roz," he said and nearly sprinted from her office. If he had to stand there another moment and look at his idea of perfection, she would have seen the evidence of his aroused state. That would have embarrassed the hell out of them both.

He was too keyed up to go back to his apartment, so he decided to go to the community center to workout and catch up on his paperwork. Walking to the community center in the cold, brisk air with sleet falling helped him refocus his thoughts away from Rosalyn and onto his work. The building was an old, decommissioned, three-level, junior high school. It had a large parking lot and an area where the kids could play outside on a grassy field. An eight-foot high, ossifying, chain link fence surrounded the property. He didn't have the budget to remodel the second and third levels of the building, so he blocked access to the upper floors.

Sometimes, he illegally let people, usually evicted families down on their luck, sleep there. They would come in dragging whatever personal possessions they could salvage. He let them stay there for a few nights until they could get their bearings. However, he didn't want to run the risk of losing his occupancy license, so he kept that activity to a minimum.

When he arrived, he checked his surroundings carefully. Over the years, there were a number of break-in attempts, usually at night. He keyed in the security code and the door popped open. Once inside, he relocked the door and quickly reset the alarm. Walking down a long, quiet, barely-lit hallway, he cast his eyes into each designated room he passed, particularly the Computer Lab. The donated computers were old and second-hand, but they provided a valuable service to kids for homework projects and adults looking for jobs and other social services.

The only library in the neighborhood was shut down due to citywide budget cuts. When the library closed, he and his crew gathered up the discarded library books, bookshelves, tables and chairs, and hauled them back to the community center. They established reading rooms, using those books and books from other closed libraries or schools; anything they could scavenge to enhance the facility.

That same round of budget cuts shut down the only prison in the area. As a result, his only family member was sent to a prison in Montana. He hadn't seen his brother, Isaac, since the day he was shipped away many years ago. It was the severely disenfranchised and disadvantaged people who suffered the most when city funds dried up.

Whenever he learned from JRock a five-star hotel was remodeling their interior, he and his crew would bargain for the furniture and what they couldn't immediately use, like beds and cabinets, they would store on the upper floors of the community center building. Sometimes, they held flea markets and sold what they could to support the center's budget shortfalls.

He was scheduled to get funds from the city for upgrading the computer software programs, but that money was promised all summer and was nowhere in sight in early fall. He knew he was going to have to put on his one good suit, shine his only pair of dress shoes, and make another trip down to the DC government office to get some answers about the funds. Telephone calls didn't get the job done anymore. Neither did talking with duly elected representatives to the city council.

At least the cost-cutting measures he instituted were working and he had enough money to pay the utility bills and salaries on Friday. With a little luck, if the weather held up, he would not have to turn the heat up in the building for a little while longer. As it was, he had the thermostat set just high enough to keep the pipes from freezing. He usually had a lot of people using the Computer Lab, which kept that room fairly warm and the electric bill high trying to manage the temperature. The kids playing in the gym and studying or watching television in the quiet multipurpose rooms kept them from noticing how cold the building was.

He stuck his head into the Nurse's Station where a group of students from various colleges and universities in the area provided free medical and dental services once a month. They couldn't do much more than routine check-ups in the facility, but to those who didn't have the wear-with-all for even that, something was better than nothing. Peckhead's Francine helped when she could. She had a list of doctors and dentists who were willing to take on elderly or indigent patients.

He noticed Slide, aka Henry Hughes, one of his home boyz who helped run the center and doubled as a night watchman, was sound asleep on one of the cots in the administrative area. He had worked all night, too, so Ice didn't disturb him, but proceeded to what used to be the principal's office he and his crew divided into cubicles to take care of paperwork that went along with running a large, multipurpose community center on a dental-floss budget.

One of his plans for the building was to start an early education, child-care program for infants through pre-school. Parents in his neighborhood needed a safe, reasonably priced place to take their preschool children while they worked or searched for employment. In this economy, it took two incomes just to survive. He had enough space for the project, but not the budget or the staff. He had been trying for years to figure out a way to make that happen.

He instituted a farmers' market and Turkish Bizaar, renting space in the parking lot twice a month for vendors to come in for three days over a weekend to sell fresh fruits, vegetables, fish and poultry, and other wares, but he didn't recoup a great deal of profit from the rental fees to fund other major activities. That money pretty much went into petty cash to fund quick repairs or maintenance he or his posse couldn't or didn't have the time to handle on their own.

He also wanted to negotiate with law schools in the area to bring their students in to help people in the community who couldn't afford an attorney for advice on legal problems or issues related to wills or trusts. Recently, people from other countries were coming in to find out how to get a green card.

Ice applied for every grant and/or charitable program he could find to raise funds to keep the community center going. Fortunately, he was successful with quite a few. Just that morning, Peckhead brought an idea to him he had heard about temporarily housing at-risk kids legally until their home situations could be evaluated; kids like Cole, Marcus, and Simone. He hadn't given the idea much thought before, but because Peckhead said the city paid big bucks on time to house at-risk kids, he was having second thoughts and had, told Peckhead to follow up and get more information. It might be the income source he needed to help fund a daycare facility. He would do nearly anything to keep the community center open, even on its current, limited, operational schedule.

Chapter 2

Rosalyn Hunter wasn't feeling the date she agreed to with Howard Gardner, a long-term relationship, but she promised. Howard was a prosperous CPA and worked for one of the big, important accounting firms in Northwest DC. He invited her as his guest for an after-hours party at his firm. She left work an hour early to get her hair done at Bubbles and Billie's, and to pick up on any gossip concerning the whereabouts of Jakima Harris. Of course, thanks to Glenda the Gossip the shop was brimming with talk about The Iceman taking care of Jakima's kids, but nothing yet about the woman's location.

She was now getting her mani-pedi at Nana's Nails, another place where gossip abounded among people who had known each other for most, if not all, of their lives. Her regular manicurist, Belva Lee, was the granddaughter of the shop's Asian American owner, and was a year or two ahead of Rosalyn in high school. Belva was tied up with another client. Because Rosalyn didn't have time to wait, she permitted LaKesha Reynolds to provide the service.

"So you know he must be trippin' or somethin' if he think I'ma be takin' care of that trick's kids, right?" LaKesha complained to anyone within earshot while she soaked Rosalyn's feet and hands in warm, sudsy water.

A simultaneous "I know you right!" came from two women also getting mani-pedi services, as they gave each other high-fives.

"I can't get a man to take care of his own damn kids, and here Ice go takin' up slack for some other third leg? *Girrrrrlllll*, I don't know, Kesha. You think one'a Jakima's kids be his? You know Coltrane, he look something like Ice; could be his daddy. He got them pretty-colored eyes like Ice got. Ice, he always be lookin' out for Jakima's kids."

Incensed LaKesha said, "Ice is a stone up sex machine. Got dick for days, but he ain't crazy enough to hug up on Jakima's rusty butt. He ain't Cole's daddy or none a thems' daddy."

"Heard dat!"

"Y'all ain't seen the bitch, have ya?" asked LaKesha.

"Saw her Saturday night at the Down Under, huggin' up on Honeybear. Trick was high as a Georgia pine. Ain't seen her since. Ice be lookin' for her?"

"Yeah. You know where Honeybear be stayin' at?" LaKesha asked.

"He been up in Jakima's spot, last I heard, but he from Jersey. I can ask my boo. He know where Honeybear be livin' at in Jersey. Last summer they went to Atlantic City to game. I can't be texting or callin' him on his celly and I ain't gonna see my boo 'til Sunday while the football game be on."

"Your boo, he still be livin' with his wife up in Northwest?"

"Naw, they moved out in Montgomery County somewhere like Chevy Chase or Bethesda somethin'. His wife, she be makin' bank, much bling-bling. She a HNIC at that big bank downtown on Fifteenth Street 'cross from Old Ebbitt Grill, but he gon' leave her, so we can be together. Bitch-ass wife be watchin' him like a damn hawk."

"Uh huh, I heard that!" LaKesha knowingly intoned while catching the eye of two other women, and then turned her attention to her client. "You quiet today, Roz. What you workin' on?"

"E-mail," she said, though she had heard every word of the conversations going on around her, particularly when those discussions turned to men and sex. LaKesha was very graphic in describing her sex life with Wesley. Roz had her iPad in her lap while she put out feelers with people she knew and trusted at the police department, like Captain Gary Bouchard, aka G-Boogie, Bubbles and Billie's oldest son, and William Porter, aka Slick Willie, an administrator at the city hospital who used to live with his parents two doors from her. She just finished putting the street name "Honeybear" and "New Jersey" into the instant message so her friends would have a place to start looking for Jakima.

"I don't know how you deal with all them bad-ass kids all day," LaKesha said derisively.

"Yeah, it's a mystery all right," Rosalyn said, with tongue planted firmly in cheek. Truth is, she loved her school and its kids and still wanted children of her own. She would be ecstatic if she could somehow get Wesley Greenfield to father her children, but that was just a pipe dream. Realistically, unless she went the artificial insemination route, her chances of having children any time soon were slim to none.

"You still seein' that accountant? Whatchamacallit, Gardner?"

"Howard. Yes, in fact I'm seeing him tonight. He and some of his co-workers just signed up a big client and as a result got a promotion."

"Least he makin' some cheddar. He took you on that trip last year to Paris, France. He's always taking you on trips and out to do nice things. All Ice wanna do wid every dime he get is fix up da hood."

"Yeah, but to hear you tell it, Kesha, that man be sexing you up good and proper six ways and double that on Sunday," one of their female contemporaries added, laughing.

"Yeah, his Johnson is huge and he know what he be doin' wit' it, but that ain't got me nowhere other than a fake French restaurant on my birthday three years ago," she said and sucked her teeth.

Rosalyn's nipples had tightened at the thought of Wesley's anatomy. She'd trade Paris for one night in Wesley's bed in a heartbeat.

"Whatchu grinnin' 'bout, Roz? Can your man bring it between the sheets?" another woman asked.

"Brotherman looks like he's packin' some heavy luggage," LaKesha teased, grinning.

"Why you be studdin' her man's package, Kesha, especially wit' whatchu got at home?"

"Hey, I got eyes, don't I? I seen him when he picked up Roz to go play tennis one day last summer. He had on a pair of dem white shorts and a real Polo shirt. Wasn't no knockoff neever. Brotherman was packin' or he was damn glad to see Roz," Kesha joked and laughed. The others joined in.

Funny, Rosalyn thought. She remembered a number of occasions when she and Howard played tennis or golf last summer, but she didn't recall his attire registered with her on any of those occasions. Yes, he was physically fit and handsome enough, but a bit too controlling and egotistical for her taste. He thought it was his duty to order for both of them whenever they were out forbreakfast, lunch or dinner without consulting her. He frequently bought expensive clothes and lingerie for her to suit *his* taste not necessarily hers.

Though jewelry wasn't her thing, he liked to surprise her with a bobble on any occasion. Yet, he accused her of not being ambitious enough by settling for a position as an elementary school principal in a rundown school in an economically challenged neighborhood, rather than accepting the position as a head mistress at a private academy that was offered to her. With her credentials, master's, and doctorate, he argued she was selling herself short. She disagreed with him, countering that her old neighborhood school and community needed her more than some highbrow academy.

Because of the bones of contention between them, she chose to reduce the amount of time she spent with Howard. Yet, when the mood struck her, she might be persuaded to go away with him for a weekend of sex. Their last trip before school started was to the five-star nudist resort, Plato's Retreat, on an exclusive, private island in the Pacific Ocean. Yes, Howard would definitely bring it between the sheets. He also liked to come up with two or three-day getaways several times a month, particularly in the summer when her school was closed.

"Brotherman is sportin' that big, fine, new Lexus, too," commented LaKesha.

"He's going to be upset if I don't get to his office on time. Are my nails dry yet?"

"Not yet. How far you gotta go? Where you gotta meet him at?"

"Downtown. K Street, the Cox Building."

"Oh, that's not too far. You got time. It's not like you got to go out in Virginia or Maryland someplace."

They continued chatting while her nails dried. A few minutes later, Kesha tested a few nails and nodded her agreement that Rosalyn's nails were dry enough. "You ought to let me put some designs on your nails."

"Thanks, Kesha. I'll keep that in mind," she said, knowing full well that wasn't going to happen. Given what spastic-looking designs Kesha had on her own talons, it wasn't positive advertisement. Nevertheless, she generously tipped Kesha, considering she had enjoyed living vicariously through Kesha's graphic descriptions of sex with Wesley. It was far better than watching a pornographic movie. She hustled to get home to change her clothes.

***

When Rosalyn stepped off the elevator, chatting with two of the wives of Howard's co-workers, she checked her watch and noted she had made it with seven minutes to spare.

Howard spotted her and immediately came forward. "I thought you planned to wear the blue dress," he urgently whispered.

"Well, hello, Howard. How are you?"

"Don't be obtuse, Rosalyn. I specifically asked you to wear the blue dress I bought for you so you wouldn't clash with my outfit. What you're wearing is all wrong."

"That's all right. We don't have to stand near each other, or, better still, I could leave."

"That's not a solution. Everyone has seen you arrive. If you leave, people will think we had an argument or something." He looked at her enigmatic expression with one raised eyebrow, huffed, and then sighed. "Look, I apologize for snapping at you. You always look pretty. I'm a little on edge because this promotion is such a big deal for me."

"For your co-workers, too, I imagine. Relax, Howard. You and your team have already been promoted."

"Yes, of course, but I led the campaign to get the client to come on board. The partners have their eyes on me, not my team, so I've got to keep them happy. I need to keep bringing in other big-money clients. I want to make partner before I'm thirty-five."

"I understand this is important to you, but I don't think what I'm wearing is going to make an iota of difference in the big scheme."

He squeezed her hand affectionately. He wasn't big on PDA, though he could turn it on and rock her boat when they were somewhere in private. He led her to the open bar where he ordered a white wine for her, without asking her preference. She rationalized that, since she was driving, one glass of wine wasn't a bad choice, so she didn't make an issue of his presumptuousness.

Taking her wine, she was able to mix and mingle, grip and grin easily. She already knew most of the people Howard worked with and their significant others from the many group outings she attended with him as his plus one.

An uncomfortable moment came when one of the partners—a tall, handsome man—had a little too much to drink and began touching her inappropriately or invading her private space. It took another of the partners—a woman—to come to her rescue, while Howard looked on, grinning, as if nothing untoward was happening. Miffed as she was with Howard, she wasn't going to berate him in front of his co-workers, staff, and bosses. She let the incident pass, but she dearly wanted to leave as soon as she could manage it.

After the drinks, dinner, and after dinner coffee and cognac were done in the executive dining room with a beautiful panoramic view of the city's skyline, she reached her limit of pretense and inane chatter. It was a good and appropriately reasonable time to leave. She had fulfilled her duty, once again, as Howard's plus one.

"It's only eleven or so," said Howard. "Why don't you come to my place tonight. You've got clothes and toiletries at my place and I'll bring you back in the morning to get your car? It should be fine in the building's parking garage overnight."

"I have a lot to do tomorrow, so I think it's best I head home."

"Okay, I'll follow you home."

"That's not necessary. I'll be fine and I really need to get some sleep."

"Then how about this weekend, we leave on Friday and drive up to the mountains? The leaves should be brilliant. We can find a B&B to spend a couple of nights and come back late on Sunday or Monday."

"Not a good idea."

He stepped back, folded his arms across his chest, and gazed intently at her. "You know, I thought it was my imagination, but I think you have been avoiding me. Am I wrong?"

Rosalyn sighed. He wasn't wrong, but something kept her from being completely honest with him. Perhaps it was guilt because all evening she mentally compared Howard to Wesley Greenfield, and Howard came up lacking. Howard clearly had the material things many women looked for in a man and he was handsome enough. He was an intelligent man, a stimulating conversationalist, and could deliver in bed, too.

Still, there was something indefinable and admirable about a man, who would fight hard to keep a community center open and operational in a failing neighborhood, do neighborhood watch patrols on foot, regardless of the weather, from nine at night to five in the morning, and willingly take on the responsibility of three children who were not his own, caring for them and about a negligent, absentee mother. Unless the women in the nail salon were right, and one or more of the children was his. She didn't really believe that to be the case. Wesley was the type of man who would have claimed his child or children out loud.

On the other hand, Howard Gardner was the type of man who would not want children of his own unless it was politically expedient for him to do so. She sometimes wondered what her children would look like if she had them with Wesley. Would they have his pretty eyes? *Silly dreams*, she thought again, but they sometimes brightened her days.

"Rosalyn, am I right?"

"No, you're not right, Howard. I have cramps, which means my period is going to start soon."

"Oh," he said, looking properly chagrin. "Well, you're about a week early this month. In that case, maybe you should hurry home. I'll walk you to your car."

"Good idea," she said. She knew any discussion about a woman's natural bodily function would quickly back him up off her. However, it was annoying he kept up with her monthly cycle more stringently than she did.

Rosalyn parked her car on the street in front of her house and checked her surroundings before opening her car door. Except for the time away when she was in college, she lived in this same neighborhood all her life. She knew everyone who lived on her block and surrounding vicinity.

After she earned her doctorate degree, her parents retired from their dental practice and moved to North Carolina for the milder winters to play golf and tennis pretty much year-round. They had transferred her childhood home to her as a parting gift. The house was a large, brick Victorian style and mortgage-free. She only had to pay taxes, insurance, utilities, and maintenance from her salary.

She loved the three bedrooms, three full and one-half baths, and twenty-five-hundred-square-foot home on two levels, with a large, unfinished attic space and a full, finished, walkout basement to a large, fenced backyard. When her parents left, she used her savings to renovate the house, knocking out walls to create an open-concept environment. Her kitchen was modern with new, high-end appliances, cabinets, and a large center-post workstation, with six high chairs forming a breakfast bar, with a clear view through the dining room to the front living room.

She upgraded all the bathrooms and a small alcove, which was a former butler's pantry between the kitchen and formal dining room, she now used for a hideaway office. Across from the living room area was a library/den that backed to a powder room and continuing to a large family room at the back of the house, all surrounding a grand, central staircase leading upstairs to the bedrooms and downstairs to the finished basement. She didn't mind clutter, but everything had a place and she wasn't someone who hoarded unnecessarily.

The security lamp in the front yard illuminated as she started up the first flight of steps, but a noise near the base of the second flight of steps which led to the covered porch had her hesitating. She didn't spook easily, but she didn't know whether she would have to take flight or fight, putting her seven years of martial arts training to work.

She vividly remembered an experience she had years ago while living in New York City and attending Columbia University for grad school. Recalling that occasion, she had parked her car on the street at the nearest parking space she could find, which was four blocks from the apartment building where she lived. There had been reports of several muggings in the neighborhood. Like now, she always checked her surroundings before opening her car door. Still, she felt at home there on the New York City, tree-lined street full of homes and small businesses. She just had to be careful not to step in dog poop along the way.

As she walked, she noticed there were not the usual groups of people chatting on the porches and sidewalks, and assumed the sudden cold snap in the Manhattan weather drove everyone inside. The absence of people created an unusual silence and she could actually hear her own footsteps. Until she realized those were not only her own footsteps, but also the footfalls of someone behind her. She deliberately slowed down and moved to the side of the pavement, inviting whomever it was behind her to pass. That was tough to do on the particularly narrow New York City sidewalk.

When no one passed, she resumed her regular pace, turning slightly around to look over her left shoulder. She caught a glimpse of a tall figure, who appeared to be a young, white male with a long, shaggy head of hair. She turned around, further facing the man who was now a few paces behind her and nodded slightly, but he did not respond. Turning back, she began to walk faster.

About three blocks from her apartment, the man stayed behind her, not moving any closer, not falling back. Rosalyn contemplated whether she should walk faster, run, cross the street, turn around and walk in the opposite direction, or confront the stranger. She opted to cross the street and was gratified to see the stranger did not cross after her.

More relaxed now and thinking about the dissertation she needed to complete, she purposefully walked toward her flat. Just as it came into view one block away, another man appeared out of the dark, facing her and blocking her path. He, too, was white and young, but he was short. At the same time, the tall guy started crossing the street and running toward her.

There was no longer any doubt in her mind she was about to be mugged or worse by the two young men she dubbed Stretch and Shorty. She was not afraid; with years of martial arts training under her belt, she felt she was ready and capable of defending herself. Just as Stretch lunged at her, she curled her body into a ball and aimed her leg at him. She missed the exact target she was aiming for, but still managed to slow him down with a hack at the Adam's apple in his throat.

He came at her again and she kicked him again, this time hitting her target. Stretch went down like a bowling pen, but she had lost sight of Shorty. He came up behind her and grabbed her by the throat. She could not wriggle free, so she stomped down on his instep with her stiletto-heeled boots, delighted at his scream of agony.

Still, he didn't completely release her neck. A sharp elbow to his solar plexus and air whooshed out of his open mouth. She head-butted him and blood spurted from his nose. As she managed to struggle free of Shorty, Stretch recovered sufficiently and punched her, landing a hard blow to her stomach. She managed to back away before he could get his hands on her again, but realized she was in trouble when Shorty grabbed her again. Keeping her eyes on Stretch, she kicked back, connecting with Shorty's knee and heard him cry out in pain.

Suddenly, a thump sounded behind her and Shorty released his grip, falling to the ground. She turned to see three imposing-looking men wearing dark hoodies, two of whom were beating on her two attackers and slamming them to the ground, face down.

"You okay, lady?" one man asked, flashing a New York City police badge he wore around his neck. The other two men, apparently also police officers, were none too gently cuffing her attackers.

"I will be. I haven't seen patrols in this neighborhood before. Thank you for saving me, Officer . . . ?"

"Lieberman. Detective Carl Lieberman. We're out of the Two-Seven. We've been covertly staking out this neighborhood from a couple brownstones because of the number of muggings reported in the area.

"What's your name, ma'am?"

"Rosalyn Hunter."

He was writing in a small notebook as she answered his questions. Then he said, *"You're pretty good on your feet."* He nodded toward the men on the ground. *"They won't soon forget the beat down you gave them."*

She also noted the detective checked her out. He wasn't hard on the eyes either.

In the confusion, she noticed the other officers had their prisoners secured and heard the scream of sirens rapidly approaching in the distance. It seemed like only moments passed before alternating, red-and-blue flashing emergency lights painted the buildings. People were peeking out of windows or coming out of their homes to watch the action.

"We need you to come into the precinct and provide a statement, so that we can book these dirt bags. Do you feel up to doing that?"

"I do, yes. Thanks again for helping me, Detective."

"You're welcome. Afterward, maybe we can get some breakfast and then I'll bring you home."

She liked his engaging smile. *That first breakfast at an all-night diner frequented by cops lead to many more.*

That incident in New York City was so long ago, but was vivid in her mind now as she mentally went on alert. Then she saw a pair of green eyes peeking out at her from behind her rose bushes and realized it was her neighbor's cat digging in her yard, again. Those green eyes reminded her of Carl Lieberman's eyes when he was in the throes of heated passion. Their affair lasted about eighteen months until she graduated and returned to DC.

"Shoo!" she said to the cat, relieved someone was not lurking, ready to pounce like before.

"Evenin', Roz," a voice came from behind, causing her to jump.

She abruptly turned, hands at the ready to fight, to see three imposing-looking men wearing dark hoodies and big overcoats approaching her. Obviously, her adrenalin had not yet dissipated. "That you, Roscoe?" she asked, recognizing his voice and peering through the dimness the street light afforded.

"You the only one still call me by my given name. Everybody else call me Peckhead."

"Your daddy and your mama didn't name you 'Peckhead', Roscoe Hubbard. So if it's all the same to you, I'll keep calling you what Mr. Ervin and Ms. Jennie named you." Then she noticed who the other men were. "Morning, Tavon, Wesley."

"Roz," they both acknowledged.

"You don't usually patrol this far out," Noted Roz.

"Old Mz. Lewis caught some crack heads tryin' to break into her basement and took her shotgun after 'em."

Rosalyn looked up toward her elderly neighbor's house down the block. The big, denuded tree-lined street, obscured her view. For the first time she noticed the lights were on, which was unusual for this time of the morning. "Is she all right?" she asked, concerned.

"Yeah, I mean she was fussin' up a blue streak, but she took a plug outta Micky D's leg and Pugh broke his fool arm tryin' to get away. Shotgun's got a kick to it and knocked Mz. Lewis on her backside."

"Oh, no. She must be eighty, if she's a day, and couldn't weigh more than a buck-o-five soaking wet. Is she home?"

"They took her to the hospital for observation and X-rays to see if she cracked her hip. Francine went with her."

"Anyone call her grandson?"

"She didn't want Buddy to know, so Francine will stay at her house just in case somebody else called him. We were checkin' the neighborhood and saw when you turned onto the street. Thought we would check out your alley. Make sure them numb nuts didn't hit anybody else's house before they got to Mz. Lewis."

"Sure, go ahead. I'll wait out here until you get back."

"Be back shortly, but I gotta say, Roz, you sure are looking pretty this morning. Smell good, too. Hot date?" Roscoe asked.

"Couldn't have been but so hot if she's comin' home alone this time of the morning, looking like new money," Little T, aka Tavon Rogers, commented.

"Let's be about checkin' out the alley," Wesley gruffly interrupted, speaking for the first time as he started away.

"Me and Peckhead got this, Ice. You hang with Roz. This shouldn't take long."

He desperately wanted to walk away with Peckhead and Little T, but didn't relish the idea of leaving Rosalyn standing alone in her front yard. It was true this street and a few others adjoining it were better lit and the houses well taken care of. Mostly professionals had lived on this block dubbed Strivers' Row and a few other streets back in the day.

Some of their children or grandchildren who were now professionals themselves, still lived in their parents' or grandparents' old homes, people like Dr. Rosalyn Hunter. This was the kind of neighborhood her boyfriend, the CPA, might have lived in, Ice thought.

Ice didn't want to admit to himself that he was glad she came home alone. Especially looking as sizzling hot as she did in that dress that stopped above her knees, showcasing her fine, dancer's legs. The dress had long sleeves and a scoop neckline that showed just enough of the top of her fleshy breasts to make his mouth water. The dress had a sleeveless overcoat that did nothing to hide her hourglass figure. The heels she wore had one strap across her toes and one just above her ankles.

If he had seen her bring that CPA home, with her looking like a walking wet dream, Ice knew he would have spent a restless night thinking about what he wanted to do with Rosalyn in his bed, instead of what that lucky S.O.B. CPA would be doing with her in her bed. He envied Rosalyn's main squeeze the privilege and opportunity to be with her.

The silence is deafening, Rosalyn thought as she mentally searched for something to say. "Is LaKesha at your place with the children?"

"Uh, no. After we closed up the center for the night, I took the kids home to get ready for bed. I wasn't going to go out on patrol tonight, but when I got called out about Mz. Lewis, I had to leave Dog with the kids."

"You could have called me, Wesley. I offered to help any time you or LaKesha need it. You've got my contact numbers, don't you?"

"You obviously had something else to do. Remember, I was in your office today when Glenda gave you a message confirming your date."

"Nothing I couldn't have gotten out of." Well, she would have had difficulty breaking her date with Howard, but for a chance to spend time with Wesley, she would have done almost anything. "Look, I know it's hard to find someone to watch the children on short notice, but I usually don't have a lot to do at night, so just call me or have LaKesha call. I can stay with them until one of you gets home." Then something dawned on her. "You said you left Chester Dillard with the children? Wasn't Kesha home? She did my nails for me, but she didn't say she was working at Sporty's last night."

"She worked Sporty's, but hasn't been at the apartment the past couple nights."

"She's pissed about you taking care of Jakima's children, isn't she?"

He shrugged. "Maybe. Probably. I haven't talked with her."

"So, if Chester is at your apartment that means you're shorthanded on your patrols."

"G-Boogie's seeing to it the cops out of the One-Four Precinct send a sector car out."

"Gary will see to it that they'll roll, but his officers won't leave their patrol cars and walk the streets the way you and your teams do."

"If one three-man team is all we can do tonight, then it will have to do. I'll rearrange the schedule tomorrow."

"Look, I'm going to get a few things out of my house and then I'm going to go to your apartment to stay with the children until LaKesha comes in."

"Roz, that's not necessary—"

"Don't argue with me, Wesley. Just wait here until I get back." She walked away without a backward glance.

"What's got Roz so hot?" Peckhead asked, coming to stand beside Ice.

Ice ignored the question. "Find anything?"

"Nah. Houses on this side of the block are buttoned up tight. This has always been a nice neighborhood. Wish Francine and me could live around here."

"Go back, finish college, get your social work degree and you can live in a neighborhood like this."

"Yeah, so could you if you'd open up your old man's ice cream parlor and bakery or a restaurant. Man, you got mad skills in a kitchen."

"Yeah, so I can end up gettin' jacked for a buck-o-five locking up my store one night."

"You know we gotchu, Ice," Little T said. "What the hell? We started walking these patrols shortly after your father got killed to keep it from happening again to anybody else."

"The problems are bigger now than they used to be. Back in the day, some numb nut might steal a bike outta somebody's yard or jack some tires off a car, but now they think they can just bust up into an old lady's house while she's home? Especially someone like Mz. Lewis? She taught math to my father when he was a boy and more than half of everybody still living in the hood was in her classroom at one point or another. She taught school for fifty-five years and then did private tutoring for free. She deserves better than to be jacked by some stupid crack heads, so they can buy drugs and a forty."

"You right, Ice," Peckhead added. "I know for a fact Killer and his Royal Red crew been lookin' to take up residence in the neighborhood since Tony the Tiger got got by the feds for interstate drug trafficking last month. I know more drug troubles gon' be poppin' off if he moves in. I gotta get my boy over here outta Killer's neighborhood 'cause my boy's baby mamma say he be tryin' to roll. She having a hard time with him 'cause Jemar don't like her new man."

"Damn, Peck! Jemar is what now, fifteen?" asked Little T.

"Fourteen. Me and Francine been beefin' 'cause she wants me to go get him and bring him to live with us. I want him to come, too, but I don't see how that's gon' work in a one-bedroom. I don't want to move out of the neighborhood to find a bigger place. Jamar's mama didn't tag me, but she called Francine on her job, pissin' and moanin' about what Jemar be up to. So, Francine was primed and ready when I walked in the door the other morning. I was too tired to be hearin' her, so I got hat and split."

"Let me talk to Jenkins. Jakima ain't paid rent in three months. Even when she comes back, she ain't likely gonna have the scratch to pay what she owe. She's got two bedrooms and one bath. With what she got in there, a couple of mattresses on the floor, Jenkins can put that stuff in a storage bin in the basement until I find out where she is and what she's going to do."

"That might work. I need to jump on that because there aren't usually any vacancies in your apartment building. At least it would get Francine off my back about Jemar living with us. Maybe get him out walkin' patrols with us if it ain't a school night."

"I'm ready," Rosalyn said, as she approached.

Ice noticed she changed her clothes and had a duffle bag over her shoulder. She wore a pair of dark slacks, ankle boots, a V-neck sweater under a dark, leather jacket and a colorful scarf around her neck that tied the ensemble together. No matter what the woman wore, she still looked like a walking wet dream of hot sex.

"Come on," she said. "I'll give you a lift to your place and you can get Chester to walk with you."

He, Little T, and Peckhead worked out the routes they would patrol for the rest of the night and morning, and then went their separate ways. Rosalyn drove them to Ice's apartment building. He told her to wait when he got out of the car and looked up and down the dark street of his neighborhood. Then he opened her car door and escorted her up the steps to his apartment. Chester Dillard, aka Dog, sat at the dinette table playing solitaire when they entered. The kids were asleep on the futon behind the screen.

"Look, Sporty's closes at two o'clock," Wesley told Rosalyn, while Chester put on his hat, coat, and gloves. "On a busy night, Kesha might work six to two in the morning. Otherwise, if she don't show up soon, she ain't comin'. You can take the bed and get some sleep. If everything is quiet, I'll be in at about five, five-thirty in the morning."

"We'll be fine."

He knew she and the kids would be okay, so he and Dog hit the streets. During the rest of the night, there was one domestic dispute; an old wino dancing around in the middle of the street half-naked without benefit of pants, underwear, or shoes; and two guys gettin' it on rump-ranger style in an alley. The sector police car did stop a few times on their rounds to talk and report any other incidents they had noticed. Otherwise, it was a fairly quiet night by the time Ice and Dog parted ways to go home just before daybreak.

He saw Rosalyn's car still in the parking lot and figured Kesha had not put in an appearance again. If she was serious about not coming back because of the kids, he needed to talk with her. It didn't matter to him overmuch if she left, but he wanted his keys back or he needed to change the locks. He didn't want her coming in and out when he wasn't there and bringing her rowdy friends in, boozing it up around the kids. He'd have to track her down later that day to see what she planned to do. Right now, he was too tired to think anymore. When he entered his apartment, the lights were out except for the little night light he had plugged into a socket for the kids. Marcus and Simone were hugged up tight to Cole though there was plenty room for them to spread out on the futon. He undressed, got a clean sheet, and lay on top of the covers next to Rosalyn. Her sweet scent followed him into a deep sleep.

Chapter 3

osalyn couldn't believe her eyes as she secretly watched Wesley undress. His body, illuminated by the streetlight coming through the window, was mostly in silhouette, but she could see he was masterfully built. Her fantasies paled by comparison to the vision that was Wesley Barrett Greenfield in the buff. Clearly, he worked out from the cut and definition in his six-pack abs, the broad muscular chest, and strong-looking arms, thighs, and legs. His penis was long and thick, even in its dormant state. Lying on top of the covers next to her, he covered himself with a sheet, and immediately dropped into sleep. It wasn't possible for her to breathe after what she had seen.

She lay next to him for a long time, trying to get her breathing under control. He seemed in a deep sleep so she waited before she lifted the sheet that covered his beautiful body. Lying on his back with his arms up beside his head, he didn't break the rhythm of his light snoring when she peeled back the sheet.

As the morning light grew brighter, she sat Indian style beside him. Looking her fill, she itched to touch his flat nipples, to run her tongue over them and suckle. Then she would visit the indentation that was his navel and pay homage to his mid-section. Looking at his face, the shadow of a beard on his square jaw and the dark brown eyebrows and lashes against his light skin, she was tempted to touch. He was always, in her view, a pretty man, but clearly all man. There was nothing soft or feminine about his features. To her eyes, he bore a striking resemblance to the actor Terrance Howard.

As the night began to lose more of its grip on the darkness, Rosalyn sat in reverent appreciation of a man her body craved, but her mind told her she would never have. Gingerly, she recovered him and slipped from the bedroom, taking her overnight bag with her into the bathroom to shower. Later, after she dressed, she woke the children one at a time, starting with Cole, and shuttled them in and out of the bathroom and to the breakfast table. They didn't seem surprised or they just didn't care that she was there, and talked with her while they ate.

When breakfast was over, the children helped clear the table, went to brush their teeth, and returned the pullout futon to its upright position. She washed dishes and placed them in the rack to drain. Quietly, they left the apartment and, leaving her car parked in Wesley's lot, she walked with the children the block and a half to the elementary school.

The morning domestic tasks added a spring to her step for the entire day. She hoped she would have other opportunities to enjoy the feeling of tending to a family, even if it wasn't her own. She wasn't delusional. The children weren't hers and neither was the man.

***

When Ice woke, he jolted out of bed. His intention was only to sleep for an hour or two before getting up to make breakfast for the kids and then get them off to school. He pulled on his jeans and padded barefoot into the living room. It was empty, the futon put back in place, and clean dishes sat in the drying rack. Then his fuzzy brain recalled Rosalyn was still there when he came in that morning.

A small pot of coffee sat on the warming base, smelling of something he desperately needed. To get his head clear and eyes completely open, he took his first hit of black coffee standing up. It was exactly what he needed while he scrambled eggs, green pepper, garlic, onion, and cheese, heated the thick, hot sausage in the tiny microwave, made grits, and grabbed the last of the buttermilk biscuits Rosalyn apparently baked for the kids' breakfast. Kesha hadn't so much as given him a glass of water in the morning, while she rode him. Rosalyn left a pot of coffee for him, sausages, and biscuits, and he didn't have to give up any leg to get it. With that hit of caffeine, the beginning of breakfast on a chilly morning, and thoughts of Rosalyn Hunter in his bed, everything was right with his world.

After cleaning up the kitchen, he went to his room to pull some clothes out to wear after his shower. When he opened his one drawer, he noticed the chest of drawers seemed lighter than usual. He generally didn't look into Kesha's drawers, but this time he pulled one of her drawers open and found it empty. When he checked the other drawers and then the closet, they were equally devoid of her possessions. Apparently, at some point, without so much as a goodbye, LaKesha Reynolds had decamped after five years. *Well*, he thought, that put a fine point on where things stood between them. He still intended to change the locks.

He headed for the bathroom to shave, shower, and get on with his day. It looked like he needed Rosalyn's help after all.

Chapter 4

The following week there was still no news about where Jakima had gone. Though Ice was royally pissed at her, he didn't let her children feel his anger or his concern.

He and Rosalyn established a childcare routine that worked. He would cook dinner each day before he left for work. Rosalyn would bring the kids to his apartment after she closed up the elementary school, help them with their homework, eat with and feed them, and then deliver them to him at the community center. She would then go to her home, run errands, like shop for groceries for him, then pack a bag and return to the center to pick up the children, take them to his apartment, get them ready for bed, and sleep in Wesley's bed until morning.

Rosalyn had lightened the load considerably by taking care of Cole, Marcus, and Simone. He even saw some sparks of hope in Cole's usually dour demeanor. Both Marcus and Simone looked up to their brother and took their cues from him. Nevertheless, Wesley knew that, unless Jakima showed up soon, he would have to do something to get temporary custody. He called his best friend for advice.

"Yeah, my brother told me Jakima up and split and you're taking care of her kids," said JRock.

"Who, Walter or Francis?"

"You know it had to be Francis. With seven children, Walter and Marie don't have time to gossip."

"It's been more than a week and no one has seen or heard from her or this dude, Honeybear, she ran with. I've got to work out what to do until she shows up."

"Look, call my lawyer, Vivian Jackson. She'll know what to do about custody. She handled it for me about my girls."

"Man! Vivian Alexander Jackson? I can't afford somebody like her. I've seen her on television. She's big time."

"I've got you, Ice. Just call her. She's tough, but she's good. I think you'll like her."

"Man, there is no question she's good. She ripped those two senators a new one on the TV show *Sweet Justice*."

"Yeah, she did, didn't she?" JRock said around a hearty laugh. "She was awesome on *Meet the Press* after she beat the pants off of FOX, too, in court. She's scheduled to be on *Face the Nation* on Sunday. *Elegance* wants to do a spread on her and her family early next year."

"Like I said, big time."

"I'll call her and tell her to expect to hear from you."

"I don't know, JRock. I'll think about it."

"Don't think about it. Just do it. I've got you. In any event, I'm glad you called."

"Why? What up?"

"I think I'll be able to move on the Baylor Plaza Park project sooner than I previously thought."

"*Yeah, boyee!* You're going to make your father's dream a reality."

"Our fathers' dreams, Ice. Your old man and mine were as tight as you and I are, along with Peck's, Little T's, Buddy's, and Dog's fathers. Baylor Plaza Park will be a tribute to the old heads who tried to make life better for everybody in our community."

"You're right. Should I pass the word?"

"No, not yet. I just hired a new architect who has some innovative ideas for the project. I've got a few other big deals cooking and, if one of them works out the way I plan, I'll have the grip to fully fund Baylor Plaza Park for the first five years."

"Man!"

"Yeah! You feel me?"

"Up and down! When will you know for sure?"

"A week or two. Keep it on the QT for now, but I'm going to need for you to come on board, Ice. I need for you to come on as project manager, my PM."

"Rock, you know I'd give you the last drop of my blood, but I'm not a suit-and-tie kind of guy. Hell, I only went to junior college for culinary school. I took one semester of business related to running a restaurant and that's it."

"Stop telling what you don't have, Ice. It's not like you. You're the only one I know can make a dollar outta fifty cents. You won't let me help you, but I'm calling in a favor. You're the right man because you know everybody in the hood and the rhythm of the street beat.

"Baylor Plaza Park is going to have some opposition because it's going to demolish most of the old community to make room for the new. People respect you and trust you. Do I have project managers I can task to do the job? Hell, yes! My people are the best in the business, but not one of them has what you have: leadership skills, trust, and respect in the hood.

"You'll have full authority to hire from our old neighborhood, institute training programs, arrange housing for people who will be displaced, and have a budget that will have room to spare. You can refit your community center, especially the second and third floors, for doing the journeyman training. Maybe even add a fourth level or a rooftop deck."

"You've got your sister. She could run the project."

"Karen or Kelley?"

"Either one."

"No go, bro. Now that Karen and Delbert's children are older, she's going back to Johns Hopkins to finish medical school. Kelley's already got her hands full running the day-to-day operation of Baylor Construction and gearing up for the new company, Baylor Design and Development. So you see, Ice, I need you."

"Man, you're not gonna let up, are you?"

"I won't do this without you being on board. This is for the old heads, too, Ice. I need you at the table when decisions are made. I want you to form a community council that will work with you. You've got to be my right hand, my eyes, and ears."

"Give me time, JRock. You've got a few weeks before you know what's what. Right now, I've got to deal with finding Jakima."

"All right, Ice. Let me know whether there is anything else I can do to help with that, but definitely give Vivian a call. I'll bet Kesha ain't too happy about it."

"Kesha ain't about it. She got hat and chucked."

"I can't say I'm surprised or sorry. I'd be lying."

"You never did take to her too tough. She tried to hit on you, didn't she?"

"How'd you know?"

"She was trying to get the 411 on you a while back. I figured she was up to something."

"I had to crack on her to get her to back up off me. She wasn't showing no respect for herself or for you."

"It wasn't like that with me and her. She wasn't my lady."

"Regardless. I don't know what she took me for, but I ain't sorry to see the back of her. So, how are you handling the kids, the center, and the patrols?

Though JRock couldn't see him, he shrugged, self-consciously. "Roz has been helping out."

"Yeah!" JRock said enthusiastically. "Now that's where you should be looking to go!"

"She's your lady."

"Roz was never my lady, Ice. We had one time and that was way back when. She wasn't into me. Don't get me wrong. She's prime and I respect her. She and I are still friends, but that's as far as things will ever go between us."

"You still hung up on Monique?"

"Like Kesha, that's history. What's past is prologue. The only reason we communicate is because I want my girls to know their mother; have a relationship with her. Kelley took the twins to visit their mother in California. Monique couldn't cope for two damn weeks before she brought the girls back to me on Black Caucus Weekend. Said Shelly and Shelby were too distracting, while she's preparing for some movie role. What did she expect?

"My girls are four years old, bright, and active. The deal was Monique was supposed to spend quality time with our daughters over the summer."

"Don't tell me. Let me guess. Monique wants you to invest in the film."

"You heard?"

Ice laughed. "Yeah, sounds like something Monique would do. Are you going to do it?"

"I asked Vivian to look into it."

"Good luck with that."

"Yeah. Look, I've got to go now, but I'll be in the neighborhood when I know more."

"Don't fret."

"Later."

Peckhead came into Ice's cubicle and sat in the chair beside his desk.

"What up?" Ice asked, not looking up as he sorted out projects and plans on his desk.

"Mz. Lewis is getting out of the hospital tomorrow."

"Yeah, I heard. Buddy called me. He wasn't too happy that nobody called him. He read me the riot act."

"He's soldiering in freakin' Afghanistan. There's no telling when he'll be stateside again. He says he wants me and Francine to move in with his grandmother while he's away. Mz. Lewis agreed because she says she's tired of hearing him fussin' about her living in that big house alone. Francine agreed she needs people around her and talked with Mz. Lewis' doctors. They don't want her living alone or up and down the steps anymore. So, Francine arranged to have one of them stair chair things installed today, going up to the bedroom, but not down to the basement where she does her laundry.

"Mz. Lewis wants to still be able to do stuff on her own. She got a linen closet in her upstairs hall next to her hall bathroom. I'm gonna see if I can fit her washer and dryer in there. It might work if I can hook it up to the water and drain in the bathroom. I need to vent the dryer to the outside, too. I can handle the carpentry work, but Screw knows more about plumbing and electrical than I do. He's going to give me a hand with it. Otherwise, we gotta get JRock to bring in a crew."

"How about Jemar?"

"Buddy and Mz. Lewis want him to move in, too. I think she was a little lonely with Buddy away all the time. That's what got Francine to agree to the move. She wants Jemar living with us. She ain't too keen on my baby mama."

"When are you gonna make the move?"

"Tomorrow morning before Francine brings Mz. Lewis home. It's Saturday, so Francine don't have to work and Jemar don't have school. Some of the guys are gonna give us a hand. We're only bringing our clothes. Everything else we'll put in storage. I need for you to take me off patrol Sunday night. Monday morning I'ma have to get Jemar transferred to the junior high school over this way.

"We worked out a schedule. Francine will stay with Mz. Lewis, get her fed and dressed until I get in from patrol in the mornings before she leaves for work. I'll get up before noon and fix lunch for me and her. Jemar should make it home from school every day before I leave for work. He agreed to stay with Mz. Lewis until Francine gets in and makes dinner, then he'll come to the center until it closes. Friday and Saturday nights he'll walk with me and whoever you team me with. I was thinking that maybe we should add some of the young bloods to the patrols on the weekends. Bubbles and Billie's youngest boy, Frank, asked to walk. He's sixteen. Said his parents were okay with it and he said some of his boyz want to walk, too."

"I don't know, Peck. You know the risk. I don't want to see no young'uns catch a bullet."

"We gotta start trainin' them sometime."

"Jemar really wanna do this?"

"He's pumped. So is Frank."

"We'll bring it up at the staff meeting. See how everyone feels about it. Then we'll decide."

"Sounds good to me."

Chapter 5

Rosalyn was working in her office when Glenda announced over the phone's intercom that she had a visitor. Since she wasn't expecting anyone, Rosalyn assumed it was a parent who came in without making an appointment. Rising from her desk, she opened her office door while putting a polite smile on her face. However, there, standing, looking at the school's wall of commendations and awards, was Howard Gardner.

Surprise didn't cover the range of emotions that ran through her mind. He never came to her office, not in all the years they had known each other and he didn't like coming into her neighborhood.

She guessed he resorted to tracking her down, considering the number of his messages she did not find the time to return in the last few weeks. Her behavior was nothing less than rude, she admitted to herself, but she was hard pressed to explain she didn't have time for him because she was spending every free moment tending to Cole, Marcus, and Simone.

Moreover, what kind of explanation could she offer when each day she lusted for the sight of another man's body in the early morning hours before dawn? Howard did nothing to deserve her disrespect and she prepared herself for his retribution when he turned around and looked at her. She couldn't read his expression and prepared herself for the worst.

"Howard, this is not a good time, but I apologize . . ."

"No, I know that you're busy and I arrived unannounced. I promise I won't take much of your time," he said, coming forward and then taking her into his arms for a hug and a kiss on her lips.

This behavior, this very public display of affection, was so uncharacteristic of him, she thought, but didn't want to have whatever conversation they were about to have with Glenda looking on with avid interest.

Then the situation got worse.

Over Howard's shoulder, while she was still in his arms, she spotted Wesley Greenfield. He, too, had an indecipherable expression on his face and in his unrevealing, golden-brown eyes. She wanted desperately to go to him, but Howard had not yet completely released his hold on her. More mortified than she could imagine ever being before, she took a deliberate step back, breaking Howard's hold on her. Turning to Wesley, she stepped forward.

"Wes, is something wrong? Did you need to speak with me?"

"It can wait. Go ahead and finish with ..."

"Howard Gardner," he said, stepping forward, hand extended, a professional smile on his face. "I'm Rosalyn's other half. Are you one of the parents? If so, I'll wait and let you go first."

"Uh, something like that, but ..."

"Wes, if you could give us just a moment, I'll be right with you," Rosalyn said, quickly ushering Howard into her office and partially closing her door. She folded her arms across her chest and frowned up at Howard. *My other half?*

"Well, not legally, but that can be arranged," he said, grinning. When she didn't crack a smile or react to his half-hearted proposal, he must have sensed he had stepped over some invisible line. At her look of displeasure, he hastened on. "Look, Rosalyn, I know coming here unannounced is inappropriate, especially when you have parents with appointments coming in to meet with you, but I needed to apologize for my behavior. I know you're probably upset with me, but I really don't do start-up accounting for small or new businesses. I thought you understood my clientele are national, multinational, or foreign companies with billions in resources. I tried to explain that to your friend, but she kept insisting I should make time to include her because you and she are such good friends. I can find out from someone in my fraternity, or in one of the professional groups I'm a member of, who does that kind of work and maybe give her some recommendations as to—"

"Stop!" Rosalyn held up both hands, halting his dissertation. "What are you talking about, Howard? What friend?"

"Your friend, uh," he said, rubbing his jaw thoughtfully while trying to recall her name. He pulled his iPhone from his pocket to access his calendar. He thumbed through it until he came to the right date. "A LaKesha Reynolds? You do know her, don't you?"

"Yes, I know her," she said, her confusion growing. "We went to high school together. She's a manicurist at a nail salon near here."

"You told her to contact me, didn't you?" he asked, his brows beetled.

"No, of course not. She told you I sent her to you?"

"Well, she kept mentioning your name and said, since you two were such close friends, …" he trailed off, then crossing his arms over his chest, he said, "Okay, if you know nothing about this, which you apparently don't, and you're not angry because I didn't help her with her business venture, then why haven't you been returning my calls?"

"I've been a little busy lately. That's all."

"You've never been too busy to return my calls before. What's going on, Rosalyn? Is this about Dwyer at the office party a week or so ago putting his hands on you—"

"No, it isn't"

"Then what? You couldn't possibly still be on your period. I know that sometimes you get a little cranky—"

"Stop speculating about it. It's simple. We've had a parent go missing. I've been helping to take care of her three minor children in her absence."

Confusion was evident on his face. "Aren't there agencies that do that kind of thing? I mean, what am I paying all these damn taxes for if these government agencies aren't doing their jobs? Now I have to suffer twice? You're wasting your time and mine taking on someone else's responsibilities and the government is abdicating its obligations?"

For a pregnant moment, Rosalyn stared, dumbfounded. "That's what comes to your mind when I say a woman is missing and her minor children may be traumatized as a result if not for people lending a hand to take care of them? The first thing you think about is how this situation affects you?"

"Really, Rosalyn, this wouldn't happen if you were dealing with a better class of people."

"Un-friggin'-believable," she said, shaking her head. "I have work to do and I'm sure you do, too."

He checked his silver Rolex. "You're right. I have a meeting I have to get to. Look, part of the reason I need to talk to you is because we've been invited to attend a four-day weekend retreat in the country by the partners at my firm. You're probably going to need a few new things to wear like a riding habit, so let's plan to get together this week. We will be expected to dress formally for each meal. We can have an early dinner then I'll take you shopping at the Chevy Chase Galleria Mall or we can go out to a boutique in Reston or Potomac. We should be able to find everything you'll need in one of those places. However, you know we haven't taken a long weekend in New York City for quite a while. We could shop on Fifth Avenue or in SoHo and then see some shows on Broadway. I want you to shine like new money when we show up for the retreat." Then his voice dropped an octave or two when he whispered something decadent in her ear about what he wanted to do to her all night long.

She backed away from him unimpressed. "Uh, Howard, what is it you didn't understand about my helping to care for three children? I also have responsibilities I will not walk away from on a whim or to suit your schedule."

He released an exasperated sigh. "Rosalyn, just get someone else to look after those children for a weekend, can't you? As for your job, it won't make a difference to these people if you take off a couple of days. After all, it's just an elementary school for Pete's sake. Your job just isn't that important. We'll talk more later. Right now, I don't have the time or inclination to discuss this silly stuff." He opened the door and started out of the office then turned back and kissed her. "I'm glad it was nothing important that kept you from returning my calls." He kissed her again and was gone.

Roz met Glenda's smug, interested expression with foreboding. In a nanosecond, she knew as soon as her office door closed, Glenda would be spreading the word far and wide about Howard's visit and about Wesley's. The woman lived to gossip. Realizing that nothing could be done about that, she beckoned Wesley into her office and closed the door.

"I apologize for keeping you waiting," She said.

"I didn't have an appointment."

"You don't need one. Have a seat. What do you need to talk with me about?"

"I'll stand. This shouldn't take long. I spoke with JRock today about the kids. He suggested I contact his attorney."

She whistled. "Isn't his attorney Vivian Alexander Jackson?"

"Yes."

"*WOW!* She's extraordinary and top notch. Of course, I've seen her on television and I've heard her speak at conferences and seminars, too. She's a fantastic orator who reminds me of former Congresswoman Barbara Jordan. I've read several of her books, too, but I hear she doesn't come cheap. If you need financial—"

"No, I don't. I'll handle it. I just thought I'd let you know I'm thinking about going for temporary custody of Jakima's kids."

"That's a big step, but I agree it's the right one. We've known these children all of their lives and Jakima, too, though she's younger than us. It's good of you to do this. I'll do whatever you need me to do to help."

"I couldn't help overhearing some of your conversation. The amount of time you're spending with Cole, Marcus, and Simone is causing you problems. I'll find some other way to cover them overnight starting tonight."

A shark attack couldn't have been more shocking or devastating, Rosalyn thought. It was as if someone had taken a big bite out of her heart. She could barely breathe. "Wes, please," she heard herself beg, but his decision seemed written in stone.

She looked forward to spending each evening with Cole, Marcus, and Simone, eating with them, and then helping them with their homework before taking them to the community center. They were such bright, energetic children. She wanted to go on mentoring them, helping them to discover the world and explore their universes. She didn't want to lose the closeness she'd developed with them.

Losing her growing closeness with Wesley was shattering as well. Talking with him now, with Glenda the Gossip just outside her office, probably listening with an ear to the door, was not feasible. She would have to make time to meet him alone to discuss it further.

Having been so focused on her own thoughts, she missed whatever else he was saying. "I'm sorry, what?"

"Look, it's none of my business."

"No, no, I'm a little preoccupied. Please repeat what you were saying."

He sighed and ran his hand over his close-cut hair and down his face. A typical thoughtful reaction she recognized. Then hands in his pockets, he said, "LaKesha is scoping out your man."

"Who?" Rosalyn asked confused.

"Howard Gardner."

"My man?" She chuckled, and then she focused more on his statement. He seriously believed that Howard, her male friend, was her man when in reality he was her bootie call, a friend with benefits. "Howard is not 'my man'."

"Whatever. She tried to hit on JRock. If she's showing up at your friend's office, she's after him."

"She did ask me where his office was located…" She recalled the conversation she had a few weeks ago while getting her mani-pedi. At the time, she was in a rush and thought nothing of it. Now it became clear that LaKesha was pumping her for information about Howard. If she really needed information about starting a business, she would have just come up with the question and asked for advice from Wesley. That was the kind of information she could get over the Internet at his community center. She smiled. Howard would be clueless about LaKesha's hidden agenda. If LaKesha's conversation didn't involve big money clients, she wouldn't get his attention. Rich clients consumed the majority of Howard's thinking, but he was still a man. She had not known him to be a philanderer. However, if LaKesha was successful in gaining Howard's time and attention, then more power to her.

"I have to go, but don't worry about the kids. I'll meet them after school and take them to the center with me. They can do their homework there. I'll take them home to eat dinner. Thanks for your help over the past few weeks."

"About that, Wesley. I want the chance to discuss this further, so let's keep the routine unchanged until we have a chance to talk more."

"No, Roz. That's a wrap. I should have an alternate plan worked out soon."

Chapter 6

Well, that was one way to solve his growing infatuation problem with Rosalyn Hunter, Wesley thought later, as he mentally patted himself on his back. While sitting in his cubical at the community center, attempting to work, he felt he was getting entirely too comfortable with Rosalyn's presence in his life. The intoxicating scent of her in his bed drove him to distraction. He actually caught himself smelling the pillow she slept on.

The domestic chores she performed around his place made his life a lot less hectic. She did the grocery shopping and housekeeping with the kids. She even took the laundry home with her and brought everything back, including his sweaty underwear, smelling clean and fresh, and put it away. It felt entirely too good to have someone share the burdens of everyday life, but not at the expense of her losing out on a long-term relationship. He wanted to be selfish and hope she and Howard would see a natural parting of the ways, but he didn't have anything to offer her in return.

LaKesha used to gossip about the rumors she heard regarding things this Howard Gardner did for and with Rosalyn; places he took her. The man reeked of money, class, and sophistication. The suit he wore cost more than Wesley made in six months. The shoes Gardner wore cost a mint.

Rosalyn deserved to have the best money could buy, maids to run her errands, do her laundry, and cleanup for her. She shouldn't have to wash dishes, make up beds, and sweep and mop his floors.

Though he never thought of Rosalyn as shallow or wanting the easy life, she must have dreams she had yet to fulfill. Maybe a husband, kids, vacations to interesting or exotic places. What did he know of those things? He never traveled for pleasure or been far beyond the boundaries of the DelMarVa (Delaware, Maryland, Virginia).

Yet, he, at one time, had dreams, too. A good bakery business and ice cream parlor, maybe even a restaurant. Those dreams died with his father and then Isaac's incarceration. There was no one left to build his dreams with or on. The hood became his home and trying to do what his father dreamed of—making life better for those in his makeshift family—became his life's work.

"You shouldn't keep a lady waiting."

Ice did a double take and then immediately got to his feet. "If what I saw you do to those two senators on television is representative of 'a lady', gentlemen are in for a rough road, Ms. Jackson," he said, extending his hand. "And these little people are?"

"My crew. My children: Glenda, Bryan, Darren, Derrick, Jr., Geneva, Dena, Spencer, Vincent, Ryan, and Roger," she said touching each one as they stood quietly before her looking up at him.

"I wasn't expecting a person as busy as you are to show up on my doorstep."

"I trust we're welcome?"

"Of course. Let me find some chairs."

"Please, no. The Jackson Crew is vibrating with their collective desire to escape me and explore your community center. Is it all right if I cut them loose on your unsuspecting clientele?"

"Yes," he said, chuckling.

"All right, you unguided missiles," she said to her children who all turned to look up at her vibrating with eagerness, "you're free for an hour." The launch was underway before she finished speaking.

"Now," she said to Wesley, "let's sit and you can tell me about yourself."

"Me? Ms. Jackson, this isn't about me, it's about Cole Cooper, and Marcus and Simone Harris."

"Trust and believe if you want a judge to give you—a single man, not a family member—emergency custody of three minor children, the first thing this is going to be about is you. And the name is Vivian."

"I see your point. I'm not sure what a judge would want to know. There's not much to tell. I'm a native Washingtonian and lived all of my thirty-plus years of life in this neighborhood. My parents and grandparents are deceased, I have one older brother, Isaac, and I'm not now nor have I ever been married. I have no children of my own that I'm aware of. I don't have a police record and I have never done anything that would deserve police scrutiny. I don't smoke, drink heavily, or do drugs of any type or description. That's about it."

She leaned back comfortably in the chair and began. "Your mother, Elizabeth Barrett Greenfield, was born in Ballard County, Kentucky, and died of an embolism in DC when you were less than a year old. Your brother, Isaac Jeremiah Greenfield, Junior, was three years old at the time.

"Your mother was an only child of an interracial couple and you were named for her father, Wesley Barrett. Like your mother, your father, Isaac Jeremiah Greenfield, Senior, was an only child. He went to college after his years in the military were over.

Like your mother, he was a graduate of Tuskegee Institute. They married shortly after graduation and had your brother within the first year of their marriage.

"Your father's parents, David and Essie Turner Greenfield, lived in the same one-bedroom apartment where you live now and took care of you and Isaac, Junior, while your parents worked. The four of you used to live on the third floor in the same two-bedroom apartment where Jakima Harris lives with her children.

"While your mother taught school, your father took over running his father's bakery and ice cream parlor after your grandfather died. He ran it successfully with a seven-person staff and your older brother, Isaac Greenfield, Junior. Your father was shot to death by a Melvin 'The Juice' Cotton. Isaac hunted for and found The Juice within twelve hours of your father's death and executed him, using The Juice's own gun; the same gun he shot your father with. Your brother then called the police, waited for them to arrive, admitted to having committed the murder, pleaded guilty at his arraignment, and was sentenced a week later.

"When your father died, his best friend, John Baylor and his wife, Sarah, though they already had five children, took you to live with them for a time and helped you to settle your father's affairs. John Baylor was the father of your best friend, J. Roderick Baylor, aka, JRock. You were nineteen years old and had finished two years of culinary school by the time your father died.

"Your paternal grandfather started the business your father left to you and your brother, along with the apartment building your grandfather purchased and he and his family had once lived in, in a two-bedroom apartment on the third floor. You currently live in that building and rent out the remaining units through Mercantile Realty, a DC-based company, who have no idea you're the absentee landlord, using the pseudonym, Jeremiah Isaac.

"You have an excellent credit rating and have no debts. You do have one credit card you recently used to purchase clothes and other necessities for Jakima Harris' children. You have been funding the community center, which you opened more than ten years ago, using the money you received from your father's life insurance policy and through your own anonymous donations.

"The concept of the community center grew out of a dream your father, JRock's father, and the fathers of the rest of your friends, Roscoe Hubbard, aka Peckhead, Henry Hughes, aka Slide, Chester Dillard, aka Dog, Richard Rainey, aka Screw, Tavon Rogers, aka Little T, Byron Lewis, aka Buddy, and, as a mentor, DC Police Captain Gary Bouchard, aka, G-Boogie, had for the unity and safety of this neighborhood. It stemmed from the 1966 March on Washington, which your fathers attended and heard Dr. King's "I Have A Dream" speech. They pledged to make that dream a reality and charged their sons and daughters to continue the struggle. They were also instrumental in arranging the Million Man March on Washington. Your fathers were veterans, community activists, and, with former Mayor Marion Barry's RAP, Inc., and Pride, Inc., projects, had a dream their sons are making into a reality in any way all of you can manage. That's what you and your posse have dedicated your lives to accomplish.

"Over the years, you have instituted a number of programs to help various aspects of your community through the center. On weekends, you have a farmers market and kind of Turkish Bazaar set up in the parking lot; job training classes, job fairs, GED classes; after school education programs for kids and programs, like music, dance, and art that the public schools no longer offer. You arranged to have free medical and dental examinations performed by students from area colleges and universities.

"How am I doing so far?"

He looked at her, dumbfounded.

She continued. "One of the many things you and your friends do for your community is walk night patrols to aid the police in keeping down the crime in this part of the city. You've been very successful. You're well respected by your neighbors and as a community organizer and activist.

"To say I'm a little miffed you didn't call me for help on a personal problem, as JRock suggested, is a gross understatement. Instead, I ended up having to track you down."

He shrugged, completely blown away by how much she had learned about him and his boyz so quickly. He had only spoken with JRock earlier that same day and here *the* Ms. Vivian Alexander Jackson, Esquire, Olympic Gold Medalist, the widow of basketball super icon Derrick 'Dunk and Jam' Jackson, attorney, mover and shaker, sat in his small cubicle, reading his life without benefit of notes like she wrote the book, chapter, and verse on him.

"Now, let's get to LaKesha Reynolds. Do you expect she will be back in your life again on an intimate basis?"

"No. Whatever there was it's done."

"Okay, I don't have to go through a bio with you on her. Now, about Dr. Rosalyn Hunter?"

"She's been helping to take care of Jakima's kids, too. She's the elementary school principal… You probably already know that."

"I do. Yes," she said and continually looked at him earnestly as she had steadily done since her arrival. "I've got her very impressive resume and background information. I've actually heard Dr. Hunter speak at a Congressional Black Caucus seminar. She's an active member of the DC Chapter of her sorority and a member of the National Women's League. JRock tells me she's also a friend of yours; a good one, as is JRock. I hope you will accept my friendship as well."

"Yes, but I can't afford—"

"Do you have a dollar?"

"A dollar?"

"American money."

He smiled at that, reached into his pocket, and pulled a dollar from the bills in his hand.

Vivian plucked the dollar bill from his fingers. "Now that you have paid your legal fees, you're officially my client and we've got some work to do."

"That can't be nearly enough."

"It is if I say it is and I do."

"Okay." He shrugged. He put the remaining bills back in his pocket. "What do I have to do?"

"Move into a three-bedroom house or apartment; furnish the bedrooms with something other than a futon for the kids to sleep on, provide furniture for their clothes; stock the kitchen with real healthy foods, plenty of fresh fruits and vegetables; and establish reliable, adult or responsible child-care providers for when you're not at home. Once that's done, I can get a ninety or a one-hundred-twenty-day, emergency, child custody decree for you. How long will that take for you to accomplish?"

"How about tonight? Is that soon enough?"

Wesley and Vivian turned toward the woman standing just outside the cubicle.

"Dr. Hunter," Vivian acknowledged, standing and extending her hand.

"Rosalyn, Ms. Jackson," she said, as they shook hands.

"Vivian, Rosalyn. JRock asked me to look you up for a number of reasons. I was going to call your office on Monday morning. First, of course, about the children and their mother. I put an investigative team together to start a search for her."

"The other reason?"

"JRock is planning to announce the start date for the development of Baylor Plaza Park. He would appreciate it if you and Wesley could prepare a list of people from the community who are interested in seeing the project move forward."

"Then I'm pleased to assist with both things. I own a home with three, furnished bedrooms sufficient to accommodate Wesley and the children."

"Roz," Ice interjected. "We've already discussed this."

"I'm going to help—"

"You already have," he said to Rosalyn and then turning to Vivian, "I need a few more days to work this out. I'll get back to you on the arrangements."

"That will be fine. In the interim, I'll prepare the brief for the judge's consideration."

They continued to talk about arranging a meeting of interested and active community members who would support the Baylor Plaza Park project until Vivian's children returned *en masse* with Cole, Marcus, and Simone in tow.

"Mommy, the computers are really old, so I called Uncle Kenneth. He said he will ship fifty new computers with new programs to the center in a few weeks," said twelve-year-old Glenda. "More if that's not enough."

"She just called him up on her phone and he said yes," Cole added in amazement.

Confused, Wesley looked from the kids to Vivian for an explanation.

She shrugged. "My oldest brother, Kenneth Alexander, owns and is the Executive Director of CompuCorrect Global. He has offices in San Francisco and Santa Barbara, California. It's a computer hardware and software development and manufacturing company. They do other things, like design security systems, other electronics, and telecommunication services. You should talk with him about your security program for the center. JRock has talked with representatives of CompuCorrect about security measures for Baylor Plaza Park."

"Your brother would ship new computers on the request of his niece?"

"You heard?" she said. "Hope you have some muscle around when the desk top computers arrive. If I know my brother, he will probably dispatch one or two of his techs to do the installations and training on the new software. His company is also an internet provider. Because you're a not-for-profit operation, he'll provide free internet service. I expect he will send laptops and flat screens, too. Everything will be cutting edge and Wi-Fi capable." She smiled, shrugging again laconically. Turning to her children she asked, "Anything else?"

"Well," Bryan hedged. "They really could use some more toys, new books, games, and all kinds of balls."

"Okay, that's doable. You make up a list, Bryan."

"But—" Ice began, but was cut off by one raised eyebrow on Vivian Jackson's gamine face.

"Are you and I going to have a problem with accepting help where it's needed?"

"Well," Wesley hedged, looking at the 'don't-screw-with-me' expression on Vivian Jackson's face. The same type of expression Rosalyn often wore. He didn't like his chances of succeeding with Attorney Jackson any better than those two disgraced senators had. JRock was right. The woman was exceptional. "Maybe sometimes."

She grew a cocky grin. "Right answer. I like an occasional challenge. Keeps me on my toes. You'll have the things my son thinks are needed on our next visit. Also, although you may not be quite ready for this yet, I'm going to ask one of my former law school professors from Georgetown Law to put together a team of third-year students to advise your clientele on issues that may come up related to the law. Someone from my office will be in touch with you about that.

"Now," she said on a windy, seemingly satisfied sigh, "it's time for me and my crew to get home." She took business cards from her pocket and handed one to Rosalyn and to Wesley. "This is my contact information. Let me hear from you when everything is settled.

"Oh, and Wes?"

"Yes?"

"Don't make me have to track you down when you need my help on anything else. Bye," she and the kids said, waved, and were heading out of the center.

Little T came to stand by Rosalyn and Ice, watching Vivian and her family leave. "*Wow!* That was actually *the* Vivian Alexander Jackson! She's taller than I thought she was and a lot younger. She's got to be younger than us and with all of those kids? Up close, she kinda looks like Jada Pinkett-Smith back in the day when she wore her hair short. Like she did in that movie, *Jason's Lyric*. Television doesn't do Ms. Jackson justice. She's a real babe! *Ms. Jackson, if you're nasty*," he sang a few lyrics from the old Janet Jackson song, and did a little dance move. Proud of his footwork, he turned back to look at Rosalyn and Ice for praise, but must have noticed the tension between them. "Uh, well, I'll go start… uh, doing…something." He quickly walked away, whistling the Janet Jackson song.

Ice and Rosalyn stared at each other until Ice gave up throwing up his hands in defeat.

"Okay, say what's on your mind."

"I have a house with three fully furnished bedrooms. One actually has two double beds in it. I have food already stocked. We've got a childcare routine established that works. We only have to change the location of where we all sleep. That's all Vivian said she needed to get the emergency temporary custody granted by a judge."

"No."

"*No?* Why not, Wes?"

"People will talk, Roz, and you know it. You have a reputation to consider and a man who is already complaining about the amount of time you've been spending taking care of Jakima's kids. He wouldn't like another man living in your house and sleeping in your bed."

"People are going to talk regardless. Those who matter know what time it is. It's not like you're my booty call, for Christ's sake! I haven't laid a finger on you." More is the pity she added silently, but his expression remained closed. She sensed he wasn't buying her arguments. "At least let's stick to the routine until you find something better."

"What about Howard Gardner?"

"He's not a consideration. Don't give him another thought. Plus, I've been sleeping in your bed for nearly three weeks now. You haven't so much as breathed on me."

Only because he was dog-tired when he came home each morning and she was gone when he woke up. He went from having sex at least twice a day to not having sex at all. He was always at half-mast around Rosalyn. Could he survive a few more days, a week at the most, with Rosalyn Hunter in his bed? He wasn't sure or brave enough to risk it.

"No, Roz. You've done enough."

He began turning off lights and moving toward the front door to meet his crew. Thankfully, Francine had agreed to spend the night with the children. Jemar would be at Mrs. Lewis' house with her, and Peckhead would still walk tonight and pick up Francine in the morning on his way home. It was Friday night, so he and the kids could sleep in on Saturday morning.

He watched as Rosalyn got into her SUV and drove away. He knew she was steamed at him, but he had to stand firm. She was too much of a temptation and he was certainly no gentleman.

Chapter 7

A week after Vivian's second visit to deliver the mountain of items her son had suggested, Ice watched from a distance and a relatively secluded location as JRock parked his expensive, custom-built, foreign car at one end of the U-shaped shopping center. He peeled his long, six-foot, seven-inch frame from the car before helping a beautiful woman from the passenger seat, but did not bother to set the car alarm. Ice and he knew alarms held no protection for a car like that one in this neighborhood. If he had locked the doors, it may have cost him a broken window. JROCK on his DC license plates was usually a barrier against theft and vandalism in the neighborhood, and not even that would deter some. Ice sent two boys on bikes to keep a lookout over JRock's ride.

He continued to watch his friend, as he seemed to be explaining something to the woman with him, as they slowly walked the shopping center. As usual, the corner drug store had metal detectors and two guards standing sentry at the doors. JRock raised his hand in acknowledgment of the guards who saluted him in return. They passed the Chinese food carryout with its counter-to-ceiling, bulletproof glass barring unwanted entry and a Plexiglas, turn-style in which money was collected and scanned before the food was delivered. The place was jam packed with customers. The dry cleaners had the same arrangement, but was closed and locked up tight for the night. At Bubbles and

Billie's Hair Emporium, JRock rang the doorbell, but only to get their attention, to wave to the occupants in each chair and stacked deep on a Friday night waiting to be served, not for admittance. He pointed out the entrance to the underground bowling alley that accommodated duckpin and ten-pin play, as well as billiards. It was a favorite hangout for crapshoots in the men's room.

The old Senator Theatre used to have great movies or live shows, but it, too, was closed and boarded up. When old Doc Stillman died, his family of doctors cleared out his office above the shoe repair shop and moved to Atlanta, Georgia. A little known insurance company now occupied the upstairs office space. They sold wigs and hairpieces on the side.

Now a multibillionaire, JRock never forgot his roots, Ice knew was planning for a revitalization of the area.

JRock and the woman reached the storefront church that had bars on the front and pictures of angels hanging behind the bulletproof glass. They approached the North East Diner where Jakima worked as a waitress. Little T's father, Big T, was the cook there before he died in a car accident. The place still had the best, melt-in-your-mouth, barbeque ribs in town, Ice thought, as he continued to monitor JRock's and the woman's slow progress.

Cherry's Liquor Store was owned by Mrs. Lewis' husband, Buddy's grandfather, whose street name was Cherry. Her son lost his life in the war and her daughter-in-law, Buddy's mama, remarried and moved to Seattle with another soldier, but left her son behind. Mrs. Lewis still owned the liquor store that anchored the development. Business was brisk nearly twenty-four hours a day, requiring complete coverage by armed guards walking around the catwalk, overlooking every corner of the store ready, willing, and able to meet the slightest provocation head on.

Patton's Shoe store had not long moved out after years of fighting the losing battle of pilfering and break-ins. Joey Patton, aka JP, used to be a neighborhood kid, and one of the boyz in Ice's crew, but his family gave up, closed up shop, and moved to Reston, Virginia, opening a boutique in a new, elite town center. Ice heard they recently opened a second location in the affluent Chevy Chase Galleria Mall and were looking at a third location in the new National Harbor Shopping Center across the Potomac in southern Prince George's County, Maryland. Joey was the new store's manager and a key element in his family's business. He occasionally donated money to the community center, but never took the time to visit anyone in his old neighborhood.

Addie's Attire was next to a discount auto parts store. The space where Icey Ice Cream Store and Bakery used to be was still boarded up with gang graffiti and old posters barely clinging to the boards. Icey was Wesley and Isaac's father's street name. They used to call Isaac, Junior Little Icey because their parents' store sold real hand-dipped and packed ice cream. Wesley's street name, Ice or The Iceman, was derived from that family history of street names. He and his brother used to work in the store with their father and grandparents from the time they learned to wear long pants.

Next to that, the second-hand furniture store was dark, evidencing that perhaps it, too, had folded like the others. Slide's father was the assistant manager until PTSD and alcohol took his life at an early age.

There were other stores and shops where young men and their women started to open businesses with small business loans after the war. Some failed for one reason or another, but some also remained, like Bubbles and Billie Bouchard's Hair Emporium. It would likely remain a neighborhood touchstone with two of the Bouchard's five children working as barbers and beauticians in the shop alongside their parents.

As usual, loud, trash-talking young people loitered outside the chain, fast food, fried chicken place for no apparent reason other than there was nothing better to do, Ice observed. He wanted to, but he couldn't afford to keep the community center open any later in the evening or open any earlier to give these youngsters something more constructive to do. In the spring, summer, and fall, JRock ran basketball camps and games a couple of times a week on the center's outside courts from six to midnight drawing a lot of interest in the neighborhood. Venders would sell food and drink making the games community events. It was moving into winter now and too cold for the outdoor events so teens and others loitered.

JRock pointed to where the public telephones were torn off the wall, usually not by vandals, but by law enforcement tired of drug dealers being warned anonymously that a raid was about to be pulled. A lonely, battered, and burned-out police cruiser sat on the littered parking lot, a grim reminder that, despite G-Boogie's efforts, calling 911 didn't always get you the help you needed in time and there had been losses on both sides of the war zone.

There was a crowd in Nana's Nails, but Ice didn't see LaKesha among the operators providing service. A quick look at his cellphone indicated she probably already left to go to her other job. She wasn't answering his calls, but he already had Slide change the locks for him.

"*Hey! JRock!*" the Iceman growled loudly, finally moving out of the shadows to where he could be seen. "Whatchu doin' up here?"

"Yeah!" growled Screw. "Think he all that!"

"He ain't knee high to nothin'!" Peckhead added with equal disdain. "Oughtta jack da punk!"

"He be frontin' on us, Ice! Ain't nobody gonna swing dat bull jive like he be a buster!" Dog added.

JRock turned to see six physically imposing men of various complexions, wearing dark hoodies, advancing on him and JaiHonnah.

The woman, Ice noted, didn't particularly seemed to care for the way he and his men surrounded them, as she inched closer to JRock's side.

"Yo, Ice, why you and your crew wanna be steppin' up to a brother cold blooded like that for?" JRock barked back at Ice, arms flaring out from his sides. "I gives you yo props! You wanna piece of me? C'mon, I'll show you your punk! I know you packin' dat 2-5!"

The woman froze, Ice noticed, at the belligerent tone in JRock's voice and the sudden shift in his demeanor to a street-wise slang, obviously unfamiliar to her. Clearly, she wasn't from the city. Ice imagined she almost believed JRock, he and his crew were speaking another language and somehow the dapper, J. Roderick Baylor—astute, intellectual businessman—had morphed into JRock, a street-wise thug. He got a kick out of teasing her with his and his crews' antics.

"Ain't my props I be wantin', brotherman. It be dat fine ass fox you be sportin'!"

"Ain't gonna be like dat, Ice. Now 'less you ready to walk the Rock, you be steppin' down from my lady."

"Yeah, we got yo Rock," Little T barked, grabbing his crotch. "You bangin' this babe—"

"Watch yo mouth 'round this lady, Little T," JRock fired back, pointing a threatening finger in Tavon's face.

A slow grin crossed the Iceman's lips and he noticed the woman seemed frozen in the spot where she stood. Then, he and JRock moved toward each other, leaving her standing unprotected. They were nearly chest-to-chest, and then, suddenly, they embraced and smiled broadly at each other. JRock towered over most of the men, hugged them as they smacked at his head and butt. Then he acknowledged the other men in a similar fashion.

JRock turned to the woman and extended his hand to her. She immediately took it, moving toward him.

"JaiHonnah Chapman, this is Wesley Greenfield, better known as The Iceman or Ice," he said, and then introduced her to the other men. "These other criminals are Roscoe 'Peckhead' Hubbard, Chester 'Dog' Dillard, Tavon 'Little T' Rogers, Henry 'Slide' Hughes, and Richard 'Screw' Rainey.

"JaiHonnah, huh? Pretty name for a stone, cold fox," Ice said without expression. "What kind of name is that, pretty lady?"

"Navajo," she said, barely audible.

"Indian, huh? I like it. JaiHonnah. Yeah, I like that." He looked her up and down before he finally cracked a slight smile.

"Native American," she said, lifting her chin defiantly.

"Whoa! She can grit on you, too," commented Screw.

"JaiHonnah is the architect I told you about. She'll be designing the Baylor Plaza Park project, Ice. I want the word on the street. Anybody touches her, they're gonna have to walk the Rock. She goes anywhere she wants and talks to anyone she wants. She's protected regardless of whether I'm with her or not—"

BANG! BANG! BANG!

Shots rang out loudly in rapid succession. Others in the parking lot jumped and ducked for cover, except Iceman, his crew, and JRock, who turned their heads slowly in the direction of the shots.

Ice nodded to two of his crewmembers. "Go see 'bout that," he ordered. Screw and Slide peeled off and moved in the direction of the commotion. Then, he turned back toward JRock. "Don't worry 'bout that, JRock. Ain't nothin' gonna happen to your lady. We'll take care of it personally.

"So, you finally got the scratch?"

"Yeah, cut a deal today that's going to fully fund the Baylor Plaza Park Project and start the build out. That plus the commitment of the Black Construction Industry League for funds to open a journeyman trade school in the hood, in your community center if you'll let me use it. You ready to come work with Baylor Design and Developers, yet? You know I need your help."

"Naw, man, can't be livin' no nine-to-five gig."

"That's seven to seven, Ice. Nine to five is for the wimps," JRock said facetiously. "You've never let me down and you've always had my back. You make this move with me, it could go a long way to putting this place where it should be, like we talked about when we were kids. It's what our fathers wanted, remember? They wanted us together taking care of each other and the hood. They were best friends like us and they went through hell in the war in Nam together, on these same streets in the 60s, 70s, and 80s, and they still made it. Here we are in the new millennium. They are gone, but the struggle continues. I want you to reopen your old man's ice cream parlor and bakery."

"Man, you had to go there, didn't you?" he said, aggrievedly.

"I'll use anything I can to get you to work with me on this project. Who knows, you might just like busting your ass twenty-four-seven."

"Like I don't already, but I like wearing them def threads," he said, grinning and fingering JRock's jacket lapel, "and having a lady like JaiHonnah on my arm."

"The threads you can buy, Ice. Ladies, like JaiHonnah, you gotta earn," he said, without a smile.

"He knows all about 'de ladies'," a female voice said, entering the discussion with a saucy lilt from behind Roderick and JaiHonnah, "Don't you, Wesley?"

They turned and looked in Rosalyn Hunter's dark, sultry eyes below half lids.

"Hey, Roz," JRock said, extending his hand.

"JRock," she acknowledged expressionless, still eyeing Wesley, but shook hands.

JRock felt the chill between his two friends. "Dr. Rosalyn Hunter, this is Dr. JaiHonnah Reise Chapman, my new architect. She's going to be representing Baylor Design and Developers on the East of the River Redevelopment Committee for the Baylor Plaza Park Project," JRock said. "JaiHonnah and Vivian Alexander Jackson were in undergrad together at Spelman College and Vivian is my legal rep on the project. Rosalyn is the elementary school principal in the community and one of the community leaders. She and I went to high school together. She graduated from Wellesley College and Columbia University for her masters and doctorate."

Rosalyn nodded toward JaiHonnah, but JaiHonnah extended her hand. Rosalyn took it and shook it lightly. Then Rosalyn turned her attention to JRock and Wesley.

"Kelley told me," she said dryly. "She called me at school today and wanted me to set up another community meeting for early next week. I told her Wednesday at six o'clock at the school would work. You gonna be there, Wesley?"

Rosalyn and Wesley stared at each other intently, but he didn't answer. His two-man crew returned and Screw whispered something at his ear.

"I gotta roll out, JRock," he said lowly, giving JRock a clasped hand, shoulder bump, brother's handshake.

"Ice, what are you going to do, man?" JRock asked not losing the grip he had on Wesley's hand.

"First, I'm gonna keep your ride from getting jacked by some crackheads. Then, I'm gonna go jack up some little nine-year-old nothing who thinks he's something 'cause he gotta piece."

"I want an answer, Ice," JRock said, as Wesley pulled away. "What's the word?"

"Peace. Out," Wesley said, moving away and glimpsing Rosalyn's stoic expression as he left.

JRock turned back to Rosalyn. "He'll be there, Roz. I'll see to that."

"Whatever," she said, as she watched Wesley leave. Then her temperament was less harsh. She was still angry with him she realized.

JaiHonnah exhaled noticeably, Rosalyn observed. Wesley's crew looked like stone thugs. JaiHonnah was probably afraid and holding her breath.

"You're still tryin' to hang, JRock?" Rosalyn asked.

"Got to, Roz. You know it. You doing all right?"

"I'm makin' it. Tryin' to keep these little knuckleheads from growin' up like that one," she said, nodding toward Wesley's departing figure. It frightened her that he could be walking into a bullet on these night patrols. "Only lost six this year."

"Ice is keepin' the chill on."

"Ice ought to learn how to chill," she said with heat. Then she turned on a slight smile. "Looks like you're learning something, JRock." She nodded toward JaiHonnah.

"Uh, business relationship, Roz. Strictly business."

"Yeah, right. Look, I've got to go pick up my dinner from the Chinese place before they close. I'll see you and your 'strictly business relationship' on Wednesday night. Nice to meet you, JaiHonnah."

"You, too, Rosalyn."

Chapter 8

If it wasn't one thing or another, Rosalyn thought, on Monday morning, as she tried to untangle the mess Glenda made of the budget needs her teachers submitted. She could not make heads nor tails of Glenda's notes and, of course, Glenda would be out today with the same flu that attacked several of her faculty members and about a quarter of the students. If this epidemic got any worse—

"Uh, excuse me. Are you Dr. Hunter?"

Rosalyn looked up from her desk to see a man and woman standing in her open door. She stood and rounded her desk, her hand extended. "I am. Yes. And you are?"

"Agents Corso and Bennett," he said, both producing identification and badges. "We're with Child Protective Services."

"I'm not aware of a problem that requires investigation in my school."

"We're following up on a complaint filed by…uh," he consulted a notebook, "Mr. Howard Gardner. He states there are several abandoned children in this school?"

"He's mistaken and I'm not sure how you gained entry without authorization or prior notice. I'll have to ask you to leave."

"The guard at the door admitted us, Dr. Hunter. We showed him our credentials and badges. We have a job to do and if you're impeding our investigation we will have to bring the matter to the attention of your superiors."

"I assure you what I am doing is protecting the security of my students, staff, and teachers. I do not release information about any of my students. You arrived unannounced, asking questions I am not authorized to answer. Now, I will accept your business cards, consult with the school board's attorneys, and have them contact your office to arrange for a time and place to discuss whatever we can without violating anyone's confidentiality or privacy. You will have to leave now. It's my job to make sure the school is secure."

When they left, Rosalyn sat, bent at the waist, and put her head between her knees. She had never been so afraid in her life. If she hadn't been quick on her feet, Cole, Marcus, and Simone might be, at that moment, on their way to juvenile services facilities.

When she got her head together, she picked up the phone and started dialing.

"Time's up," she said to Wesley. "I need you in my office PDQ."

She hung up without waiting for a comment and then dialed another number.

"Vivian Jackson," she answered.

Surprised she gave them a direct number, Roz was momentarily flabbergasted. She fully expected to have to wade through a battery of office staff before she could reach Vivian directly, if at all.

"Rosalyn? What's up?"

"I, uh, I didn't expect you to...never mind. That's not important. About fifteen minutes ago, agents from Child Protective Services showed up, acting on a complaint lodged by someone who I'm going to commit justifiable homicide on after we straighten out a few things. I've already called Wesley to come in. He only lives a block and a half away and should be here shortly. So far as I know, he's been negotiating with a few property owners, but he hasn't found suitable housing in the neighborhood for himself and the children."

"Is your offer still open for him to move in with you?"

"It is, yes."

"Okay, give me your address and other contact information. Then, I need the names of the agents and their contact information."

While Rosalyn talked with Vivian, giving her the information she requested, Wesley was buzzed into the building by the school security guard and walked into her office. He looked flushed, as if he had been out running as he usually did daily, or that he had run all the way to the school from his apartment. Rosalyn put Vivian on her cell phone loud speaker so Wesley could also hear and participate in their conversation.

"All right, Roz, tell me exactly what happened," Vivian said.

"Well, as I said, Agents Corso and Bennett showed up as a result of information their office received about three abandoned children. I gave them a song and dance about security measures, unannounced visits, privacy issues, yadda, yadda. I didn't acknowledge that there were any children in need of their services. I couldn't think fast enough, but what I did say got them out of the building. I don't think that will be the last we hear from them."

"By the way, I don't practice criminal law," said Vivian, "but what you described might constitute premeditated murder, not justifiable homicide, so be careful how you commit the crime. Who is this soon-to-be-deceased informant?"

Rosalyn chuckled and then took a couple quick, calming breaths before continuing. "Howard Gardner. He's a person who believed my decision to help with the care of the children was a monumental inconvenience for him. He hasn't seen inconvenience yet! If we lose these children to child welfare, Howard Gardner will rue the day he meddled in my business!"

"*O-kay*, still a little hot under the collar, are we?"

"A tad!"

Vivian's laugh was warm and comforting, Roz thought.

"Well, I think you know what has to happen."

"I do. Wesley is here now and he's listening to this conversation. I'll discuss this with him."

"Great! Convince him, Roz. I know you can do it, if anyone can. Listen to her, Wesley. Believe me when I tell you, you don't want me and JRock on your back. Give me a few hours. I'll be back to you both shortly."

"Thanks."

"You're welcome."

They hung up. Rosalyn turned and watched Wesley while he paced the floor, head down, hands in his pockets. He seemed to be deep in thought. She remained quiet, waiting for him to reach the same inevitable conclusion she had. Finally, he stopped pacing, turned, and looked at her.

"Are you sure about what you said? About your relationship with Gardner? You would cut your ties with him to keep the kids?"

"In a heartbeat. I will see the soon-to-be-departed Howard Gardner after we settle the issue of living arrangements for the children. I don't want them to have any idea there is the possibility child welfare would have any say over their lives, Wes. Please. Don't fight me on this. Let me help. We can do this together."

"You really care that much for them?"

"I do, yes. More than I can express. I want them and you to move in today. If Vivian can get a judge to approve the emergency, temporary custody petition, then child services can take a long walk off of a short pier!"

He grinned at her. "Give your keys to me. I'll go get the kids' things from my apartment. Their clothes are already in boxes."

"Take my car. That's too much to carry."

He hesitated only a moment. It was difficult for him to accept help for things he considered solely his responsibility. He had his father's vintage T-Bird in storage, but he never drove it. It cost to maintain and insure a vehicle in his neighborhood. Instead, he channeled every bit of money he could into the community center. Generally, he used public transportation to get where he needed to go. Occasionally driving LaKesha's hoopty was no big deal, but driving Rosalyn's BMW SUV was a major step for him.

***

Walking on to the polished, heated, marble floor in Rosalyn's home at the wide vestibule was another major step. As instructed, he disarmed the security system immediately. The openness of the main floor with a library/den to his right and to his left, the front living area he liked immensely. There was a pleasant scent in the air like what it smelled like in certain stores and boutiques. A big fireplace and a spacious dining area all the way to the to-die-for, ultra-modern kitchen were accessible. The family area in the rear where a big flat screen hung on a wall above another fireplace looked like a magazine cover. All the furniture looked like it was comfortable and the colors and textures perfect for the spaces.

Double French doors led to a wide, deep deck and grassy, fenced backyard beyond. She had a monster outdoor rotisserie grill on the deck, comfortable-looking chairs and tables. He eyed the grill again. How he would love to get his hands on that baby. It wasn't even chained.

His knees went weak looking at the kitchen setup. He was salivating over the modern gas, six-burner range with center grill, double wall ovens with warming drawers below, big double-door refrigerator and freezer with ice and water dispenser in the freezer door, and the dishwasher. There was even a tall wine cooler next to the refrigerator fully stocked with white and red wines at different temperatures. All of the appliances were stainless steel. The cabinets and built-in pantry were custom, solid Brazilian cherry wood set off by the light quartz counter tops and glass-tile backsplash. Hardwood, perhaps bamboo, floors spanned the entire area, wide hallway, powder room, and what appeared to be a hideaway office when he opened the doors. He pocketed the extra set of house and car keys Rosalyn told him he would find in the center desk drawer.

Steps from the family room area led downstairs to what was an open game room with a high ceiling. He sensed and then squatted to touch the floor. Just as he suspected, heated stone tile. A pool table was set in one area, a ping-pong table in another, and groups of comfortable seating throughout with a bar and bar stools against a far wall.

There was a fully equipped kitchenette behind the bar. Another large flat screen hung on an adjacent wall with an assortment of electronic games stacked on shelves beside a brick fireplace. A full, four-piece bath and, in another room, a storage area with plenty of vacant shelves included a utility room.

The theatre room blew his mind with its reclining club chairs and foot rests. A popcorn machine and beverage cooler sat across the back wall next to a bar with bar stools.

Then he stepped into another room that contained her in-home gym and exercise equipment with mirrored walls, a long ballet bar, and other apparatus he couldn't identify. An opposite wall held pictures of Rosalyn as she had appeared in various performances, apparently from the time she was a little girl through college and perhaps beyond. Unlike other parts of the basement, this expansive room had light-colored hardwood flooring. She apparently still kept up her fine shape and legs with her ballet routines.

The kids would go crazy when they saw this space that didn't resemble any basement he had ever seen.

Ice brought in the boxes, carried them upstairs, and stacked them in the two extra bedrooms where the children would likely sleep. Two double beds with nightstands and lamps were in one room with a double dresser, a double chest of drawers and a corner desk and chair. In a smaller, yet still spacious bedroom similarly furnished as the other one held one double bed. There was a nice size four-piece bath with heated floors off the hallway next to a compact laundry room with a large stacked washer and dryer, iron and board, and heated drying racks. All of the modern conveniences, Ice thought, still awed.

When he finished placing boxes in the appropriate bedrooms, he entered Rosalyn's master bedroom and *en suite* bath, which was the size of a small bedroom and goggled. She had a sitting room with a flat screen on a wall above a fireplace flanked by full bookcases. Deep, comfortable, extra-wide seats, both with ottomans, sat catty-cornered with a small, glass-topped table between them.

Yet, the *pièce de résistance* was the highboy, California king-sized bed with a tufted, leather headboard. On one nightstand was a stack of popular novels—mystery and romance. On the other were a remote control, telephone, and Bose clock and radio.

Attractive area rugs covered the hardwood floors and flowed into a walk-in closet large enough to double as a bedroom with built-in shoe racks, drawers, and plenty of hanging space on three walls. A waist-high cabinet centered the room with clear drawers containing jewelry and fine lingerie. One complete wall with shoe racks and built-in chest of drawers was empty. He placed his meager belongings on that side of the closet.

Then he went into the spa-like bathroom. There was a large, frameless, glass-enclosed, stand-up shower that could easily accommodate four people simultaneously and a deep, wide, whirlpool tub, large enough for two comfortably. He didn't want to think about Rosalyn all wet, warm, and soapy in that tub, but, nevertheless, the image came to him unbidden. There was also a separate water closet and double, under-mount granite vessel sinks in Brazilian Cherrywood vanity cabinets behind large mirrored doors. She had pretty pots and bottles attractively arranged on one half of the long counter top. He lifted what looked like an expensive bottle of perfume, sniffed, and smiled at the intoxicating scent. He placed his shaving kit under the counter at the opposite end.

Homes in this neighborhood were large and actually had stairs up to a huge unfinished attic space above the bedrooms and baths, but he never would have guessed what Rosalyn had done to her place since her parents moved out. Her home looked like something out of *Better Homes and Gardens* or *Architectural Digest*. It was going to take a little getting used to for him and for the kids to actually live there. Still, he would do almost anything to keep them from being separated and subjected to the child welfare system.

Ice reset the alarm in the coat closet at Rosalyn's front door and started down the first set of steps toward her car when he heard the booming base from a couple of black, tricked-out SUVs. They rolled slowly down the street and paused briefly in front of Rosalyn's home. The rear window of the second SUV slid down and a face appeared. It was Killer, aka Levi Hall. He and his crew, the Royal Reds, Ice knew, were scoping out new territory for his drug sales. He grinned at Ice, his gold tooth glinting, and then flashed a gang hand sign.

Ice and his friends, including G-Boogie, worked hard, covertly, and steadily to get the previous, big-time, drug dealer, Tony the Tiger, aka Tony Taylor, out of the neighborhood. He wasn't about to let another one move in. The small-time dealers still in the hood only sold pot or designer pills. In time, Ice had plans to rid the neighborhood of those parasites as well.

Killer may also have been scouting for Peckhead's boy, Jemar, he thought, who now lived up the street in Mrs. Lewis' home. It would be a real feather in Killer's cap if he could jump Peckhead's son into his Royal Reds. Peckhead wasn't about to let his son get caught up in the drug scene. Peckhead told him if Killer came looking for Jemar to initiate him into his drug gang, he'd ship Jemar down South to relatives there to keep him from getting caught up like so many other kids had been. Admittedly, fewer and fewer kids were turning to a life of crime. He hoped the work he and his posse did in the community contributed to the lower loss numbers.

As Killer's crew pulled away, Ice continued quickly down the second set of steps while he called the community center to alert his own crew there was unwanted company in the hood. It had been a long time since his crew had to walk the neighborhood strapped, but if the circumstances called for it to protect Jemar or others, they would strap up. They were all licensed and had permits to carry concealed weapons. He would also alert G-Boogie at the One Four Precinct and his contacts at the FBI, just in case something started jumping off as Peckhead predicted. He drove to Rosalyn's school and returned her car and house keys to her. She was on an important call and didn't have time to talk. He only had time to warn her to be careful because the Royal Reds were in the neighborhood.

Chapter 9

osalyn's heels clicked a quick staccato on the concrete garage floor. She couldn't move fast enough in her pencil-straight skirt and icepick heels, but she had such a head of steam going that when the elevator doors opened on Howard's floor, people quickly moved out of her way. She marched past Howard's executive assistant before the woman even knew she was there. When she entered his office without knocking, Howard was seated at his conference table with his team deep in conversation, with projection screens up and operational on several walls.

"We need the room," Rosalyn announced when she entered and held the door open for his team's hurried departure. Since there was not a smile for his co-workers anywhere in the vicinity of her face, like children responding to their teacher's authoritative voice, people got quickly to their feet with various looks of foreboding toward a stunned Howard, then just as quickly exited his office. Without taking her eyes off Howard, Rosalyn firmly closed the door behind the last person.

"Rosalyn, what is the meaning of this?" he asked, sternly. "Didn't you see I was in a meeting?"

She was on him, swinging his chair around to face her, trapping him in his seat, and in his face before he could get to his feet. "Did you call social services and lodge a complaint about the children we discussed?"

"Of course, I did. It took one of my assistants hours through a morass of government bureaucracy to find the right place. You can bet my congressman is going to hear about it from me! Still, that's no excuse for you to come barging into my office, like your Ghetto Fabulous Queen friend, demanding—"

"How dare you interfere in my business this way!"

"You're not a social worker, Rosalyn. You have a doctorate in education, not as a social scientist. You're ill-equipped to deal with some cast off pick-a-ninnies when you should be—"

"Don't you dare presume to tell me what I can and cannot do! I am a grown, professional woman! I do *not* need nor do I want your advice or guidance about how I live my life, spend my time, or conduct my business. Since you think I'm such an imbecile who needs guidance, lose my phone number and address. I never want to hear from you again!" She pushed his chair away from her and turned preparing to leave.

"This isn't about some damn children, Rosalyn, and you know it! This is about some rowdy roughneck you've been sleeping with, isn't it?" he demanded, standing, pushing his chair further away so hard it banged loudly against a wall.

She slowly turned to look at him, her confusion apparent. "What are you talking about?"

"Are you going to deny you've been sleeping with some man who goes by some silly, childish name like Ice or Iceman?"

"Sleeping with as in being intimate with him?"

"Yes, of course!"

"You think so little of me you would believe I'd sleep with you and another man at the same time?" she asked incredulously.

"Can you deny it?"

"Without hesitation, but I resent I would have to deny it to you. Yes, I've spent the last few weeks taking care of children who need some normalcy in their lives and I've consistently slept in a bed other than my own, but I have only been intimate with you for more than two years. No one else."

"That's hard to believe. Some man slept in a bed with you and didn't touch you? He had to be a eunuch or gay to manage that miracle. You turn me on when you're standing still or as angry as you are now. I'm getting hard just looking at you."

"He, for damn sure, isn't a eunuch or gay, but not once did he touch me. Frankly, Howard, I don't give a flying fig what you think or believe. These children are all I care about right now and if Vivian Jackson can't undo the damage you've caused—"

"*What? Wait!* Vivian Jackson? You mean *The* Vivian Alexander Jackson, Esquire?"

She drew back, brows furrowed, and looked at his overly excited interest, surprised by his eagerness and what looked like a woody. He looked almost orgasmic.

"You actually know Vivian Jackson?"

"Yes," she said cautiously, "we've met."

"Do you realize she's one of the wealthiest women in the world? I've tried for years to get an appointment with her so I can get her business and I couldn't get past her administrative staff. You actually know her? Her law firm is one of the most prestigious in the country. Her law partners include William Chandler, attorney to the stars, sports and media icons, the über rich and famous and the people who made them. He's a publisher and superstar model, too.

"Alan Lightfoot is Attorney General to the Native American Nation. Can you imagine what kind of financial windfall the Native Americans generate from their casinos annually? They need someone, like me, to handle all of their financial accounting.

"Melissa Charles, David Carter and Gloria Towson Carter, all of them are wealthy and in need of my specialized guidance.

"Ms. Jackson's brother is Kenneth Alexander. He owns one of the fastest growing tech and communications companies in the country. These are extremely wealthy and influential people!"

"So?"

"*So?* What do you mean '*so*? Why haven't you introduced me to them? Do you know what this could mean to me, to my career, for us after we're married? We're going to need a bigger house in the right zip code," he said as he started pacing, deep in thought. "We will have to invite her and her friends and family over often. We'll encourage them to bring more people to our parties. I could start my own accounting firm with them as my clients." He finally stopped pacing and turned to look at her. "I've invested a lot into you because, despite the disgusting neighborhood you grew up in, you have the right pedigree to be my wife, but I'll fix that. To your credit, you do come from a long line of professionals. Although you're politically an independent, you belong to some of the best organizations, like Jack and Jill of America, Inc., a large sorority, The Links, and Mensa for Pete's sake. It would be your duty to foster my career… Why are you laughing?"

"Because you've got jokes. You're a great lay, Howard, and I'll admit I've enjoyed you these past few years, but I have no intention of marrying you. I never did. Moreover, after the stunt you pulled, I would never even consider becoming your wife. You have no social conscience."

"I'm politically ultra-conservative, Rosalyn. I make no apology for my views. You've known me long enough to understand that. I don't believe in social welfare. We have certainly debated the issues, *ad infinitum,* but despite your progressive leanings, you had to know where this relationship is going. I've introduced you to all of the important people in my firm and in my social circle. I never would have done that if I didn't intend to groom you to be my wife."

"'Groom me'?" she said and laughed.

"Of course! I took you to all the best stores and bought clothes and jewelry to make you look presentable to be with me."

"You sure as hell put all of your eggs in the wrong basket, pal, because this relationship has surely gone to hell in that hand basket. Better luck next time."

She walked out of his office through the group of his co-workers and staff who stood in stunned silence as she passed by.

***

Cole, Marcus, and Simone were as goggle-eyed as he was when Ice opened the door to Rosalyn's home for them and ushered them in out of a cold rain. He had to encourage them to move from space to space, their fascination apparent.

"Ice, do this be where Mz. Hunter be livin' at? All by herself?"

"Yes. Now we are going to live here with her until we find your mother, Cole."

"Man!" Marcus declared, "Maybe it gonna take a long, long time to find Jakima."

Ice had to smile at that sentiment, too. Just the idea of sleeping in that awesome, king-sized bed was nearly enough to make him want the morning not to come sooner rather than later.

"Let's go upstairs and put your clothes away."

The upstairs was as awe-inspiring for the children as the first floor had been. He left them alone, putting their clothes into the closets and drawers, while he went to the kitchen to prepare their dinner. He had so much fun in the dream kitchen he planned to make everything from soup to dessert as if it were a very special occasion.

First, he fed them a snack and then worked with them on their homework for a few hours while dinner cooked. With the extra bathrooms, they were showered and dressed for bed in record time, but it was still early and Rosalyn had not yet come home. He kept checking the time, worried about her safety, but he didn't know where she was or what was on her schedule. He left dinner in the warming drawer for her and then took the children to the basement game room as a special treat. They were speechless from the moment their feet touched the last step.

That's where Rosalyn found them after she arrived home. They were so involved in the Wii game they didn't immediately notice her presence. When they did, the children gathered around her, looking up at her with such hope and devotion that she could do nothing but kneel, gather them in her arms, and hug them tightly.

Then, as if choreographed, they turned and included Ice in the group hug. When they parted, they were all a little misty eyed. Ice was thrilled to see her unharmed.

***

"I apologize for coming by so late at night, but I thought this was important enough," said Vivian Jackson. "My investigators have reported that Jakima Harris was killed, along with Phillip 'Honeybear' Brown, in a car accident over a month ago in New Jersey. The accident was so severe that the occupants were burned beyond recognition. We will have to confirm her death through dental records. The only thing that survived the crash was part of the license plate. The car was registered to Ms. Eldora Harris who my investigators believe to be Jakima's mother. She died more than two months ago. Initially, the police thought the car might have been stolen when they found out Ms. Harris was deceased and didn't check any further. It was only through death records that my investigators found the name Jakima Harris as the informant on her mother's death certificate. They determined Jakima was an only child of the elder Ms. Harris and she was likely the person in possession of her mother's car. No papers had been filed to change the ownership registration of the car or the insurance policy. The insurance policy was paid up for a year. The New Jersey police pretty much gave up on trying to locate any next of kin."

Wesley and Rosalyn sat in her living room in stunned silence, listening to Vivian. Tears glistened in Rosalyn's eyes. Wesley reached for her hand and she clung to his with both of hers.

"What now?" Wesley asked.

"In light of this new information, which I received late this afternoon, after speaking with you, the good news is that, a little over an hour ago, a night court judge granted joint, temporary custody to you and Rosalyn for one-hundred-twenty days while a search is conducted for the children's next of kin. As I said, Jakima, we believe, was an only child and my investigators have found no living relatives for her mother. Her father is unknown, but we will have a DNA test run on her remains to determine whether we can find a familial match. Jakima didn't know or didn't identify the father of any of her children on their birth records, so DNA testing will be conducted to determine whether a match can be found on them, too. That's a hit or miss situation and a long shot. Until the results are known, the children will remain in your custody.

"Someone from social services will visit you, likely Corso and Bennett, to establish for the record you are both who you say you are, to inspect your home, and do a background check on both of you. They will inspect not only your home, but also your places of business and interview your friends, family, and acquaintances.

"As your legal counsel, a copy of their report is required to be provided to me. Wesley, you will need to change the address on all of your legal documents, including your driver's license.

"Now, I had to stretch the circumstances of your relationship a bit. The documents I filed with the court state you have been in a 'close' relationship since high school, but only recently started living together. The implication I left the judge with was that you two are in a long-term, committed, intimate relationship and decided, for the children's welfare, to move in together to provide a stable home environment. The fact you would do this for the children went over really well with the judge. Also, that you 'may' even be contemplating marriage. So, are either of you uncomfortable with that interpretation of the facts?"

They looked at each other, still holding hands.

"These 'facts' helped to gain the judge's approval?" asked Roz.

"They were pivotal as was the fact you have known the children's mother, who would certainly want her children cared for by life-long friends rather than strangers. People who have known the children all of their lives and can provide a sense of, community, continuity, and economic stability in their time of need."

"Then I'm comfortable with your interpretation of the facts," Said Roz.

"I am, too," Wesley added.

"Good! Now, I can bring in a child psychiatrist to break the news—"

"No, that won't be necessary. I've been with them and so has Wesley for more than a month. I remember enough of my children psych classes and medical rotation to do this, to gently break the news to them. We also know them well enough to gauge whether they need further intervention." Rosalyn looked at Wesley for agreement.

He nodded. "We just finished reading bedtime stories to them. They are asleep now, but we'll discuss it and find a way to tell them tomorrow. Is there anything else we need to do?"

"You may want to arrange a funeral or memorial service; put a notice in the newspaper. I'll take care of the details regarding any estate Jakima and/or her mother may have and set up a trust fund for each of her children. The accident wasn't Jakima's fault. A woman who was driving under the influence was charged with reckless endangerment and vehicular manslaughter. This is not her first time being arrested for a DUI. She's in jail and her insurance company is looking to settle all claims quickly and out of court.

"If we find no relatives, at some point before the end of the temporary custody, we will have to discuss whether you want to petition the court for permanent custody or adoption."

"I don't know why I hadn't thought that far ahead," Rosalyn said, still saddened and shaken by the news of Jakima's death. She had yet to release Wesley's hand and he had not pulled away from her. "If their fathers don't show up or if any one of them doesn't want all three children, I would be interested in adopting them; all of them. I think I could handle the court's scrutiny. Wes?" She looked at him.

If she continued to look at him like that, like he was her hero, he could deny her nothing at all. "I don't know whether the courts would consider me reputable enough."

"You're a community organizer just like former President Obama was," said Roz.

"Yes, but he was also a Harvard Law graduate, United States Senator, and a scholar."

"Details," Vivian said glibly and then rose from her seat. "I've given you a lot to do and to think about. Talk it over. The court petition would be stronger with both of you on the document.

I'll check back with you next week unless something else comes up before then."

Ice and Rosalyn rose as well.

"Thank you, Vivian. You've made a very difficult situation easier to handle," said Rosalyn and hugged Vivian.

"You're welcome," she said hugging Rosalyn and then Ice. "Call if you need anything. You two make a great team."

"I'll walk you out," Wesley said.

When he returned, Rosalyn was waiting at the front door.

"May I get anything from the kitchen for you before you leave?"

"I'm not on patrol tonight. I got Slide to take my place. I wasn't sure how the kids would handle moving in here. I didn't want them or you to think I was pawning them off on you and abandoning them."

"They seemed okay when I came in."

"They were a little hesitant initially, but once they saw the game room, they were fine. The sheer size of your home is a little intimidating."

"Are *you* okay with all of this?"

"I'll handle it."

She nodded. That was probably the best she could expect from him for the time being. She wanted him to think of her home as his, too. Only time and patience would determine whether they could make this arrangement work over the long haul.

"Look, it's late. Let's go to bed. We have a long, difficult day ahead of us," he said.

With the kitchen clean and put to right, he started the dishwasher, then checked doors and windows, turning out lights, and setting the alarm.

Rosalyn waited for him and they climbed the steps together. When they checked the boys' bedroom, they found all three children in one bed and snuggled up under Cole. Gingerly, they moved Simone and Marcus into their own beds and covered them. Tomorrow would be a hard day for them all.

Wesley went into the hall bathroom to shower and shave, while Rosalyn used her master bathroom to shower and then find something to wear to bed that didn't make her look like an exhibitionist. When finished oiling her skin and wrapping her hair in a silk scarf, she turned out the bathroom light and eased into bed. Wesley was already in bed and, for a change, he was under the covers instead of on top. He stared at the slowly turning ceiling fan with his hands folded under his head. His massive shoulder and arm muscles were in full view. She marveled at how truly handsome and sexy he was. Terrance Howard never looked this good, particularly about the color of his eyes in the bedroom lighting.

"I think I want to go for adoption," he said, then turned his golden gaze on her. "I want to talk with the kids about it first. They may not want me as a father."

"You'll make a great father, Wes."

"For sure, I'll try my best. I never really thought about becoming a father before, but I know what it feels like when people you care about unexpectedly get taken away from you."

She turned on her side, facing him with her hands stacked under her head. "You're thinking about your father and Isaac."

"Yes. Always. One day everything's fine. I'm floating through life without a care. I finish culinary school and continue working in the store with my father and brother, making good money. I'm nineteen years old and I'm thinking, maybe I'd save up because I'd like to open a restaurant someday. Not a big one downtown, but a soul food place where people can eat in or take out. Something bigger than my father's bakery and ice cream parlor.

"I had been talking about it with my father that day and for a few weeks before that. He wanted me to work out a business plan and, if I was serious, he said he would help me get started. He sent me to make the bank deposits. Afterward, I went home early to write down some thoughts on the type of restaurant I wanted, the food I'd serve, and to get started on my plan.

"I was going to hang out later with the boyz at this club downtown. I was just getting out of the shower when Peckhead came with the news that my father had been shot and Isaac had gone looking for the shooter. I was afraid whoever shot my father would kill Isaac, too. In just a few seconds, everything was over and done.

The next week, I buried my father next to my mother. Isaac went to prison in Montana because there is no prison in the area anymore, and I closed up the store. It simply wasn't the same without my father and Isaac there. I probably could have kept the bakery and ice cream parlor open, but I couldn't dream anymore or drift anymore. Everything got real, real fast.

"That's what Cole, Marcus, and Simone are going to feel tomorrow. Like the rug has been pulled out from under them. Jakima wasn't the ideal mother, but, on top of losing their grandmother two months ago, she was all they had."

"It's true, their sense of security is going to be shattered. We won't let them down, Wes. Just like Mr. and Mrs. Baylor were there for you, we'll be there for Cole, Marcus, and Simone."

"I took this on me, Roz. I never wanted to get you tangled up in it. Now, where you had a nice orderly life, you have been invaded."

"Do I look intimidated?"

He laughed. "It's only the beginning."

***

Wesley and Rosalyn talked into the night settling some issues about household expenses. Rosalyn reluctantly agreed to share the expenses equally, but Wesley insisted he be solely responsible for the kid's expenses. They were deadlocked on that proposition. Rosalyn was determined to participate in any costs involving the children.

The morning found them asleep in each other's arms. Rosalyn's head was pillowed on his left shoulder, her arm and left leg across his torso. Wesley's left arm and hand held her fleshy rear securely. Sleep was slowly losing its grip on them.

"Roz?"

"Hmm?" she hummed, barely awake.

"I need to get up."

"Why?" she asked, sounding aggrieved and then snuggled closer.

He moved her left hand and placed it on his early morning erection.

"That's no reason to get up." Blindly, sleepily, she reached into her nightstand and retrieved a condom. She wasted no time covering him. "That's an excellent reason to stay in bed."

"Are you sure about this?"

"Let's not waste a perfectly good boner."

With no further encouragement needed, Ice rolled on top of Rosalyn and slowly sank into her heat.

It was better than her imagination, Rosalyn thought, when she could think at all. Sex with Wesley was off the charts; so huge, so indescribably delicious. He wasn't a big man, built more like a Class A, middle-weight, prize fighter, but he was solidly muscular and she felt every one of those muscles as he helped her climb to another peak and over into a dazed wonderland. Heaven knew she craved his body for years, but never in her experience had any man taken her to such heights. LaKesha was right. He was well endowed and he knew what to do with it.

Ice was in another reality with the feel of Rosalyn beneath him. Her scent and body alone had him on a plain where he had never been with any other woman, including LaKesha. Rosalyn was a woman who enjoyed being touched and didn't rush the euphoria or bounce on him to serve only her own needs. She gave and he met her at the point of no return for him. He came harder and longer than he could ever remember.

He also realized he had said things to her he had never said to anyone else; not even JRock. She was a good listener and found he enjoyed talking with her. With LaKesha, they rarely ever talked; they just more or less grunted at each other and let that suffice for conversation.

"Do you still have to get up?"

"I couldn't if I wanted to, which I don't."

That brought a chuckle from her as she snuggled closer to his heat.

Sleep claimed them both for more than an hour before Ice was forced out of bed to relieve himself. When he went into her bathroom, his bare feet hit warm, floor tiles. Surprised, he looked down at the floor and noticed the condom he had yet to remove was leaking. Suddenly, he forgot about the comfort the heated floor provided. He took care of his needs and padded back into the bedroom. Sitting on Rosalyn's side of the bed, he gently woke her.

"What's up?" she asked, rolling over and looking at the concern of Wesley's face.

"The condom broke. Are you on any other form of birth control?"

Rosalyn sat up in bed and reached into her nightstand drawer. "Uh, no, I'm not. I can't take the pill and I'm afraid to use IUDs."

She held an unopened condom in her hand and looked at the 'use by date'. "Expired," she said on a lengthy, frustrated sigh. "I'm sorry, Wes."

"What are the chances?" he asked.

Looking at the date on her clock, she sighed. "Oh, hell."

Wesley rubbed his face hard with both hands. "That can't be a good 'oh, hell.' How long before we'll know?"

We? She focused on that part of his question for comfort in a fretful situation. He was not shrinking from his part in her possible pregnancy.

"I don't know. I've never been in this situation before."

"Do you have a doctor we could see?"

"Wes." She sighed. "Don't worry about this now. We'll face that bridge if we come to it. We've got to tell Cole, Marcus, and Simone about Jakima and then make some kind of arrangements for a memorial or funeral."

"I know, but if you're carrying my child, I want it understood between us I'm in this one hundred percent. I would not want you to consider not having it."

"Don't fret. I would not do that. I'm over thirty years old. At this point in my life, if I'm pregnant, I would be very happy to be an expectant mother."

"If you are pregnant, this could affect what the judge does about custody. It cost to raise three children. I'm ready for that. A judge might not think I can support four."

"You are not going to be the only support for these children, even if it's four. I'm committed to this in every way you are, including financially."

"I take care of my responsibilities, Roz."

"I take care of mine, too, Wesley, but for now we can't keep playing the 'what if' game. Let's worry about things that are facing us where the children we have now are concerned."

"First, we'll get rid of your supply of expired condoms, because I hoped you weren't finished with me yet," he said and, for the first time, grinned at her.

She grinned and lay back in bed, removing the cover from her nude body, an invitation for him to get back into bed. "We could try doubling up? That's one way of getting rid of my supply."

So, they did.

Chapter 10

By Sunday morning, Wesley and Rosalyn were still closely monitoring the children's reaction to the news about their mother. As expected, they had questions about her death, what would happen next. With both Wesley and Rosalyn explaining they had asked a judge to let them stay where they were and the judge had agreed, the children seemed to breathe easier, but were still somewhat pensive. So, Rosalyn decided they needed a diversion. Rather than sit in the house all day, she convinced Wesley to go with them to Annapolis Mall in Maryland to buy clothes for the memorial service they decided with the children to have once Jakima's body was returned to DC at a neighborhood funeral parlor.

The huge, indoor, shopping mall was a new experience for Cole, Marcus, and Simone and somewhat intimidating. The boys walked, each holding one of Rosalyn's hands, while Wesley carried five-year-old Simone who fiercely clung to his neck, her eyes wide, trying to take it all in. He tried to soothe her fears, but the mall was crowded with energy bouncing off other kids, excited teens, and harried adults.

Once they got the children outfitted in new clothes and shoes that Rosalyn insisted on paying for, they browsed most of the other stores in the mall and then went to the food court, another new experience that had the children wide eyed. There were things for the children to do and to ride or slide through or around in. Bungee jumps, net-enclosed springboards filled with rubber balls, bumper cars, and a kid-sized choo-choo train for them to ride on. Even Simone left the security of Wesley's arms to join her brothers on some of the rides and slides. She frequently checked to make sure Wesley and Rosalyn were still at the lunch table nearby, but otherwise she seemed to be having fun.

Although it was still fall, the stores were gearing up for Christmas. Wesley and Rosalyn talked about making plans for the holidays. Halloween was over, but Thanksgiving, Christmas, and New Years were right around the corner.

"This was a good idea," Wesley admitted. "Maybe we should do something like this once a week or a couple times a month."

"Yes, we should. There's a lot I want them to do and experience. They're ours now, Wes, and I want them to feel safe and secure with us. They haven't had much joy in their lives. In fact, I've never seen them smile like they are now," she said, as she lifted a hand to return Marcus' wave as he came down a ceiling-high, winding, air-filled, rubber sliding board.

"I never would have known Cole was interested in astronomy if we hadn't gone into that toy store. Or, that Marcus liked building things."

"Simone is going to be our diva."

Wesley smirked. "She'll have to have a four-year, college degree before she even *thinks* about a career in entertainment."

Rosalyn laughed at the serious expression on Wesley's face. "Look at you, *Papi*, laying down the law for your daughter."

"Damn straight! She's not going to end up with some roughneck like me."

"She'd be lucky to find a man as fine as you, Wes, and I don't mean how handsome you are. I mean a man who cares so deeply for others."

"You think I'm handsome?" he asked, a grin edging his lips.

"I didn't kick you out of bed, did I?"

He gave her a full-wattage smile and spontaneously kissed her mouth; something he hadn't done while they were having sex. He had nibbled on her ear, her neck, her breasts, but hadn't ventured beyond. Not that she was complaining. As far as she knew, Wesley and LaKesha were not sexually involved with anyone else since they began living together five years before. That probably limited the amount of experimentation they had outside the box, so to speak. She wasn't necessarily going to force Wesley to read *Fifty Shades of Grey* or watch the movie version, but a copy of all three E. L. James' novels were stacked on her nightstand on his side of the bed. If he picked up any one of them, they might shock him right out of her home. However, if he found them intriguing, they could embark on a whole new journey into intimacy and discovery. She was accustomed to creative, sexual exploits with Howard Gardner and other former lovers in college, grad school and while working on her dissertation, including Carl Lieberman. She wasn't used to having to teach anyone in the bedroom, but if Wesley wanted to learn…experiment…well.

"Why do you have that devilish light in your eyes and smile on your face?" he cautiously asked.

"Just thinking about that first morning."

He sat back in his seat, crossed his arms, his muscles bulging. "What about it?"

"We haven't had sex since. I mean, do you need the little blue pill already?" she teased.

He shook his head, amused. "Believe me, it's not because I haven't thought about it. I didn't want you to think I was taking advantage of you or the situation. I mean, I bought a large, new box of condoms, but this living together thing came about quickly.

You were in a relationship already a few days before we moved in on you. Now I'm sleeping in your bed."

"You don't like having sex with me?" she asked, with a tease in her tone.

He smirked. "I didn't kick you out of the bed, did I? I even did you twice."

A giggle bubbled up and out before she could control it. She threw her wadded up paper napkin at him. Then she leaned in close to him, dropping her voice to a sexy purr. "Since the center is only open for a few more hours today, maybe after we go to the movies we can drop off the children and spend some time warming the sheets?"

"Yeah, and everybody will know just what I'm up to if we do that."

She sat back frowning. "Are you still worried about my reputation?"

"Yes, I am. I mean, I don't want people to think you're some easy, round-the-way girl, Roz. People respect you. You've got credentials up the wazoo. People shouldn't think you'd settle for someone like me."

"Un-friggin'-believable. Not two weeks ago, Howard thought I was beneath him and now you think you're beneath me?"

"Look, Roz, you know me. I'm just one of the street corner boyz. I always have been. I never aspired to do much more than survive. Maybe cook for a living. You were voted most likely to succeed. One of the best and brightest in high school. You finished college top of your class, grad school, and even got a doctorate degree. You've traveled extensively to other countries. I don't even have a passport. We're walking on uneven ground in this relationship."

"Bull! You're one of the bravest men I know. You spent your inheritance to open a community center, for Pete's sake.

You've successfully run that center for the past ten plus years and organized a neighborhood watch program that has considerably reduced the crime rate. You're also initiating programs to serve the needs of the community and making them work. You act like that's nothing."

"I've only done what came next. I didn't have a clue or a plan after my father was killed."

"Yet, look at what you've accomplished. I would be ecstatic if people considered me your woman. I'm very proud of you."

Her saying that, that she was proud of him, shifted something monumental, like tectonic plates moving inside him. No one said that to him before. People said, "Thank you" or "I appreciate" something he did for them, but, in his memory, no one said they were proud of him. Somehow, it made all the difference coming from Rosalyn Hunter.

"We'd better round up the kids if we're going to catch this movie and then get them home in time to make dinner," he said, gathering the debris from their lunch table on to a tray and stacking the others. "We've still got to check their homework before they get ready for bed."

"I'll round them up," Rosalyn said. "We still have about fifteen minutes before the movie starts."

He waited with their purchases, while she went to get the children off the various contraptions they were playing on. Watching her sexy walk, his dick was at three quarter readiness, and she wasn't even trying to entice him.

"You have a nice looking family, young man," said an elderly man sitting with a younger woman at a nearby table. "Your children are very mannerly. They don't make a lot of noise or run around like wild things. Your wife is beautiful. I was just telling my daughter how nice it is to see families like yours spending quality time together."

"Oh, they're. . ." he started to correct, then trailed off as he looked at Rosalyn when she tickled Simone's tummy. It caused the little girl to giggle and then wrap her arms around Rosalyn's neck. The boys were looking up at Rosalyn, smiling like she hung the sun. He turned back to the couple and said, "Thank you, sir."

***

A week later, the children got such a kick out of bathing in the big whirlpool tub in the master bathroom that Rosalyn let each of them have a few extra minutes. "Ladies first," she cautioned, and her budding five-year-old diva pranced her way into the bathroom, carrying her multitude of new tub toys. Marcus was next with his motor boats and then came Cole who claimed he was too old for tub toys. He lay in the churning water, looking up through the skylight at the moon and stars.

"All right, which story do you want Cole to read to you tonight?" Wesley asked, as he picked up the assortment of new books they purchased at the big, mall bookstore the previous week.

"This one." Simone spoke up first and grabbed the book. She handed it to Cole and settled back in the crook of Wesley's arm to listen to the new story.

Before long, Simone was asleep as was Marcus. Wesley tucked Marcus in first and then lifted Simone to take her to her room.

"Ice?"

"Yes?"

"I kinda liked what we did last week like a real family. They was other peoples with they family and we look just like them. Jakima, she never done nuffin' like dat before."

"We'll do more things like what we did then, Cole. All of us together."

That seemed to satisfy the boy and filled Wesley's heart to overflowing. Cole slid down in his bed and turned off the bedside lamp. Wesley pulled the covers up over his shoulders, and then took Simone to her bed tucking her in. She snuggled up to a pink stuffed whale they bought for her last week and sighed contentedly. He leaned down, planted a kiss on her hair, and then patted her head. He was going to have to take the kids to Bubbles and Billie's again soon, but he didn't mind that so much.

When he turned to leave, he found Rosalyn leaning against the doorframe, arms crossed under her impressive breasts.

"You are already a great father, Wes. You've been wonderful to them this past week since we got the news."

He turned just enough to look over his shoulder at a peacefully sleeping Simone. "Yeah, and I think I'm gonna like it."

"I hope so, because so far it's been a week and my period hasn't shown up."

He turned back to her, searching her beautiful brown eyes for her possible reaction to the prospect she might be pregnant.

She smiled at him. "Scares you, doesn't it?"

He shrugged and his eyes drifted down to her very flat stomach. For some reason, it wasn't difficult to imagine her belly swollen with his child. He reached out a hand to touch her where his seed may have taken root and another new sensation jarred him. Fatherhood. Life was no longer something he merely had to survive. Now he had to have a plan. He actually had a family and likely a child on the way. There were people who were depending on him to make their path through life smoother. Now he had a reason to step up to the task.

Should he do it? Should he take JRock's offer to be the project manager for Baylor Plaza Park? He could move Peckhead into the lead position at the community center and give Little T a shot at managing the night patrols. It could work, he thought, as he continued to rub his hands over Rosalyn's abdomen. He looked up at her slumberous expression and sultry, bedroom eyes. With his hands spanning her narrow waist, he lifted her. She wrapped her firm thighs around his waist and her hands on his head, guiding his mouth to hers.

There, in the hallway, he consumed her mouth. Somehow, he found his way to the master bedroom with her still in his arms, closed and locked the door, and headed for the bed. One handed, he unzipped his jeans, lifted her nightgown, and sank into her moist heat like a runaway jackhammer, hard and fast. He couldn't seem to get enough of her as she rode him just as furiously, their mouths still melded together.

He swallowed each of her cries of release, but still couldn't seem to pull out of her. He was like a man possessed. Her moans, intoxicating scent, and decadent words and voice in his ear edged him ever closer to a white-hot collision with destiny. She latched on to his nipples with her mouth on one and her fingertips and nails on the other, his body going into overdrive. Flesh slapped flesh and, if she hadn't stripped his long-sleeved crewneck sweater from his body it would have ended up a wet, soggy mess from the moisture their two bodies produced.

Near asphyxiation from the heavy breathing, Ice ran smack into an orgasm that suspended his ability to breathe and wrenched a cry of tortured completion, from which he nearly blacked out.

"Wes?"

"Yeah?"

"I don't know what stoked you up, but tell me what it was so that I can make sure you have an ample supply."

Although he was still sensitive and buried bareback inside her, Ice had to laugh at that. She sounded as serious as a Lotto game winner.

Chapter 11

"You and JRock, y'all got something deep going?" Ice asked, as he and the architect, JaiHonnah Chapman, walked slowly through the neighborhood in the bone chilling, November air.

Ice looked down at the ground, as they walked, not noticing much of what was around them. He had seen it all before—dilapidated, boarded up buildings; broken glass, litter and other debris strewn everywhere; iron bars on windows and doors; skeletal remains of abandoned and stripped cars that were now children's playgrounds; refuse from illegal dumping; yellow police tape left tied in long strips protecting the sanctity where another heinous crime was committed; dried, dead grass between cracked, crumbling sidewalks and miles of ossifying, grayish, chain-linked fences.

He needed to schedule a clean-up day for this block. This was a part of his neighborhood, the place where he, JRock, and the others in their crew survived the harsh, sometimes violent, and dangerous streets. He didn't have to look at it to know it was dying a slow, miserable death and unless something drastic happened, he feared there was nothing he could do to stop it.

"Deep? Well, we're friends, if that's what you mean, Ice," JaiHonnah said, answering his earlier question while snapping pictures of the westward area where the center of the park would be located. She was capturing the architecture of the old neighborhood so that she could reproduce the façades on the new structures.

"Friends? Burt and Ernie are friends." He snorted. "JRock has a lot of Burts and Ernies around him. A few Big Birds, too. He don't look at none of them the way he be scopin' you out. Man got himself a big-time jones going."

JaiHonnah only smiled her understanding of Ice's comments, but continued to take the pictures she needed for posterity as they walked.

"You, Roderick, and the other guys have been friends for a long time, haven't you, Ice?" she asked, as they began to walk back toward a Baylor company car.

"Seems like all our lives we've known each other. His ol' man, mine, Peck's, Little T's, Buddy's, some of the others, were running buddies back in the day. They were all in Viêt Nam together. Some didn't make it back, but those who did became surrogate fathers for those who lost their fathers in the war.

"When they came home, they said drugs and crime had taken over the streets in the neighborhood while they were away. They tried, with Marion Barry's RAP, Inc. and Pride, Inc., to clean up the neighborhood and get out-of-work men, especially former military, into job training programs.

"Ol' man Baylor was a community organizer, even way back then. He worked two jobs full time, and was hell on wheels, but all the knuckleheads gave him his props because they knew what he was about. He didn't take nothin' off of nobody though. He'd tell us all, '*Be in the house before them street lights come on*'," Ice said, mimicking John Baylor and remembering him fondly. "Knew we had to be there, too, else that ol' man would be dead on us, and he didn't care whose kid we were. He didn't cut his own kids no slack either."

"Tough, huh? Sounds like my father." JaiHonnah shivered purposefully. "Tell me, what was Roderick like as a child?"

"Shorter." Ice laughed. "Well, I mean we used to get into our share of stuff—with da ladies, you know. He had this big-time love jones going for Roz, but JRock, well, he was always the thinking one of all of us. He wasn't buck wild or nothing, but he was deep. You know, like always planning stuff. Like how he was gonna go to college and how he was gonna get in the NBA. Then how he was gonna start his own business. Man, he had it all mapped out from the time when he was a little kid. He knew where he was going. He got his mind fixed on something and it wasn't no changing it.

"He wasn't like the rest of us." He absently shrugged his big shoulders. "Yeah, he'd hang out on the street corner under the lamp post and make like we was Boyz II Men, but his chores and homework was done." He laughed at the memory.

"Mostly though, he'd be ballin'. Man! Could he handle the rock or what? You know that though. You've seen him on the court. Sweet shot! Take ya downtown, uptown, 'round town and lose ya comin' and goin'. Man, he owned that hardwood real estate! He was a better ball man than Dr. J, Magic, or Jordon, or Kobe Bryant. Even LeBron couldn't handle JRock. He was up there with Vivian's husband, Derrick "Dunk and Jam" Jackson. Now Vivian's brother, Gregory, aka, Alexander the Great, owns the court. JRock said he wasn't gonna let basketball use him, he was gonna use basketball to get where he wanted to go.

"We'd be hanging out doing a blunt and a forty, but not JRock. Said the stuff made you stupid, that's why they call it dope. Dudes tried to play him for a chump, got they asses kicked though. Man give you the shirt off his back, but he didn't want nobody trying to use him or trying to push him around. Whew! Don't nothin' get to JRock like somebody using somebody. Then, man, look out!"

JaiHonnah talked about how she could imagine the tough little kid, JRock, who grew up into the suave, debonair business personae that was now J. Roderick Baylor. She mentioned that he had shared some of the stories of his juvenile behavior with her, much of it very daring and reckless. He gave thanks to his parents, siblings, neighbors, and the boyz in the hood for his survival.

Suddenly, loud music blared, interrupting their conversation. JaiHonnah noticed Ice's demeanor instantly transformed. His changed comportment caused her to tense. Three black, tricked-out SUVs rolled up, two of which hopped the street curb, effectively surrounding him and her on three sides. The elementary school's high, chain-linked fence was a barrier at their backs.

"No fear," she heard Ice hiss through gritted teeth without moving his mouth.

Instinctively, she knew it was a warning to her—not a pledge he made to himself—but fear, she did. She had become accustomed to the bawdy neighborhood sounds, but this was distinctly different. The loud boom-box speakers mounted on the top of one of the cars kicked out obscenities that would befall a woman, degrading images conjured up by the references to bitches and whores. It made the hair on the back of her neck stand on end, but her hand instinctively covered her abdomen.

Men, looking like the Unabomber in black, got out of the vehicles, stalking and circling Ice and JaiHonnah. They fixed their stare on Ice through dark sunshades. JaiHonnah noticed Ice put one hand behind his back, inside his jacket.

"Sup', black?" a tall, dark-skinned man with a deep vertical scar down his right cheek asked Ice. Up close, he looked like the actor Michael K. Williams.

The man's voice was low, demanding, and ominous. He wore a red, patterned bandana around his baldhead, an over-sized, black, hooded warm-up, dark sunshades, and layers of dark clothing. His neck was inked with sculls and crossbones.

"Killer," Ice acknowledged. "You wanna piece of me or you just window shoppin'?"

"Heard you done punked out," he growled, looking at Ice from head to toe. "You look like a punk. Doin' a gig like them other nine-to-five suckers."

"Yeah. I got chore sucker, right here in my hand," he said grabbing his crotch. "I don't be lookin' up your itinerary, Killer," Ice said with an indecipherable façade.

Suddenly, guns were drawn in motions too quick for the eye to capture. Ice held a 9-millimeter to Killer's head and Killer's gun was centered at Ice's heart.

"You 'bout to be assed out," Killer growled, his chest rising and falling in rage.

"You won't live to see me go," Ice growled back, his light, golden-brown eyes darkening and blazing with deadly quiet anger.

JaiHonnah shuttered visibly, unable to believe what she was witnessing. She glared at the two men. Pregnant, tense moments passed, while the men glowered at each other. Time seemed to stand still. JaiHonnah's eyes flitted back and forth between the two warriors. She swallowed a lump in her throat. "Uh, you gentlemen have a reason for stopping us?" she tentatively asked.

"Who dis?" Killer growled, nodding toward JaiHonnah.

"Dis be JRock's woman," Ice answered, still holding the gun to Killer's head.

"Dis dat bitch been up at dem meetin's, huh?" he said, still holding the gun to Ice's heart.

"Ain't no bitch 'round here 'cept you, Killer," Ice growled.

Another tense lifetime passed, while JaiHonnah's mind worked feverishly to find something to quell her rising fear and to deflate the tense situation. Neither man had lowered his guard.

"Uh, hello, uh, I'm Jai Chapman," JaiHonnah said, extending her shaky hand.

Killer looked at her hand and then at her from head to toe. "You JRock's piece, huh?" he growled. "Yeah, you be da one."

"Piece?" JaiHonnah flared, her emotions swinging from fear to furious in a finger snap. She thought there was a reason not to like this man, but now there was no question. "Who are you calling *'a piece'*?"

With his free hand, Ice grabbed JaiHonnah's arm, moving her further aside. His gun clicked. His teeth clinched, as he leaned into Killer's gun at his chest. "I done told you, Killer. You don't be bringing no shit up in here. You and the Royal Reds don't have no passport in dis hood."

"Just scopin' the territory. Heard they was 'bout to raze this muver focker."

"Sightseeing's for tourist. Take your jive-ass crew down on Capitol Hill."

"You ain't no muver fockin' chief no mo', Ice."

"That so?" Ice asked, as cars suddenly screeched to a halt, surrounding the Royal Red Crew. Car doors flew open. Heavily armed men and women climbed on truck beds or car hoods, or car rooftops. Guns clicked into action. "It'll cost you to find out," Ice said, with a sinister grin.

If possible, the air was thicker with more deadly tension than before. JaiHonnah swallowed hard and began snapping pictures of the Royal Reds.

"What you think you doin', bitch?" Killer's voice rumbled.

"I'm no 'bitch', but I'm capturing a part of history," she said, dissipating her fear and replacing it with more confidence. Faces she had come to know as friends surrounded them now, buoying her strength to action. "If you didn't already know it, you're history.

Like the gunslingers of the old west, your time has come and gone."

Both men's eyes swung toward her. Ice grinned.

"Yeah, *Le-vi*. Like de lady said, you history. Now be gone."

Police cars streamed and screamed into the once desolate street, however the officers who poured out of the cruisers quietly stood alert and at the ready, but made no attempt to intervene. G-Boogie sat on his cruiser's hood, relaxed, a Tec-DC 9 cocked and resting on his shoulder.

Furtively casting his eyes around at Ice's crew, the cops from the drug store, Bubbles and Billie, with their guns drawn and trained on him, and the police and then back to Ice. They were clearly out-gunned and out-manned. "Dis ain't over," Killer growled as he slowly backed up to his car and got in.

"I say it's over. Don't bring your crew up in here again," Ice growled, lowering his weapon. He watched while the three cars pealed out with a police escort before he put his weapon away in the small of his back. He turned to JaiHonnah, folding his arms across his ample chest and grinning lopsidedly at her. "Since when did you become a historical photo-journalist?" he asked quizzically.

She cocked her head to the side, a grin curling her lips. "It was either take the pictures or hit Mr. Killer with the camera," she said with hands on hips. "I may be Native American, but I wasn't into taking hostages today," she said, laughing nervously.

Ice looked at her for a moment and then stifled his amusement. He turned to Peckhead. "Who dropped the dime on them?"

"Roz," Peckhead said, with a nod toward the elementary school behind them.

Ice and JaiHonnah both turned in time to see Rosalyn Hunter walking back into the school.

"Take JaiHonnah back to the center. Leave Dog with me. Put out the word to watch the hood. I want the kids on bikes riding the hood two-by-two. Make sure Killer and all of his crew left. I'll be out in a minute." He turned and walked into the schoolyard and, after being buzzed in, past the school security guard, who had yet to holster his weapon, Wesley went to Rosalyn's office.

Glenda stood pensively by her seat, tears on her face, and her little gun on her desk. He opened Rosalyn's closed office door and went in, closing the door behind him. She was standing with her arms wrapped around herself, looking out her office window at the children playing in the back schoolyard.

He walked up behind her and put his arms around her. Her head fell back against his shoulder and she seemed to melt into his embrace. A low keening cry escaped her as he turned her in his arms. She clutched him fiercely and cried violently into his neck. He just held her tightly, saying nothing. Finally, he guided her to the sofa, sat with her on his lap, and kissed her hair, her forehead, her nose, and then her lips.

"Okay, enough of that. It's not good if you're carrying our baby," he crooned.

"I thought if you decided to work with JRock you wouldn't be in any danger like you are when you walk the streets all night." She looked up into his eyes, hers still brimming with tears. "Then I saw you surrounded right in front..." she choked. "I was so scared, Wes."

"I'm fine, thanks to your quick thinking, Roz."

"You don't understand, Wes. I was being selfish. I'm in love with you and I saw my whole life getting ready to go out in a flash."

Did Dr. Rosalyn Amelia Hunter just say she was in love with him? It stunned him to hear those words come from her. He took her face in his hands, wiping her tears with his thumbs.

"Say that again."

"What? That I'm in love with you?"

"Yes, that." He kissed her, holding her tightly until they heard a commotion outside her door. Abruptly they stood up.

When the door opened, Cole was fighting off Glenda, trying to get into Rosalyn's office. Fear etched on his face.

"It's all right, Glenda," Rosalyn said.

When Glenda let go of him, Cole ran straight to Wesley and buried his face in Wesley's chest, with his arms tightly around his waist. Wes hugged Cole, running his hands soothingly over the boy's small shoulders, head, and back. "I'm all right, son. Everything is all right."

"Stoker said Killer had his gun on you."

"Look at me, Cole." When the boy looked up, he said, "It's never a good thing to try to settle an argument with a gun. That's not what I'm about, but times may be scary for a while. Your job is to take care of yourself and our family. You stay cool and don't let anyone psych you out. Okay?"

The boy nodded, but again buried his face in Wesley's stomach.

Chapter 12

“Well, that seems to be it,” Juan Domingo-Garcia said, as he gave Wesley a clasped hand, shoulder-to-shoulder bump in parting.

“We appreciate what you and CompuCorrect did for us,” Ice said, as Juan and another electronics technician, Bob Stark, continued their farewell with him and his crew.

“It’s the kind of thing Kenneth Alexander likes to do when we find a need,” said Bob.

“Still, your boss paid for you two to be here for weeks, nearly a month, installing the computers and training everyone on the new software.”

“Like I said, that’s what we do. Give us a call if anything comes up. I’ll be back in touch with you after the New Year to make arrangements to bring those eleven kids out to California for the summer to train as computer techs. They have a real aptitude for computer science. Remember, we’re going to need parental releases to make this work. We’ll provide transportation to and from California, chaperones on our end, and pick up any other costs associated with their trip for training, but if you want to send someone or several people out with the students, we’ll cover that cost, too.”

“I’ll take care of that.”

“Great. *Adios.*”

“Safe trip.”

Juan and Bob waved and climbed into a waiting SUV that would take them to the airport.

Ice and his crew stood in the computer lab surrounded by forty of the fifty sleek, new, desktop computers Kenneth Alexander sent on his niece's say so. New flat screens hung on the walls that were used during the weeks of training the CompuCorrect's lead technician and his helper provided free of charge to everyone who wanted to learn. Old and young alike flocked to the training sessions, sometimes having to double up at each computer station to accommodate the crowd. Ice and his crew extended the operating hours of the center to accommodate the training sessions for everyone.

The remaining computers and ten laptops were to be used in the administration cubicles or as replacements or when needed to work from home. The old computers were upgraded with new programs and refurbished as training tools for kids with technical skills. Eleven preteens and teens showed a real interest and aptitude for computer science and engineering. Juan singled them out for special training classes. He was so impressed with their skill and ability to pick up complicated computer codes and mapping that he asked whether their parents would let him bring their young people to California for the summer for more extensive training at CompuCorrect's Santa Barbara facility. All expenses would be covered by CompuCorrect. In the interim, those eleven young people, both male and female, would conduct training classes for anyone who wanted to learn how the new programs worked.

The old computers the students refurbished were going to be raffled off at the community center's holiday party. A potluck dinner would be sold and small gifts would be distributed to the children and teens by the neighborhood fire department and the

One Four Police Precinct. Contributions would be accepted from local businesses in the community, also for gifts for the children and those who were in need. They were also unveiling a miniature scale model of the Baylor Plaza Park Project.

Ice still hadn't given JRock a final answer, but he kept up with the project and did what he could through regular meetings at the center with JaiHonnah Chapman and other interested people selected to be on the project council.

Little by little, he was easing Peckhead into the center's leadership position and Little T into taking over the night patrols. He still kept his hand in, but everyone knew JRock depended on Ice to take the project manager's position when they had final approval to start demolition of the old neighborhood. Excitement was really growing among people who had lived there nearly all their lives. It was conceded that JaiHonnah's plan of a woodland village concept was nothing less than brilliant.

The project wasn't as large as the seventeen-hundred-acre Rock Creek Park in Northwest, Washington, DC, but much larger than the forty-two-acre Fort DuPont Park in South East, DC. Baylor Plaza Park would be the only one of its kind in the northeastern quadrant of the city. It wouldn't have the expansive waterfront view of East Potomac Park, but the plan was to clean up the Anacostia River, restoring it and the National Children's Island to pristine condition, along with the Langston Golf Course.

New, more innovative, interactive schools, stores, and shops intermingled with homes and plenty of green space for children to play anchored the design. Stores would be designed with the old brick and block cityscape façades with housing above the shops the way it used to be before urban renewal removed the character elements from the neighborhood. It would be a walkable community again. No concrete streets, but walkways leading out from a central park, like the spokes of a wagon wheel to the outer reaches, merging with exiting city streets and public transportation. Electric trams would provide conveyances or electric golf carts for residents to public bus stops or the planned subway stop in the park.

Ice never heard of using the huge shipping containers he saw pulled along highways by eighteen wheelers as housing, but he was fascinated after seeing a demonstration of how the containers were welded together to form a strong house with definable rooms, windows and doors. Four to six containers could make a four-bedroom house above a store, ready for occupancy, within thirty days at a ridiculously low cost per unit.

JRock wanted him to institute and manage the training programs to use this new, unique type of housing construction. JaiHonnah showed videos of how shipping containers were stacked up, all but abandoned in shipyards at all of the major seaports. For a relatively nominal fee, each of the containers could be purchased, welded together, and outfitted with plumbing, electrical, and cable services as homes and businesses.

Also, JaiHonnah planned to use geothermal energy instead of electricity provided by the local power company to heat and cool the homes they would construct. She would also employ a rain-barrow system for the community's water supply to flush toilets, water yards, wash clothes, or take a shower. Some of the water would be diverted for further filtration and purification to become drinkable or for cooking. Covered, rooftop hydroponics gardens would provide residents with fruits and vegetables to use or to share in the community market year-round.

Ice found it fascinating to see how much new technology was going to be instituted in the new construction to reduce costs while maintaining high quality, energy-efficient homes and businesses that looked like the old neighborhood. Ice was beginning to feel more and more attuned to taking on the job. At least for the first five years it would take to build out the model project to completion. Then, with the extraordinary amount of salary he would earn, he could save more than enough to open a restaurant in the community village. More importantly, he would have the necessary income to convince a judge he could take care of three and probably four children and a wife.

"Hey, Ice?" Little T hailed.

"What up?"

"You remember when you said there was a two-bedroom in your old building where Jakima used to live?"

"Yeah?"

"You think it's still there?"

"Probably." He shrugged. He knew very well it was still vacant. "Why?"

"Since Peckhead didn't take it, I'm thinking about moving outta my mama's house; me and my sister, Charmaine. She got one more year in high school after this year and she wants to go to college at UDC, but all my other sisters keep moving in with they men and kids. Now my momma got a new man. The house is too crowded. Charmaine's having a hard time studying with all the noise and she don't have a bedroom to herself no more. Some of them men be tryin' to check her out when I ain't around."

Little T had five sisters, but he was the only boy in the family. In age, they were a year apart. Four of his sisters were older than him with kids of their own. Charmaine was the baby of the family at sixteen years old; a late surprise birth to his parents just before his father died.

"Want me to talk to Jenkins?"

"No, man, I'll do it. I just wanted to make sure the place was still available. It's the only place I can think of where ain't no rats and roaches and it's clean with the laundry in the building."

"Go for it. Let me know if Jenkins gives you beef."

"Yeah, I'll do that," he said and left the office.

Peckhead stood up to stretch in his cubicle. "That's huge for Little T," said Peckhead. "I didn't think he would ever move out of his mama's house."

The name, Little T, was a euphemism, a misnomer. He actually stood six-foot, five-inches tall, the second tallest in the crew to JRock's six-foot seven inches. Tavon's father, Tavon Senior, who played football as a linebacker in high school and college, stood taller than Tavon. A sports injury and poor grades got him kicked out of a North Carolina college after two years. Because he was a big, burly man, his nickname on the street was Big T.

"We must be growing up or something," Ice joked. He checked his watch. "I gotta hat."

"You takin' your brood for checkups?"

"Yeah, physicals and dental. Have to make sure they have all of their shots, too. Vivian arranged for a friend of hers to do this at Georgetown Hospital."

"I like her, Vivian, I mean. Kelley Baylor told me Vivian and DJ Jackson adopted all but one of her kids before he died and she still adopts children now. DJ Jackson grew up in an inner city, Philadelphia neighborhood like ours. When he married Vivian, they adopted his patients from an orphanage. Mostly, Vivian still adopts children who have some type of medical problem and nobody else wants. She's got all that money DJ made playing ball like JRock, but she's still a regular person."

"I'll tell her you approve the next time I see her," Ice said on the way out the door to get the kids. He didn't know that bit of information before. Of course he knew Derrick "Dunk and Jam"

Jackson was a street kid who left the hardwood at the top of his game and became a pediatrician, but he didn't know how Vivian had so many children. She was younger than DJ by at least ten years and younger than him and his crew. That might be why she was moving heaven and earth to help him and Rosalyn get permanent custody. She had done it herself many times.

"Hey, Glenda," Ice hailed, as he entered Rosalyn's outer office where Cole, Marcus, and Simone sat waiting for him to arrive.

"Hey, Ice."

"Is Roz in her office?"

"No, she had an outside appointment this morning."

"Oh, she didn't mention it."

"She didn't tell me where she was goin' neever," she pouted, aggrieved.

He and Rosalyn had established a routine in the mornings now that he didn't often walk night patrol. With Little T in charge and recruiting more men and some women to patrol, he was only called out if they were shorthanded or there was a problem. So every morning, he and Rosalyn started the day with a rousing bout of energetic sex. Well, more like lovemaking, he admitted. Kissing and touching, whether they had sex or not, then carrying their morning activity into the shower together before getting dressed for the day. He would make breakfast and lunches, while she got the kids up, dressed, and ready for school. Rosalyn and the kids would leave and he would clean up, do the laundry, general housework, cleaning the bathrooms and kitchen, and begin preparation for dinner. On the weekends, they would do the grocery shopping and other errands together with the kids.

If she weren't too busy, Rosalyn might come home for lunch, a little afternoon delight, and then drop him off at the community center before she went back to work or to an outside appointment. He oversaw the management of the center and the neighborhood watch programs while picking up the slack for JRock in the community. His days were full of community meetings and identifying potential men and women for JRock's training programs.

Over breakfast, he and Roz usually talked with the kids about their plans for the day. That's why he was surprised she hadn't mentioned a late morning meeting. He even had her drop him off at the community center because he had that last meeting with Juan Domingo-Garcia and Bob Stark. He didn't think it was anything to worry about, so he and the kids left for their doctors' appointments.

Hours later, he took a taxi home from the hospital. The kids had extensive tests, checkups, teeth cleaning, and were given necessary childhood immunization shots. Needless to say, they were not happy campers. So, rather than take them back to school, he took them home, gave them lunch, and tucked them into their beds.

When he came back downstairs, he was surprised to find Rosalyn at home, sitting in the kitchen at the prep island, fingering a box of condoms.

"I didn't hear you come in. It's early. Is everything all right?"

She looked up at him with tears in her eyes. That caused alarm until she smiled at him.

"I was wondering what we could do with this big box of new condoms now that we don't need them anymore."

"Why wouldn't we need…" he started and trailed off as that bolt of lightning struck. "Well, now, we could raffle them off at the Holiday Extravaganza with the computers. Or, I could hand them out to the teens . . ." he trailed off, again, as tears leaked from her eyes down her smiling face. "Oh, hell," he said, smiling, pulling her into his arms and kissing her with enough passion and energy to fuel a small country. "Is that where you were today?"

"I had an appointment out of the neighborhood's prying eyes and gossip grapevine to see an OB/GYN doctor Vivian recommended, Savannah Logan. She, JaiHonnah, and Vivian were in undergrad at Spelman College together."

"Is everything all right? I mean, oh hell, I'm so pumped I don't know what I'm saying."

"Could we go up to our bedroom, light a fire in the fireplace, and could you just hold me for a while?"

He stood, lifted her in his arms, and carried her up to bed. She undressed, while he lit the fireplace logs, locked the bedroom door, and turned on some soothing music.

They snuggled under the covers, her back to his chest as they watched the flames devour cords of wood, and listened to the music. When it started to rain, Ice thought it was the perfect backdrop to an ideal afternoon. The perfect time to grow up a little more, he believed.

"Roz, would you marry me?"

She looked over her shoulder into his beautiful eyes. "You don't have to do that, Wes. I mean, yes, I would marry you in a heartbeat, but I don't want you to feel trapped into marriage because I'm pregnant."

"I don't feel trapped. I feel so much right now, all of it good. I'm thinking about something Cole said when we first took them to Annapolis Mall. He said he saw families that looked like us and he liked it." He told her about the elderly man and his daughter. "I want what Cole wants, Roz. I imagine what Marcus and Simone want, too. I want to build this family with you. With them. Do you think you can want what me and the kids want enough to take a risk on us, and marry me?"

She was so choked up she could only nod, let her tears flow, and kiss him into a long, lovemaking session.

Chapter 13

"With the power vested in me by the State of Maryland, I pronounce you, Wesley Barrett Greenfield, and you, Rosalyn Amelia Hunter, husband and wife," the Justice of the Peace concluded.

They accepted the well wishes of the witnesses and began to leave. They wasted no time and told no one of their plans. The children were warmly bundled into the SUV as they drove through rain that was turning into snow, and rush hour traffic to and from the small Town of Elkton, Cecil County, Maryland, where there was no waiting period to be married.

Though the children were there with them, they were still groggy from the series of childhood immunizations they received earlier that day. So, after the quick ceremony, which made them husband and wife, they drove back to DC, fed the children dinner, and put them to bed for the night. Wes and Rosalyn then had a quiet, romantic dinner alone as the snow fell and went to bed early to share their first night together as a married couple.

***

"That was my parents on the phone. They just left a Cracker Barrel restaurant somewhere in Virginia. They're making good time, they think. They should be here sometime before dinner tonight," Rosalyn said brightly. "They're so excited about meeting the children. They didn't think they would ever have grandchildren."

"Oh, boy," Wesley lamented and made Rosalyn laugh.

"Stop worrying. My parents are looking forward to seeing you again, too."

"I haven't seen them in years. I'm surprised they even remember who I am."

"They used to buy fresh bread and pastries from your father and real ice cream that he made and hand dipped. I used to love the smells in the shop when your father was baking. I watched him decorate the donuts and cupcakes when they were fresh from the ovens. He made the best birthday cakes, pies, muffins. We were in the shop all the time to buy dessert for dinner. Of course, they remember you. My parents used to tease me because I used every opportunity I got to come in to see you working. Plus, we all came to your father's funeral."

"I don't remember any of it clearly. The funeral, I mean. If it wasn't for the In Memoriam book people signed, I wouldn't know who came. I was in a fog."

"I know," she said, hugging him around his waist from behind, her right cheek between his shoulder blades. "That was a really hard time for you." She rubbed his chest soothingly.

Wesley continued to wash the huge turkey inside and out while enjoying Rosalyn's attention. Because his in-laws were coming, he began planning for Thanksgiving dinner a week in advance.

"It still seems like only yesterday."

"Did you get a chance to call Isaac?"

"Yes, I spoke with him last night."

"How is he doing?"

"He's handling it. He's in a Montana penitentiary where no one ever comes to visit with him, but he says he gets to cook every day and that makes the time pass. He's even started writing a cookbook of his recipes. He says he's going to make a copy and send it to me."

"Did you tell him about us?"

"Only what we've told everyone else; that we have custody of Jakima's kids and that because of them we're living together."

"Maybe you should fly out to Montana to visit him."

"I offered to come before to visit, but he doesn't want me to do that. He said it would be too hard on him for me to see him in a place like that."

"I believe it's just as hard on you not seeing him in all this time."

"I'll handle it," he said, as he lifted the turkey to drain. "Here, hold the bag open so I can put the turkey in it."

She moved from behind him and held open the mouth of a huge, clear plastic bag filled with briny water and seasonings.

"That sure is a big chicken," Marcus commented when he came into the kitchen from downstairs, ahead of Cole and Simone.

"It's not a chicken. It's a turkey," said Cole.

"Whatever. It's a big whatever it is."

"It's got to feed a lot of people tomorrow for Thanksgiving dinner."

"Like who?" asked Simone, as she pulled herself up on the bar stool at the center post work station to watch. Marcus and Cole did the same.

"Well, let's see. My parents, Daniel and Etta Hunter, are on their way. They should be here before dinner tonight."

"They live in North Carolina, right?" asked Cole.

"Yes, in Charlotte. Then there's Mrs. Lewis, Roscoe, Francine and Jemar. So that's how many people including all of us, Marcus?"

"Eleven," the seven-year-old piped up brightly.

"Exactly right."

"Can we set the table tonight?"

"You mean *'may'* you set the table tonight?"

"Oops."

"Yes, you may. That's a good idea. You can get the dishes, silverware, and glasses out of the China cabinet and put them in the dishwasher. Then, we'll dress the table and buffet after dinner."

"Why do we have to wash clean dishes before we can eat on them?" Simone wanted to know.

"Because the dishes are dusty and we want everything nice, clean, and sanitary for our guests, don't we?"

"I guess," she answered uncertainly. "Are we only going to eat the big chicken on the sani—sani? I can't say that word."

"Sanitary. We'll work on it as one of your new spelling words," Wesley told her. "I thought you might help me bake a ham, broil the roast beef on the outdoor rotisserie grill, and make candied yams, mashed potatoes, and corn pudding. How about cornbread turkey stuffing and mac and cheese? We could have fresh fish, too. Maybe some salmon. We're going to need giblet gravy, mint jelly, and cranberry sauce. For vegetables, we'll have string beans, collard greens, and steamed cabbage. Might even throw in some turnips and turnip greens. Hot dinner rolls, buttermilk biscuits, and Mexicali cornbread. We could make a Waldorf salad, Ambrosia, fresh, field-green salad with pecans, Mandarin oranges, cranberries, and raisons. For dessert, how about apple pie, pumpkin pie, carrot cake and homemade cherry and pistachio ice cream?"

As he continued to speak, the kids' eyes got bigger and bigger.

"All that?" Marcus asked.

"Oh, that's just to start," Wesley teased.

"Wow!" Cole said, and then turned around to look critically at the long, trestle, dining room table. "I don't know," he said, shaking his head skeptically. "Do you think the table will hold all that food and dishes, too?"

Wesley and Rosalyn both laughed at Cole's seriously concerned expression.

***

Mrs. Lewis sampled the pot liquor and meat from the thick ham hocks in the collard greens for the third time. Then, she shifted over to the turnip greens and snagged a turnip and red pepper with her fork. "Boy, you must have put your big toe in them greens," she declared, smacking her lips. She had been liberally sampling the wine, too, since her arrival. That was her contribution to the dinner from her store, Cherry's Liquors, a case of assorted wines and a case of beer.

"You in my pots again, Mz. Lewis?"

"You keep cooking like this, boy, and I may have to move in with you and kick Roz out," she said and cackled.

"Can't expect me to stay out of the kitchen either, with all these good smells," Etta Hunter commented, as she peeked into the top, then the lower wall ovens again and took a deep sniff of the bottom warming drawers that were packed full of dishes, hot and ready to be served. "That fish smells so good."

"You fell into some luck there being with a man who can cook like this," Mrs. Lewis said to Rosalyn and then plucked a fat olive from a tray of assorted hot pickles and peppers, relishes, garnishes, and condiments that Rosalyn had just finished putting together. The cold cooked shrimp appetizers and cocktail sauce were disappearing rapidly, too.

"I'll say. I have to work out extra hard and long to keep the pounds from settling on my hips from all of the good food Wesley cooks every day."

"What you got cooking in that pot over there?" Francine asked, reaching across Wesley to get a look at the string beans with onions, garlic, and almond slivers. "Mmph, mmph, mmph, looka here, looka here at these green beans!"

"All right, out of here, all of you who are not me," Wesley said, shooing everyone out of the kitchen. He did it more for form than necessity. Not that anyone paid any attention to him or moved. They just kept moving aside so they could snitch a sample of everything he made.

He really liked having people around, enjoying themselves and snacking while he cooked. There were many years when he ate alone. Rosalyn's house was a perfect setup for enjoying family and friends. The fireplace was ablaze and the flat screen was on in the family room, in clear view of the kitchen, with an unobstructed view through the dining area to the more formal living area. Everything was festive in the Thanksgiving theme with scented candles lit everywhere.

"Look how pretty the table looks with the candles and Thanksgiving decorations. You've even got all the silver chaffing dishes lined up on the buffet with the sternos already lit. You must have been working and cooking half the night and all day, too," Daniel Hunter commented, as he got a beer from the tall, glass-fronted beverage cooler for himself, Wesley, and Peckhead.

"Not so much. Roz and the kids set the table and the buffet last night after dinner. I prepped everything yesterday before you arrived and then started cooking this morning. It didn't take long to dry fry the turkey. It's all about preparation and timing," Wesley said, as he took a swig of the ice-cold beer.

The family thing was working out easier than he could have imagined. When the Hunters arrived the previous day, everything fell right into place. They were thrilled with Cole, Marcus, and Simone as were the kids with them. The Hunters were even making plans to take their new grandchildren to Disney World for a week during the Christmas holiday school break.

They were having such a good time together it was hard to get Rosalyn's parents and the children out of the basement to eat breakfast that morning. After breakfast, they spent most of the day back in the basement, playing games together. That's when Wesley found out several of the sofas in the basement converted to comfortable queen-sized beds. When he moved in, he could have stayed in the basement instead of moving into Rosalyn's bedroom space. Now he understood why there was a four-piece bath in the basement. He had no complaints though. He loved sleeping with her on the few occasions when he actually let her sleep. There was something about knowing she carried his child that wouldn't let him keep his hands off her.

When Mrs. Lewis, Peckhead, Francine, and Jemar arrived early for dinner, Etta Hunter gave up her place in the basement shooting pool and came up to the family room to visit with Francine and Mrs. Lewis. They were all under foot at one time or another in Wesley's kitchen ever since. Dinner would be ready soon enough. The cloverleaf dinner rolls he made from scratch had risen to his satisfaction. He just had to butter the tops and pop them into the oven to bake a few minutes and brown.

Rosalyn hopped up from her seat next to Mrs. Lewis when the front doorbell rang.

Wesley was stirring the giblet gravy when someone behind him said, "Uh, I decided to bring the cookbook to you in person. I think you probably need it."

When Wesley turned around, he was facing his brother, Isaac. He choked, tore off his oven mitts, and grabbed his brother in his arms, hugging him tightly.

"Lord, be praised!" Mrs. Lewis screamed.

Her shriek brought everyone up from the basement on a dead run. People stood in silence, tears moistening their eyes as they watched Wesley and Isaac hugging each other and fighting back tears.

"Boy, don't you burn that bread," Isaac joked, as he and Wesley held each other at arm's length. "Didn't Dad teach you better?"

Rosalyn pulled the large baking sheets of beautifully browned dinner rolls and buttermilk biscuits out of the oven to join the golden brown Mexicali corn bread and set them on the counter.

Wesley couldn't take his eyes off his brother. Peckhead handed a beer to each of them.

"Can we eat now?" Simone asked, exasperated, as she looked up at everyone with her hands on her small hips.

That broke the tension in the room and everyone erupted in laughter.

"Yes," Wesley said, lifting her in his arms and kissing her tiny nose. "Everyone's here now," he said, looking at his brother. "We have a reason for a real Thanksgiving celebration."

After Mrs. Lewis blessed the food, the cook, the return of a missing son of the neighborhood, and those soldiers serving in the military worldwide, including her grandson, everyone served themselves from the piping hot chafing dishes lined up on the room-length buffet and then tucked into the feast.

"So, I had no clue what was going on," Isaac was saying. "I was in the kitchen putting on my apron at five o'clock in the friggin' morning, getting ready to start making breakfast when this guard came for me. They had already boxed up my cell, and led me out to Discharge. It was like, here's your hat, what's your hurry?" Isaac said, perplexed as he cut into a melt-in-your-mouth tender piece of roast beef. "Then, I'm outside with the pen at my back. It was as cold as a witch's tit out there, but this SUV was waiting with the motor running. This man opened the back door and put me inside. The next thing I know, I'm being loaded onto this private jet and in the air, bag and baggage in hand. We landed at BWI, a car meets me at this Adventurer Executive Air Transportation Terminal, and I'm delivered here and told to ring the doorbell."

"No one said anything to you?" Rosalyn asked, fascinated by the story.

"They gave me my papers. I was being released for time served. I don't even have to report in to a parole officer. I'm a free man."

"That's really strange," Peckhead commented. "I've never heard of anything like that."

"I really wouldn't care at this point how it happened," Francine said, and scooped up more corn pudding. "We're just glad you're home, Isaac."

"I'll drink to that," said Daniel Hunter, and took a sip of his dinner wine. "So what are your plans now?"

"I really don't know. I'm just coming to grips with the fact that, after all these years, I'm actually outside of the prison walls. This morning I was an inmate at a Montana prison and now I'm back home in Washington, DC, having Thanksgiving dinner with my family and friends."

"Never should have gone to prison in the first place," huffed Mrs. Lewis, before she took another sip of wine. "Your daddy was a good man. A really good man. Raised you boys right after he lost Libby. He didn't deserve to be killed like that. If I had known you were going to plead guilty to shooting The Juice, I would have boxed your ears."

Everyone smiled at the eighty-plus-year-old former math teacher.

"Thank you, Mz. Lewis, but I did the crime. I deserved the punishment."

"It was self-defense, Isaac. If you had let someone help you, you may not have gone to jail at all," Mrs. Hunter added.

"Maybe, but I felt guilty for not thinking first. I confronted The Juice without any idea about what I planned to do, but when he pointed his gun at me, I just grabbed it. We struggled, and then the gun went off. The Juice was dead. I immediately realized I was going to go to jail and I was sorry for what I was going to put Wesley through."

"Now that's all behind you, Isaac," Francine said, wiping a tear.

"Why are you crying, babe?" Peckhead asked.

"It's just been such a wonderful day with family and friends around, especially having Jemar and now Isaac with us. The food taste so good and that's what pregnant women do when their hormones go haywire."

Everyone stopped eating and stared.

"We're…we're pregnant?" Peckhead asked, stood straight up from the dinner table, and then immediately fainted.

Between bouts of chaos, tears of joy, and unbridled laughter, order was finally restored, Peckhead revived, and the Thanksgiving dinner was a rousing success. No one paid particular attention to Wesley and Rosalyn as they grinned at each other and held hands under the table.

Chapter 14

"It's not much," Wesley said, as he sat with Peckhead, Little T, and Isaac in his old apartment.

"It's plenty space for me. Just knowing I can open that door and walk out of it any time I want to is enough for me. This is the same apartment Granddad and Grandmamma Greenfield used to live in, and you, Dad, Mama, and I lived upstairs. In a strange way, being back in this same building where we grew up, it's like coming home to all of them."

"It should be enough to get you started. There are sheets, towels and other stuff I didn't take when I moved into Rosalyn's house."

"Is Addie's store still there?"

"Yes, it is."

"Good. I'm going to need clothes and shoes, a coat and stuff."

"I can take you to one of the malls if you want."

"No, I want to be able to walk down the street again."

"Well, we're out," Little T said, as he and Peckhead rose to grab their big winter coats, skullcaps and gloves. "If you need anything, Isaac, I live right upstairs in 302 with my sister Charmaine in your old apartment."

"You mean you walk the streets all night, every night? Even on a holiday?" Isaac asked.

"Yep. Keeps the rats in their holes," Little T said, pulling up his hoodie over his skullcap and then pulling on his big, insulated coat, and a warm scarf around his neck, and part of his face. "It's good having you home, Icey. Come walk with us sometimes."

"Count on it," Isaac said, giving both men brotherly handshakes and bumps.

Peckhead and Little T left and Wesley and Isaac sat staring at each other.

"I still can't believe it," he said, shaking his head in wonder. "It's so good to have you home."

"You can't imagine how good it feels to be here. It just doesn't feel real yet. I feel like I'm dreaming and when I wake up I'll be back in my cell."

"I hope it doesn't take long for you to realize you're really home."

"Seeing everybody at Thanksgiving dinner today helped a lot. Talking about everyone else and what they're doing, and what's been going on since I was locked up," Isaac said, shook his head, and grinned at Wesley. "Roz was always going to be a pretty woman. And Jakima's kids?" he shook his head again, this time sadly. "I still remember her when she was a kid herself. Now she and her mama's gone. It's good of you and Roz to take care of them kids."

"We're planning to adopt them if their fathers don't show or don't want them. Or, even if they do. We want to keep them together. They're a unit."

"You and Roz seem to be a unit, too."

Wesley hesitated, but for a moment. "We're more than that. We're married with a kid on the way. We want to keep it on the down low until we can apply for permanent custody and then adoption after the first of the year."

Isaac's smile was a mile wide. "Man, this is really great. I was already happy being an honorary uncle to Cole, Marcus, and

Simone. Now there's going to be another Greenfield."

"Yes, but, as I said, keep it on the quiet for now. We're going to tell her parents before they leave on Sunday to go back to Charlotte. Other than me, Roz, and the kids, no one else knows."

"I can do that."

"Look," Wesley said, reaching into his pocket for his wallet.

"Don't offer me money, Wes. You've done enough, letting me move into your old apartment."

"That's not it, Isaac," he said, presenting a passbook for a savings account to Isaac. "You're going to need stuff like food and clothing until you decide what you want to do. This is yours. Your part of the inheritance from Pop."

Isaac opened the passbook and whistled. "How did it get so huge?"

"After all of Dad's expenses were paid, I divided what was left equally between us and put it in this account for you. He had a life insurance policy. Your part I added to this savings account. This apartment building is also half yours. It's paid for. I didn't know that Grand Pop bought it and then Dad owned it until after he died. Nobody, but JRock, knows that we own it now. I pay rent here to old man Jenkins like everybody else in the building. Pop's old store equipment, furniture, and utensils are half yours, too. Sometimes I take some things out to use in the community center, but for the most part, I've kept everything in storage, including Pop's car. The store is boarded up, but if you want to open it up again, you can afford to do it. You may want to take a look at what JRock is planning to do first with the Baylor Plaza Park development."

"What's this Baylor Plaza Park project everyone talked about at dinner?" Wesley explained the concept and plans. "I'll take a look at Pop's old store and then at the new plan before I decide.

I don't want to sit around doing nothing. With what you've done for me, coming back home won't be so hard."

"I'm up and out, brother," Wesley said, rising. "Roz is going to worry if I'm not back soon."

"You always had a thing for Roz Hunter. Now she's your wife. You're a lucky man."

"I know it," Wesley said. "Come by the old junior high school building tomorrow. Peckhead is going to open up around ten in the morning because school is closed. That's where the community center is that I started after Pop died."

"I'll be there."

They hugged again tightly before Wesley left.

Chapter 15

A few days later after Thanksgiving dinner, Ice banged on the door and then rang the doorbell to wake his best friend out of a deep sleep. It was three-forty in the morning. A television monitor came on and a familiar face appeared on the screen. When the telephone beeped, he picked it up.

"Ice? What? Never mind. I'm buzzing you in. Take the elevator to your right and come to the third floor."

As the elevator doors opened, the Iceman stepped out. Without a word passing between them, Ice followed JRock into the living area.

"You want something to eat?" JRock asked, moving toward his bar.

"Naw, man." Ice said as he casually looked around the room. "I'll take a brew, if you—" Ice took the bottle of beer that was in his hand before he finished speaking.

JRock uncapped his bottle of beer, tossed the cap into the recycle bin, and sat the bottle on the fireplace mantle in the open expansive, concept living, dining, and kitchen space. He put more logs on the nearly dead embers and stoked them back to life. Soon the flames caught the new timber and blazed up. JRock went back to the bar and retrieved more beer before he sat down in an easy chair.

"Nice place. Awful big though. I never would have thought it looked like this inside. You could live anywhere. Why you wanna live down here in the warehouse district anyway?" Ice asked.

JRock tried often enough to get Ice to come for a visit, but never succeeded. He knew this was not a social call, especially not at three on a cold morning. Something catastrophic must have happened, but he also knew when Ice was ready to talk, he would.

"My business offices are on the ground and second floors. This warehouse gives me plenty of space for my trucks, two-level parking garage, for my employees, and storage for equipment and supplies. It doesn't make me feel claustrophobic because the ceiling is so high.

"Since my home is here on the third and fourth floors, my daughters have access to me all day. I have live-in help to cook, clean, and look after my girls.

"Most of all, it's quiet. After three or four in the afternoon, there's usually no one around, unless Kelley or some of my crews are working late on projects. There usually isn't anyone around on weekends.

"The yard out back is large enough for the girls to play and my employees like to eat lunch or take breaks out there when the weather is good. I had it landscaped with a swimming pool, tennis and basketball courts the employees use, too. My girls like to watch the planes take off and land at Reagan National Airport. The Potomac River is out back, so I keep my boat there in the marina."

"You still like the water. Man, when we were kids you used to sit by the Anacostia River for hours, just looking. Never could figure out what you were looking for."

"Peace. I was looking for peace. I still am."

"Yeah," Ice said solemnly. "Well, you found it all right. You were always a strange bird. Never liked getting it on. If you weren't at the river, you were always on the basketball court shootin' hoops. Man! You were one helluva rockman. Dribble that rock between your legs, fake a brother out, shake and bake, and could run the real estate on a fast break and score," Ice mused, smiling slightly at the memory.

"Peace. I found a different kinda peace there. There I could see my enemy and I knew how to control him. I could control him with the rock and that gave me peace."

"Well, ain't no peace no more," Ice groaned before turning the bottle of beer up to his lips to drain it.

"Who caught the bullet?" JRock asked, instinctively.

"That kid I went after the night you and JaiHonnah was first up in the hood."

"Thought you took the whistle from him."

"Yeah, I did," he snorted. "I turned it in to G-Boogie. Then the little nine-year-old knucklehead bully went and got himself another one. Well, he won't see ten years old now," Ice lamented coldly. "A twelve-year-old bully saw to that." He gulped down his second beer. "That's two that Roz has lost from her school this semester."

"Sofa over there in the den area lets out into a bed. Pillows and blankets in the closet. We'll figure out what to do about it later in the morning," JRock said, handing another beer to Ice as he rose from his chair.

"JRock," Ice called, as JRock started to leave.

"Yeah?"

"There's got to be a better way. I can't let my kids grow up like that. I couldn't take it if anything happened to Cole, Marcus, or Simone. That's why I'm here."

"I know. Put some more logs on the fire, if you want. Turkey salad in the refrigerator. Some of Kelley's pound cake is on the kitchen counter."

"Hey, JRock, how'd you know? That I came over here 'cause of that kid, I mean?"

"Lived there, remember?" he said and kept going to his bedroom. "You're the reason I got out alive."

Ice remembered. There were nine or ten year olds playing a pick-up game on the basketball court at the junior high school. JRock won the game with a sweet, three-point shot. A sideline kid didn't like that he and his friends from another part of town lost the game and pulled a gun on JRock, intending to shoot him. Ice and some of his posse tackled the bully and took the gun away from him. That bully was Killer, aka Levi Hall.

Chapter 16

A week later, after Rosalyn stripped him bare and had her way with him, Ice crawled out of bed and pulled on a pair of Jockey's that had somehow ended up on the floor near the foot of the bed. Whoever was incessantly banging on the front door and ringing the doorbell wasn't going to give up easily.

He was tired after being called out again in the middle of the night. Little T and Isaac had stopped an attack on two teenaged girls by some out-of-the-neighborhood thugs after a house party. Little T had identified the thugs as part of Killer's Royal Reds crew.

The number of violent incidents involving the Royal Reds was increasing since the showdown in front of Rosalyn's school. Ice's crew was strapped now, but Little T successfully recruited more men and women, some former military just returning home from active duty who wanted to help patrol the neighborhood. Pleased with the decrease in the crime rate and not wanting it to rise again, they volunteered what time they could contribute to the safer streets. Little T arranged for more police presence on night patrols and worked up plans for day patrols to provide more protection for the neighborhood merchants. Everyone was equally excited about the plans for the new Baylor Plaza Park project, which resulted in more eyes in the neighborhood, including Isaac who hadn't missed a night patrol since his return from prison.

When Ice came in off the icy streets this morning, Rosalyn was already up getting the children ready for school, but made time to show him that he was missed and loved. Afterward, he went into the kitchen to prepare breakfast for his family. After breakfast and a review of homework, including spelling words for Simone, math questions for Marcus, and a discussion on current events for Cole, he bundled his family off to school, cleaned the kitchen, and crawled back into bed. He planned to do the laundry later and start dinner while he cleaned the rest of the house.

Whoever was at the door was going to get a piece of his mind. When he opened the front door, Howard Gardner stood there dressed in all of his Savile Row glory.

"You're Greenfield? I've seen you somewhere before, haven't I?"

"We've met."

He stared a moment and said, "Look, it's cold out here. May I come in?"

Ice's brow bunched. "Uh, sure, but if you're looking for Roz, she's at the school this time of the morning."

"I know. I'm here to see you, not her," he said, stepping inside the vestibule. "I stopped by your office at the community center. I was told you were still at home this morning and wouldn't be in until later today.

Ice shrugged noncommittally, closed the door, and said, "Have a seat while I put on some clothes."

When he returned to the living room, Gardner was reviewing the pictures displayed on the fireplace mantle that had been taken during Thanksgiving Day while his in-laws were in town. Rosalyn and the children printed the pictures off the computer and planned to create handmade scrapbooks as Christmas gifts for those who were at the dinner.

Ice let Gardner continue his perusal of the photographs uninterrupted.

"I understand you own and operate the community center."

As an opening statement, Ice thought it a bit strange, shrugged, but still answered, "I do, yes. Why?"

"I want to make a donation," he said, producing a certified check, which read for a staggering amount of money.

Suspicion grew and Ice's face showed it. "What is it you want in exchange for that much money?"

"Nothing. There are no strings attached."

"*O-kay*," he said, not believing one word of that statement. "If you're just looking for someplace to park your annual charitable contribution before the end of the tax year, the center is a certified not-for-profit organization under the federal tax codes. We have a federal tax identification number."

"I know. I had one of my assistants do a thorough review of your license and city and federal filings. You appear to be a legitimate operation adhering to all of the city codes for occupancy."

Ice shrugged again. Gardner wasn't saying anything that wasn't true, but still there seemed to be something more to this visit on a personal level. If Gardner simply wanted to make a donation, he could have put a check in the mail or delivered it when he stopped at the community center. There had to be more to this visit. He only had to be patient and wait.

When the silence seemed to drag on without purpose, Ice said, "If that's all you wanted," he started moving toward the front door. "We appreciate your generous donation."

"That's not all. I also have another check in the same amount made out to you personally."

"For this additional amount you want what?"

"This will help you and those children to get out of Rosalyn's house and life. You see, I don't intend to lose her to some two-bit, hood rat like you. I intend to marry Rosalyn as soon as she gets over this silly infatuation she has with those ragamuffins. I don't want anything and certainly no children disrupting the lives I've planned for us to have together. I've invested a lot of time and attention into making Rosalyn acceptable to be my wife and a member of my circle of friends and associates.

"Now that she has moved into the higher echelons of society with her association with people like attorney Vivian Alexander Jackson, architect JaiHonnah Chapman, and businessman J. Roderick Baylor, we may be ready…." He paused, arching his brow. "You're laughing? You think this is a joke?"

"Uh, have you discussed your plans for Rosalyn's life with her recently?"

"This silly tiff between us won't last. She will soon come to her senses."

"Uh huh, just as I thought. You haven't spoken with her about your plans. Well, I'm not interested in your assistance. No amount of money would induce me to move or get out of Rosalyn's life. She's a grown woman and she makes her own decisions about what she does or does not want to do."

"You don't deserve a woman like her."

"We agree on something," He said flippantly.

"You have nothing to offer her. You should stay with that ghetto fabulous girlfriend of yours, that LaKesha Reynolds tramp. She's the kind of low-class, gutter rat you deserve."

Ice grinned. "Banged her, did you?" he said, more as a statement than a question, and smiled fully when Howard flushed. "You should catch her show five nights a week at Sporty's in northeast. She'll give you one hell of a lap dance for an extra fee, but she doesn't work Sunday or Monday nights." He stepped into Howard's personal space. "Don't ever come into my face and disparage her after you've fucked her."

"I won't dignify—"he huffed, incensed. "I warn you that you're making a huge mistake."

"It won't be my first."

"This one could cost those children—"

That comment snapped Ice's spine ramrod straight and wiped the amused expression from his face. He moved closer into Howard's personal space and bared his teeth, delighted at the little show of fear that crossed the other man's face. With his unshaven face, unkempt hair, and appearance, he knew he probably looked like a criminal. He could thug up in a heartbeat. He wasn't that far removed from surviving life on the streets that he would back down from a challenge. "If you do anything to threaten my family, you had better grab your hairy ass and kiss it goodbye."

"You don't scare me. I can buy ten of you for a dime a dozen."

"I'm not for sale," he said, shredding both checks into confetti and placing them in Gardner's hand. "And you can't buy Rosalyn's respect. Now get the hell out of here."

"You'll regret this."

"So you've said several times. I'm still not impressed."

Howard left, but Ice was too angry to go back to bed. He emptied the dishwasher, did the laundry, started dinner, and took out his anger on the punching bag in the basement gym. He finished up with half an hour in the sauna before making lunch for himself, Rosalyn, and the kids using the last of the turkey and ham from Thanksgiving for sandwiches.

"This is a nice surprise." Rosalyn smiled, as she closed and locked her office door. She had been thinking about Wesley all morning. He was called out on patrol last night, and she hadn't gotten her full morning dose of loving him before she and the children left for school. Those quiet morning times were precious to her now and she looked forward to spending time with Wesley anytime she could get it.

Ice took her into his arms for a warm and thorough kiss. "I brought lunch." He smiled at her as he felt her up. He wondered how he deserved to be so lucky. Dr. Rosalyn Hunter was any man's ideal fantasy and she was in love with him. He kissed her again just because he liked to and because she was his wife and he could.

"Mmm, if you keep this up, babe, lunch may have to wait a while," she whispered in his ear while feeling his hardened penis through his jeans. She unzipped them and reached inside.

"Oh, no. The last time we got busy in your office, you had three incidents and two important phone calls to deal with. I had to go to work that day with a hard-on. We'll have to save our pleasures for after the kids are asleep tonight."

She pouted prettily for show, zipped up his jeans, and then kissed him again before moving toward the picnic basket to see what gastronomical delights her husband had prepared.

"Ah…" She sniffed the hot container. "You made soup?"

"Potluck vegetable."

"And hoagies. Ham and turkey."

"And the last of the red velvet cake. I already dropped off lunch for the kids. I made a peach cobbler for tonight's dessert."

"Mmmm, what else is for dinner tonight?"

"Pot roast. I put it in the crockpot to slow cook before I left home. It should be ready around six tonight. Carrots, celery, onions, and white potatoes are bagged in the frig. If I'm late getting home, would you add them to the pot for about thirty minutes before you're ready to eat? I also baked a loaf of the rye bread that you like."

She had been with Wesley every day and night for many weeks. He was her husband now and she was thrilled every day to be with him. Though they were feeling their way through this new experience of living together as man and wife, she knew him well enough to know when something was bothering him. "What's up, Wes? I know this is not the first time you've brought lunch for me and the children, but it usually means there's something on your mind."

"The last time I did that was because I was horny as hell and I needed to plant myself between your thighs."

"Anytime, lover," she said and grinned at him, "but what's up today, besides your libido?"

He looked at her and marveled again that she was his. "I like that you know me so well I don't have to explain things to you."

"We're getting really good at it, too. So tell me."

"I had a visitor this morning shortly after you and the kids left."

Her brows drew together. "Someone who woke you up and upset you?"

"Howard Gardner."

It took a moment before it set in. "Was he looking for me?"

"No, for me." He went on to tell her everything as they ate their lunch.

When he got to the part about Howard offering him a bribe to move out, she had to cover her mouth as she laughed.

"Oh, to be a fly on the wall when you told him what he could do with his checks. What a pompous ass he can be sometimes."

"You heard? Kesha must be giving him the four-one-one about what's going on between you and me. I think he's banging her."

Laughter bubbled up and out of Rosalyn to the point of tears leaking from her eyes. "Oh, hell, Howard probably scared poor Kesha to death." She howled in laughter again.

Ice frowned. "Why?"

"Howard Gardner is the living embodiment of Christian Grey, the main character from the E. L. James novel *Fifty Shades of Grey*." At his blank look, Rosalyn took time to explain the premise of the book's character and series. "So as you might imagine, Howard's sexual proclivities are on the exotic and rather erotic side. From what I've heard LaKesha say in the nail salon about her experiences, she's somewhat parochial. Howard would scare her to death."

"Uh, Roz, you were with him as his lover for what, two years?"

She laughed. "Longer. We met at a party given for me and four others when we received our doctorates." She searched his face for any sign of concern. Finding none, she continued. "I wasn't a virgin and I've had my share of intimate relationships."

"I'll say," Ice said and grinned, "but perhaps we need to read the E. L. James novels together. You can point out some things I might have overlooked in my education. Obviously, we've been walking on uneven ground in the lovemaking area, too."

"Babe, all I need to know about our sex life is that I'm not walking on shaky ground. I promise you there is absolutely nothing wrong with our lovemaking. However, practice makes perfect, and I do enjoy practicing with you between my thighs," she teased, then sobered. "Do you think I should contact him? I mean, I haven't been accepting his calls and I made it clear the last time I saw him I didn't want to hear from him again."

"You know him better. Do you think he's capable of causing us trouble with our petition for permanent custody or adoption?"

"Capable? Yes. Howard is certainly capable of going after anything he wants and doing whatever he has to in order to make it happen. He's a control freak. On general principle, he doesn't like social welfare programs, but he would prefer that to allowing me to adopt the children."

"What would he do if he knew we're married and expecting a child?"

Rosalyn shook her head. "I don't know and I couldn't even hazard a guess. I don't want him to get wind of those facts though. He can be ruthless if he believes he's been crossed or made to look the fool. Image is everything to him."

"Then I say we give Vivian a heads-up about his visit, his threat, and do nothing else for the time being where Howard Gardner is concerned."

"I agree," Rosalyn said.

They finished lunch and called Vivian.

Chapter 17

"Hi. You're Wesley Greenfield, right?" asked the pretty brunette, with sparkling blue eyes and pink cheeks chilled by the blustery cold day, as she stood next to his cubicle and extended her hand.

He stood and shook her hand. "Yes, and you are?"

"Melissa Charles. I'm a lawyer and one of Vivian Jackson's partners in the firm."

"Oh, yes. Please have a seat," he said, removing a stack of files from his side chair, offering her the seat beside his desk. He was getting the center's books in order in preparation for issuing W2s and filing taxes. "I've appointed Roscoe Hubbard as the new community center manager, but he's out at a city council meeting this morning. Vivian mentioned someone from her law firm would be in touch about setting up an advice clinic for legal matters."

"Yes, she asked me to handle it for her some time ago. I apologize for taking so long to get around to this, but our firm has been inundated with new clients. For me, this is the fun part of my job. You see, we used to do this type of thing when we were law school students at Georgetown. Professor Gus Fehey, the former senator, was our advanced scholars program's leader. He still has the student volunteer program, but they're spread pretty thin throughout the city."

"Oh, okay. I guess that means you can't do it then."

She chuckled. "Oh, no, we are going to do it. We're just going to use some of our first year, junior law partners instead of students to do it, along with Professor Fehey's students and Constantina Justice's law call center that operates twenty-four-seven. I just need to see the space where you plan to set our people up so I have an idea of how to build out the space and add a bank of telephones and computers." She waited a beat. "Uh, are you all right? You seem to be in a state of shock."

"I had no idea she, that Vivian had such an extensive program in mind."

Melissa chuckled again. "Vivian does nothing by half. Do you mind taking me on a tour?"

"No, not at all. Let's go."

They walked through the entire facility on the first floor and discussed the various unused spaces.

"What's up there?"

"That's completely vacant space. It's pretty much the same layout as this floor except for the space above the gym/multipurpose room."

"May I see it?"

"Sure," he said and unlocked the gated doors that were installed to prevent access to the second and third levels. They walked up the steps to the second level hallway that led to the former classrooms.

"I like this space," she said, as they stood in one of the old classrooms that must have been a science lab. "It's larger than the empty rooms you have left on the first floor without having to knock down walls. This will do nicely. We'll have to get JaiHonnah in to take a look around. We're going to need a few elevators installed."

"Elevators?"

"Oh, uh, yes," she said absently, as she made a note in her iPad. "We will have to comply with the Americans with Disabilities Act, the People with Disabilities, and the Affordable Care Act. The halls are wide enough to accommodate wheelchairs. The bathrooms will have to be renovated and new, more efficient windows installed. The doors look to be wide enough, but we'll have to double check to be sure," she said, making more notes in her iPad. "Heating and air conditioning, too, will need to be upgraded, but that shouldn't be much of a problem. JRock is already planning to keep your community center in tact on the new Baylor Plaza Park concept. It will, of course, be completely renovated and renamed for your father …"

Wesley stared blankly at her, mouth partially open.

"You didn't know any of this, did you?"

"No, I didn't know. I thought this center would be torn down to make room for something else. That a new center would be built to replace it."

"Oh, no. It was never JRock's intention to demolish your community center. In fact, he wants to help reimagine it to become a full service and vital part of the new village plan. He has already bought all of the available land he needs for Baylor Plaza Park."

"On the plan I've seen, this area was whited out."

"Only because it wasn't a part of the demolition plan. He's going to need substantial space on the third floor of your building temporarily for the on-site construction headquarters and maybe add a fourth floor. He's planning to convert one of your empty classrooms on the main floor on the back of the building into a reception lobby and install a new set of stairs and elevators to the third and potential fourth floors. He needs additional parking spaces, too, on that side of the building. Again, he's got to comply with federal and local laws. He also didn't want the construction activity interfering with your other programs for the children, teens, and adults you serve. Didn't he talk with you about this?"

"He mentioned it months ago, but we haven't made time to talk about it much recently."

"You should really come on board fully, Wesley. I can give you my notes, but JRock refuses to assign anyone else to take the leadership role on this project. He's still waiting for you to work with him. Now that your brother's home, we all hoped you'd have more time for this project while it's still in the planning stages."

"My brother?" he asked, his brow bunched.

"Yes, Isaac, right?"

"Yes, but how do you know about him?"

Melissa chuckled. "There is absolutely no one at our law firm who doesn't know about your brother. Vivian had her investigators going over the details of his murder case months ago. She doesn't practice criminal law, but her friend, Constantina Justice, the woman who has the *Sweet Justice* television show, has a bunch of lawyers working in her call center who do practice criminal law. Vivian and Constantina were in undergrad together at Spelman.

"Vivian just set up a competition for our lawyers and Tina's to come up with evidence and reasoned arguments to convince a judge to release your brother from jail. Three lawyers who teamed together won your brother's freedom. They received an all-expense-paid, two-week vacation to anywhere in the world they wanted to go and a huge bonus. They were transported to and from their choices on one of Vivian's Adventurer Executive Airline jets. And I see by your expression you didn't know any of this either."

"I had no idea. We didn't know how it happened. How or why Isaac was released from prison."

"Oh, hell. If Vivian didn't tell you or your brother about it, she probably didn't want you to know about her role in his release. Do you think we can keep this just between us?"

"I have to tell my brother and one other person, but I'll ask they not mention her generosity to anyone else."

"*Whew! Thanks!* You've really saved my life. Vivian loves me like a sister, but she'd skin me alive if she finds out I've spilled the beans."

Ice smiled at her serious expression. They continued to talk about the timeline for construction of the new law center. It was going to take approximately six months before it would be up and operational.

Just about the time his and Rosalyn's baby would be born.

Chapter 18

It was a few weeks before Christmas and Wesley had to smile at his family decked out in new clothes and shoes to attend a performance given by the Alvin Ailey American Dance Theatre at the Kennedy Center for the Performing Arts. Rosalyn scored comp tickets from some of her friends who were dancers for the troupe of entertainers. She attended exercise classes with the company while she was in college in New York City and had even performed with the troupe at summer stock. They were scheduled to perform one of her favorite routines, *Firebird*, and she had designed a costume for Simone to wear to the theatre.

Cole and Marcus were not thrilled with having to wear a shirt and tie with dress slacks, a pullover long sleeve sweater and new, hard-bottom shoes just to see a bunch of people dance, but Simone was beside herself with joy. She could barely finish her lunch at the Italian restaurant where they ate near the Kennedy Center.

Rosalyn was insistent on introducing the children to authentic foods from other countries. The week before their lunch or dinner excursions, the children were required to read about each country and its customs and cuisines. They even had to speak a few words of each language.

Marcus' attention grew when he got a look at the Kennedy Center for the first time and he was absolutely bowled over when they entered the vast structure.

Wesley had to admit, watching a matinee ballet performance wouldn't have ordinarily been on his to-do list, but after the show was over and they were backstage with the performers, he, Marcus, and Cole had nothing but good things to say. Simone was speechless; she was so enamored with the costumes and beautifully, made-up dancers.

Though people oohed and aahed over Simone, who wore a Firebird Halloween costume of her own, there were plenty of hugs and kisses for Rosalyn, too, Wesley noted. She seemed to know everyone in the dance company. That earned Simone an opportunity to walk out onto the grand stage with the spotlights on her while she tried out some of the ballet moves Rosalyn taught her. Her face was made up in the Firebird personae. A few of the show's performers danced with Simone, while Rosalyn took scads of pictures and videos. Of course, everyone autographed Simone's pink tights. It took nearly two hours before they were permitted to leave the theatre. By the time they got home and sat down to dinner, the conversation was all about that day's excursion. In true diva fashion, Simone still wore her costume and makeup.

It was typical that after morning chores were finished, they went out every Saturday afternoon to do something different. The first Saturday they visited the Air and Space Museum and then walked on the National Mall. Cole was a bubbling fountain after that experience. He loved everything about the possibility of space flight. The next Saturday, they went to a home show at the DC Convention Center where they watched college students construct a home in a matter of hours. Marcus was like a sponge soaking up every tidbit of information. He even impressed JRock with what he learned. He was the leader of the cheering squad to get Wesley to take the project manager's job. He had visions of working with Wesley during the summer on the job site for Baylor Plaza Park.

They had one more Saturday before the holiday. Plans were made to go to Tyson's Corner Mall in Virginia to buy last minute gifts and clothes for the children appropriate for Florida weather in the winter. Rosalyn's parents were returning to Washington, DC to pick up Cole, Marcus, Jemar, and Simone to take their grandchildren and friend on their first airplane flight to Walt Disney World. They would not be returning until after New Year's Day.

Wesley and Rosalyn would have the house to themselves for seven days. Since Rosalyn's school would be closed for the holidays, Wesley intended to spend as much time together with her as possible. They planned to have friends over on New Year's Eve, including Buddy Lewis who would be stateside from Afghanistan to visit with his grandmother. Everyone looked forward to seeing him.

Wesley mused, watching his family. If someone had told him, in less than six months, his life would turn around and upside down again, the way it was now, he never would have believed it. He had the beautiful and dynamic Dr. Rosalyn Amelia Hunter as his wife, three great kids and another on the way, in-laws who were loving and supportive, his brother was back from prison (thanks to another dynamic woman, Vivian Alexander Jackson) and a community center that would become full-service in the ways he had wanted for many years.

At the first of the year, the city council would vote up or down on the Baylor Plaza Park project. JaiHonnah and JRock were tag-teaming members of the City's Zoning Commission and the DC City Council. Smart money was betting the vote would be favorable. With everything coming together, Wesley felt more confident about taking on the project manager's job. It didn't hurt that the construction office would be housed on the third floor in his community center where he could keep an eye on what went on under Peckhead's and Little T's leaderships. When he discussed it with Rosalyn, as he did with most big decisions that had to be made concerning them and their family, she said he would have her support regardless of what he decided to do. He planned to stop in at JRock's office the next day to discuss it with him.

***

"What do you mean JaiHonnah's not with your company any longer?" Ice asked JRock, surprised and concerned.

"I fired her or she quit. I don't know which. Either way, she's gone."

"I don't understand. What happened?"

"She planned to leave anyway and work for Lionel Porter."

"Porter? You mean the dude your ex-wife had an affair with years ago? The guy who lives in Atlanta?"

"Yeah, him. He left a message for Jai, confirming their plans to meet in Atlanta over the holidays to discuss her employment package. I was planning a trip for us to go skiing in Vail, Colorado, and then I find her meeting with her estranged husband at the Shadows Restaurant. She accused me of not trusting her. So, I fired her or then she quit. The sequence of events is irrelevant at this point."

Ice shook his head as if to clear it. "That doesn't sound like something JaiHonnah would do. I mean, from what I've seen of her, she's dedicated to this plan and all of the Baylor Company projects."

"It's true. I never would have believed it if I hadn't seen it myself."

"I'm sorry this happened. What are you going to do for a lead architect and civil engineer now she's gone?"

"The Baylor Plaza Park project and all of the others will go forward. The construction plans are complete, including the scale model. I'll make the presentation to the City Council myself when I get back. I'm making plans to buy an architectural and engineering firm to handle Baylor Design and Development projects going forward."

"You've got out-of-town business at Christmas? What about your girls?"

"My sister left this morning to take Shelly and Shelby to California to visit Monique. She'll stay with the girls at my house in Malibu and then bring them home after the New Year. I'm going to take a vacation and go skiing like I planned."

"You're going to be alone during the holidays?"

"I'm taking Savannah Logan with me."

"JRock—"

"Don't, Ice. I know what you're going to say. Yes, it's probably too soon to get into another relationship, but this won't be the first go-round between me and Savannah. I need a diversion to get JaiHonnah out of my head."

"As long as you and she know what time it is."

"I won't let Savannah get to me the way JaiHonnah did."

"Take it light, man. Safe travels."

"I'll see you when I get back. Hey, by the way, why did you come to see me? This isn't like you."

"To invite you and JaiHonnah to come to the house for New Year's Eve and to tell you that I'm going to take you up on your offer, if it was still open."

"Sorry, I can't make the party, but your decision to come on board is the best news I've heard this year. Welcome to Baylor Design and Development."

"Thanks. We'll talk more when you get back with a clear head."

***

"So, I've decided to take JRock up on his offer," Ice finished, as he sat in his old apartment with Isaac and his crew, including Buddy Lewis.

There was a round of enthusiastic whistles and pats on his back and head.

"It's about time!" Peckhead expressed demonstratively.

"You ain't said nothin' but the truth!" Little T added.

"Man, I wish our fathers were still alive to see this day," Slide said.

"True that," Dog added.

They bumped beer bottles and drank.

"You ain't the only Greenfield with good news," Buddy said. "Tell everybody what you told me, Isaac."

"I got a lease on my Pop's old space in the shopping center and a license to operate from the city. As soon as I build out the old space, reinstall the ovens, that kind of thing, I'm opening for business. I probably need some elbow grease painting the place, but otherwise I pretty much have everything I need. Later, I'll be talking with you about a new space in the Baylor Plaza commercial area plan."

"You're right. That is good news."

"Not many of Pop's old employees are still around so I have to hire some new blood. I checked with the culinary school at JUCO, the junior college, to see what the new crop looks like."

"That's a good move. I'll help whenever I can. I don't think Roz would mind if I did some baking after the kids are in bed."

"She's holding the hammer, huh?"

Ice laughed. "Nothing is permitted to interfere with quality time spent with Cole, Marcus, and Simone. Simone is my right hand in the kitchen these days. She wants to learn to cook, so I'm teaching her. She'll probably want to come to work with her Uncle Isaac this summer. The boys just want to plant their feet under the table while the food is served. They don't mind doing the set up and cleanup, though, so you might get Cole to come in to set up and bus tables for you, but Marcus wants to work construction. He'll shadow me and maybe sweep up the construction sites."

"You and Roz, y'all done right by those kids," Slide said. "Nobody, not even Jakima, could've done better."

"Yeah, they're handling the tough stuff. Grades are still good and they're eager to learn. They don't have a choice with Roz around. She makes everything a teachable moment and learning experience. They're serious about working out, too, in Roz's exercise area. We got them some free weights for Christmas."

"A bunch of other good stuff, too, to hear Jemar tell it," Peckhead added, laughing.

"Not a lot from me and Roz, except clothes and books, but we couldn't keep her parents from buying out Toys "R" Us and then taking them to Walt Disney World. They took Jemar with them, too. The Hunters have a time-share in Orlando."

"Still, it's good what you and Roz done," Isaac said.

"Since Peckhead is taking over the center and JRock is leaving on vacation, I can give you some real time while the kids are away."

"I don't know anything about cooking, but the eating part," Buddy said and grinned, "but my grandmother wants me out from up under her twenty-four-seven. I can give you a hand whenever someone else is with her."

"I appreciate that."

"Do you want Pop's old car, too?"

"Nah, leave that in storage for now. I like old cars. I might want to polish it up and check the engine and tires, but I probably need to buy or lease a truck I can use for the business. I'm thinking about doing some catering. I need wheels for that to get around town and out into the burbs. Something with that new GPS thing in it. I've been away so long a lot has changed and I don't know my way around anymore.

"Anyway, JRock asked me to cater his holiday office party. I need to buy a bunch of chaffing equipment with sternos, table clothes, dishes, glasses, and silverware. Bar set ups and a lot of trays.

"He said to make sure I have business cards to hand out and flyers, but I don't have any of that stuff. A lot of his clients and customers are gonna stop in to the party."

"I can help you with that at the community center. I can do the simple stuff for you, but my boy, Jemar, is real good with designing business cards and stationary, too. He's not bad with designing web sites either. You'll probably need one of those for your business. Juan picked him to go to California for the summer for more training. The boy's got skills."

"Thanks, Peckhead. See, I got all this new stuff to learn about, along with reopening Pop's bakery and ice cream parlor business."

"Pop would probably have wanted to retire by now, so it's your business. With adding catering, you're making it a new business. I suggest you make it a specialty coffee and tea shop, too. You've got all of us to help you with the other stuff."

"I'm glad you said that because I want to call the new place Greenfield Brothers instead of Icey's."

Wesley was touched by his brother's gesture. "It's a fine name," he told Isaac and the crew touched beer bottles again in salute.

Chapter 19

Snow was still piled high on the ground outside the DC Courthouse on this bitterly cold day in mid-January. "Well, are you two ready?" Vivian asked.

Roz put her hand on her jittery stomach above her hidden baby bump, exhaled sharply, and nodded in the affirmative. Then she turned her head to look up at Wesley.

"Good. And you, Wesley?"

"I'm ready, but, if I'm not mistaken, that's Howard Gardner and LaKesha Reynolds coming up the hall."

Vivian, Rosalyn, and Isaac turned in the direction of the long hallway.

"Oh, hell." Rosalyn sighed.

"Don't react," Vivian said. "Let me handle this."

Howard led with an outstretched hand. "Mrs. Jackson, I'm Howard Gardner. It's a pleasure to finally meet you. How fortuitous that you would be here today. If you would allow me just a few moments of your time, I would like to speak with you about my company's accounting and auditing services. You see—"

"Mr. Gardner, is it? If you hadn't noticed, I'm here for a child custody case. Not to discuss any other business. Is this your wife?"

"*Wife! Hell no!* She's just a concerned citizen and here to object to this silly custody petition, just as I am."

"Your name is?"

"Kesha? I mean, LaKesha Reynolds? Who does your nails?" she asked Vivian.

"I do."

"You got all that money and you do your own nails?" she asked incredulous.

"Every penny counts. Are you two represented by legal counsel?"

"You mean, like a lawyer or somebody?"

"Uh, yes, Ms. Reynolds, someone like that."

"He didn't say nuffin' 'bout no legal stuff," LaKesha said, casting an evil look over her shoulder at Howard. "He just say if I wanna get Ice to come back to me, I gotta come and say how me an Ice been together like for a long time and this man, a judge, can make Ice move back with me and get rid of them kids. You see, it be like dis: I can't find me no place decent to live in on what I make, so I need to move back with Ice 'cause he like paid for everything? But now, he be like livin' at Roz's place and all and his brother be like livin' where me and Ice s'pose to be livin' at together like always. Howard, he say when I get Ice back livin' with me, he gonna like give me a lot of money."

"That's not what I said . . . exactly," Howard interrupted.

"You's a lie! That's what you said, with your freaky self!"

"I said you had to tell the judge about you and Ice living together for a long time. That he's not fit to be someone's daddy and those children would be better off in the child welfare system."

"That's going to be your testimony?" Vivian asked LaKesha.

"My what?"

"Is that what you're prepared to swear to under oath and under penalty of perjury to the judge?"

"I guess?" she said uncertainly.

"Am I late?" JRock asked, as he rushed up to the group in the hall. "I had a hard time trying to find somewhere to park near here. Most of the streets are still blocked with snow."

"No, we haven't been called yet," Wesley said, still frowning at LaKesha. If Vivian hadn't told him not to react, he would be giving LaKesha a piece of his mind. Then he felt Rosalyn's forehead between his shoulder blades. She seemed to be vibrating. Initially, he thought she might have been crying, but when he put his hand behind his back reaching for her hand, he realized that she was trying desperately to stifle her laughter. She squeezed his hand. That made him relax somewhat.

Isaac's hand on his shoulder grounded him as well. It felt great to have his brother back in his life and sharing this experience with him. Then G-Boogie, Police Captain Gary Bouchard, joined the growing crowd of supporters for Wesley and Roz.

Howard stepped past Wes, nearly on him to shake JRock's hand and chat him up the same way he had attempted to do with Vivian without any success. Before long, Rosalyn's parents returned from the restrooms with the children.

The courtroom doors opened, their case was called by a bailiff, and everyone filed in. They stood when the judge entered and the docket was read by the Clerk of the Court. They were the only ones in the courtroom for the hearing.

"Are these the children named in the petition?" the judge asked, peering over his eyeglasses at the first row of seats where the children sat with Rosalyn's parents and Isaac.

Vivian stood. "Yes, Your Honor. I am Vivian Jackson, appearing for the Petitioners."

"As if you need an introduction, Ms. Jackson. I heard your keynote address at the Judiciary Dinner. Gus Fehey still argues the other way on that Supreme Court decision that you cited, but I prefer your interpretation of the law since it happens to agree with my views as well."

"Thank you, Your Honor."

"I take notice you generally don't argue cases in Family Court."

"That's correct, Your Honor. Though I've been in Family Court many times as a petitioner, this is a special situation involving my friends, people I know and respect."

"All right, let's see what we have here," he said and started reviewing the files before him. "Is Social Services in attendance?"

"Yes, Your Honor," the attorney said, standing. "Robb Hardy, acting as Guardian Ad Litem for the three minor children. Also in attendance are Child Services Investigators Corso and Bennett."

"Your father is Major Hardy, US Marine Corps, isn't he?"

"Yes, Your Honor."

"I've played golf with him a time or two."

"Yes, Sir. He mentioned that at dinner last night at the Officer's Club."

"Good, tell him that as soon as the weather breaks, I want to get back out on the golf course."

"Will do, Sir."

"First, I want to see only the children in my chambers with you, Ms. Jackson, and you, Mr. Hardy. Then I'll hear from other interested parties."

Vivian rose and escorted the children into the judge's chambers. Robb Hardy followed.

Wesley and Rosalyn sat holding hands, chatting with her parents, Isaac, Gary, and JRock. Howard and LaKesha sat on the other side of the small courtroom, not speaking. Howard kept grimacing and looking at his watch, while LaKesha picked at her fake nails, and continually popped a wad of bubble gum.

Nearly an hour later, Vivian returned with the children and the judge returned to the bench.

"All right, are there people here to speak in support or opposition to this petition?"

"Yes," Howard said, springing to his feet. "We are. We are here to oppose the petition." He prompted LaKesha to stand up. She did so slowly.

"Are you represented by legal counsel?"

"No, sir."

"All right then, first I'll hear from Social Services, the Investigators, and then those who are here in support of the petition."

The investigative report had been favorable finding both Wesley and Rosalyn fit people to parent the minor children.

JRock made an impressive witness in support of the petitioners, too, as did Rosalyn's parents and Captain Bouchard. When they concluded, the judge turned his attention to the opposition.

"I will hear your complaint now. The Clerk will swear you in."

After Howard gave his statement, it was Vivian's turn to question him. He looked decidedly uncomfortable when she approached him.

"Mr. Gardner, you claim you and Dr. Hunter are currently in a committed, long-term, exclusive relationship?"

"That's correct. Dr. Hunter and I plan to marry as soon as those children," he said with a flick of his hand in their direction, "are taken into custody by the duly responsible agency."

"Didn't Dr. Hunter sever her ties with you last year, explicitly citing her decision that she no longer wanted to see you because of your position about the children?"

"She was just being unnecessarily emotional, but she can't help it. After all, she's only a woman and she gets that way sometimes before her monthly . . . you know. She just needs time to come to her senses."

"In the interim period, have you had intimate relations with anyone else?"

Howard blanched. "I don't see how that's relevant in this situation."

"You claim your relationship with Dr. Hunter is exclusive. So my question goes to credibility."

"Answer the question, Mr. Gardner," the judge instructed.

"Well, yes, I have, but it meant nothing. I'm entitled, you see, but she isn't. I'm a man, after all."

"Uh huh, and who have you had intimate relations with, Mr. Gardner?"

This time he pouted before indicating with a flick of his hand toward LaKesha.

"Let the record show Mr. Gardner has indicated he has had sexual relations with Ms. LaKesha Reynolds."

"So noted," the judge said.

When LaKesha took the stand, she was also sworn in and given an opportunity to state her opposition to the petition. Her testimony ran pretty much as it was stated in the hallway.

"So, Ms. Reynolds," Vivian began, "your reason for coming forward today is because you want Mr. Greenfield to resume living with you without the children?"

"Well, *duh!* Yeah!"

"Yet, you've been intimate with Mr. Gardner?"

"Only one time, see 'cause he wanted to know what was goin' on between Roz and Ice. So I told him I was lookin' for a new man and if he wanted me to tell him what Roz and Ice be doin' he had to like serve it up in the bed and wid the long green. I wanted him to take me places like where he took Roz."

"So you essentially blackmailed Mr. Gardner into sleeping with you in exchange for providing information concerning Dr. Hunter and Mr. Greenfield? And in addition, he had to pay to have sexual intercourse with you and take you on trips?"

"Yeah? I mean we didn't do no sleepin'. He just wanna do freaky kinda stuff to me, but it wasn't like normal stuff, ya know? So, I didn't like it. I mean, like I gave him free lap dances and all and a BJ, but he wanted to spank me. I ain't never gonna let no grown ass man spank me," she said, pouting.

Rosalyn noticed, as LaKesha continued to answer Vivian's questions, the judge was having a hard time keeping a straight face. His complexion turned a few shades and he continually wiped moisture from his eyes. She was having the same problem.

"I see. I have no further questions of this complainant at this time. However I reserve the right to recall."

"So noted. You may step down, Ms. Reynolds."

"As a rebuttal witness, I call Dr. Rosalyn Hunter to the stand."

After she was sworn in, Vivian resumed. "Dr. Hunter, you have heard the sworn testimony given by Mr. Gardner and Ms. Reynolds?"

"I have, yes."

"Do you agree with his statement that it is your intention to marry Mr. Gardner if or when the children are removed from your custody?"

"It is not now nor has it ever been my intention to marry Mr. Gardner. That is a fact I made perfectly clear to him in his office. His staff, I believe, heard me loudly and clearly. If it becomes necessary, they can provide supporting evidence of my statement. Moreover, I certainly would not want to continue an intimate relationship with Mr. Gardner after having heard Ms. Reynolds testimony about her sexual exploits with him."

"Why not?"

"Because I am already married to Wesley Greenfield and have been for some time. Long enough for us to be expecting a baby," she said, grinning.

"How did you know?" Ice asked Vivian after court adjourned and he and Rosalyn were granted permanent custody, pending conclusion of the search for relatives.

"My investigators, Richardson Investigations and Security, are excellent at what they do. They know I do not like surprises that could jeopardize my clients' cases. So, they dig deeper and keep digging until a case is closed.

"Now am I to prepare adoption papers for you two to sign?"

Wesley and Rosalyn looked at each other and smiled. "Yes," they said in unison.

***

"So what do you think?" Wesley asked Cole, Marcus, and Simone. "Do you want to stay with us always and be a family?"

"Do we call you like our father and mother?" Marcus asked.

"Yes, you may, if you want. You would take us as your real father and mother and we would take you as our real sons and daughter."

"If you like, your last names would change to Greenfield, like ours. You would be Coletrain Cooper, Marcus, and Simone Harris Greenfield."

"It would be for real and everything? Like a real family? For always?"

"Yes, for always."

"The welfare peoples can't come and take us away?"

"That's right, Simone. No one can come and take you away from us ever again."

"Ms. Etta and Mr. David would be like our real grandma and grandpa?"

"Yes, they would like that very much and so would your Uncle Isaac, too," Wesley added. "We'll be having a new little brother or sister, too, this year."

"You're going to adopt more of us?" Marcus asked, incredulous.

Wesley and Rosalyn smiled at each other, and then Wesley placed his hand on Rosalyn's abdomen.

"Right here is your new brother or sister," he said and then Rosalyn placed each of their hands on her abdomen.

Just then the baby moved. The children stared at Rosalyn in varying degrees of wonder.

"Can the baby come out and play with us?" Simone wanted to know.

"Not yet," Rosalyn said. "We have several months to go before you'll have someone new to play with."

"How is it going to get out of there?" Marcus wanted to know, concerned.

"Very carefully," Wesley said, smiling. He and Rosalyn had talked about how to tell and talk with the children about the baby, but the purpose of their after dinner discussion in the family room was planned to talk about the adoption. So far, none of the children said they wanted to be adopted. They had wandered away from their primary topic. "So, do you want time to think about whether you want me and Rosalyn as your father and mother?"

"Is it okay if we like love you, too?"

Ice was too choked up to speak, but found comfort when Rosalyn took his hand and squeezed.

"It is very okay because Wesley and I love each one of you and each other very much." Rosalyn said it, but Wesley had yet to say the words to her. She knew, without doubt, he loved the children, but she felt his feelings for her were nebulous or ambiguous at best.

"The new baby, too," Simone said, seated on Wesley's lap, snuggling deeper into his embrace.

"Then I guess it's all right," Cole said, sitting next to Rosalyn and speaking for his younger brother and sister.

Rosalyn squeezed both Marcus and Cole to her sides and then kissed each one on their fresh haircuts. In turn, they both kissed her cheeks.

"So, when your grandparents come back around Memorial Day to pick you up for your summer trip, we'll have an adoption ceremony, okay?"

The children nodded their agreement. Daniel and Etta had asked to take the children with them on vacation after school let out for the summer until the baby was due just before the Fourth of July. They were traveling via motor home to Martha's Vineyard for a Howard University dental school reunion of their classmates and other alum.

Wesley and Rosalyn agreed to her parents' plans because the construction of the enormous attic space in their home was to be converted into two bedrooms with a Jack-and-Jill bath and a roomy study/play space while the children were away. Each space would be bright and airy with operable skylight windows, and reversible ceiling fans. There would be ample walk-in closets and storage spaces for each boy. Baylor Design and Development was handling the renovations and believed they would have the project completed in four weeks or less.

Rosalyn would be out of the house most of the day after school closed for the summer. She planned to volunteer at the community center and help Roscoe set up summer camp and programs for the children and teens. Many of her teachers would also help as paid summer aides and employees. JRock planned to pick up the tab for all the neighborhood kids to participate in the summer programs, including the food expense and excursion fees. While the preteens would be in summer camp at the community center, the teens would be taken to a summer camp in the western Maryland mountains at Cumberland State University. They would return just before school opened again for the fall term. Other neighborhood teens, who could not attend the away summer camp because of family obligations, would hold summer jobs at Baylor job sites in and around the city.

Rosalyn had plenty of plans for Cole, Marcus, and Simone once they returned from spending time with her parents.

"You look happy," Rosalyn said, hugging Wesley from behind, as he stood before the kitchen sink, scrubbing a sticky lasagna pan. Her left hand slid under the bulky cable-knit sweater her parents gave him for Christmas to latch onto his flat, left nipple. Her right hand unsnapped the button on the new jeans she gave him for his birthday to find his member warm and responsive.

"The kids," he began.

"Are in the basement playing that new Wii game," she said, as she unmercifully continued to fondle him. "That's why I'm not going to get you naked in the kitchen and have my way with you on the center prep station again."

His memory of her attack on New Year's Eve, just before their guests started to arrive, was vivid in his mind. She was a very creative lover.

"I am happy," he said, and sucked air through his teeth. His wife was not only creative, but also very skillful. She knew just how to touch him to bring on the most pleasure for them both. "For the first time in a very long time I know what happy feels like."

"Me, too, Wesley. Me, too. They want us to be their parents. I feel honored and humbled by their love for both of us, my parents, and Isaac," she said, as she rested her forehead at his back and continued fondling him.

He let the pan slide into the hot, sudsy water, wiped his hands dry, and then turned in his wife's arms.

"Now, let's see how much happy we can have in fifteen minutes or less," he said, scooping her into his arms and carry her quickly up the stairs to their bedroom. They took thirty minutes, but the water was still warm in the sink when Wesley resumed scrubbing the lasagna pan. His lovemaking was so thorough his wife was still asleep.

Chapter 20

Ice sat in the audience at the city council hearing room, while other developers at the podium discussed their projects for different places throughout the city. In the month since he accepted the project manager's job, he immersed himself in the demolition and construction plans for his old neighborhood. He spent some late nights studying the layout of every utility and the placement of every home and business. JRock assigned several of his specialists and drafting technicians to work with him to refine points in the plan. He took the plans to the community council to have them signed off on the agreement.

Instituting hiring and training programs took up much of Ice's time and attention. There was no shortage of men and women looking for an opportunity to gain work experience on the project and jobs to feed their families. Ice resolved to hire and train as many destitute members of the community as he could manage. He knew he may not be successful with all of the derelicts he planned to bring on board, but some of the faces he saw for years, scrounging in dumpsters and trash cans and living in abandoned buildings, were old friends of his father's and his crews' fathers. They would get a fair shot at turning their lives around to become productive members of the community again. For the chronically homeless, who were in training for jobs, he brought in trailer homes that comfortably slept four adults or adult parents with children to set up on vacant land around the job site. Along with job stipends while in training, Isaac would cater breakfast, lunch, and dinner in the community center's cafeteria for the indigent trainees and any family members at a nominal fee. He had a bunch of retired seniors who wanted to volunteer to help in any capacity needed.

Ice was so busy now that some days he didn't get to take a break to have lunch with Rosalyn, but she didn't have to force him to break off to spend time having dinner and quality time with her and his family. Because he was up and out of the house by six in the morning, he didn't often get a chance to make love to his wife and eat breakfast with his children before he was in his office, on the third floor of the community center, working with his team and sometimes with JRock in attendance.

Though Rosalyn was bearing up under the changes in their household rhythm, she was more round, carrying their child. He taught Cole, Marcus, and Simone how to sort the clothes and linens and how to do the laundry. They were also learning how to do other housework to relieve Rosalyn of the more strenuous bending and stretching. Still, because Rosalyn and the children were home hours before him, she took on more of the cooking duties. His absence meant she was on her feet more when he felt she should be relaxing. He would still do the cooking on the weekends, sometimes making multiple meals to freeze and eat during the week. He made and froze a lot of soups, stews, and casseroles to make mealtime easy for Rosalyn to prepare. The children pitched in to help with the set up and cleanup. Sometimes, they came to the community center and had dinner with him in the cafeteria.

Rosalyn's birthday was coming up and, as he sat in the city council meeting waiting for their turn to give the Baylor Plaza Park presentation, he tried to think of something special to do for her. He had come up with something he thought might please her, but he was still going to have to enlist his in-laws' help.

***

Carla Allen, Isaac's date, was telling a joke that had everyone's attention. She was a very animated woman whose hand gestures and facial expressions had people laughing so hard there were tears in their eyes. Isaac was talking with Kelley Baylor, away from the group and his date. Carla fit right in with this group of Rosalyn's family and friends at the surprise birthday party, Ice thought.

Isaac met Carla at the junior college's culinary school when he was looking for cooks for his business, Greenfield Brothers. She was an assistant culinary school administrator and had a list of talented students she could recommend to Isaac. From that first meeting with both Isaac and Ice, she asked to come to Isaac's facility and, although it wasn't opened yet, he agreed. He ended up inviting her to attend the New Year's Eve party Ice and Rosalyn hosted, but not necessarily as his date. Nevertheless, Isaac and Carla had been seeing each other socially since then.

She was a nice fit, Ice thought, as he watched her and other people circulating around what was a makeshift party room at the community center. A couple of days before her birthday, he took Rosalyn to stay at a McCoy Hotel, one of the city's most exclusive and had dinner at Blue's Alley, a jazz club in Georgetown. The next morning, he had her scheduled for the works at the hotel's spa. While Rosalyn was being pampered, his in-laws, he, and the children decorated a former classroom at the community center with birthday balloons and streamers, while Isaac started cooking for her surprise birthday party. When he brought Rosalyn to the party the next day, she was so touched by the gesture she cried like a baby.

Ice just finished replenishing the hot food trays on the buffet and checking the beer, wine, and soda barrels. Francis Baylor, JRock's older brother, set up his deejaying equipment to get the dancing started. He was a popular radio personality and television show host who produced a few shows on MTV.

Peckhead's Francine was filling another plate when she looked up and grinned at Ice. "How ya doin', Ice?"

"Okay. How are you, Francine?"

"Pregnant," she said and laughed. "Your food is always good to me."

There was pure joy in her radiant smile.

"So I've heard every day from Peckhead since you made the announcement at Thanksgiving dinner."

"We're stupid happy about having a baby. We're even talking about getting married."

"You've been together, off and on, since you were in puberty. Might as well take it to another level."

"We're planning to do that. Also, Roscoe is thinking about going back to college to complete his degree." She smiled broadly. "He only has about eighteen credits to go. Jemar and this baby have him wanting to step up his game. It didn't hurt that you trust him enough to make him the new director of your community center. Would you talk with him? He looks up to you, you know?"

He hugged Francine. "He looks up to you, Francine. You're a good woman and he knows it."

"Hey, unhand my man, woman," Rosalyn teased, as she moved into Wesley's left side, her right arm circling his waist.

Wesley grinned, squeezing both women into him. "There's enough of me to go around," he joked, "but Peckhead's got you right where he wants you, Francine." He kissed her temple. "Pregnant and about to make an honest man out of him."

She smiled pleasantly. "He is a good man," she said, as if affirming a well-known fact. "Now he's heading the community center, he's working harder than ever and loving it. Even the paperwork makes him happy. It was a great idea of his to open a senior center during the day."

"You're right, Francine," Rosalyn said, still holding Wesley around the waist, her head on his shoulder. "I've heard he had sixty plus seniors come in every day since the program started."

"It's been a big success," said Ice, "especially since there are funds available for this type of program. All those baby boomers get to help out with the breakfast, lunches, and dinners Isaac makes for the Baylor Plaza Project trainees and workers. Volunteering gives them purpose. Some of the seniors are here as early as four in the morning to start breakfast."

"I know. Isaac said when he comes in off patrol, nearly everything is ready for him to open the doors at six to let the workers and their families in for breakfast," commented Rosalyn.

"The seniors are all volunteers and they work hard. I think it's good for them, too, because, as you said, they feel useful and have a nice camaraderie with people they've known and are in their age group," added Francine.

Ice said, "When breakfast is over at eight, the seniors sit down for their own meal before cleaning up and getting ready for lunch at noon until two o'clock."

Francine nodded her agreement and stated, "Usually, another group of seniors takes over for the lunch cleanup and starts the prep for dinner while Isaac gets some sleep."

"How are the renovations for the at-risk kids' rooms going?" Daniel Hunter asked, joining the group.

"Nearly complete," Francine said. "Roscoe said he'll have the final inspection next week. The seniors have formed a group to work with the babies and toddlers. The city has completed their background checks. Everyone passed, so there are twenty-two volunteers for that program. Thanks to Rosalyn, seven of her single teachers, both male and female, who wanted the extra money to work with the at-risk children after school hours and overnight, have signed on. Since they get to sleep in the center and get meals as a part of their employment package, it works out very well as far as second jobs go."

"Did you hear Buddy is thinking about coming in to work with the at-risk kids?" asked Francine.

"Really?" Rosalyn asked, surprised. She looked up at Wesley. "You didn't tell me that."

"It all depends on what his doctors say," Wesley said. "His injury could result in a medical discharge from the Marines."

"I didn't realize his injury was that serious," Rosalyn commented.

"The bullets in his left arm and shoulder severed a few nerves," Wesley continued. "He still has the use of his left arm, but a few of the fingers on his left hand don't function well. So, he may be discharged or given desk duties. That's why I haven't said anything. If he's discharged, he definitely wants to come home to be with his grandmother and to work with the at-risk kids. He's a decorated officer in the Marine Corps. He has the academic background and experience working with young male and female soldiers. He wants to go back to school to get his master's degrees in education and sociology while working in the at-risk program."

"That's a great idea," Rosalyn said. "That way he can spend time every day with his grandmother."

"We bring Mrs. Lewis to the center every day to have breakfast with us and other seniors, before I leave for work,"

Francine said. "Then she's part of the cleanup crew that preps for lunch. She gets such a big kick out of it. After lunch, Roscoe takes her home to take a nap and stays with her until Jemar gets home from school. When school closes, Jemar will be off to Santa Barbara, California, to study computer design and engineering. It would be great if Buddy is back home by then so Mrs. Lewis is not home alone in the afternoon until I get home at five. Of course, once our baby is born, I'll be home on maternity leave."

"With the center opening every day at nine in the morning, it's been busy," said Ice. "We've got the Baylor Plaza workers in class on the third floor, the call center for legal programs and the at-risk kids program going in on the second floor; the early education and child care programs and the cafeteria going from six in the morning until the center closes at eleven at night."

"Isaac's the one who's busy. Walking patrol every night from eight o'clock until four in the morning and then cooking every day for more than a hundred and fifty people. I'm surprised he has time to date," said Francine.

"He cooked for a lot more people than that while he was incarcerated," Wesley said. "After breakfast, he places his food orders for the next day and prepares lunch. The seniors do the set up for lunch. That allows him to sleep from nine in the morning until time to prepare for dinner. So far, Carla has been coming by to have dinner with him or on the weekends, she may come to have lunch. When time permits, we work on Dad's old T-Bird. Isaac's going to get the registration and insurance on it and then he's going to put it on the road."

Wesley noticed JRock sitting alone. He seemed to be in a pensive mood, so when the conversation drifted in another direction, he excused himself and moved away. He picked up a few beers and headed toward JRock. "Hey, got something I want to talk with you about," he said to JRock and walked out of the party room.

JRock stood slowly and followed Wesley down the long hallway away from the party to his old cubicle. He took the beer Wesley passed to him.

"So what's up with you?" Wesley asked while uncapping his beer.

"You saw the revised plan for the Olympic-sized pool?"

"Yeah, I saw it. It's a great addition to the community center. I like that it will be a year-round pool with the heating elements and the retractable doors. Peckhead and I have still got to hire lifeguards and swimming instructors. It's on my agenda, but I'm glad you added it."

"It wasn't my idea."

"Oh? Who suggested it? Kelley? I know she likes to swim."

"JaiHonnah."

"Oh," Wesley said and looked away. He took another swig of his beer. "How is she?"

"I don't know, but she's pregnant."

"Oh, man," Wesley said, aggrieved. "Is it yours? Your baby, I mean?"

"Probably not. We only slipped up one time. She left just before Christmas. I heard she was back in San Antonio, Texas, from a woman who knows her. I met the woman on the ski trip Savannah and I took at Christmas. It's probably her husband's baby."

"I know Jai wore wedding rings, but I never got the impression her marriage was solid. Kelley said her husband is some type of international financier who lives most of the time outside of the country. Someplace like Copenhagen, Denmark."

"Before Jai moved back to the states, she lived in Milan, Italy. That's where she got her double doctorates."

"So you think they lived together in Italy?"

JRock leaned his six-foot, seven-inch frame forward with his elbows on his thick, muscular thighs, his hands clasped around his beer. "I don't know. I saw her husband at the Black Caucus banquet last year, but, at the time, I didn't know who he was. I saw him again that same weekend at The Watergate where Jai was staying in Vivian's condo. The last time I saw him with her was at the Shadow's Restaurant on the same day JaiHonnah quit. So, obviously, they were still together, though they were not living in the same place."

"You think their marriage was strong enough to produce a baby?"

"I didn't think so, I mean, I overheard a woman at the banquet admit to JaiHonnah she had been sleeping with JaiHonnah's husband. Apparently, she wasn't the only one and it wasn't the first time. It also wasn't news to JaiHonnah."

"She seemed like a strong woman. Not like someone who would put up with her husband slippin' and trippin'. She stood her ground that time Killer rolled up on us."

"Man!" JRock said, closing his eyes against the image. "When I heard about that . . ." He shook his head. "Anyway, Chuck Montgomery told me after Jai quit she ended up in the Emergency Room at Georgetown with food poisoning. She apparently left the city after that and went to Texas."

"You're still in love with her."

"I am. Yes."

"Then go to Texas and tell her."

JRock shook his head. "I won't do that. I know what it feels like to be cheated on; made to look the fool. As long as she's married, I won't play a part in her domestic drama." He downed the last of his beer and looked Wesley in the eye. "Marriage to Roz seems to be good for you."

"It's working out, I think. The kids are holding up since their mother died. They're legally ours now; name officially changed and everything. So far, Social Services hasn't found any other relatives for any of the children.

"You were right about Vivian. She works very hard. She's real people and she's been a good friend to all of us through this process."

"I'm talking about you and Roz."

Wesley shrugged. "I know you are, man. It's hard for me to put us into words. It's like too many good things have happened after so much bad. I'm married to a woman who I know I didn't deserve back in the day and don't deserve even now. She tells me she's in love with me." He shook his head in disbelief and denial. "We're about to have a baby and we have three great kids. Isaac is home, free, and doing good things for himself. I've got a job I like and my community center is going to be everything my father and yours would have wanted it to be.

"Because of you, the old neighborhood is starting to turn around. Little T and G-Boogie have pretty much cleared the neighborhood of the pushers and pimps. The rest are on notice their time is up. The working girls, well they moved their business off the block and inside to that old apartment building over on Nixon Street."

"See, you did it again. What about you and Roz?"

"You want the truth? I'm afraid to be happy. That's the truth, JRock. Things are so good for me with her, I'm afraid something is going to happen to take it all away. I feel like I'm holding my breath so I won't do anything to screw stuff up."

"If you're in love with her, then you won't lose her."

"I don't know what love looks like. It has never happened to me before. What I was with LaKesha wasn't love. It was sex and

I settled for that. We probably would have gone on just being fuck buddies. We weren't even really friends. With Roz, it isn't about sex. I want things with her I never even thought about with LaKesha. I feel more with Roz. I want to talk with her every day and we never get tired of talking with each other. I want to hold her and kiss her and have her smile at me like I'm her hero or for no reason other than she's happy to be with me. I want to be a good man because of her. To sleep beside her every night and have her reach for me in the morning. Just to hold her is a privilege.

"Man!" He shook his head and briefly closed his eyes. "Everything I think about involves her and our family. Is that love?" he asked rhetorically. "I've been alone for so long, even when I lived with LaKesha, that I don't know, but if it's not love, it's the next best thing. I'm holding on to it as tight as I can. I don't want any of it to slip away."

"Sounds like love to me, brah. As for everything else, we never know what's around the corner. I say breathe, really exhale, and enjoy everything you have today, regardless of what may happen tomorrow. If I had taken my own advice, I may still have JaiHonnah in my life. Instead, I let fear of a repeat performance like what happened with Monique destroy what I might have had with Jai. Now all I have are memories and regrets. Don't let fear rule your life, Ice."

"*Hey! Ice!*" Little T yelled through the halls, his tone urgent, getting Ice's and JRock's immediate attention.

"What up?" Ice asked, moving swiftly down the hall toward Little T.

"I've got to roll out. I got a call from a contact at the One Four. Some of the Royal Reds took over that apartment building over on Nixon. Says it's theirs now. That's their new headquarters."

"The building where the hookers live?"

"Yeah. The PoPo are evictin' they asses, but the girls gotta go, too."

"Man," Ice said, thinking quickly. "I've got two, empty, double-wide, trailer homes that sleep four each. Take the women there until they figure out what they need to do." He handed two sets of keys to Little T who left immediately with six of his posse. He turned to look at JRock, his brows beetled. "That's what I was saying. Things are just too good."

"Take that building down tomorrow. Demolish it. I own it and it was slated for demolition later, a couple of years down the road in the process. I won't have any drug gang use one of my properties to move into this neighborhood. I'll have Kelley find out if the women see themselves doing something other than tricking. If so, have Little T and Dog see what we can do to help. If not, maybe they'll want to relocate somewhere else out of the neighborhood. If someone gives you lemons, Ice, make lemonade."

Ice clamped his hand on JRock's back. "I feel you, man."

They returned to Rosalyn's birthday party to find everyone up on the floor doing a line dance. His children and others were adding energetic movements to the basic dance steps, locking and blocking. Even Mrs. Lewis was trying to dance along with some of the other seniors.

Wesley grinned at her and then at his very sexy, pregnant wife, as she moved her beautiful body and great looking legs in tandem with the steps and music. It only took one of Rosalyn's smiles to have him joining her on the dance floor.

***

Rosalyn sat down on Simone's bed and picked up one of the multitude of stuffed animals she arranged among her many pillows to enjoy the new décor. After the court granted permanent custody to her and Wesley, they encouraged the children to decorate their bedrooms to their own taste. Cole picked a cool blue, while Marcus picked a nice sage green color. So, they planned to do wide lateral stripes around the boys' new attic bedrooms using variegated shades of those paint colors. They also had new linens with their favorite colors and new draperies to match. Each boy had also picked pictures or posters to hang on their individual bedroom walls. Cole had a picture of the solar system as his primary focal point he wanted to put on his ceiling, while Marcus had an aerial shot of the towering buildings of Dubai as his.

However, their little diva, Simone, picked a wall mural with pinks, oranges, purples, and other shades in the red family. She had large stars and butterflies with gossamer wings and fairies hanging from the ceiling and attached to her walls. Pictures of fairy-sized dancers of all genres were strategically placed to her precise direction on the mural. The bedspread alone was a study in fine quilting with appliques of her favorite colors. It was a birthday gift from her grandparents. Her world was rosy, attesting to her newfound happiness. The bedroom fit Simone to a tee.

This was the first time Rosalyn was permitted into the bedrooms for over a week. Wesley, Isaac, and the children did all the finish work, including the decorating. They refused to let her anywhere near the paint fumes, although they paid extra for paint that had no appreciable odor or off gases.

Nevertheless, she was exiled to her siting room to read or to the gym to exercise while the work was underway. She had to admit, they did a great job on every room down to the last detail.

As she stroked her abdomen, she wondered what other adjustments they were going to have to make to accommodate the new baby. Maybe even more than one. Even with her knowledge and experience with little people, she didn't think she was equipped to handle as many children as Vivian Jackson had, who was still adopting abandoned children with health challenges. With all of her high-profile cases and activities, Vivian also played on a women's basketball team of lawyers, female law students, and judges call Final Justice, for heaven's sake! They had gone to several games to watch her play. Where her new friend, Vivian, found the energy to do all that she did, had to be the eighth wonder of the world.

Rosalyn thought maybe she could manage one or two more children before time ran out on her reproductive years. If so, they would run out of space and either have to move or remodel the house, yet again. However, the converted attic was so large it could accommodate additional bedrooms and baths beyond what was there now. Cole and Marcus' old bedroom was repurposed into a guest room again for now, in preparation for her parents extended stay once the baby was born. At Wesley's insistence, for the time being, the baby's bassinet would be in the sitting area of the master bedroom for the first six weeks. He wanted to be an integral part of their child's experiences. Later on, this new baby, or maybe others, would want and deserve to have a space of its own.

If they were going to have more children though, she would have to run the idea by her very handsome and virile husband first. She smiled to herself as she continued to rub her abdomen and think about Wesley. She could go damp just visualizing him. He had the prettiest eyes she had ever seen, particularly when he had that sexy grin on his face. She hoped their child would have Wesley's eyes.

She loved the way her husband was learning new ways to make love to her. The new ways she was becoming more comfortable with making love to him. Like last night when she sat on the bed after her shower, putting lotion on her skin. He knelt on the floor before her and put lotion on places she could no longer reach, like her feet, legs, and thighs while they carried on a conversation about the woman, Carla Allen, Isaac had brought to the party. When Wesley wanted to put lotion on her bottom, she turned over on the bed. He had raised her hips, dropped his jeans, and taken her from behind all while still putting lotion on her hips and back. His hands were magical and clever on all of the right places and together with the lotion, he had her in a state of euphoria the likes of which she had never experienced before. Now she knew there was a difference, at least for her, between having sex and making love with a man she was in love with.

Though Wesley never said the words 'I love you' to her, she felt them in the way he looked at her, touched her, and the way he took care of her and their children. They had been together for less than a year. For now, it was enough.

Chapter 21

"Yes," Rosalyn said, urgently shaking him awake. "Honey, wake up. I think my water just broke." Wesley quickly stirred at the sound of his wife's strained voice. "Are you having pain?"

"Some, but it's getting harder."

"Sit still, babe, while I get dressed and get your father up." He looked at the clock on the nightstand. It was three-thirty in the morning on July 2. Daniel and Etta had just returned two days earlier with the children after their vacation traveling to and from Martha's Vineyard in their RV.

"Hurry, honey," Rosalyn urged, holding her burgeoning belly.

Wesley wasted no time dressing and going into the guest bedroom to wake his in-laws. He didn't wake their children. Wesley helped Rosalyn change into dry clothes and carried her from their bedroom to the car. His father-in-law already seated behind the wheel and his mother-in-law brought up the rear, carrying Rosalyn's packed hospital go bag.

In less than an hour, they were on their way into Georgetown Hospital's Emergency Room. Roscoe and Francine, who was very pregnant herself, after Wesley's call, came to stay at the house with the children.

They practiced what to do in the Lamaze classes they took in preparation for the birth of their child. Wesley was with Rosalyn every step of the way as were her parents in the same birthing room for the seven hours until little Elizabeth Etta Greenfield made her appearance. With moist eyes all around, little Elizabeth's family was there to welcome her into the world.

Later that morning, Roscoe, Francine, and Mrs. Lewis brought Cole, Marcus, and Simone to the hospital to meet their new baby sister. Scads of family portraits were taken for the few hours before everyone, except Wesley, left the hospital. He curled up on the wide bed with Rosalyn, holding his daughter and continuing to marvel at his beautiful child.

"She's perfect, isn't she, Wes?" Rosalyn asked, still looking at their sleeping baby cocooned in Wesley's arm. She looked up at Wesley when he didn't answer and found him looking at her with moist eyes. "Wes? Is something wrong?"

"I love you, Rosalyn. I am so much in love with you." He kissed her.

"I know, baby. I know." She smiled through her own tears while she used her thumb to wipe his tears away. "I love you so much and you have made me the happiest woman in the world." She kissed him again. Then she turned her head to look down at their daughter in his arms. "Look at what we've done," she said reverently and then kissed their sleeping baby's button nose.

"I didn't know I could be this happy, but you've made it all happen, Roz. You and our family have made it all happen."

"*We've* made it happen together. Back in high school, I used to daydream about being with you. I wanted to be your girlfriend because you were so handsome and sexy. All of the girls wanted to be with you for all of those superficial reasons, never realizing there is so much more to you than what's on the surface. I didn't stand a chance then. Now? I can't believe how lucky I am to be with you and to really know and respect the person you are. You are such an unbelievable gift for me, Cole, Marcus, Simone, and now Elizabeth. You take care of us and make us feel safe, secure, and cherished all at the same time. You make us feel loved, Wesley. I couldn't be happier."

"I never knew that, Roz. About back in high school. If I had, I wouldn't have hesitated in stepping to you. You talk about luck? I'm the lucky one to have you as my friend, my lover, and my wife. Sometimes when you look at me, I feel like I'm ten feet tall. I want to be for you everything you need me to be and so much more. I don't ever want to disappoint you or myself in what we are building together."

***

It was the Fourth of July holiday. Grills were smoking across the backyards in Wesley and Rosalyn's neighborhood. People stopped by all day to see baby Elizabeth and many brought gifts. The Greenfields and Hunters opted to stay at home rather than go to the community center where the crowds promised to be pretty large for the picnic, dance, and fireworks display.

"I'm glad you stopped by, bro," Wesley said to JRock, as he turned the corn on the grill and then placed the sliced, fresh pineapple between the steaks, ribs, and chicken parts. Kelley Baylor sat on a chaise lounge holding Elizabeth while she talked with Mrs. Lewis and Rosalyn. In the yard, a round, twenty-foot, inflated, waist-deep swimming pool held Daniel and Etta Hunter and Cole, Marcus, and Simone. Their delighted and excited squeals, giggles, and laughter lit up the hot July air.

"I had to come see my new god child. Kelley and I are going over to Walter and Marie's for a cook out. My girls are already there or I would have brought them, too. They spent the night with their cousins."

"How did your meeting go with your ex-wife and her attorneys?"

"Settled. I cut back Monique's annual financial allotment. She's fit to be tied, but she can't threaten me with a court battle to take away my daughters anymore."

"So the DNA test proved the twins are really yours and not that Lionel Porter guy?"

"It did, yes. All this time I thought Monique was telling the truth. That Shelly and Shelby were fathered by Lionel because of their light complexion. Maybe she was. It is possible she didn't know who fathered the twins or she really wanted them to be Lionel's. However, the test proved conclusively they are mine."

"I thought that Lionel would shit a brick when you took his company away from him. I hate to see a grown man cry like that, but he deserved it."

"He screwed my wife and then tried a hostile takeover of my business, but he didn't have the juice to pull it off."

"You did have the juice."

"It wasn't something I wanted to do, initially. I was willing to let it lay between us. I got over the fact that a frat brother slept with my wife while Monique and I were still married and living together, but he stepped over the line when he went after JaiHonnah." He paused, shaking his head. "I heard his company, Silver, Porter and Dare, was in trouble after they won the Olympic stadium deal. I would have offered to help him because he was a frat, but then he wanted to come after my company to shore up his? Uh, uh, wasn't gonna happen."

"So, Kelley's moving to Atlanta to take over Lionel's company?"

"Yeah, temporarily. There are over two hundred employees, mostly architects, civil and structural engineers, and technicians

I have to figure out what to do with. Kelley's going in to evaluate what needs to be done about the existing architectural and engineering projects and how I'm going to absorb it all into Baylor Design and Developers."

"Sounds like a lot of work."

"It is, but Silver and Dare are good men and managers. They want to stay on and I'm considering letting them buy a minor interest in the company. The people you're training are doing really well. I want to put them under the same corporate umbrella with the Atlanta group. That means you'll be working directly with them and Kelley. I'm also thinking of opening a journeyman training center based on the model you created.

With the money the Black Construction Association is putting up in partnership with Baylor Developers, we will be able to supply the construction industry with talented experts in building with shipping containers for homes and businesses. The question is whether to locate that new business and partnership here or in Atlanta. People in the Midwest around Tornado Alley need this type of construction the most because it can withstand the adverse weather events when properly anchored to the ground. The same is true for California and other areas where earthquakes happen frequently."

"You're not going to ask me to move to Atlanta, are you?"

"No, I need you here, but I may ask you to help set up the program regardless of whether I locate the training school in Georgia or here. Setting up somewhere in the Midwest isn't a bad idea either. Still, it's probably easier and more cost effective to put the containers on railway cars and trucks to get them to job sites."

"Whew!" Wesley sighed. "That's a relief."

"However, if I move those Atlanta employees to DC and open a training school here, I'm going to ask you to head it up."

"Man!" Wesley said, sighing and shaking his head. "I only planned to do this for Baylor Plaza Park for the initial five years and then open my restaurant."

JRock laughed. "Look at what you've done here, Ice. You've got nearly every homeless man and woman off the streets of our old neighborhood. They're training for new, productive, construction industry jobs in a new field of construction that not many other developers have discovered yet. We're going to corner the market on low-cost, high-quality construction, using containers and have the Baylor Plaza Park Project as a model to show how it's done. Our workers will be the experts. With a few exceptions, Baylor Plaza Park will be the only planned park community in the world built entirely with shipping containers and new technology for utilities.

"You're providing medical and dental care at a nominal per person cost, legal advice, and guidance, safe housing and balanced meals, and new career opportunities for people who had no hope to live a productive life again. That's another first in the building trades and contributes to a stabilized economy at a low, up-front cost. Why wouldn't I take advantage of what you've done and expand it?"

"Let me get beyond the deconstruction stage of Baylor Plaza Park before you hand another task to me, JRock."

"See the big picture, Ice. Time's money. Now that I've got both Lionel and Monique's drama off my radar, it's time to move on and keep bigger companies, like BlackHawk International, from swooping in and trying a hostile takeover of my business."

"I know you've got your hands full, but so do I," he said, looking across the deck at his wife and new baby. "At the moment, nothing is more important to me than my family."

JRock followed his line of sight and nodded in agreement. "For now, enjoy your free time and your beautiful new baby."

Wesley looked at Rosalyn as she sat nursing Elizabeth and talking with Kelley and Mrs. Lewis. His in-laws were having a ball splashing in the pool with Cole, Marcus, and Simone. He and Rosalyn had the aboveground pool constructed as a surprise for the kids. Daniel and Etta, both retired dentists, were helping at the community center when they were not helping with the kids, especially baby Elizabeth. They wouldn't be in town much longer. They were heading back to North Carolina in a few weeks.

JRock was right, though. Time is money. Shortly, he would have hundreds of acres cleared and before fall, the trenches would be dug for the new underground utilities under the first phase of the build-out of Baylor Plaza Park. The new community still wouldn't be as large as Rock Creek Park in northwest Washington, DC, but larger than Fort DuPont Park in the southeastern area of the city.

The plan called for plenty of woodland, green spaces to explore. Boating, swimming, fishing, tennis, basketball, a golf course, hand ball, and racquet ball courts, football and baseball fields, the Children's National Island Playground and picnic areas on the Anacostia River with the music pavilions, ice rink and roller skating arenas, the equestrian bridle, bike and jogging paths, water features, an aquatic garden, and nature walkways.

Before long, they would be able to showcase the exteriors and interiors of the homes and business footage and open up the sales office for the properties. Although the façades would resemble their old neighborhood, it would have a village feel like the old days. Wesley purchased the old decommissioned public library from the city for a dollar and planned to have it remodeled as the Baylor Plaza Park sales and conference center. The scale model would show how the homes and businesses would be intermingled in the trees and vegetation in the park. Everything would be low rise, allowing him and Isaac to save both the community center and their apartment building.

Since Isaac was doing mostly catering, he hadn't spent a lot of personal time on the retail side of the business. Nevertheless, the bakery, ice cream parlor, and new coffee bar were flourishing, particularly because his breads, cakes, pies and other pastries were of higher quality than his competitors in the chain store markets.

Thanks to Isaac's lady, Carla Allen, he had eight competent and eager employees, not counting his niece, Simone, and nephew, Cole, who were eager to work part of their summer days in Greenfield Brothers, bussing tables and sweeping up. The kids had only been back from vacation with their grandparents a few days, but already they fit right in to the routine.

Down the road, he and Isaac picked an ideal new Greenfield Brothers location that would expand nicely to accommodate a soul food restaurant with an art gallery featuring themes from the fifties, sixties, and seventies. They were looking at other locations in the city for their unique combination shop, art gallery, and soul food restaurant. Anacostia and Georgetown were their target locations for now. They were also thinking about somewhere in southwest near the Washington Nationals baseball stadium.

Wesley wanted a legacy to pass on to his kids as his father and grandfather did for him and Isaac.

His household was up early every morning, but at Rosalyn's insistence, they all sat down to breakfast with no distractions, except to discuss their plans for the day. Daniel and Etta claimed their grandparents' rights, took charge of feeding Elizabeth her six A.M. bottle, and started breakfast preparation, while Wesley and Rosalyn spent some quality time of their own in the shower together before they dressed for the day.

Cole and Marcus loved their new, completed, spacious, attic space. They each had their own bedrooms with walk-in closets, built-in drawers, and shoe racks. A Jack-and-Jill bath connected the two bedrooms, but each had a private lavatory and shared a stand-up shower and whirlpool tub. They had arranged pictures they had taken while on vacation around their community area where they kept their books, computer, and flat screen.

Wesley knew that losing Jakima was still hard for the children, but they were resilient and acclimating to their new home and family. It was less than a year since he took responsibility for Cole, Marcus, and Simone, but he didn't regret one minute of his decision. Especially since that decision brought Rosalyn and Elizabeth Etta into his life. He had other challenges ahead, but with his family and his friends at his back, his future looked bright.

Rosalyn wondered what Wesley was thinking about. He and JRock were talking, while Wesley grilled. She was talking with Mrs. Lewis and Kelley Baylor particularly about Buddy's progress and recovery from being shot several times in the shoulder while in Afghanistan. He decided to take his medical discharge and come home.

At Buddy's and Mrs. Lewis' insistence, Roscoe and Francine agreed to continue living in Mrs. Lewis' home. There was still more than enough space for all of them. Roscoe was enrolled at the University of the District of Columbia for the summer and planned to continue through the year to complete his degree.

With the help of Baylor Design, before Buddy was discharged and came home, he had his grandmother's walkout basement converted into a fully-equipped, two-bedroom, two-and-a-half bath apartment.

Mrs. Lewis loved having them all in the house, especially now that Francine was near term on her pregnancy. Still, Roscoe and Francine were planning to buy one of the new container homes that would have four bedrooms and three and a half baths. It would be within walking distance of the community center. The medical practice where Francine worked as a registered nurse wanted to open a new office in the new Baylor Plaza Park community. Francine would manage that office which meant she would be within walking distance of her home. Their child would be in Roscoe's childcare facility at the community center he now headed. They agreed to stay with the Lewis' for a while longer until their new home was completed. The section they wanted to live in and the style of home they wanted was more than a year away from completion, though, so they would save toward furnishing their first home in the new Baylor Plaza Park.

Buddy already applied to Howard University to work on getting his master's degree. Mrs. Lewis was beside herself with joy about having her grandson home permanently.

Rosalyn looked up again to find Wesley watching her with a rather serene expression on his handsome face. She smiled at her husband, as she continued to nurse their daughter.

"It's good you and Wesley named this little golden nugget after his mama. Elizabeth was a good woman and she loved her man fiercely," said Mrs. Lewis. "She and I taught in the same school. She would be proud of how her boys turned out."

"Even though I never met her, I think so, too. My parents knew her. They say she had Wesley's and Isaac's golden-colored eyes and buttermilk-biscuit brown complexion."

"Just like this little angel. Elizabeth Greenfield was a tall shapely woman. She turned plenty of heads in her day. Even my boy, Buddy's daddy, thought she was something else, but Isaac Senior was no slouch either. He was a pretty man like his daddy, Jeremiah, before him and his sons. Though Isaac and Wesley have more of an edge to them than their daddy did, more like their granddaddy. He was a strapping man," Mrs. Lewis, said, smiling coyly. "Jeremiah Greenfield turned plenty heads in his day, too."

"Yours, too, it seemed," Rosalyn said, smiling impishly.

"We stepped out a few times together, yes, before I married, but my Michael was as solid and dependable as they come. He was handsome, too, but he had eyes only for me. Jeremiah had eyes for a lot of women and them for him. Your daddy, too, Kelley. John Baylor was a big, tall man with muscles that were so thick he could crack walnuts in the crook of his arm."

Kelley and Rosalyn laughed.

"You knew them all, didn't you, Mrs. Lewis?"

"Knew 'em, and taught them their numbers. Most of them, that old school crew, married neighborhood girls. Mostly the ones that went away to college, like Isaac Senior, married girls they met in college like your daddy did, Rosalyn. Your daddy met Etta Mae at Howard University. He done well picking her, too. She comes from good people who taught her well in North Carolina."

"I don't remember my grandparents," said Roz.

"They were old folks already when your momma was born late in their lives. They never thought they would have a child. I only met them one time when they came north when you were born. They were married for sixty-eight years and died within three months of each other. Your mama was an only child, and had to take care of everything about their estates, but just like now your daddy was your momma's best friend. They opened that dentist office together and worked side-by-side all their lives. They're like two peas in a pod."

"They're enjoying their lives now. They love to travel in that big RV of theirs. Now they've got their grandchildren hooked on RVing," said Roz.

"I've seen a lot in my time and, Lord willing, I'll see my Buddy married to a good woman before I finally close my eyes, but this little bit of sunshine here," Mrs. Lewis said, patting Elizabeth's feet as she slept, "is a happy addition to this next generation. Now, I still got to get you, Kelley Baylor, married off, but you work so long and hard with that brother of yours, JRock, you don't have time to find a man," she huffed. "However, now my Buddy is home—"

"Oh, no you don't, Mrs. Lewis. Buddy is like a brother to me and I'm older than he is. Don't worry. I date plenty of available men. When or if I want to marry, I will. Buddy is a handsome man and a good one. He'll find someone special when he's ready."

What Rosalyn, Kelley, and all of Wesley's crew knew was that Marine Corp Captain Byron "Buddy" Lewis was gay. His grandmother didn't know and as in his military life "Don't Ask, Don't Tell" had been in effect. For Mrs. Lewis, there would be no granddaughter-in-law, or great grandchildren, Rosalyn mused, as she looked down at her sleeping daughter. By silent agreement, Wesley and Buddy's crew would never divulge what they knew about Buddy to his grandmother. They just shared their lives and children with the senior citizen who was one of the neighborhood treasures.

Chapter 22

"It's good to see you, Vivian," Rosalyn said, as she and Wesley entered Vivian's plush, yet comfortable, law office in the Georgetown section of northwest Washington, DC.

"I'm glad to see both of you, too. I wish I could have come by your home to see your new daughter and the other children, but my schedule since I got back from my families' Fourth of July reunion has been tight."

"You said you had news related to Jakima?" Wesley asked, getting directly to the point.

"Yes." They sat down in the lounge area of her spacious office. "First, I have papers for your signature regarding Cole's, Marcus', and Simone's trust accounts. The insurance company paid the accident claim and, since I had your Power of Attorney, I accepted their settlement offer. It was in line with precedent cases for this amount for each child," she said, handing a copy of the settlement agreement to both of them.

"Wow!" Rosalyn said, surprised. "If Howard Gardner saw this he'd be singing a different tune about the children."

Wesley whistled. "That much?" he asked. "That's a fortune."

"It should take care of them for the rest of their lives."

"I'll say," Rosalyn said. "What do we tell them about this, Wes?"

"I'm not sure I want to tell them anything about this yet."

"I agree with you," Vivian said. "It's a lot to comprehend for children at their ages. For now, I've deposited the funds in their trust accounts. You'll have access to it for whatever you deem appropriate."

"We're able to take care of them," Wesley said. "Since I took JRock's job as PM for Baylor Plaza Park, Roz and I shouldn't need to touch this money."

"That's fine. The money will draw interest and each year my accounting department will provide documentation of the status of each account."

"Vivian," Rosalyn said, reluctantly, "I don't mean to pry, but you must have had to deal with this with your own children and your extraordinary wealth. How do you handle it?"

Vivian laughed. "I let them see what things cost. Money isn't an issue for me or my children, but they don't live in a bubble where expenses are concerned. We hold family meetings to pay the bills and plan for expenses. We work within a set budget. They don't receive an allowance. Although we have live-in domestic household staff, I've established chores and associated a dollar amount to the satisfactory completion of each task. They can make as much pocket money as they like. The dirty jobs, like cleaning the bathrooms, get higher amounts. They clean their rooms, but don't get paid for it. They may have to pay a penalty if their rooms aren't neat and clean by Saturday noon, though," she said, laughing. "Needless to say, the penalty jar is often empty."

"That's certainly creative. What do they spend their money on?"

"Usually each other for birthday or Christmas presents. They make cards for other family members—their grandparents, aunts, uncles, cousins—and we have a lot of family. They know they're wealthy, but I try not to let it adversely influence them.

For example, they voted to donate those gifts to your center out of their own funds and I matched what they gave. Then they spent time deciding what to buy based on their budget. Of course, every chance I give them, they drag me to your community center and play with the gifts they gave," she said, smiling.

"They're great kids, Vivian. You've got to be very proud of them."

"I am, but I'm equally proud of how they handle their health challenges. They work hard in school, too, just as I understand your children do."

"They do, but they always have worked hard even when Jakima was alive. They didn't have anything else to do with their time. Jakima was younger than us and she liked to party all the time. She was barely at home, so they had to, pretty much, take care of themselves. Mostly, Cole took care of Marcus and Simone."

"Now they have you two as their primary support system, your parents as the secondary support system, and Isaac as the extended family they needed to sustain them."

"That's true and I think they appreciate what they have now. We'll just have to figure out how to introduce this new wealth to them as they grow older."

"Along those lines, you may have to introduce Cole to a potential family member. The DNA test came back to a match with a man who was a police officer for five years at the One Four Precinct. He later enlisted in the Marine Corps and died in Afghanistan two years ago. His name was Brenton "Brent" Cooper. He was born on a farm outside of Pittsburgh, Pennsylvania. His parents are deceased, but he has a sister, Alberta Cooper. He never married. I've seen a picture of Brent and Alberta. They both have red hair and blue eyes. She isn't married, but she and her brother have aunts, uncles, and cousins from both sides of her family. She owns a highly productive farm that's been in her father's family for many generations.

"Social Services informed her about her brother's paternity and she wants to meet Cole. She says her brother didn't like farming or living in the rural area outside of Pittsburgh. He liked the city and moved to DC to become a cop. My investigators showed a picture of Brenton to some of the officers at the One Four and to people at the North East Diner where they hang out and where Jakima used to work. Several recognized him and said he and Jakima were definitely lovers for a while, approximately ten years ago."

Wesley and Rosalyn were holding hands, concern masking their faces. "Why does she want to meet Cole?"

"I don't know, but don't start worrying she'll want custody of him. Still, I don't see any reason to avoid them meeting. You should prepare him for this, though. Tell him about his biological father, who he was and what he did. This may be pretty hard on him, coming on the heels of finding out about Jakima last year and his grandmother before that. You can try to control some of his anxiety by letting his aunt meet him in familiar surroundings where he's comfortable and feels safe.

"Ms. Cooper has been informed that Cole didn't know anything about his biological father. She wants to fill in some of that information for him; show him pictures and give him some background about who he came from."

"I suppose we could invite her to come for a visit," Rosalyn said tentatively, looking into Wesley's worried expression for support.

"What can we do if she wants custody?"

"Wesley, I can't predict what might happen in a court action, but I would do everything I can to insure you and Roz retain custody of Cole. A judge would likely be unwilling to separate

Cole from a stable home environment in favor of a place he's unfamiliar with or with someone he hasn't had a relationship with. Still, what a judge might do is grant visitation rights to Ms. Cooper, if she wants them.

"However, we're getting ahead of ourselves. At this moment, we don't know what Ms. Cooper's intentions are beyond what she told Social Services. I've got my investigators working to determine her character, so we will be prepared regardless of what we have to face."

"Okay. Give us a day or two to talk with Cole, and then we'll let you contact Ms. Cooper to arrange for her to come to meet him and us. Also we want you to start billing us for your services and for that of your investigators. This work you're doing for us is costly. Certainly more than the dollar I paid you."

"Are you trying to screw up my tax return? This is *pro bono* work for me and I get a really good return on my investment. We get great pastries whenever we want. Just ask my children, if you don't believe me. Since I can't cook, they love to come to the center or your home to eat and Greenfield Brothers for dessert," she said, laughing.

***

"So, she wants to meet you," Wesley finished.

They were gathered in the family room with Cole sitting between Wesley and Rosalyn. Marcus was sitting next to Etta Hunter, while Simone sat on Daniel's lap with her head on his shoulder.

"You'll still be my adopted father, right?" Cole worriedly asked Wesley. "Because we had that adoption ceremony and everything. I adopted you as my father and you adopted me as your son."

"Yes, that's right, Cole. You are now Coltrane Cooper Greenfield. You're my son no matter what and Rosalyn is your adopted mother."

"Okay, if she just wants to come and meet me then she can, but I don't want to go live with her."

"That's fine. I'll tell Ms. Vivian it is okay with you that Ms. Cooper comes here to our home to meet you."

"Can we . . . I mean, may Marcus, Simone, and I go play downstairs now?"

"Yes, you may," Wesley said and ran his hand over Cole's head and shoulder before the children got up to go downstairs.

"You handled that well, son," Daniel said, when the children were out of earshot.

"You did," Etta said, nodding in agreement.

Rosalyn moved closer to Wesley, laying her head on his shoulder. "He's had so much to contend with in such a short time and he's only nine years old."

"He'll be ten in September and in October it will be a year since Jakima died."

"Well, I'm not leaving until I know what this aunt is about," said Daniel with Etta's agreement. "I'll not have someone come in and take my grandson away no matter whom she is," he huffed.

"You're welcome to stay as long as you like, but we don't want you to miss your golf tournament," said Rosalyn.

"Psshaw!" Etta scoffed. "This is more important than any golf tournament. Plus, I haven't collected all of my kisses from Eliza's sweet cheeks yet."

They all laughed at Etta's obvious affection for her grandchild.

***

"Mr. Greenfield?" asked the woman with bright red hair and startling blue eyes.

"Yes, please come in. You must be Ms. Cooper."

"I am, yes. Thank you for letting me come."

"You're welcome. This is my wife."

Rosalyn extended her hand. "It's a pleasure to meet you, Ms. Cooper."

"Please, could you just call me Alberta?"

"Yes, that's fine. I'm Wesley and my wife is Rosalyn."

"You have such a lovely home."

"Thank you. If you'll follow me to the family room, I'd like to introduce you to my parents."

"Is Coltrane here?"

"Yes, he's downstairs with his younger brother and sister. We call him Cole. That's what he prefers," Wes said, leading her into the family room where Daniel and Etta sat playing with one-month-old Elizabeth.

"Oh, what a beautiful baby!" Alberta exclaimed.

"This is our daughter, Elizabeth Etta, and these are her grandparents, Daniel and Etta Hunter."

Daniel stood with the baby in his arms, proudly showing off his granddaughter.

Rosalyn slipped downstairs to gather the children. When they came up to the family room, Alberta stood and stared at Cole.

"Hello, Cole," she said, her voice full of emotion. "I'm Alberta Cooper, your aunt."

"Hi," Cole said and stepped forward to offer his hand, as Wesley and Rosalyn had taught him to do. Then he turned to Marcus and then Simone to introduce both of them.

"It's a pleasure to meet you, Marcus, and you, too, Simone," she said, but her eyes immediately returned to Cole.

"Why don't you have a seat, Alberta?" Rosalyn offered.

"Thank you," she said, still looking at Cole who sat on a sofa between Rosalyn and Wesley. "I understand you have a birthday coming up, Cole. You'll be ten years old. I have a picture of my little brother when he was ten. May I show it to you?"

Cole first looked to Rosalyn for permission before shrugging in agreement. At her nod of consent, he said, "Sure."

Alberta reached into a tote bag she carried and brought out the picture.

Cole stepped forward to take it and then sat back down between Rosalyn and Wesley. "He looks like me, but he was white?"

"Yes, he looked just like you, except your hair is darker and curly and your complexion is tan. You have hazel-colored eyes instead of blue. His name was Brenton Aaron Cooper, but we called him Brent. Brenton was our mother's, your grandmother's, maiden name. When he was a little boy, Brent liked to play outside in the hot summer sun. His skin would look like a boiled lobster and his skin would burn more brown than yours," she said, laughing with moist eyes. Her smile faltered at the memory and a tear fell down her right cheek. She batted the tear away and took a deep breath. "I promised myself I would not cry, so please forgive me."

"It's okay," Cole said. "My mother died, too."

"That's what I hear. Would you tell me about her?"

They sat for over an hour talking, the conversation becoming easier as time passed.

"Alberta, I hope you'll join us for dinner." Rosalyn said.

"I don't want to impose, but I admit the delicious smells coming from your kitchen have my mouth watering."

"There's no imposition. My husband is an excellent chef and he always has our mouths watering."

Later, after dinner, Rosalyn sat on the deck holding Elizabeth with Etta and Alberta watching Daniel, Wesley, and the children playing in the backyard swimming pool. They chatted amicably and then Alberta quieted.

"Rosalyn, I have to admit I was surprised when Social Services contacted me to tell me Brent had a son. At first, I didn't believe it because Brent never mentioned fathering a child and he would have because we were very close. I thought someone made a mistake or was just claiming paternity because they wanted a part of what was his. I didn't know what to expect when someone as famous as Vivian Alexander Jackson invited me to meet with all of you and Cole.

"I look at him and know, without question, he is my brother's son, my nephew, and I want to take him in my arms and hug him tight. I know it's too soon for that. He's a very perceptive child, but he's not ready to trust me yet. I didn't..." she faltered. "I thought I was alone. I have relatives, but we're not close."

She hesitated, seeming to have a war with herself. "I usually don't tell people this and I hope you aren't offended, especially you, Mrs. Hunter, but I'm, um, a lesbian. Although I haven't been in a relationship in many years, my orientation is an affront to my aunts, uncles, and cousins and their puritanical ways. It offended my parents, too, but not Brent. He was okay with who I am.

"However, my relatives are a narrow-minded group who won't be inclined to welcome Cole into the family because he's part Black. I don't care about them or what they think. I've lived independent of them for most of my life. What is important is what Cole thinks and what you and your family think. If you'll let me, I want to get to know my nephew and all of you. Do you think that we can do that despite my inclination?"

"I know we can, Alberta. Your being a lesbian isn't an issue for us. My husband and I will have to work with our children to teach them about the meaning of being gay. It's not something we have focused on, but we will."

"This doesn't offend me, either," said Etta. "My husband and I are from a different generation than you young people, but it's not like being gay or lesbian is a new fad or some silliness like that. From what I understand, it's not a choice. You are born with a romantic 'inclination,' as you put it, toward people of the same sex. There are millions of people in the world of all nationalities who gravitate toward people of the same sex for intimate relationships."

Alberta released a deep breath. "Thank you, Mrs. Hunter, for your understanding, and you, too, Rosalyn. I would like it if you would bring Cole to the farm for a visit. After all, the homestead is part of Cole's legacy. Now I know he is my nephew, I plan to put his name on the property as Brent's heir and mine, too. You should tell Ms. Jackson that Cole is entitled to certain military benefits, also. I'll send the paperwork about the farm to her and to you, also. If your attorney hasn't already done so, I want her to set up a trust account to receive profits from the farm for Cole."

"Thank you, Alberta. Ms. Jackson has already established a trust account for Cole. You may deal directly with her about any financial arrangements you want to make, but you really don't have to worry about that. My husband and I are financially able to care for the children. I'll talk with him and the children about coming to visit your farm and let you know."

"Yes, I'm sure that you are, but Cole is entitled to inherit from his father's family, too, so I would appreciate it if you'd let me do this for him."

"That's fine. I'll tell Vivian what you've said. You're not going back to Pennsylvania tonight, are you?"

"No, I thought I'd find a motel and go back tomorrow. I've never been to Washington before. Would you recommend someplace to stay?"

"Yes, you're welcome to stay here."

Alberta shook her head. "You've already been so gracious."

"If you can, stay here with us for a few more days. It will give you more time to spend with Cole."

A tear leaked down her cheek. "Thank you."

***

"So, I guess I have to put a weekend trip on my schedule," Wesley said, snuggling Rosalyn against his sated body, after having mind-blowing sex with his wife.

"Maybe more than one."

"Oh?"

"Vivian and JRock want me to look at the school system in Summer County, South Carolina."

"Why?"

"Dr. Bernard Alexander, Vivian's father, is the former Dean of the Summer County Academy. The county's school system has a unique program that's producing exciting results. They are open year-round and the students take only one class all day for six weeks. Then they're out of class for two weeks. When they come back, they take another class for six weeks."

"That does sound different."

"It is and they have a nearly perfect attendance record across all age groups. Their test scores are higher as compared nationally and they incorporate junior college curriculums as well as trade schools in their academic program. JRock wants my opinion on whether we can institute that type of program here in the Baylor Plaza Park schools. If so, he and Vivian want to fund a new school system. They believe inner city school students will benefit from a new approach to education. They've asked me to head it up.

They are prepared to allocate space for a new campus that will accommodate preschool through two years of college. Essentially, to mimic what Dr. Alexander has done with the Summer County school system. It would be called Baylor Park Academy."

"You sound excited by the prospect of designing a new system."

"I am, but I want this system to be able to compete on a global basis. Not just compete against other American school districts. America is so far behind globally, our students are at a competitive disadvantage in the new world economy. We spend more resources per child and achieve less for our educational dollars than other countries with fewer resources. If JRock and Vivian are going to fund a new school system that I'm to head, I want to change that dynamic."

"If anyone can do it, you can, babe. When do you want to go?"

"I'll talk with Vivian and see what she suggests. Maybe we can take a few days to go to the beach?"

"Okay, just how much time am I taking off?" he asked, laughing.

She smiled at him, running her hand up and down his body. "Oh, maybe seven to ten days total."

"Babe," he sighed, "I need to stay on top of what's going on at the job site." He grunted when she latched on to his still sensitive penis, massaging him aggressively.

"The only thing you *have* to stay on top of is me."

Then she kissed him and everything else left his conscious thoughts.

Chapter 23

"That sounds like it's running smoothly," Wesley commented to Isaac after he shut off the motor of their father's old T-Bird.

"It's ready for the road," Isaac said while toweling off the sweat on his face and neck.

It was another hot, muggy August day. Isaac and Wesley were in a rent-by-the-day garage space with only a ceiling fan circulating the moist air. They were putting the finishing touches on their father's car. Isaac grabbed a couple of ice cold bottles of water from a Styrofoam cooler chocked full of ice and passed one to Wesley. They both took long swallows, nearly downing all in one gulp.

"I, uh, wanted to talk with you about something," Isaac said, tentatively.

Wesley shrugged. "Sure, what is it?"

"It's about Carla."

"I haven't seen her lately. Is something wrong between you two?"

"I, uh, well, I haven't . . . Oh, hell. She gave me an ultimatum."

Wesley's brows bunched. "*O-kay*? What for?"

"She wants to sleep with me."

Wesley stared at his older brother while he downed the last of his water. Then he leaned both hands on the car, dropped his head between his massive shoulders, and shook it. He looked up, frowning. "What? You're telling me that in the last seven plus months since you've been seeing Carla, you haven't slept with her?" Then he stood, arms folded across his chest, and his expression changed. "Are you trying to tell me that, like Buddy, you're gay? I mean, it's not a problem for me or the crew if you are—"

"Hell, Wes! I'm not gay. I just . . ." He struggled, with anguish written on his face. "It's been years since I was with a woman. A woman like Carla Allen deserves better than me. I'm a convicted felon just out of the joint. I'm getting my shit together with the catering and Greenfield Brothers. You were right. People are really into that coffee shop and teahouse thing. They are standing out the door at six in the morning for coffee or tea and a hot bun. The way things are going, I'm giving Dunkin' Donuts and Starbucks heartburn. I'm making a good profit, too, with my cakes and pies. The store is running good for bread, rolls, and biscuits for area restaurants. I'm gonna hire two more people because we're doing so good."

"What do you mean by 'better than you'? Cut the crap, Isaac. You're stalling. What's the deal?"

"I want my self-respect back before I step to someone like Carla. I don't want to start something that I can't finish."

"Why wouldn't you be able to finish?"

"I don't want to just screw around because it's there. I want to have a relationship that's going somewhere. I want a relationship like what you and Roz have; like Roscoe and Francine. Someone who's going to be in my corner and have my back like Roz does with you."

"Roz and I didn't start out planning a relationship together. She was sleeping with someone else and I was sleeping with LaKesha Reynolds for five years until a few weeks before I moved in to Roz's home. The only plan Roz and I had was to protect Cole, Marcus, and Simone from getting snatched by Social Services. Though I wouldn't change anything that happened, Elizabeth was a result of equipment failure the first time I slept in Roz's bed. What we have now grew out of our mutual need to keep the kids, particularly after we found out about Jakima's death. Now, Roz and I work every day to lay a foundation that wasn't there when we started out."

"I thought you two must have been together for years to get to where you are now."

"Months, Isaac, less than a year. We got married because Roz was pregnant with Elizabeth. I didn't want rumors out that Roz was just my baby mama. If we were going to be sleeping together, I didn't want anyone to disrespect her or my child because of me. I didn't realize it was more than respect I felt for her until the day I held Elizabeth in my arms for the first time. Roz and I married long before I knew I was in love with her. I was living with Kesha and, as you know, I was sleeping with her off and on since junior high school. Yet, in all of that time, I never felt for her anything like what I feel for Rosalyn. In so many ways, Rosalyn is my dream come true. She completes me."

"She's prime. That's for sure. She's got Cole, Marcus, and Simone talking and acting like you see on TV. Like Vivian's kids talk and act," said Isaac.

"I had to step up my game, too, because of her, the kids, and being around JRock in business meetings with these big-time, money people. I feel you though when you say you don't just want to screw around. If Carla's not it for you, then next."

"She is. I mean she makes me step up my game, too. She knows about me being incarcerated and the reason for it. She says she doesn't care about that. I want to build a relationship with her, but I don't want to move too fast. Plus, I want to be able to bring her to a nice place. I haven't done anything to the apartment since I moved in. I really just haven't had time. I want to spruce the place up. In fact, all of the units could stand a makeover and updating. Would you be willing to go in together and remodel the apartments in the building?"

"Yes, I would. We could talk with JRock about contracting his company to do the remodel."

"They did a great job for a reasonable rate on that huge attic space for Cole and Marcus. It doesn't even look or feel like an attic. So that's a lock for me on using them for this job. I like what Roz did at y'alls place. Do you think she could give me a hand with decorating my space once it's remodeled?"

"She's got a good sense of style. Ask her, but what about Carla? If she's what you want, don't you think she would like to help you decorate?"

"Maybe, but I want to think about her ultimatum. I learned to control my sex drive while I was incarcerated. I won't be pushed into something until I know what I want from her and what she wants from me."

"Good idea. She'll just have to understand only good things come to those who wait," he said, laughing. "Seven damn months? Really? Man, I'd have tapped that hard by now! I can't go for more than seven hours before I need to be with my wife."

***

Wesley signed the contract, then the check, and handed both to JRock's assistant. "When will you get started?"

"For you and Isaac, I'll put a team on it the first of next week. You've got, what twelve units in that building? If we can throw enough people at it while they're not on other job sites, we should be able to knock out the whole building in six to seven weeks. The problem is going to be in getting your tenants packed and moved out for a few weeks while each unit is renovated," JRock said before he leaned forward and rubbed his face vigorously, as if frustrated.

Wesley noticed. "Isaac and I put together a schedule that should take care of it." He hesitated before he asked, "What's up with you, man? You seem . . . I don't know, out of it or something. You haven't seemed yourself since you met with that big guy from Texas, that Jake Hawkins character."

JRock shrugged and then stood up, looking out of the French doors to a view of his backyard, swimming pool, and his yacht docked in the marina. He dug his hands into his pockets. "I guess you heard that Vivian and Chuck Montgomery are getting married."

"Yeah, Roz and I got an invitation. We plan to go to see the school system in Summer County, South Carolina, anyway, so this fits right in. Are you going?"

"Yeah, I am. Chuck asked me to be his best man."

"You don't sound happy about this. Did you and Vivian have something going on? I know she's your lawyer and that you two work together on some of your projects. She took you to the hoop at the Three-Point Shootout Tournament. I see why she is an Olympic Gold Medalist. She hit every one of those three-pointers. Pure net! That woman can ball! Was there something more between you?"

"No, nothing like that. Vivian is like a sister to me. Both her first husband and Chuck and I have been good friends since our days in the NBA. I love her, but not in the way you mean."

"Okay, if not that, then what's up?"

"JaiHonnah. Vivian told me she's going to be in the wedding, too, in case I wanted to back out. I was tempted not to go, but I couldn't do that to Chuck or to Vivian. I agreed to take Chuck and his groomsmen for a sail on *The Navajo Princess* down to Atlantic Beach, South Carolina, on a booze cruise and to do some deep-sea fishing along the way. The groomsmen will have ten days to two weeks before the wedding to make the trip and then stay at Vivian's great grandaunt's home on the beach. Then we'll drive to Vivian's family's compound a few days before the wedding.

"That Texan who bulldozed his way into our meeting, Jake Hawkins, is JaiHonnah's father. He picked up a sixty-billion-dollar bank promissory note of mine I had out with another financier. He told me he's calling the note due in sixty days or, if I promise to stay away from JaiHonnah, he'd destroy the note and I'd owe him nothing."

Wesley smirked. "Jai's father, huh? The man's got big, brass ones. I'll give him that. He bogarted his way up in here on your turf? Not a smart move. So are you worried about seeing JaiHonnah again?"

"You heard?" he said. "I'm still in love with her, Ice. No way in hell I'll stay away from her, but if she shows up with her husband, I don't know whether I can cope with seeing them together."

"I haven't seen you this hung up on a woman since you were bent over Rosalyn back in high school. You weren't even this hyped up over your ex-wife."

JRock turned from the backyard view and walked to the front of his desk, leaning his butt against the edge, facing Wesley. "You made the last year of high school, particularly the prom, a good memory for me. I didn't have two dimes to rub together back then. I spent all of my time studying and playing ball. I played on Boys and Girls Club teams every summer and never even held a part-time job. My parents had four children in college at the same time. They didn't have any extra to pay for all those senior high school perks for me—trip to the Bahamas, the prom with new clothes and shoes, class pictures, class ring. My father worked two, full-time jobs and my mother worked a full-time job, and all the overtime she could get at the post office. Still none of that was in their budget, but you spent the money you earned working in your father's store to make sure I got to do everything that everyone else got to do that last year of high school. You even sent money to me while I was in college. Then, when I signed my first professional NBA contract, you wouldn't let me pay you back. You still won't accept anything from me, except gifts for the center."

"It wasn't about the money back in the day and it's not now. We were boyz, JRock. Together since we started crawling. I couldn't do all those things without you, Peck, Little T, Slide, Dog, Screw, Buddy, and Isaac. We're still boyz because the struggle to save our hood continues. So, get that gratitude stuff off your back. Besides, quiet as it's kept, my father paid for the trip to the Bahamas for us and two others, and Isaac paid for the rental car we used to go to the prom. I know Bubbles and Billie Bouchard, Mrs. Lewis, and others put into the pot, too, to make sure that everybody got to enjoy our last year of high school. Now, look at what you're doing to honor what our parents did for us and the community.

"If it weren't for you and JaiHonnah, none of this would be happening. She's still submitting good ideas, even though she doesn't work for you anymore. What do you think that's about? Kelley said your girls call JaiHonnah every day to talk with her. Five-year-olds don't know how to get it wrong yet. I know these things. I'm an expert. I've got a five-year-old daughter. So, if for no other reason, tell her daddy to stick it where the sun don't shine. Then go to Vivian and Chuck's wedding to say thank you to Jai, up close and personal, for helping with the struggle."

Chapter 24

It was seven days before Vivian's wedding to former basketball icon, seven-foot-tall, Charles Patrick Montgomery, a Johnny Depp look alike, known in the sports world as Chucky P, another multi-billionaire. He was now an Emergency Room doctor at Georgetown Medical Center in Washington, DC. He was also building a practice and a hospital outside of Washington in a nearby, rural area of Prince George's County, Maryland.

Wesley, Rosalyn, and their children drove to Charlotte, North Carolina, a few days earlier in time to see Daniel and Etta play in a seniors' golf tournament and stay at their home for the weekend. They were now on the road again headed to Summer County, South Carolina, for Chuck and Vivian's wedding, and to evaluate the school system. They were driving Daniel and Etta's spacious RV that slept six comfortably and could accommodate more in a pinch.

Charlotte to Summer County wasn't a long ride. Nevertheless, the kids got a big kick out of riding up high in the RV and having a panoramic view out of the huge front and side windows. Wesley had to admit, if only to himself, he enjoyed it, too. He and Rosalyn were thinking about taking more family getaways in a mobile home of their own. Cole was riding shotgun with Wesley driving, while Rosalyn, Marcus, and Simone played a board game at the dining table. The nearly two-month-old Elizabeth was awake, cooing at everyone, including her own hand, as she sat strapped into her padded and secure travel chair.

They left Charlotte early that morning after breakfast, with a promise to come back and visit longer with Daniel, Etta, and their circle of retired friends and neighbors. Wesley was listening to Cole's excited chatter about the junior space cadet's program Rosalyn found at the National Aeronautics and Space Administration's facility in Prince George's County, Maryland. She enrolled Cole in the program as an extra curriculum activity for after school and/or weekend programs. She also found a dance class for Simone at the Duke Ellington School in downtown Washington, DC. Marcus was just happy to go to the construction office each day to work with Wesley at the community center and sit in on site planning sessions. Rosalyn also arranged for all three children to take martial arts classes and swimming lessons.

That brought back pleasant memories for Wesley of his father teaching him and Isaac how to swim when they weren't much older than Cole and Marcus. With the children around, he was beginning to remember good things about his own childhood with his father and Isaac, not just the bad things that changed his life.

Wesley found it cathartic to drive the long distances on the open road away from the city because it allowed him to spend quality time talking with each of his children, his wife, and just having time to think. Although Wesley didn't often drive a car, they now had a larger SUV to accommodate their growing family. It was tethered to the back of the RV on transit wheels.

He marveled at the fact that less than a year ago he was the head of a struggling community center and shacking with LaKesha Reynolds in a sparsely furnished, one-bedroom apartment and calling that existence a life. Now he was heading a multibillion-dollar city design, development, and construction project, employing and training hundreds of people and married to Dr. Rosalyn Amelia Hunter with four wonderful children.

Problems he struggled with for more than ten years, like funds for his community center's growth and development, were no longer an issue. He was able to up salaries and pay his crew amounts equal to what their tasks deserved. Though the center maintained its not-for-profit status, word was spreading about the Baylor Plaza Park project and the influx of donations allowed them to do more projects and activities. What Baylor Design and Development paid to lease space in his community center building alone more than compensated for all costs associated with operating a multifaceted facility. They also had more volunteers in every aspect of their operation, further reducing their operating costs. They actually now had surplus funds at the end of their budget year. They would actually start the new fiscal year on October 1 with a huge plus on their balance sheet.

As more of the old, run down, dilapidated neighborhood disappeared and the land reclaimed for the new Baylor Plaza Park Project, excitement continued to build for the future. Wesley felt good about his role in what was taking place and in his new family's life.

"In one mile, turn right at Goodwill Lane," the disembodied voice of the GPS system announced. *"Your destination is one mile ahead on your right."*

Wesley slowed the RV on the narrow, rural road and marveled at the beauty that surrounded them. A bunch of tall, wide, weeping willow, sycamore, oak, and pine trees overhung the road, creating a canopy or cathedral-like corridor. The branches, draped with a gray, ringlet shroud, swayed in the heated breeze. A granite post on both sides of the road read: WELCOME HOME as they entered the small, quaint Town of Goodwill, Summer County, South Carolina, a place where time had not encroached. He loved its simplicity and homey style. It was so much like the designs JaiHonnah produced for Baylor Plaza.

There was a wide, grassy town square separating the roadway to the right and left. Someone wearing a big, straw hat knelt at the edge of freshly turned earth, planting a tray of border flowers, ringing a huge tree. The street was bordered on both sides of the square with colorful, old-fashion, wood-framed shops, a post office, and a wide array of mom-and-pop stores. Flower boxes hung below shop windows and not a sign of security bars anywhere in sight. Shop doors stood open and welcoming. There were gazebos, walkways, benches, and water features cutting through the town square, again overhung by weeping willows, oak and pine trees. It was absolutely picturesque, like something out of a Currier and Ives reproduction. Complete strangers walking on the boarded sidewalks raised a hand in a friendly gesture of acknowledgement and smiled as the RV slowly drove past.

About a mile beyond the town, they were surrounded by well-tended farms, sheltering beautiful and stately homes, the likes of which Wesley never would have expected to see in the rural south. Some of the homes seemed ultra-modern, but still fit comfortably into the wooded landscape, while others ran the gamut straight out of the movie *Gone With The Wind* with large antebellum features.

They pulled the RV to an open gate where people on horseback with iPads were halting a long line of RVs of every type and description. One young woman rode up to the driver's side window, which Wesley opened.

"Good morning," the woman wearing a baseball cap said brightly while steadying her horse. "My name is Nora Benson. Are you here for the Jackson-Montgomery or the Jordon-Dixon wedding?"

"The Jackson-Montgomery wedding. We're the Greenfields, Wesley and Rosalyn," he said. His children were nearly in his lap to get a look at the horse the woman was riding.

"Oh, yes I have you here," she said after consulting her iPad. "Vivian and I are cousins. She arranged for you to stay at Summer County Academy, but since you arrived in an RV, if you'd prefer, you may camp here on the Alexander farm with the rest of the family. We have hook ups for your utilities and even satellite television service. There's no charge. It's your choice."

"Can we, I mean, may we stay on the farm, Dad?" Cole asked. "Ms. Vivian said this is where her children would be."

Wesley's heart nearly burst out of his chest when Cole called him *Dad* instead of Ice for the first time. "Let's ask your mother," he suggested and ran a hand over the boy's fresh haircut. He simply had the need to touch *his son*.

"Mom?" Cole called back toward Rosalyn.

"That's fine with me," she said, her voice full of emotion, too. "I'm very proud of you, Cole, for remembering the correct way to ask a question."

Cole beamed a broad smile at Rosalyn.

"Then I guess we'll be camping," Wesley said to Nora.

"Great!" Nora said. "Just follow the RV ahead of you and take the next available slip. Someone, one of my brothers, probably Bo Benson, will help you with your hook-ups once you're parked. This wedding packet will give you information about the facilities and activities for the week.

"We welcome you and your family to Goodwill, Mr. Greenfield," she said, handing over the thick packet she took from one of her saddlebags. She pulled away, directing her horse to the next RV behind them.

As instructed, Wesley followed the RV ahead of him to a shady spot under tall trees near a park-like enclave with a woodland backdrop and pulled in beside another RV. More mobile homes pulled past and parked as he had under the cover of tall shade trees. There had to be at least a hundred other RVs tucked back on the manicured, golf-course-like grass in the shade. He cut the engine, set the brake, took a deep breath of the pine and honeysuckle-scented air, and just sat a moment in quiet appreciation of the beautiful, picturesque farm. Rosalyn hugged him around the neck and shoulders and cheek-to-cheek shared the scenery outside the huge windshield.

"Mama Roz, make Marcus let me open the wall," Simone fussed.

"You may open one and Marcus may open the other one."

"See! Mama Roz said I can open one, too!" Simone boasted.

The bickering continued until Cole swiveled in his seat from his quiet appreciation of the landscape and said, "Cut the noise. Elizabeth's sleeping."

The noise instantly ceased and both Marcus and Simone, with exaggerated motion, tiptoed to look at their baby sister who was, indeed, asleep.

At the tap on the driver's side door, Wesley stepped out of the RV to help Bo Benson hook up the utilities. While unhooking the SUV from the back, Wesley was surprised to see Vivian and her children standing at the RVs front bumper, talking with Rosalyn. He raised a hand in acknowledgment of her presence, a gesture she and her children returned with infectious smiles.

"Glad to see you made it," Vivian said, with a warm hug and smile for Rosalyn and the children. "What a beautiful RV."

Other RVs were still continuing to pull into available spaces on the grass, as they talked.

"Thank you. It belongs to my parents. This is a gorgeous farm, Vivian. It looks like a park or country club."

"Thank you. It's where my many generations of great grands settled. We'll talk about it more when we're not baking in this hot sun. For now, relax and enjoy. I have instructions from my children to take your children with me and mine while we greet people as they arrive. You may claim your children at lunch over there," she said, pointing to what looked like a big, white circus tent where grills were set up and smoking around picnic tables arranged inside the tent.

"We'll see you there, Vivian, and thank you for the invitation to see the school and to attend your wedding."

"You're welcome on both accounts. You're also welcome to attend my cousin's, Donald Dixon's, wedding to Cecile Jordon. It's on the same day as my and Chuck's wedding," she said and waved goodbye, taking the children with her.

Cole, Marcus, and Simone each hugged and kissed Rosalyn, listened to her instructions about behavior and then waved to their father before they ran to catch up with Vivian's kids.

Rosalyn went inside the blissfully cool RV. The air conditioner was on and since Elizabeth was still sleeping peacefully, Rosalyn stretched out on the king-sized bed for a quick nap. When Wesley entered the RV, he immediately peeled off his damp T-shirt and jeans. At the rear of the RV, he sat on the king-sized bed next to where Rosalyn was napping and began to review the packet of information Nora provided.

There were many events planned for the week leading up to the weddings on Saturday, but there was a special packet of information for Rosalyn involving the Academy and a meeting schedule for her to see the school. There was also an invitation for all of them to have lunch at Vivian's parents' house on Wednesday at noon.

It amazed Wesley that, in the midst of this huge gathering of Vivian's family and friends, she, a high profile, multibillionaire, and attorney, would carve out time for an exclusive social with them. He admired her for her selflessness in adopting health challenged, orphaned children, as well as her kindness to him, Rosalyn, and their children, and for her generosity to Isaac and their community center. He looked forward to meeting her parents. He presumed they had to be extraordinary people to have raised a woman like Vivian Alexander Jackson and a generous businessman like her brother, Kenneth Alexander.

He looked over at his napping wife and was about to have a little private time with her when Elizabeth made her displeasure with an empty stomach and a poopy diaper known. He got up and went to her, automatically shifting from one pretty lady to another. After he changed and fed her, all was right with her world again.

Wesley sat talking with his daughter and marveling at what a beautiful wife he had. Rosalyn wore buckwheat-colored shorts and matching tank top tucked into the waistband over her almost flat tummy. She exercised religiously and the results were evident in her stacked shape from the top of her head to her pink painted toenails. When Elizabeth fell asleep again, Wesley put her to bed in her travel bassinet and returned to pleasure his wife.

Rosalyn woke when a violent orgasm crashed through her system. Her husband lay on his side with his right hand palming his head, a sexy grin on his handsome face, mischief in his beautiful eyes, and his clever left hand inside her shorts and thong between her thighs. She closed her eyes on a long, tortured moan when he put two fingers inside her and began to stroke. It didn't take long for her to climb that pinnacle again and leap into another orgasmic release.

She kept her eyes closed, but reached inside his Jockey's to find him hard, hot, and heavy. One handed, she wiggled out of her shorts and thong while he continued to stroke her. With both hands, she pulled down his briefs while he lifted his torso off the bed. He removed his fingers and replaced them with his penis, moving hard, strong, and slowly in and out of her.

Wesley kissed Rosalyn while he pleasured himself and her. He couldn't put too much of his weight on her upper body, but she locked her legs tightly around him. Her breasts were large and full of milk. She had to pump her breasts several times a day to release the pressure. They had a freezer full of breast milk for Elizabeth. He could get excited just watching her nurse their daughter.

Although Rosalyn was an organized soul, he and the kids became adept at preparing bottles for the baby. For now, he kissed her swollen twins, loving the way they jiggled while he pumped himself in and out of her like a slow-motion jackhammer.

"That felt so good."

"Every time I see you in bed, I think about the first weeks we spent taking care of the kids in my old apartment. When I came in at five in the morning you would pretend to be asleep."

Her eyes widened and her mouth dropped open. "You knew? How?"

"Roz, please." He smirked. "You weren't fooling me. Don't you think I could hear the change in your breathing when I came into the bedroom and took off my clothes?"

"You never said anything."

"Why should I? If you wanted to see me naked, why should I care? Plus, I was too tired at that time of the morning to do anything but sleep."

"Thank goodness you're not too tired now," she said and took him to a place in their euphoria where only consummate lovers played.

***

Freshly showered and dressed in shorts, T-shirts and sandals, Wesley and Rosalyn walked hand-in-hand across the grass from their RV to the tent. Elizabeth was comfortably tucked into a shoulder sling across Wesley's chest.

A crowd was building for lunch. There had to be several hundred people gathered in the surprisingly cool and breezy tent. Overhead huge fans dissipated the heat and circulated cooler air. Tables and chairs were arranged away from the cooking grills, each laden with a variety of meats, vegetables, fruits, and fish. There were so many food stations that there were no people standing in lines to get plates. Wesley and Rosalyn walked around to each station in the connected tents that were easily the length and width of a football field.

Cole, Marcus, and Simone came running, their faces bright with widened smiles of joy.

"We saved you seats over there," Cole said, as he took the diaper bag from Rosalyn's shoulder and Marcus took the lightweight baby stroller from Wesley's hand. Simone burrowed between Wesley and Rosalyn, taking each one's hand to swing between them while they followed Cole and Marcus to their seats. The tables were round and easily sat twelve. There were already two couples seated at the table. They rose and extended their hands as Wesley and Rosalyn approached.

"Hello, I'm Vivian's oldest brother, Kenneth Alexander. This is my wife, JeNelle, our brother, Benjamin Alexander, and his wife, Stacy. You must be the amazing Greenfields, Wesley and Rosalyn."

"Pleased to meet you," Wesley said, as they all shook hands and settled in.

"Amazing?" asked Rosalyn amused. She noted that both of Vivian's brothers were eye candy and their wives very different, but beautiful women.

"According to your children, you two walk on water," Benjamin said, laughing.

"We are mortal regardless of what our offspring say," Rosalyn said, smiling first at her husband and then at the group at large.

"Kenneth, I'm glad to have this opportunity to thank you in person for the computers, flat screens and your generosity in training the kids from our community."

"You're welcome. We've benefited from having them in our training facility. They have worked very hard, long hours all summer and show real promise for computer and software design. We'll be sorry to see them go in a few weeks. We hope you and your community members will let them return next summer. Two of the older teens, who will graduate high school this coming year, we'd like to offer paid internships and admission to our trade school program. We will also help them with scholarships for enrollment in a four-year, California college or university program, if they chose to attend."

"That's great, Kenneth. I don't think we could stop them from wanting to return next year. From all reports, each one of them has thoroughly enjoyed the experience," Rosalyn said. "The internships and scholarships are an added bonus. I'll talk with the two students and their parents about their post high school plans, and have them get in touch with you."

They chatted amicably while they ate the delicious lunch, sampling a wide variety of food from different stations. Wesley learned many of those manning the different grills were actually Alexander family relatives. A set of twins, Donald and James Dixon, truly had a great variety of grilled offerings that tantalized Wesley's taste buds. However, something about Donald Dixon piqued Wesley's curiosity. He sensed Donald had an edge about him Wesley could identify with and appreciate. Something like the way Buddy was now. Wesley though that, like Buddy, Donald Dixon was a warrior.

Strangely enough, he got that same vibe from Stacy Alexander. He learned both Benjamin, Benny to his family and friends, and Stacy were active duty military. Yet something about Stacy, other than her exceptional beauty, screamed danger. Between the two Alexander brothers, there were sixteen children. Kenneth and JeNelle had nine, with three sets of twins and one set of triplets. Benny and Stacy had two sets of triplets and an older daughter, Whitney Ivy. It was obvious with Vivian's crew, the Alexanders believed in large families. The children seemed to be great friends as well as cousins and spent time talking with the Greenfields.

Wesley also learned that the patriarch of the family, Bernard Alexander, was a twin and one of thirteen children in his family. Stacy was also a twin and her grandmother had two sets of triplets. Wesley learned a great deal about their family from them.

An hour later, Wesley and Rosalyn looked up to see JaiHonnah Chapman approaching the table with her tray of food. Everyone stood to greet her.

"It's so good to see you," JaiHonnah said enthusiastically, hugging first Wesley and then Rosalyn before she circled the table to greet Kenneth, Benny, and their wives. She and Vivian were in undergrad together at Spelman College, so she met Vivian's family at college events.

"So you have twin boys?" Rosalyn asked, as she fed Elizabeth.

"Yes, they're a month or so older than this little beauty," JaiHonnah said, smiling at Elizabeth. "You look great, Roz. I understand from Vivian that you and Wesley got married and the custody issues have been settled."

"Thank you, Jai. Yes, we married, but didn't announce it until after the first of the year. All is well in the Greenfield household.

The children are ours now, but Social Services found out Cole does have an aunt," she said and went on to explain the circumstances.

"So she's not going to challenge you for custody?"

"No, but she does want to have a relationship with Cole. We drove up to her farm outside Pittsburgh and stayed the weekend. The children had a really good time on the farm, so we plan to take Cole to visit at least once a quarter and we'll have Alberta come for visits as often as she can manage it. Particularly during holidays, we want to have her join us. Wes thinks once Cole gets use to Alberta, we can let him visit her for longer periods of time over the summer. She agrees with that approach. She doesn't want to force herself on him or make him feel pressured. She also wants all three children to come for visits, not just Cole."

"I can't imagine Wesley letting the children out of his sight for a day. He's so protective of them. This must be your influence to get him to agree."

"We both want to expose the children to all types of positive experiences. Like this trip. This is the first vacation Wes has taken since high school. He has worked all of his life and until we took on Cole, Marcus, and Simone, Wes had never taken time to just enjoy himself. We're heading to the beach once we leave here for a week before we head back to return my parents' RV to Charlotte, North Carolina, and then drive home."

"Exposing them to positive experiences is very important in the early stages. When you're ready to travel abroad let me know. I have homes in Paris, London, Milan, and Madrid."

"Thank you, Jai. I'll certainly do that. I, uh, have to ask, though, are you ever coming back to Washington to live? You're missed there, you know."

She shrugged elegantly, but with a sad expression on her gamine face. "It's not likely. I've decided to stay in Texas for now and not go back to Europe for the time being. I've started taking on architectural and engineering projects. They are mostly small projects for now while my boys are so young."

"Oh, where in Texas?'

"Hawkinstown. It's just outside San Antonio. On one of your family excursions, you should come and bring Wes and the children for a visit and stay at the ranch with me. I'd love to show you around San Antonio and Hawkinstown. Maybe even visit my grandmother on the Navajo Reservation near Ship Rock, New Mexico. The children should really enjoy visiting the Res."

"I'll definitely put that on the family agenda for next year. The children get such a big kick out of traveling in the RV. If it's all right with you, I'd like to bring my parents, too."

"Definitely. We have plenty of room on the ranch."

Rosalyn wanted to, but didn't ask whether the "we" JaiHonnah referred to was her husband.

They continued to chat until an announcement was made that the sports arena and swimming pool were open and the hay wagons were loading for the trip to the Academy.

Teams of horses pulled up to different stations to load passengers on to the hay-filled wagons. The children bundled together in several wagons and sang songs all the way to the school where they unloaded and went inside one of the school buildings that housed sports activities. Most people gravitated to the Olympic-sized pool, while others dispersed to other sports venues like the basketball court and game rooms.

Wesley distributed swimwear and took Cole and Marcus into the men's side of the dressing rooms, while Rosalyn took Simone with her to the women's dressing area. The children splashed around in the shallow end or the kiddy pool while Rosalyn and JaiHonnah looked on from the deck. Wesley stroked the length of the pool with Kenneth, Benjamin, and their children and their youngest brother Gregory, who was more eye candy to Rosalyn's way of thinking.

Their twin cousins, Donald and James Dixon, James Dixon's wife, Janice, and their children and Donald's fiancée, Cecile Jordon and their son, Donald, Junior, joined them. While talking with them, Rosalyn learned Cecile and Janice were friends since their undergrad days at San Diego State University. They both held doctorates—Cecile in oceanography and Janice in biochemistry. Cecile won the Nobel the year before for her work in oceanography and climate change. So best friends were married to twin brothers.

While others swam, Rosalyn, JaiHonnah, JeNelle, Stacy, Cecile, and Janice sat on the pool ledge chatting and keeping an eye on the younger children.

One by one, Cole, Marcus, and Simone rode on Wesley's back as he swam the length of the pool. Then he took them together, teaching them each how to swim. They swam until time to return to the big tent for the evening meal at six.

By eight o'clock, the music began and people were taking to the makeshift hardwood dance floor down the middle of the tent. Every age group's music was represented in sections of the big tent and each had an opportunity to strut their stuff. Cole, Marcus, and Simone had plenty of dance partners with Kenneth's, Benny's, and Vivian's children, and the rest of their extended family.

By ten o'clock, Wesley had to carry a tired Simone in his arms, while Rosalyn carried Elizabeth back to the RV. The children each showered quickly, were tucked into bed, and fast asleep by eleven o'clock.

Wesley pulled Rosalyn into his left side, before kissing her goodnight. They fell asleep to the faint sounds of the party still going strong in the big tents.

Chapter 25

"So the students are in session for six weeks before a break?" Rosalyn confirmed her understanding of the Summer County Academy program. It was nine o'clock on Wednesday morning. Instead of going to the big tent, the Greenfields opted to make breakfast in the RV and have it picnic style on blankets on the grass. Wesley was baking a surprise for Vivian and her family.

By eight o'clock, the thick, moisture laden, summer heat began to rise and Vivian's, Kenneth's, and Benny's children, along with Donald's and James' children came to collect Cole, Marcus, and Simone for a morning full of activities. They would meet at Vivian's parents' home for lunch. Wesley unhitched their SUV and he, Rosalyn, and Elizabeth drove to the Academy, less than two miles from the Alexander farm for a scheduled meeting with Dr. Bernard Alexander, Vivian's father.

"That's right, and they are out for two weeks before sessions begin again," answered Dr. Alexander, who was also the former Dean of the Summer County Academy, presently a state senator. The current Dean, Jefferson Logan, a former US Ambassador, his wife, Dakota, and their five children—three sons and two daughters—were visiting his wife's family in Hawkinstown, Texas. JaiHonnah and Dakota, aka LaiLoni Skai, were sisters, both daughters of the wealthy Jake Hawkins. Dr. Logan and his family would return before Vivian and Chuck's wedding. Ambassador

Logan was also the brother of Dr. Savannah Logan, Rosalyn's OB/GYN. JaiHonnah, LaiLoni Skai, Savannah, and Vivian were all Spelman College alumni.

Dr. Alexander, Wesley, and Rosalyn were walking down a long Academy hallway. Beautiful, huge, hand-painted murals hung on the walls of the buildings they were touring on the college-like campus.

"So, the students master six subjects in a year just as student do in other school districts in compacted nine-month programs. We don't have harsh winters here, so the Academy usually does not have to close for inclement weather."

"That's for more than six hours a day?" asked Wesley.

"Yes, for as much as ten-hour days and sometimes for six days a week, depending on the subject. We found young people have a greater capacity for learning than we sometimes give them credit for, particularly, if they are very interested in the topic. It's all in how the material is presented. Of course, they have breaks and lunch, but they can accomplish so much more each day and still have an extra curriculum activity of their choice, in addition to the set curriculum. They progress at their own pace in each subject while they are thoroughly immersed. They don't have to divide their attention with other subjects. If they need additional help, their team pals are available."

"That's a good idea, to have teams working together in the classroom," said Roz.

"Sometimes another student can relate to a classmate better than the class leader can."

"So you don't call them teachers?"

Dr. Alexander laughed. "It's a perception thing. The class leader is a counselor there to facilitate the learning process and experience. They keep everyone on course and encourage the students to have discussions about a subject, for example, math. Young people like to talk if only to hear themselves. We find ways to slip learning into the dialog. They discuss the concept of how to add, subtract, multiply, and divide, which is, as you know, Dr. Greenfield, the basis for all math. Then they do projects that reflect those theories. The process encourages total interaction, immersion, and participation by each of the students. That way, they have buy-in for what they learn and accomplish."

"I've read your papers and those of Ambassador Logan published in *The New Educator* magazine. You certainly have stirred a great deal of discussion, but no one disputes your approach produces extraordinary results at an incredibly low per-pupil cost. Your students are in training for years longer than average and you have infinitesimally low truancy or behavioral problems," said Roz.

"That's correct. However, we're dealing with a relatively small student population and we have the resources to invest in each aspect of a student's education. We have a low counselor-student ratio, too. Usually no more than a ten-to-one ratio and even that's pretty high. And, we're fortunate we have so many university students interested in our program. As a result, we get university volunteers and interns in education and the social sciences.

"We are essentially a private school and the only school, pre-school through what would be considered junior college status, in the county. We are fully accredited by the state and several national accreditation boards, including Mensa up through our college level courses. I understand you're a member of Mensa, so you understand what the accreditation means."

"I am, yes. It is one of the reasons your program intrigues us," Roz said.

"To maintain our integrity, we don't take state or federal funds for education. Our local tax base does support education for the Academy, so we are in a public/private partnership with the county. This campus serves all of the academic needs of county residents, and functions pretty much the same way Vivian tells me your community center does. We have a very good senior education and literacy program. The nursing school, cosmetology programs, construction specialties, like electrician, plumber, carpenter, and mechanic, are all served from this facility."

"One-stop academic shopping, so to speak," Wesley said, as he continued to push Elizabeth in her stroller down the halls.

"Exactly," said Dr. Alexander. "Here we can meet the needs of every person in the county for education, information, and career objectives. We have the most sophisticated library in the state."

"I understand, from my research, you're taking boarding students now?" suggested Roz.

"That's a fairly new aspect instituted by Jeff Logan. For now, we're only taking a select number of young, preteen South Carolinians into the boarding school and some foreign exchange students. You see, with our county day students, we know everyone in their families back before they were gleams in their daddies' eyes." He laughed. "Their parents and grands, aunts, uncles, cousins, someone from their family is likely to be on the campus at some point on any given day. So, Jeff gets to know the students' families, too. Most parents are only a hop, skip, and a jump away from campus, and the students know it. So, they're not apt to misbehave. Not true when we admit students from outside the county or the country. So, we're being very selective there and feeling our way through."

"How do you select your students for the boarding school?" Roz asked.

"Need. We have a need-based selection process. If we can make a difference in a child's life, then we're willing to do so."

"What about disciplinary problems?"

"There's a Student Council for that. If there is something they shouldn't or can't deal with, then that's where Jeff Logan steps in to resolve it with parental participation. So far, we haven't had any referrals from the Student Council. Both Jeff Logan and I have had students come to us directly to help them solve a problem that may involve their home environment. We encourage our students to trust we want to help them academically or otherwise no matter what the circumstances. In traditional school systems, teachers are not encouraged to get personally involved with the students. Here, our counselors are encouraged to get involved, particularly to discover what, if anything, might block a student's ability to learn."

"Vivian said you don't have a regular police force in Summer County. Is that true?" Roz asked.

"It is, yes. We have a sheriff and deputy, but they mostly handle court actions like serving summonses or traffic issues. We haven't had a need for a police force. Instead, we have councils for each of the municipalities in the county and they constitute the county council. If you've got a problem, you talk with your mayor. Usually that's all it takes to solve whatever it is. My sister, Olivia Dixon, is the Mayor of Goodwill. She's been the Mayor for more than thirty years. She does such a good job that no one challenges her for the post." He laughed.

"Dixon? Is she related to Donald and James Dixon?" Rosalyn asked.

"Yes, they're her sons. Her husband is Romello Dixon."

Rosalyn laughed. "Romello," she said. "He's a character. He really knows how to tell a joke."

"He does. He's the life of any party. He's also an astute businessman. He heads Alexander-Dixon Industries (ADI) and he and his son, James, do an excellent job for our company."

"I've been looking at these murals. They are extraordinary. Did the students do these?

"Yes, they did. My daughter-in-law, Stacy, I believe you have already met, her mother, Helen Greene, and brother, Russell Greene, are artists and volunteer as art counselors. Their students are responsible for these murals."

"Russell Greene, the artist?" Rosalyn asked, surprised.

"Yes, he is very young, but he's quite famous now. He used to be a student here."

"You say his mother is an artist, too?"

"Yes, she's usually in residence, while Russell likes to travel the world. Helen, her husband, Willis, and their son, Russell, moved here after Stacy and my son, Benjamin, married. Willis owns the gas station and garage in Goodwill. He also teaches car maintenance and repair here periodically. Russell is on the road right now. He's in Africa painting a series of landscapes he'll exhibit in London and Japan. One of Vivian's partners, Bill Chandler, represents him and his work. Russell took seven of our students with him on this last trip. They'll be gone for three months."

"So the Academy encourages travel-based learning?" Roz asked.

"Definitely. Jefferson Logan, as you might know, is a former United States ambassador. He instituted the exchange program and I agree with his approach. What good is it to only read about history in foreign lands or learn other languages and not experience them or other cultures first hand? We have several of our languages counselors leading tours for six weeks in other countries. In fact, five different groups are in Italy, France, Spain, Greece, and Germany, in addition to the group with Russell in Africa."

"You have that type of specificity that you can send the students to different countries?"

"Thanks to Jeff's experience as an ambassador, we bring in counselors from different countries all over the world, in fact. People who were born and raised in various countries and cultures make some of the best counselors for our students. For six weeks, they get to go home with a group of our students and immerse them in their native culture while the students learn the language and customs. As I said before, we take foreign students into our boarding program. Again, that's Jeff Logan's doing. That's why I offered him the job when I stepped down as Dean of the Academy."

"You do that with other specialties, too? For example, your son, Kenneth, took a group of our community preteens and teens for the summer to his offices in Santa Barbara to learn computer programming and engineering. He's offering to continue with those students next summer and offering internships and scholarships to two graduating seniors."

Dr. Alexander smiled. "Yes, I know, and my son, Benjamin Staton, and daughter-in-law, Stacy, are in the military and are both stationed in Tokyo, Japan. Benjamin is in the Air Force and Stacy is in the Navy. When the students go to Japan for six weeks, in addition to learning to speak the language, Benjamin and Stacy introduce them to the possibility of Foreign Service or service to this country through the military.

"My youngest son, Gregory Clayton, though he's currently a professional basketball player for New York, he spends his off season building an investment house on the New York Stock Exchange. He takes math, science, and finance students for several sessions with their counselors. We have to work around his away schedule during the basketball season for now."

"Do you have children you press into service for each specialty?" Rosalyn asked, laughing.

Dr. Alexander laughed, too. "We only have one more child, Aretha Grace, out of our five. She's the youngest and a student at Harvard, but she volunteers with The Peace Corp when she's out of school for the summer. And, yes, she takes students with her for two, six-week periods. However, we have aunts, uncles, cousins who are a part of our life-learning programs everywhere.

"Since the students get a six-week session per year for extra-curriculum choices, they may choose from any number of tracks or specialties or repeat one if they like."

"How do you determine whether a student passes to the next grade?" Wesley asked.

"It's not about grades or test scores as it is in traditional school settings, and look at where that process has led us on the world stage. For us at the Academy, it's all about learning. We get our day students when they are as young as three months old. As you know, they are like sponges for the first five years of life, so we start early stimulating their brain cells. If we haven't got them thirsting for knowledge and eager to be in a learning environment for ten hours a day, sometimes six days a week, then we aren't doing our jobs. The biggest problem for young people is that they have short attention spans and they bore easily. Our job is to get them engaged and keep them that way, wanting to be an aggressive member of the learning process. Every one of our students has a talent and maybe sometimes more than one. It's up to us as counselors to identify that talent or talents and help the student exploit it or them. Everything is used as a teachable moment for us.

"Testing is voluntary and the students use it to determine whether they are meeting the marks they set for themselves and to determine whether they need to repeat a subject or need more intensive sessions. However, they do grade the counselors," he offered, laughing.

"This must be an expensive system to fund. Beyond the local taxes for education, how do you pay for everything?"

"We own the campus free and clear, so we only have to keep up the maintenance on the buildings and grounds. We have plenty of volunteers for that from parents and others in the county. Some limited amount of funds comes from families of the boarding students, but not a lot. More often than not, our boarding students come to us from homes that may be a challenge to survive. We receive referrals all the time from school counselors, teachers, or principals who believe a particular student deserves a different, more robust learning environment. We have accepted students who have been sponsored financially by a church or philanthropic group.

"We don't have utility expenses because we're off the grid. We use geothermal and solar energy to power the facilities. New technologies are another learning experience for our students. A well and septic system and a water barrel system that we refine into potable water have proven to spark a lot of interest by our pupils. My family members are farmers. We have hydroponics farms, livestock, and fisheries. ADI donates a certain percentage of our annual yield to the Academy through ADIs family foundation.

"The murals you see here are sent on tour each year for a handsome return. We don't have a lot of administrative overhead because so many of our counselors, like Helen, Willis, and Russell Greene, are volunteers. We do have salaried counselors and we pay into health programs, retirement accounts, and state and federal taxes. Those who donate time determine for themselves the value of their activities that support the Academy. I'm a dollar-a-year man myself. My day job is as an elected Senator to the State South Carolina government in Columbia. My family business supports me, and my wife works as the head of the nursing school and the head of nursing at the county hospital," he said, laughing, "So, I can afford to donate my time. We're a not-for-profit institution just as I understand your community center is, Wesley."

"Yes, sir, we are. And, I understand how volunteers make our programs and projects possible. You seem to have active sports and entertainment programs."

"Very active. We've won state championships in football, baseball, tennis, basketball, and soccer. Recently, one of our teams won a national chess tournament. They will go on to compete in a World Cup for chess in Madrid, Spain."

"Your campus is beautiful, Dr. Alexander."

"Thank you. Again, Jeff Logan deserves the credit for our continued success. I expect he and his family will make it back before Vivian and Chuck's wedding, so you should have an opportunity to meet with him.

"The students, through the Student Counsel, have a great deal to do with the landscaping and water features you see here. Much of the campus living architecture resulted from senior-year or college level, student projects."

"The students are out of class for two weeks now?" asked Rosalyn.

"Yes, that's why Vivian Lynn and Chuck and Donald and Cecile scheduled their weddings for this time, so they could use the campus for some of the wedding activities and not disrupt the students. Of course, they are paying to have the whole facility available for their wedding activities. That contributes to the Academy coffers."

"There certainly are a lot of people attending the wedding."

Dr. Alexander laughed. "Two weddings. This is a small gathering of family compared to our annual Fourth of July family reunion. People were just here for the eleven-day event, so not everyone will be able to make it back for the weddings. During our family reunion, we have wedding ceremonies because that is the largest gathering of family members each year and their friends are welcome to come to our family reunions. For Labor Day, the young cousins, who are still in school, camp out in tents at my wife's aunt's house on the sand in Atlantic Beach."

"That's where JRock said he, Chuck, and the other grooms are staying."

"That's right. They docked late last week, but they'll be here today for the rest of the weeks' activities.

"Chuck and Vivian Lynn are adopting a little five-year-old boy, Ronnie Smith, who is a victim of abuse. The boy had to be hospitalized for fractures in his legs and arms and he was traumatized. For some reason, he attached himself to Chuck who took care of him in the Emergency Room. For a while, Ronnie was inconsolable when Chuck wasn't around. He's better now, but Chuck took him on the cruise with the grooms instead of letting Vivian Lynn bring him with her and my other grandchildren. He's still acclimating to Vivian Lynn's other children. It will take time, but we've got nothing but time to help him. The children will stay here with us until Chuck and Vivian Lynn return from their honeymoon."

"Your daughter is a phenomenal woman, Dr. Alexander. She's done so much for us," Rosalyn said.

"Thank you, Rosalyn. I agree. My wife and I are proud of all of our children. They're all going to be at the house today with my grands. Let's see the rest of the campus and then we'll head over to the house to see what Sylvia made for lunch."

Chapter 26

So you liked what you saw?" Vivian asked as they sat on a large, screen-enclosed lanai with big ceiling fans turning lazily above. They were finishing lunch while the children, Chuck, Vivian's brothers, their wives, and Wesley frolicked in the backyard swimming pool in an energetic game of water volley ball at Bernard and Sylvia's farm house.

"I did, yes," answered Rosalyn. "I'm thoroughly impressed with what your father and Jefferson Logan have accomplished. You've obviously invested time and money into the school, too."

"We all have including Jeff Logan. We established an educational foundation to insure the children who come through our school system are able to continue through college and beyond. They work hard to earn the financial backing the foundation provides. It's not a handout; it's a helping hand and they are expected to give back by contributing time to those who come behind them.

"Many of my mom's nursing students go on to other careers in medicine."

"I'm proud to say I have nine former nurses in medical school, and six who have become medical doctors or dentist," Sylvia Alexander said as she poured more sweet tea into ice-filled tumblers with lemon slices and mint juleps before sitting down.

"My nurses, both male and female, are ranked at the top of their classes."

"They dare not be otherwise," Bernard Alexander teased, as he kissed his wife's temple before he set a long, pineapple, upside-down cake on the table.

"That looks professionally done," Sylvia commented.

"It is," said Rosalyn. "My husband graduated from a culinary school program and he and his brother, Isaac, began working in their father's bakery and ice cream shop before they were teenagers. Wesley still does most of the cooking in our household. My brother-in-law reopened their father's shop and turned it into a coffee bar, teahouse, and bakery shop. He's doing a brisk catering business, too. When Wes can, he gives Isaac a hand."

"Wesley baked this cake just this morning?"

"He did, yes. He wanted to do something to express our appreciation to you."

"Mmmm, and it's so good I'm not going to worry about the extra pounds I'm going to gain," Sylvia said sampling another moist bite.

"Mrs. Alexander, I wish I could look as fit as you do after having five children," Rosalyn said, laughing.

"Great metabolism and good genes so I can't take credit for it."

"Wow! That felt good," Wesley said, coming onto the lanai, dripping wet from the pool with a large beach towel around his shoulders.

"You looked like you were having fun."

"Who wouldn't, but your grandchildren must be part fish. They've really got Cole, Marcus, and Simone swimming very well."

"Simone seems to be more interested in Ronnie," Vivian said, and then exclaimed, "Oh, look! Simone made Ronnie smile," she said, her voice full of emotion. "Did you see that? He actually smiled. He hasn't smiled since he was brought into the Emergency Room by the police."

"Chuck was his doctor?" Hanna Ivy Benson, Sylvia's eighty-plus-year-old aunt asked her grandniece. "Chuck stayed with me all week and never said a word."

"Yes, Chuck's like that. He was on duty when Ronnie was brought in. The little boy was in such a bad shape. His parents are meth addicts and were running a meth lab out of their foreclosed home. They both lost their jobs as chemists and started mixing meth. They sampled their product, but took their animosity out on each other and Ronnie. They've given up their parental rights and are serving time for a host of charges including child abuse and endangerment."

"That's so sad," said Sylvia Alexander.

"The downturn in the economy has affected so many in such unexpected ways," Bernard commented.

"Did the economy have an adverse impact here in Summer County?" asked Wesley.

"Not so much," said Bernard. "We're mostly an agra-economy. People eat no matter what and because we grow year round in our hydroponics farms, we supply the northern colder regions with fresh fruits and vegetables, flowers and fisheries when their growing and boating seasons are over."

"You have quite a cottage industry with canning those fruits and vegetables."

"Indeed, we do. Canning is a lost art in many parts of the country, but it's a thriving business for us here in Summer County. Most of the people in the county are in the farming industry."

"This is something I'd like to introduce for Baylor Plaza Park. We have land we can set aside for hydroponics farming.

Homeowners can also have rooftop gardens along with their solar panels. We could sell to local boutique stores," suggested Wesley.

"Exactly. We supply to a few regional chains, but, for the most part, our biggest clients are the boutique stores and high-end restaurants. Because we can our fruits and vegetables produce fresh daily, they retain their nutrients and flavor. Despite the reference to canning, we don't use medal or plastic in our canning process, only glass jars. We also have a return and recycle policy for the jars. We sterilize and reuse them."

"We have a type of farmer's market a couple of times a month, but I want to expand and establish a more permanent fresh, whole food market on site in conjunction with Burk's Big V, the community grocery store. We have the space, but we're not ready to do livestock on the available land. We're trying to maintain a low-density project, and livestock would require too much of a commitment of land, but we might be able to manage a few chicken coups for eggs."

"ADI may be able to help you with a few hundred setting hens, and counsel your people on how to set it up and how to maintain it. You've met my nephew, Dr. James Dixon, and his father. James' double doctorates are in Animal Husbandry and New Technology Farming"

"Yes, I've spoken with him. I'd like to talk with him again about his specialties," said Roz. "I could use it in the new school system to train our students on how farming works and its benefits to society." Smiled at her husband. "Maybe convince Wes to squeeze out an acre or two for a working farm."

"See! That's what we're all about here in Summer County. Using the old ways in new ways to benefit our community."

"Vivian told me your family came from a long line of farmers."

"Actually, as the oral history goes, the original members of the colony were from Alexandria; a small pharaonic town founded by Alexander the Great, hence the family name that survived through the generations of my family. An ancestor from Alexandria, Egypt, on the Mediterranean Sea, was a privateer. He and his five sons owned ships that raided slave ships, freed the captives, looted and then stole or sank the vessels. They hunted in packs. One of the sons spotted an English Man of War vessel attacking a passenger ship off the coast of Barbados and attacked the British galleon. My relative lost his own ship and got separated from his brothers in the battle, but managed to save the Barbadians and their ship. Among the passengers was a girl of only about fourteen or fifteen years old, who was being sent by her father to a wealthy Greek merchant in exchange for horses and other livestock. Though they couldn't speak a word of each other's language, my relative fell instantly in love with her.

"Because the Barbadian ship was severely damaged in the battle, they had to sink her off the coast of what is now known as South Carolina. The Egyptian sailors and Barbadians had to hide from other British ships that were hunting for them and other pirates in the area. They went into the deep woods and swamp and formed a colony living in harmony with the Native Americans—the Catawba, Neighbors, Cusabo, and Cherokee— in the area and then intermarrying with them. The Egyptian and Barbadian sailors never saw their homelands again, but lived here in isolation avoiding slavery and helping enslaved people escape their captors. The Underground Railroad made a path through the dense woods and great swamp to the colony and then moved north or west from here. Some of the escaped slaves stayed in the colony and raised families intermarrying with the Barbadians, Native Americans, and the Egyptian sailors. Many years later, around the late eighteenth, nineteenth century, that colony became Summer County.

"Most of the people who live in Summer County descended from those early settlers and the Native Americans who inhabited these lands before they were invaded."

"That's fascinating. Is that true for both sides of your family?"

"Only my father's side, the Alexanders; not my mother's," Bernard said. She was Emma Grace Smithy, the illegitimate daughter of a slaveholder and one of his slaves. Her mother was sold by the slaveholder's wife because her husband brought her into his bedroom to live and sleep with every night. My mother never saw her mother again.

"My wife's family originated in the coastal area around Charleston. An area called Goose Creek, Saint James," Dr. Alexander finished.

"My people didn't escape slavery the way that Bernard's father's family did," Sylvia Benson Alexander said as she picked up the oral history. "They worked the rice patties and made indigo ink. They descended from the Gullahs on the Sea Islands. My grandparents and great grandparents left the Islands and were entertainers. They traveled Europe with the great Josephine Baker and lived there until the war chased them home. Isn't that right, Aunt Hanna Ivy?"

"Indeed it is, child. My grandfather never took to working for somebody else's welfare and not his own. He had seen his own grandfather and father trying to survive on little or nothing while the Europeans invaded and claimed the land that rightfully belonged to the Native Americans.

"Still, the European landowner lived lavishly and took anyone of his grandfather's female children to his bed. The landowner even fathered children with his enslaved people with little or no regard for the girls or women he assaulted. Every night he took a different woman, sometimes two or more women, to his bed, especially during the winter months as bed warmers and other things. It didn't matter whether the woman was already married or mated with a man or how young she was. He took the younger girls when they were twelve or thirteen.

"My grandfather was disgusted with what he had witnessed his father and grandfather suffer. As soon as he could, when he grew up and married, he took his wife and children away from the Islands where his parents and seven brothers and sisters still lived and brought them to the mainland. He started working in the bars and hotels singing with my grandmother and at times, all of their children sang on stage. They had a regular vaudeville show going on. Along the way, my father and mother met in the theatre, married and had me and my sisters and brothers while on the road traveling from place to place to perform. Eventually we had a cast of twenty-two performers.

"One day someone who knew Josephine Baker, told her about us and she sent for us to come to see her. We did and we performed for her. As they say, the rest was history. She was a huge hit it New York.

"Because of what my ancestors were subjected to, we were our own rainbow coalition. It was still hard for people of color in that society. So, we went to Paris where we were readily accepted and Ms. Baker opened in *La Revue Nègre* at The Théâtre des Champs-Élysées. She and her troupe, who included us, gained instant success for the erotically nearly nude dancing we did. Some of us learned to work in other backstage trades and capacities, like costume design or playing instruments or set construction. We were a complete ensemble of touring actors, singers, and dancers. Our family toured all over Europe with Ms. Baker and sometimes on our own to standing-room-only crowds every night. When we returned to France from one tour, we opened with Ms. Baker at The Folies Bergère."

"Is it true she performed the *Danse Sauvage*, wearing only a string of artificial bananas?" Rosalyn asked, fascinated.

"It is, yes, and she was the toast of Paris and much of the European and North African continent. Ms. Baker was born in Missouri in 1906 and died in 1975 in Paris, but her name is still spoken with reverence in France. Like Vivian Lynn, Ms. Baker fostered twelve children.

"My grandniece, Mariah, Sylvia's sister, lives in Paris and owns the restaurant and jazz club where our ancestors performed. She's also a performer and has a terrific floor show that's very popular. It is reminiscent of my grandfather's show and Ms. Bakers'. People have to book weeks in advance to get a seat in the restaurant and the show. She's known as The French Mariah and has starred in foreign films, stage, and in British music television shows. She has toured Europe, Asia, and Africa to perform. She's the only one in the family so far who is still in the entertainment business.

"When we came back to the United States just before the war, though we were very popular in Europe, we weren't favored here. Ms. Baker returned to France to work for the French Resistance. My family settled back in South Carolina in Goose Creek, Saint James, outside Charleston, and built other careers."

"How did you meet Dr. Alexander," Roz asked Sylvia.

"My parents and grandparents saved quite a nest egg after being in Europe all of those years and when they returned to the United States, they didn't trust the banks and because of their suspicions fortunately survived the Great Depression. They made sure all of us, their grands and great grands went to college. I met Bernard at Howard University. He was in grad school in education and I was in my last year of nursing school. After we graduated, we married. Bernard brought me here to his family's homestead in Goodwill where he began teaching in the county school system. I began working as a private duty nurse and continuing my education. Later, after Bernard earned his doctorate, he became the high school principal and I became the head of a new nursing school at what is now Summer County Academy. Bernard is a State Senator representing Summer County at the state capitol in Columbia, South Carolina, and I'm the head of nursing at the Summer County Medical Center."

"That's interesting. My parents, Daniel and Etta Mae Ross Hunter are Howard graduates in undergrad and the School of Dentistry."

Bernard and Sylvia both laughed. "We know them, but Sylvia and I haven't seen them in years. It's truly only six degrees or less of separation between a person and everyone else in the world. After we graduated and married," Bernard continued, "we raised all five of our children here on this land as have my eleven brothers and sisters and their families. My family farmed this land for many generations while they learned other skills and endeavors, but farming is our base and has paid for all of our children's education and business ventures. While you're here you'll, no doubt, meet many more of my family members who still live here in the county or come here for reunions and other family gatherings. We are legion," he said laughing.

"Chuck's family is huge too as was my first husband's family," Vivian said. "All of them, both the Jacksons and the Montgomerys, are in attendance for the wedding."

"They know each other?" Roz asked, surprised.

"They are neighbors, friends and there have been two marriages between the families. Derrick and Chuck became friends when they were preteens. Chuck comes from a family of farmers too, artisans, and construction workers. The seven sons were living in a trailer camp outside Philadelphia while working on an inner city project in the neighborhood where Derrick and his family lived.

"In the summer when Chuck was out of school, he used to go into the city to work with his brothers. During lunch break, he would go watch the kids play basketball on a neighborhood court. He didn't know how to play, but he was a big, tall kid for his age even back then. Derrick was one of the most accomplished basketball players in his community at an early age. One day Derrick tossed a ball to Chuck and subsequently taught him how to play.

"Chuck was supposed to be sweeping up the construction site, hauling supplies, a general dogsbody, but more often than not, he was on the basketball court with Derrick learning the game.

"Eventually, Derrick and Chuck started spending weekends over the winter at each other's homes. The next year, the Montgomery's invited the Jacksons to come for a vacation on their farm in Monroe County, Pennsylvania. Within three years, Chuck's brother, Bob, and Derrick's sister, Sheila, married and now have six children.

"Derrick's father worked for the Post Office, but grew up on a farm in Mississippi. Derrick's mother is a beautician. Mr. Jackson always wanted to get back to farming, so when he retired, the Jackson's moved out of their inner city neighborhood in Philadelphia and onto a farm on land that the Montgomery's sold to them.

"Derrick was older than Chuck, but they went to colleges geographically close together; went into the NBA two years apart; and went into medicine together after they retired from basketball. They were best friends and closer than brothers."

"Obviously, their families care a great deal for you."

"They do care for me and I for them. We lost Chuck's mother and Derrick's father, but Chuck's father and Derrick's mother are hail and hearty. My children are like their shared grandkids. We have to split time between both families in Pennsylvania and my family here in South Carolina. As I said, you'll meet many of them from Derrick's and Chuck's family."

"What I want to know, Wesley, is whether you'll bake some cakes for Vivian and Chuck's wedding?" Bernard Alexander asked. "This pineapple upside down cake is the best I've ever had."

Everyone laughed.

"I'd be happy to."

Chapter 27

Wesley turned off the car engine and sat back to take a long slow breath, as he perused the quiet neighborhood. It was ten-thirty at night and they made the long drive from Charlotte, North Carolina, after spending the morning at Carowinds Amusement Park. They ate a late lunch with Daniel and Etta, went through all the hugs, kisses, and teary goodbyes, before hitting the road, heading home.

After they stopped for dinner somewhere in Virginia, the car was quiet, except for the gentle snoring from his sons. Everyone was asleep, including Rosalyn. He placed his hand on her thigh and rubbed it. Her eyes opened slowly and then smiling, she leaned over and kissed him.

"We're home," she said a breath away.

"We're home," he acknowledged.

"How tired are you?" she asked, rubbing his thigh.

He grinned at her. "Not very."

"Good. Then let's put the children to bed and meet in the whirlpool tub."

He kissed her in agreement. His wife was a sexually creative soul, so he knew what a meeting in the wide, deep tub would likely mean. He was looking forward to having an ambiance night by candlelight.

Wesley checked the neighborhood again before he got out of the SUV, while Rosalyn began waking Cole, Marcus, and Simone.

He took Elizabeth in her carrier and her diaper bag up the first set of steps, but stopped before he reached the second set of stairs to the porch.

Something was wrong, he sensed. The security light in the front yard should have come on before he reached it and triggered the porch lights. That didn't happen.

"What's wrong, Wes? Why are you just standing here?" Rosalyn asked, coming up behind him, carrying a sleepy Simone in her arms and Cole and Marcus trailing her, carrying their bags.

"Go back to the car, Roz, and take the children with you," he said, turning them around.

"What is it?" she asked, but followed his instructions.

"I want to check the house before we go in," he said after re-securing Elizabeth's carrier in the safety seat.

"Not alone, you're not, Wesley," Rosalyn said, firmly. "See who's on patrol and where they are. If you think something is wrong, call your crew."

She was adamant, he realized, and frightened for him. Her tone brokered no argument. He recalled how afraid she was when Killer and the Royal Reds had him and JaiHonnah cornered against the fence in front of her elementary school. Her tears nearly broke his heart. He wouldn't put her or his children through that type of fear again. He reached into his pocket and pulled out his cell phone.

"Little T, who's out near my neighborhood tonight?" he asked and listened. "Yeah, Roz and I just got home. Something's up," he said and then hung up.

Less than a minute elapsed before the first team cut the corner on a dead run. Then two more teams followed and a minute later, Peckhead came running out of Mrs. Lewis' house in his underwear and tennis shoes, with Buddy Lewis on his heels. They were all strapped.

High-powered flashlights in hand, two teams of two went around through the alley, while Little T, Isaac, and Wesley went in the front door. Buddy stayed by the SUV with his gun at the ready.

From what they could see, using high-powered, halogen flashlights, the damage was horrendous. It covered everything on every floor, the attic, and the basement, too. Furniture was shredded, walls spray painted with obscenities, kitchen smashed beyond recognition, with food from the overturned refrigerator and freezer rotting on the floor. Not one thing was left untouched.

"What the fuck?" Peckhead said succinctly, as he toured the wreckage.

Alternating, emergency red-and-blue light bars and strobe beacons painted the walls as two police cars silently rolled up.

"*Oh, hell, no!*" Captain Gary Bouchard, aka G-Boogie, exclaimed, rendering the air blue as he surveyed the damage to Wesley and Rosalyn's home. The captain was out of the One Four Precinct. He and his wife, Mildred, were guests at the Greenfield's New Year's Eve bash and partied hardy until the wee hours in this lovely home. "*On my watch?*" he thundered into his cell phone, his jaws tight. He barked orders for his best two robbery detectives to get their asses out of bed and in gear. Then, he reamed his Watch Commander a new one for failure to have this neighborhood patrolled more closely.

The captain was the eldest son of Bubbles and Billie Bouchard and a full ten years older than Isaac and Wesley, but treated Isaac, Wesley, and their crew as *his* boyz. Though he lived elsewhere, he still considered himself a son of the neighborhood because his parents and siblings still lived and worked there. His precinct was responsible for patrolling and protecting the area. He declared heads would roll in his precinct and, if he were right about who had perpetrated this crime, the precinct where Killer and the Royal Reds lived would also feel the heat.

Later, nearing dawn, Wesley held Rosalyn in his arms in the shower room. They were in one of the new, double-wide trailer homes that sat adjacent to the community center on what used to be a field of grassy playground area. The trailer was designed much like the RV, except it was larger and sat on cinderblocks.

They did what they could to calm Cole's, Marcus' and Simone's fears and anxiety before they got them to sleep, but Wesley did not let the children see the damage to their home. Rosalyn's jaws were tight after the electric company got power restored to the house. The vandals had cut the power lines and accessed the house through the French doors at the rear basement level by cutting a hole in the glass large enough for people to walk through. None of the neighbors heard or saw the vandals come or go.

None of the windows were smashed, which should have tripped the alarm system before the electricity was cut off.

Rosalyn hugged Wesley tighter and looked up into his golden eyes. "I guess this isn't the best time to tell you that we're pregnant again, huh?"

For a moment, Wesley just stared. Then a slow grin grew around his mouth and into a smile. He shook his head and then kissed his wife's mouth. "Considering what we've seen, it's the best time for this news."

"I think so, too."

"Are you worried about having babies so close together?"

"Are you going to love me when I get fat again?"

"You didn't get fat the last time, but I'll love you more than ever this time."

"Then I have nothing to worry about."

"Did you think I would ever cheat on you?" he asked, concerned.

"Well, the Alexander wives, JeNelle and Stacy, and the Dixons' wives, Cecile and Janice, are very interesting, bright, and attractive women."

"Are they?" he asked, smiling smugly. "Frankly, if I was ever remotely interested in kicking you to the curb, it would be for Sylvia Alexander or Helen Greene."

Rosalyn laughed. "They're both attractive women, but they're old enough to be your mother."

"I wouldn't mind being a boy toy for either one of them," he said, laughing when Rosalyn slapped his naked butt, but then sobered. "Except no one, not even Mrs. Alexander or Mrs. Greene, could make me happier than you have since the day we had our first problem with equipment failure.

"I'm in love with you, Rosalyn Hunter Greenfield, and crave making love to only you. So you can get as fat as you want. I'll love every inch of you for the rest of my life."

She kissed him for that, shut off the shower, and led him to bed. This time, she got on top and pleasured him with her mouth and hands, as the dawn grew brighter. An hour later, they slept cocooned in a blissful slumber.

***

"I have the police report, Mrs. Greenfield," the insurance adjuster said, as they finished touring the wreckage that was once her home. "You've kept good records of your expenses to renovate and on your purchases. It was a good thing you had information stored on your laptop that you had with you when this happened.

With a slight adjustment for normal wear and tear, I think the repairs and replacement costs should be around this amount," he said, providing a sheet for her review and signature.

She took her time reading the evaluation sheet and then passed it off to Kelley Baylor who also reviewed the estimated amounts. With knowledge and experience in construction, Kelley Baylor was an expert in renovation costs. At her nod of agreement, Rosalyn initialed the forms where indicated. She accepted the check he offered and turned to Isaac and Little T. "We can get started carting the larger items out to the dumpsters now," she said while putting the check folded into the back pocket of her jeans. "Wes should be here shortly with Cole, Marcus, and Simone after he drops Elizabeth at Mrs. Lewis' house."

"Is Francine up to watching both her baby and Elizabeth? Remember Jemar isn't back from California yet. His flight gets in tomorrow night," Isaac reminded her. "If you agree, Carla wants to help, too."

"Thanks, Isaac. Yes, would you please give Carla a call and see whether it's convenient for her to come to Mrs. Lewis' house to help Francine with little Rose and Elizabeth?"

Isaac took his cell phone from his pocket and made the call.

Little T moved toward the front door and beckoned young Frank Bouchard and his crew to enter. "First, go to the backyard. Move that swimming pool to the dumpster to get it out of the way. Then, you and your crew start in the basement and haul the large pieces out the back door to the dumpster in the alley."

Frank and six of his neighborhood friends followed Little T's instructions and headed out back to get to work. Slide, Dog, Screw, Buddy, and Little T, with his sister, Charmaine, headed upstairs to the bedrooms.

"She's on her way, Roz," Isaac said. "I'm going to start in the kitchen, loading up the spoiled food." He grabbed a large industrial-sized rolling trash can, a box of trash bags, and went to work. Indeed the house reeked of spoiled food and breast milk from the refrigerator and freezer. Broken beer and wine bottles littered the floor, their contents going sticky in unseemly puddles.

Rosalyn just wanted to cry for the damage the vandals had done, not so much to her home and possessions, but for what it did to Cole's, Marcus' and Simone's sense of security. When they awoke this morning and dressed before breakfast, not even Wesley's French toast and sausage, a family personal favorite meal, could cheer the children's spirits. Their mood remained pensive and seemed to rub off on Elizabeth who was uncharacteristically cranky and out of sorts, too, that morning.

They were all overly tired after having such a fun-filled vacation, visiting with her parents and attending Vivian's wedding, followed by a week at the beach. Vivian's grand aunt, Hanna Ivy Benson, upon hearing the Greenfields were planning to be in the Myrtle Beach area after the wedding, insisted they stay with her at her Atlantic Beach home. She was another eighty-plus-year-old woman who didn't know how to take no for an answer. Rosalyn thought she would love to get Ms. Benson and Mrs. Lewis together. They would get a real kick out of each other. So, the Greenfields ended up traveling to Atlantic Beach, following JRock's SUV to where his yacht was still docked.

Ms. Benson's home was a big, three-level, wood-framed, decorative antebellum Victorian with wide covered verandas on each level, accented with rich, attractive colors on the frame and gingerbread cutouts. She inherited the house in Atlantic Beach and one in the Georgetown section of Washington, DC, from a wealthy spinster who she used to work for as a nurse, housekeeper, and companion. The woman had no living relatives and bequeathed her substantial holdings to her companion of more than twenty-five years, Hanna Ivy Benson. Ms. Benson, also an unmarried woman, sold the house in Washington to her great grandnephew, Benjamin Alexander, and returned to the warmer climate of South Carolina to live in the big Victorian on the beach.

The beach house was bright and airy. They slept in big bedrooms with high ceilings and four-poster beds. The windows were wide open to the night breezes from the Atlantic Ocean yards away from the base of the house. During the days, they sat on the veranda and people watched while JRock's twin daughters and Cole, Marcus, and Simone played on the sand at the water's edge.

Ms. Benson delighted in having them there and didn't put up a fuss when Wesley took over the cooking duties.

They went sightseeing in Myrtle Beach to places like Broadway at the Beach, Ripley's Aquarium, but, for the most part, they spent their days and nights in pursuit of rest and relaxation. Board games with the kids and card games with Aunt Ivy, as they were instructed to call her, were the extent of their major activities. They thought it strange she beat the pants off them at poker. JRock's and Wesley's refusals to play strip poker with her became an enjoyable inside joke.

After five days of pure laziness, JRock loaded his girls on his yacht and headed home, while the Greenfields headed back to Charlotte to return the RV and start their own journey home.

Rosalyn was hard pressed to remember their idyllic vacation, as she stood amid the wreckage and watched shattered pieces she carefully selected to furnish her home being walked out the door to a big dumpster in front and in the rear of her family home. Though the pieces were relatively new, they weren't anything she couldn't afford to lose or replace. More importantly, her family wasn't in the house when the vandals broke in. Her most precious possessions, her family members, were all safe.

At least for now.

As the police indicated, this didn't seem to be a robbery because nothing that could have been sold or fenced was taken, but everything was smashed. All the electronics, kitchen appliances, and clothes were still in the house, but destroyed. It appeared someone took a sledgehammer to the cabinets in the bedroom, bathroom, and the walls. Bleach was liberally splattered on all the hardwood floors and hacked to smithereens. Dry concrete mix was poured into the sinks, toilets, tubs, the washing machine and dishwasher, and the water turned on and left running so that the floors were soaked.

Just material things, Rosalyn silently reminded herself, as she turned to see her husband and children come in the wide-opened front door. Marcus ran to her, wrapped his arms around her waist, and cried, while Cole and Simone just stood angrily and stared.

"Cole," Rosalyn said, getting his attention while smoothing a comforting hand up and down Marcus' back.

He turned to look at her, his face expressionless. "Yes?" he answered with no inflection in his voice.

"Would you take Marcus and Simone upstairs to see whether anything can be salvaged from your rooms please? Just be careful of the men and women moving stuff out."

He stared at her for a moment, then nodded at her in such a grown up way it hurt her heart to see it. He was such a man-child at only nine years old. He said, "Come on. You heard Mama Roz. Let's do this," to his siblings who all went upstairs to do as instructed.

When the children were out of sight, Wesley opened his arms. Rosalyn walked into them, and buried her tears against his chest.

He wrapped his arm around her waist and palmed her head under his chin, kissing the top of her head. He rocked her for a while and then whispered, "It's time to do what comes next, babe."

He took her head in his hands and kissed her mouth, wiping her tears with his thumbs. "I left your breast pump and a supply of bottles with Francine. Go over there while I help the children here. Elizabeth should be waking up shortly and want to be fed." Rosalyn pedantically nodded and with one backward glance, she followed Slide who carried another piece of her devastated home out the front door to the dumpster.

"It looked bad in the dark," Isaac said to Wesley, as he finished shoveling another load of ruined dry goods into the large trash barrel in the kitchen.

"It looks worse in broad daylight. Did anyone see the Royal Reds in the neighborhood while I was away?"

"Some showed up at the Labor Day picnic and party at the community center, but since they didn't do anything, but scope out the ladies and dance, we didn't have a reason to make them leave. Kelley Baylor said someone loosened nuts and bolts on some of the Baylor heavy-duty equipment. Some of his other rigs got severely damaged because someone put sugar in the gas tanks, so we moved the equipment into the playground yard and put stationary patrols around the perimeter."

"Anything else?" he asked, frustrated as they continued to work. No matter what he did to keep the project on track and problem free, someone was working against them.

"Renovations are nearly complete in the apartments on the first floor. I think some people, particularly Fred Jenkins, are suspicious about my involvement in the renovations. I told everyone JRock appointed me to handle it for him since I live there and you would be away. Jenkins said it should be his job to oversee the renovations and handle the money because he's the super. He complained to the management company. Our ownership might come out if they start digging for information on Jeremiah Isaac."

"How do you feel about that?"

"I agree with you. I don't want people to know we own the property. They know you bought the junior high school for a dollar, and renovated the first floor with the money you inherited from Pop. They don't need to know more than that."

"I agree. So Jeremiah Isaac will call the management company and say he has a contract with Baylor Design and Development to do the work and Baylor reports directly to him."

"That should work. Would JRock agree to that?"

"I don't see why not. It's the truth. How do the renovations look?"

"Good. Really good. All of the windows have been replaced in the building and, since there is a new heating and air conditioning system in each unit, there's no need for the window units anymore. All of the electrical and plumbing were updated. The walls have been insulated with that spray-foam stuff and the hardwood floors sanded and refinished. All the painting has been finished in the second and third floor units and the new appliances installed. We just need to finish the first floor units and we can turn on the new security system for the front and rear entrances. The last things will be the new landscaping and repaving the parking lots. Now that each unit has its own stackable washer and dryer, the units in the basement can be moved to the community center on the second floor for use by the at-risk program. The new appliances in the kitchens, particularly the dishwashers, are energy efficient, but it's still going to cost more on the energy bill for each unit."

"It will, yes, until we get the geothermal and solar systems installed and operational. The additional stuff, like the ceiling fans in each room, the new lighting fixtures, dishwashers, radiant energy floors in the bathroom and kitchen, and laundry equipment were going to increase the cost per unit anyway. We won't have to do any more major renovations for at least another twenty or thirty years. These upgrades will pay for themselves in five to seven years since we won't have to pay utility expenses and maintenance."

"Hey, Ice, Isaac, the yard bird's here," Little T hailed from the empty living room. He and Slide brought a card table and folding chairs from Mrs. Lewis' house and set up buffet style, so they could eat while they had a crew meeting. Slide and Screw were coming in the front door, carrying a Styrofoam cooler filled with water, ice-cold beer, and sodas. They each grabbed a chair and then filled a plate from the chicken buckets and side orders. Isaac had cooked for the occasion. Dog distributed a container of wet wipes.

"So when are you and Roz leaving, Ice?" Screw asked.

"Monday. We're going to drive down to one of the furniture outlets in High Point, North Carolina, and pick out all the furniture for the house, then go to these outlet malls to get everything else. Roz says there is a big outlet place on I-95 in Smithfield that has clothes, shoes, sheets, towels, pots, pans, dishes, silverware, all that stuff. There's even an auction house in Richmond, Virginia, that has high-end kitchen and bathroom equipment."

"How long do you think you'll be gone?"

"Not sure, but Roz is determined we are going to be living in our home in a month or less."

They looked around at the damaged walls, ceiling, and floors.

"I don't know, Ice. That's a lot of work in a short time."

"We cleaned out four floors in this house with Frank and his crew in half a day. I've got a Baylor crew coming in on Monday to start taking down the damaged walls and putting up new wallboard by Friday. If the new hardwood floors go in over the weekend and early the following week, we'll make her deadline. Then we will only need the kitchen cabinets, appliances installed and bathrooms before we can have the new furniture delivered."

"Good thing y'all had insurance on this place. It's a big mother inside, if you ask me," said Little T. "It looked nice and smelled good in here," he said and reached for another piece of chicken.

"It will again, if Roz has anything to do with it," said Peckhead.

There were nods of general agreement.

Chapter 28

"Hey, Ice," Kelley hailed, as she entered the Baylor satellite construction office on the third floor of the community center. A solarium was being added as the fourth floor of the building. "I didn't know you were back."

"We got in last night."

"Did you get everything you needed for your home?"

"We did, yes."

"I guess Roz is back in school?"

"Yes, she and the children, except for Elizabeth, were out early this morning. She has a full schedule at school, so I brought Elizabeth with me."

"She is such a beauty," Kelley said, peering at the sleeping baby in her carrier. "So is Rose. I just saw her in Peckhead's office."

She sighed and Wesley noticed. "Are you getting maternal on me?" he asked, as he continued to review the paperwork that accumulated in his absence.

"Bite your tongue, son. Do you know how many nephews and nieces I have? That's the best birth control device I've discovered."

"You're not planning to have children?"

"Not on purpose, no. I much prefer being the single, unattached aunt who can fulfill any maternal urges by keeping my nieces and nephews for a few hours or even a few days and then returning them to their parents."

"Speaking of your nieces' parent, where is JRock? He should have docked by now from his trip to Vivian and Chuck's wedding. It's been more than a week."

"Oh, he did," she said, grinning. "He got back while you and Roz were furniture and clothes shopping. Then he took his girls with him to Texas to pay a debt."

Wesley's brows beetled. "Texas? What debt did he— Oh," he said, as understanding dawned. "Jake Hawkins and the sixty-billion-dollar bank note."

"And Jake Hawkins is—"

"JaiHonnah's father and—"

"She is in Hawkinstown with her father and her twin boys on their family ranch."

"Exactly," he said. "We saw her at the wedding, but her husband wasn't with her. Neither were her boys. Did her husband stay in Texas with their sons?"

"Oh, no, because JaiHonnah isn't married anymore and the boys are Baylors, Rodney and Reise Baylor," she said, grinning from ear to ear.

"*What the hell?*" Wesley exclaimed. "You're *shittin'* me."

"Nope! Apparently, JaiHonnah's been divorced from her former husband, Calvin Chapman, for many years, but JRock's former wife, Monique, convinced Jai she and JRock were still married. Not many people know JRock divorced Monique the year after his girls were born. Monique lied and told JaiHonnah if JRock ever cheated on her again she would take Shelly and Shelby away from him. Jai didn't know Monique was the unfaithful one in the marriage, not JRock. Jai thought if Monique found out about her twin boys, his sons, JRock would lose custody of his daughters. So she kept her pregnancy, JRock's paternity, and the birth of her twins a secret."

"Wow! So what up?"

"Don't unpack yet. My brother is going to marry Jai A.S.A.P. and then bring his family home."

***

"We're getting pretty good at this traveling thing," Wesley said to Rosalyn, as they danced at JRock and JaiHonnah's wedding reception on Jake Hawkins' sprawling ranch in Hawkinstown, Texas.

"When all we have to do is climb aboard a 747 and we land on a private runway on a ranch the size of this place, that's not hard work," Rosalyn said, laughing.

"It's worth it to see how happy JRock and Jai are," he said, looking at the newlyweds dancing while gazing into each other's eyes.

"When are they coming back to DC?"

"A couple of weeks. JaiHonnah's grandmother wants to take JRock's daughters and their sons to the Navaho Reservation for a week, and then bring them back here to the ranch for a week while they are on their honeymoon at an undisclosed location." Wesley laughed.

"Jai's father seems pleased she and JRock married."

"I think he is pleased not only with their marriage, but also with Kelley. He can't seem to take his eyes off her."

"I noticed that, too. Since Kelley has been living in Atlanta, apparently Jake Hawkins has taken up residence next door to her townhouse and has been in hot pursuit."

"He really isn't that much older than she is, but his oldest son, Jacob, Junior doesn't seem to be particularly pleased about JRock's marriage to his sister."

"Jai's other brother, Adam, doesn't seem upset about it."

"No, I spoke with him earlier. He seems like an okay person. Both he and Jacob, Junior, head parts of their family business, BlackHawk International. Adam also races Formula One cars in the big races like the Grand Prix and La Mans. He and his team have won some big ones."

"Isn't BlackHawk one of the top one thousand companies in the world?"

"It is. JRock was concerned they would try a hostile takeover of Baylor Design and Development once he took his company public. That was before he learned Jai was Jake Hawkins' daughter and Jai owns a part of her father's company as do Jacob, Junior, and Adam."

"You don't think JRock married her to avoid a hostile takeover, do you?"

"I know he didn't. He's been miserable since she left him just before the holidays last year. He couldn't even get up the enthusiasm to pursue a relationship with your doctor, Savannah Logan."

"When Savannah figured out JRock and I are friends, she told me they used to date a while back. I was really surprised, but I didn't mention JRock and I dated back in high school. Jai knew that, but Savannah didn't. JRock kept his relationship with her on the down low."

"He did because everyone thought he and Monique were still married. Still, women kept coming on to him. Even LaKesha tried to hit him up while she was still living with me."

"It's a good thing we don't have to keep JRock and JaiHonnah's marriage a secret. Still, the press and news media are going to want to exploit every detail of this marriage. I can see the headlines now: The basketball icon weds the BlackHawk heiress. Film at eleven."

Wesley laughed and shook his head. "JRock is determined his family is not going to be hounded by the press. I've issued orders at the job site that, if any reporters come snooping around, the words are 'no comment'."

"You don't think BlackHawk has anything to do with the problems you and JRock are having at the job site, do you?"

Wesley looked away from his wife's concerned face and she noticed.

"You do, don't you? You think BlackHawk is involved."

"We have no proof, but these problems didn't start up until JaiHonnah came to work at Baylor. It's just something JRock and I have been kicking around to see what shakes out. He's been catching hell at his other job sites, too, so he knows something is up. He just doesn't know what it is yet. What he does know is whoever is behind it is well financed. Initially, he thought it was Lionel Porter because he took his company away from him, but Porter doesn't have the juice to pull off something like this. We also considered Monique. She's angry enough at JRock to do just about anything, but she doesn't have the head for this kind of systematic vandalism. We even wondered whether Howard Gardner might be involved."

"Howard? Why in the world would you think of him?"

"The way he stomped out of the custody hearing tells me that he wasn't a happy camper. You even said he could be unpredictable. Because of JRock's testimony in court, he knows JRock and I are tight. Perhaps he would try to get back at me through JRock. We've both racked our brains trying to figure out who is doing this; regardless of how far-fetched the scenario might seem. We want to put a stop to it before someone gets hurt."

"What about Levi Hall?"

"Killer? Yeah, we considered him, too, but again, according to G-Boogie, he's a big time drug dealer in a small pond. He's got a lot of heat on him right now. Gary is keeping an eye on him."

"His older, half-brother was Melvin 'The Juice' Cotton and Isaac shot him."

"If Killer was going to start something with us over Isaac killing his brother, we think he would have done something long ago."

"Tony wouldn't let Levi get a toehold in his territory before this. Now that Tony is doing life without parole in a federal pen, maybe Levi thinks it's time for some payback."

"Maybe, but Isaac is the one who shot his brother, not me or JRock. I mean, the situation between me and JRock against Killer and the Royal Reds goes back to our childhood. He's had plenty time to take revenge if it was about me or JRock."

"Just sayin', babe. I want you to be safe for a number of reasons. Most of all, I like getting you naked and having my way with you," She said grinning up at him.

He pulled her closer letting her feel his excitement. "Uh, what time is that jet supposed to take off to take us all back to DC?"

She snuggled closer kissing his throat just above his dressed shirt collar. "About two hours from now, why?"

"Because I may have to use the Bridal Suite for a while or you're going to become a member of the mile high club," he said, grinning.

What she whispered in his ear had him looking for a secluded space to take urgent matters in hand.

Chapter 29

"This is a nice place, JRock," said Wesley, as they sat on the deck of JRock and JaiHonnah's new home overlooking the Wicomico River and Charleston Creek in Southern Maryland that bordered them on two sides. It was early spring and the air still held a hint of chill from a recent late winter snowstorm. Clumps of snow still covered the ground in places, but spring flowers were blooming on the well-landscaped backyard and trees were budding in the bright sunlight.

"I have to admit, I like it. Jai's father gave it to us as a wedding gift. I didn't want to accept it and I even tried to pay him for it, but he wouldn't accept the money. He said if I didn't want to live here, I should, at least, keep it to board Jai's horses. He gave her six thoroughbreds from his ranch. Two of the horses are prize winners and KnightHawk won the Kentucky Derby two years ago. Jai loves to ride and so do my girls. I couldn't deny them anything. So Jai remodeled the place and we moved in before Christmas."

"I see you docked your yacht here, too."

JRock laughed. "Sometimes it's faster to get to my office by water than it is by road."

"Yeah, it took us over an hour to drive here. It must be hell at rush hour."

"Yeah, it is. I have to leave here extra early to get to work and I'm late getting home all the time. The children are usually asleep by the time I get home. Because of her pregnancy, Jai usually doesn't wait up for me to get in at night. It's hard on her. Mr. and Mrs. Betterman keep an eye on her and the children to make sure she doesn't do too much."

"Your butler and cook, where are they?"

"In New York. It's their thirty-fifth wedding anniversary. We gave them an all-expenses-paid, weeks' vacation in New York City, complete with theatre tickets, spa appointments, shopping spree, the works as an anniversary gift."

"I need to think of something to do for Roz for our anniversary in the fall. You know we never went away for a honeymoon after we got married."

"Now you've got her pregnant again in less than two years and you haven't taken her away for a honeymoon?"

"Man, you've got me working from can't see in the morning to can't see at night."

JRock laughed, but Wesley noticed something in his eyes. "Something's up with you, brah. Want to talk about it?"

JRock shrugged. "Like you said, this is a nice place, particularly for our children. Shelly and Shelby really love living here and although Reise and Rodney are still too young to appreciate it, this will be a great place for them to grow up."

"But what?"

"Man, I'm pure city. I spend too much time just getting to and from home. I'm missing out on my children's lives. I'm not comfortable with that."

"What else?"

"I miss the old neighborhood and being with my friends there. You, Peckhead, Little T, and the others. I want to be able to walk my children in the park and in the village. I want to walk them to and from school the way we used to do. Now that Rosalyn has designed the new school system, I want my children to go to school there with your children, Peckhead's, and the others if or when they settle down and start families. That's what this project is all about. Generations of family and friends. It takes a village."

"Then build one of the container homes for yourself and your family."

"I'm thinking about it, but I'm not sure I can ask Jai to move back to the city and use this place for weekends and getaways."

"Nothing beats a try but a failure."

***

"Hi, Roz," Belva, her regular manicurist acknowledged, as she sat down in front of the high, pedicure chair. "How are you feeling?"

"Very pregnant, Belva." She smiled, rubbing her full baby bump. "This is my friend, JaiHonnah Baylor. You're busy tonight."

"We're happy to have you, JaiHonnah. Sorry that we're short-handed. I haven't hired anyone to replace LaKesha yet."

"Oh, I didn't know. Come to think of it, I haven't seen her in here lately."

"She up and quit while you were on vacation down south. If you don't mind, I'll let you soak for a few more minutes while I check a few customers out at the register."

"Fine, Belva. I'm not in a hurry."

"This shop isn't usually this busy?" asked JaiHonnah. Her feet were in hot, sudsy, churning water, too. They were sitting side-by-side in Nana's Nails.

"Belva has a steady, regular clientele, but without a full complement of staff, it can get pretty hectic when she gets a bunch of walk-in customers. I'm surprised LaKesha left though. She's worked here since we got out of high school."

"Is she, maybe, working at a different shop?" asked JaiHonnah.

"Possibly. I don't know. The last time I saw her was in court. She's also a dancer at a men's club in DC. She used to live with Wesley."

"Oh, for how long?"

"At least five years. She moved out because he took in Cole, Marcus, and Simone. She didn't care for kids. In fact, when she came to court, she was with a man I used to date. They both testified in opposition to the custody petition Wesley and I filed. I really haven't seen her or him since then."

"Sorry to take so long, Roz," Belva interrupted, as she resumed her seat and began to work on Rosalyn's feet.

"Not a problem. Belva, what happened with Kesha?"

"Well, you know it was getting like a soap opera in here once Ice took in Jakima's kids. She moved out of Ice's place thinking it would force him to get rid of the kids to have her come back to him. Well, when that didn't work, Kesha was fit to be tied, but when he moved into your house? Lord, the woman went mental, claiming you put him up to taking in the kids just to take Ice away from her. She had more conspiracy theories than a murder mystery about you and Ice. Everyone knows she was after that other man you were seeing," said Belva.

"Howard Gardner?" asked Rosalyn.

"Yeah, him. She was all the time talking about how she was gonna take him from you because you took Ice from her with those kids. Then all of a sudden, she didn't want to have nothing to do with Gardner." Belva shook her head.

"I tell you, Roz, that LaKesha is one hot-pants woman! She went after men she should have left alone, even Killer. He hit it and quit it a few times and then told her it was payback to Ice. That made her good and mad. The next thing I know, she comes struttin' in here wearing some phat boots that she says JP bought for her and she up and quits."

"Whoa, Joey Patton? Isn't he married with a couple of children?"

"Oh, yeah, but he always had a thing for LaKesha. He didn't do anything about it because of her relationship with Ice. But now, Sister Woman is footloose and fancy free. She quit Sporty's, too. Seems Joey put her up in an apartment or condo somewhere on 16th Street, Northwest. You know his family owns all those shoe stores, right?"

Rosalyn could only shake her head. She knew Joey Patton, but didn't know his wife. Though he was once one of the neighborhood boyz, she remembered he seemed more quiet and introspective than Wesley and the rest of his crew. He wasn't a particularly handsome kid. In fact, he was a little overweight. She hadn't seen Joey since his family closed up their shoe store in the neighborhood strip shopping area and moved to Reston, Virginia, years ago.

"You seem worried," JaiHonnah commented when Belva got up to check out another customer and guide a new customer to a pedicure chair.

"No, not so much. It's one thing if Joey is just being kind to an old high school friend and helping her out of a tough spot. I just hope LaKesha doesn't take advantage of him and isn't trying to insinuate herself into Joey's marriage."

"There are women who think nothing of having an affair with a married man. That happened often with my former husband. He raised the practice to an art form and fully expected me to go along with it. However, until I found out differently, I thought Roderick was still married to Monique and I went after him anyway. I'd be a hypocrite to say anything about that type of behavior."

"Roderick wasn't married though. If he were, he never would have let you get next to him. You're not saying you're worried about JRock and another woman, are you?"

"Well, he and Savannah Logan used to date. My brother claims he caught them together recently in a compromising position at our business offices."

"Scratch that, Jai. Roderick isn't that type of man. He was miserable when you quit working with him and went back to Texas. Now he's married to you with twin sons and another baby on the way. I haven't seen him this happy in a long time."

"I think he'd be happier if we lived in the city again and not in the country."

"Well, that may be true. Both Wesley and Roderick are city boyz." She laughed. "I don't believe any of their crew would enjoy living outside the city."

"I think you're right. He and Wesley are spending an inordinate amount of time working. Then it takes more than an hour for Roderick to drive to and from home."

"I know what you mean. The children and I gave Wesley a watch with an alarm on it for his birthday and set it for five-thirty so he knows he has to be home for dinner by six. So far it's working."

"I should have thought of something like that to get my husband home on time."

"You're really worried, aren't you?" Rosalyn asked her friend.

"I can't deny it. I am. Not so much about him and other women. I know that he loves me and the children. It's his drive and ambition that got him to the top as an athlete and as a businessman. Roderick is working harder when I want him to put in fewer hours at the office and spend more quality time with me and our children."

"Maybe once the problems with the vandalism are resolved, he won't have to put in so many extra hours."

"I hope that's the case, but I'm not that patient. If something doesn't improve soon, I may have to take action to get his attention."

Chapter 30

"JRock, man, we've got big trouble," Ice said anxiously over the telephone. "I tried to handle this, but . . ."

"Chill, man. What is it?"

"You'd better come to the site and see for yourself."

"I can't leave my office right now. I've got another meeting in ten minutes, and I want to leave the office on time for a change to go home and spend time with my family."

"JRock, the inspectors are here and they're threatening to shut down the work. Mallory was hurt on the job and he's on his way to the hospital . . ."

"I'm on my way," JRock said, as he hung up the phone and hurried out the door.

Ice was still arguing with the city inspectors when JRock arrived at the job site.

"Sorry, Mr. Greenfield, Mr. Baylor, but we have to shut you down," one of the inspectors said, handing a Stop Work Order to Ice.

"Shut us down? For what?" JRock asked, confused.

"You name it," the inspector said. "It's all in the report," he said, as he and the other inspectors began to leave.

Then one of the inspectors stopped and walked back to where JRock and Wesley were still standing.

"Look, Baylor," he said, pulling them aside. "I've inspected a number of your job sites, so I know what's going on here isn't the way you usually do business or handle your projects. In fact, you're one of the best developers in the area. That's why I know something is going on you're not aware of." He furtively looked around and then drew JRock and Ice in closer. "We've been getting over-the-transom tips for some time now. Someone's trying to make you and Mr. Greenfield look real guilty…someone with a lot of juice. We got a tip yesterday this site needed an inspection first thing this morning because, according to the snitch, it was unsafe and someone could get hurt if something wasn't done. Of course, now you've got a man injured and in the hospital. That says this incident is not a coincidence to me."

JRock and Ice looked at each other.

"Who is the snitch?" Ice asked through gritted teeth.

"No clue," the inspector whispered.

"Is there anything else that you can tell us?" Ice asked.

"I probably shouldn't have told you this much, but, well, like I said before, Mr. Baylor, you've made every effort in the past to run a clean, safe operation. All of the inspectors in my office know that to be the case. I've personally inspected plenty of your job sites before, so I know what I'm talking about. I'd watch my back though, if I were you. Whoever is doing this might not stop here. You've got active sites all over the city and out in the suburbs, too."

"Thanks," JRock said, shaking the inspector's hand. "I'll have this cleared up by tomorrow."

The inspector nodded and walked away. JRock began to read the Stop Work Order again, and then looked at Ice.

"Why didn't you tell me what was going on?" JRock asked.

Ice looked away in frustration. "Man, you've been catching hell. You're working crazy hours dealing with the big shit. Somebody had to watch your back. Besides, you pay me stupid big bucks to handle shit like this. I wanted you to know all the time, money, and effort you invested in me and this project wasn't wasted. Besides, I bought into this dream. I want to make it happen just like my old man did. Just like you do. Little T and I thought putting extra security on at night would stop all of this vandalism and dirty tricks, but it's been getting worse. I don't know who is doing this or why. What I can tell you is that it's not someone from the neighborhood."

"Despite what's going on, we're going to make it happen, Ice. You and me together. So don't hold back when there's trouble."

After JRock and Ice clinched hands in a brother's embrace, they turned and walked toward the crowd of workmen and women. Before this project, many of the faces that now stared back at him and JRock were lost souls, ex-cons, derelicts, bums or substance abusers, the homeless, the unemployable. Now they stood on their own two feet, putting their lives back together, building marketable labor skills.

JRock told the over one hundred workers they would continue to be paid regardless of the shutdown.

"Nah, that ain't right, JRock." A husky man wearing a hard hat stepped forward. "We done finished with welfare!"

"Yeah!" the other men and women vehemently agreed.

"We work for our pay. We work for our self-respect!" another yelled.

"You done a lot, JRock. You and Ice together. Peckhead, Slide, Dog, Screw, Little T, and Buddy, too. All'a y'all. Gettin' us back in school at the community center to get a GED and opening dem trade schools! Most'a us ain't had a decent place to live 'til you brought in dem mobile units!"

"Yeah, and dem doctors and dentists, too, for dat health plan and dey didn't charge us hardly nothin' for dem services neever!" another added.

"Those law school students helped me get my veteran's benefits!"

"What about all dem hot meals you been making sure we get every day?! No, man, somethin' wrong, we gotta do right by you and your boyz!"

"JRock, you and Ice just go fix dis mess up down city hall! They can't stop us from working on our own."

JRock and Wesley were speechless as the crowd started chanting, *"Go, Rockman! Go, Iceman!"*

***

"Hey, JRock, I'm heading home for the day. Why aren't you on your way home yet?"

"There is no reason for me to go home."

"What? Wait! Why not? What's going on?"

"JaiHonnah took the children and left me yesterday."

"Then why are you still here? Man! I don't know what's wrong with you! Catch the first thing smoking and go find your family."

"I know where she is, but even if I go to her, nothing will change. I have to solve the question of who is trying to destroy me, my business, and Baylor Plaza Park. If it's her father, then I know this will tear JaiHonnah apart. I don't want that to happen, so I'm going to make a play to see who comes out of the woodwork at the Board of Directors meeting next week in Texas. I want you and my attorney with me when I do this. My life with Jai depends on the outcome of that meeting with her father."

"I'll be there to back you up, JRock."

***

"So that's why you were late for dinner tonight?" Rosalyn asked, as she comfortably snuggled in her husband's arm in their bed.

He lazily ran his fingers through her silky hair. The lights were low and rain peacefully drummed on the rooftop. "Yes, I couldn't just walk out after JRock said JaiHonnah left him."

"I was afraid something like this might happen."

"Why? You knew she was planning to leave him?"

"No, but Jai was frustrated with the amount of time he was spending outside their home. I don't think she is giving up on their marriage. I just think she's giving JRock some space to figure out his priorities."

He kissed the top of Rosalyn's head and squeezed her more securely to his side. "I don't ever want anything to separate us like that, babe."

"I think we're doing fine, Wesley. We don't have any major problems to deal with. You work hard, but you always make time to spend with me and our children. I have no complaints on that score. I don't think I have to compete with other women for your attention either."

He craned his neck to look at her, even in the low light, his brows beetled. "You're right, Rosalyn, you don't have to worry about me and any other woman. What brought that up?"

"JaiHonnah and I had a pregnancy pamper date last week at Nana's. She thought that JRock might be seeing Savannah Logan again."

"Not likely. Dr. Logan did stop by the office a few weeks back and so did Jai's brother, Jacob, but I walked Dr. Logan to her car. She said something about running late for a date with some guy named Nathan Flack. I don't believe that anything is jumping off again between JRock and your doctor. He doesn't have time to do anything other than work, but he has a plan in the works to end these problems we're having and save his marriage."

"Good. I hope it works out for both of them.

"By the way, speaking of old flames, did you know LaKesha quit working at Nana's and Sporty's?"

"No, I didn't. I haven't even seen her since we went to court."

"Apparently, from what Belva said, LaKesha quit while we were away on vacation. Is it possible Joey Patton would get involved with her?"

Ice laughed. "Yeah, it's possible. Even probable. JP had the hots for LaKesha since before she and I used to screw around in junior high school. He once accused me of trying to beat his time with her. What he didn't understand was that I wasn't chasing her, she was chasing me."

"Wow! That really takes me back old school," she said and chuckled.

"Yeah, but I wouldn't trade what I have now," he said, rubbing her burgeoning belly, "for anything back in the day."

She climbed on top of him and inserted him into her body. "Good, because I'm not letting this good thing go for anything else."

He couldn't agree more, as she rocked his world for the better part of the night.

Chapter 31

Two weeks after the showdown in Texas, where JRock and Ice learned the forces behind the hostile takeover attempt of Baylor Design and Development and the sabotage of his plant and equipment were perpetrated by none other than JaiHonnah's brother Jacob Hawkins, JRock's former wife, Monique, her lover, Lionel Porter, and business financier, Rothman Child. Even Levi Hall, aka Killer, was recruited to keep the heat on locally at Baylor job sites. JaiHonnah's father uncovered the plot and brought the perpetrators to the attention of the proper officials. All were now facing local and federal criminal charges, including her brother Jacob.

"Speaking of hearing things, I've heard Killer is trying to cut a deal to get out of spending the rest of his life in prison for vandalizing your job sites and equipment. If he is convicted, it will be his third strike," said Ice.

"Yeah, G-Boogie told me the district attorney is considering a plea bargain in exchange for information leading to the arrest and conviction of Killer's drug suppliers and every member in his crew. Killer's attorney is holding out for witness protection. He says if Killer gives up everyone in his crew and his suppliers, he would get shanked the first day in jail no matter where he serves a reduced sentence," said JRock.

"I have no sympathy. He trashed Rosalyn's house. For that alone they should incarcerate him and throw away the key," said Ice.

"The thing is he swears six ways to Sunday neither he nor anyone in the Royal Reds hit your place," said JRock.

Ice sat starring at JRock, his brows beetled in disbelief. "If not him or his crew, then who?"

JRock shrugged. "It sure as hell wasn't Micky D and Pugh. It's not their style and, besides, they're still locked up from breaking into Mrs. Lewis' home."

***

When he opened the front door, Howard Gardner's eyes registered surprise. "Well, you're obviously not here to tell me you've dumped your bad-boy fetish." Nevertheless, he pulled his front door open wider so Rosalyn could enter and walked away, leaving her to close the door behind her. "So, to what do I owe the pleasure of your company?" he asked, sarcastically, as he picked up a mug of coffee to drink while watching her over the rim of the cup.

"I just have one question for you, Howard."

"Really? And, you expect me to answer it after you made a fool of me personally and professionally? Would you believe people are still telling me I was a fool for letting you go when they have no idea I didn't have you in the first place?"

"I'm not here to rehash that aspect of our relationship."

Howard violently flung his coffee cup into the fireplace where it shattered. He stabbed his hips with his fists and paced. "*Rehash our relationship*' she says," he mumbled, looking up as if communing with The Almighty. His laugh was bitter as he shook his head. "I was a bootie call for you, Roz, because I was convenient and dependable. I could deliver what you wanted in bed and you didn't have to do anything—"

"Cut it out, Howard. I gave as good as I got when we were together. It was what it was, a mutually satisfying sexual relationship, nothing more. We weren't in love; we were lovers. Now it's over. If you want to continue to make yourself unhappy, do it while I'm not around. The only reason I'm here is to ask you whether you trashed my home or had someone do it?"

He looked at her as if she had grown two heads. "What the hell? I'm not a juvenile delinquent, Rosalyn. *I'm a man!*" he shouted at her, pounding his chest with his fist. "You live in a neighborhood where that type of thing is commonplace! So don't come into my home accusing me of doing something so stupid!"

She nodded her acknowledgment. "I believe you, Howard. I apologize for disturbing you." She turned to make for the door, but his voice stopped her.

"I never had a chance, did I?"

She turned to face him. "No, you didn't. We weren't suited for the long haul, Howard. We wanted different things out of life."

"You're an extraordinary woman, Rosalyn, and very beautiful, even though you're very pregnant, *again*. You're the complete package any man would want for the rest of his life. Greenfield doesn't deserve you."

She gave him a Mona Lisa smile. "That's what he says, too, but he keeps working harder and harder to earn and keep what we already have together. He's not perfect, but he's all the man I'll ever need for the rest of my life. Goodbye, Howard," she said and left.

***

When the apartment door opened, Joey Patton's face was almost comical as it froze for ponderous moments. "Uh, hey, Ice. Uh, long time no see."

"Yeah, I'm seeing more of you than I want to at the moment. Do you want to go put something on?"

Joey's handsome face flushed. "Uh, I thought you were someone else."

"Obviously, if you answer the door naked."

"Uh, I just got out of the shower. Yeah, well, uh, come on in while I get dressed."

Ice walked in and closed the door behind him. He surveyed what had to be new furniture, rugs, and draperies because the tags were still on them and there were boxes of new goods everywhere.

When Joey returned wearing sweats and tennis shoes, he seemed nervous and fidgety.

"Why did you stop by, Ice?" he asked while moving toward the kitchen and shifting boxes out of his way to pass.

"I came by to see LaKesha. Is she here?"

"Uh, LaKesha, no, she's not here."

"She lives here, doesn't she?"

"Look, Ice. LaKesha told me she's done with you. She doesn't want to come back to you so you should just stop calling her all the time, trying to get her to come back. I mean, really, man, I hear you're married to Roz Hunter now, with a couple of kids and another one on the way."

"LaKesha told you I've been after her to come back to me?"

"Well, yeah. Everybody knows how crazy you are for her. You wouldn't let her out of your sight for five years, but you made her work two full-time jobs just so you could keep your community center open. Then, when you took up with Roz, you kicked her out because Roz has more money to put into the center. She said you told her Roz isn't half the woman she is and you want her back as your side piece."

Ice shook his head and stared at Joey. "That sounds like me to you, JP? Is that the kind of thing you think I would do or say?"

Joey looked away, obviously too embarrassed to look Ice in the eye. "Man!" Joey moaned, his voice anguished. He interlocked his fingers around the back of his neck and began to pace in the limited space. "I've wanted LaKesha for so long I would have believed anything she told me. I bought this condo for her and all this furniture and stuff because she said if she didn't move away from the old neighborhood, you'd keep coming after her twenty-four-seven for sex. She didn't have anywhere to hide from you. Kesha has been out every day spending my money and running up my credit cards. I don't know what I was thinking. If my wife finds out, she'll take my children and leave me so fast she won't even leave skid marks!"

"Go home to your wife, JP. I think your problem will be over today."

An hour after Joey left, LaKesha opened the front door and danced her way into the condo, hauling a lot of shopping bags in each hand.

"Hey, boo! I'm home, baby! Me and Victoria got a lotta secrets for you! Bring your fine ass…." she trailed off and unceremoniously dropped the packages when she spotted Ice sitting comfortably on one of the sofas. "What are you doing here?" she sneered. "Where is Joey? Joey!" she yelled. "Come put this man outta my house! Joey!"

"He's not here, Kesha, but I am."

"What do you want? You tired of that bitch, Rosalyn?"

"I want to know why you trashed Rosalyn's home?"

"Who said I had anything to do with what happened? Nobody saw me—" she faltered. "I mean, I wasn't nowhere near that backstabbin' bitch's place!"

"You left your fingerprints—"

"You's a lie! I'm not as stupid as you and that freak, Howard Gardner, think I am because I had on gloves!"

A mental giant she wasn't, Ice thought sadly. "Is that enough, G-Boogie?" Ice asked, still looking at LaKesha with no pity in his eyes.

"Yeah, that'll do it," he said, as he and other police officers came into the living room from the bedroom. "LaKesha Reynolds, you're under arrest for . . ." Captain Gary Bouchard continued to Mirandize her while LaKesha screamed obscenities at Ice and fought the arresting officers.

Epilogue

"**W**ake up, pretty mama," Wesley crooned to his sleeping wife.

Rosalyn's eyes opened slowly and then she smiled at her husband who was holding their wide-awake, three-week-old son, Hunter Barrett Greenfield. She sat up in bed and took her son to her breast to nurse, while Wesley got comfortable and looked on. "How did it go today?"

"It was busy, but we have seventy-five homes pre-sold. Who would have thought a bunch of former hookers could sell real estate?"

"Kelley did. She worked hard to get those women to take classes in real estate and get their licenses."

"She was right then. Now Kelly is married to JaiHonnah's father and living in Africa."

"We have another wedding coming up in a few months."

"True that. Isaac and Carla are planning to start a family right away. They put a deposit on one of the five-bedroom homes next door to Peckhead and Francine. They'll move in a few weeks. It's above the new Greenfield Brothers location. Now that the old shopping center has been demolished, that's the last of the demolition work that needed to be done. Now all of the businesses are interspersed in the village area and operational. We're getting great reviews from HGTV and DIY Networks. They've been watching the progress and shooting a lot of film and video footage for their new series, Urban Dream."

"I know. I've been watching each episode on television.

"Roscoe's graduation is coming up just after the wedding," Rosalyn continued. "He's planning to go on and get his master's like Buddy did."

"Did you meet Buddy's man?"

"Staff Sargent Shawn O'Brady, yes. Eye candy. Apparently, they were in Afghanistan together. I'm interviewing him for a deputy position at Baylor Park Academy. I think he'll fit right in."

"Now that Mrs. Lewis is living in South Carolina with Hanna Ivy Benson and loving it and the milder climate, Buddy can live a more open life with Shawn."

"JaiHonnah stopped by to show me the secret plans she designed for the new container home for her and JRock."

"I haven't seen the plans yet, but she asked me to hold one of the large lots that border a deep part of the Anacostia River for her building site. She wants to have the site built before she tells JRock about it as a birthday gift. So far, everyone has kept it from him."

"What time will the children be home?"

"Your parents called while you were sleeping. They were leaving Alberta's farm within the hour and should be here before dinner."

"What are you making?"

"I'm baking chickens, making mashed potatoes and gravy, string beans and biscuits. Isaac and Carla are coming over to talk about the wedding plans over dinner and to welcome the children home. He's bringing strawberry shortcake for dessert. As soon as this young man finishes his lunch and before Elizabeth wakes from her nap, I'm going to have some private, quality time with my wonderful, sexy wife."

Rosalyn's Mona Lisa smile bordered on salacious.

About the Author

Ann Jeffries, the critically acclaimed author of the Family Reunion—Wisdom of the Ancestors series, is a native of Washington, DC. As an only child, she enjoyed the benefits of a private school education at Allen in Asheville, North Carolina, and a public education at the University of Maryland. Ann began writing fiction for her own amusement.

Ann is the recipient of many awards for leadership and public service. A keynote speaker at colleges, universities, conferences, and conventions, she has extensively traveled the North American continent, Asia, and Europe. Among other endeavors, she is an entrepreneur, an avid supporter of public television, and a voracious reader.

Her pride and joy are her family, particularly her Fabulous Four grands. She lives in Maryland and South Carolina.

Follow Ann on her website www.annjeffries.net, her publishing house site, www.newviewliterature.com, Facebook: @Ann Jeffries, and on Twitter: @Ann Jeffries.